TIME TO LIVE AGAIN

MADRONA INN
BOOK 1

KRISTINA BECK

Copyright © 2024 Kristina Beck

This is a work of fiction. Names, characters, organizations, places, events, and incidents are either products of the author's imagination or are used fictitiously. Any resemblance to actual events, locales, or persons living or dead are entirely coincidental.

No part of this book may be reproduced, or stored in a retrieval system, or transmitted in any form or by any means electronic, mechanical, photocopying, recording, artificial intelligence, or otherwise, without express written permission of the publisher.

This book is licensed for your personal enjoyment only. This book may not be re-sold or given away to other people.

For Sarah
Live your life to the fullest!

OLIVE AND LEO'S PLAYLIST

"Somebody To Love," by Queen
"Kiss," by Prince
"I Gotta Feeling," by Black Eyed Peas
"Unstoppable," by Sia
"Titanium," by Sia
"Roar," by Katy Perry
"her," by JVKE
"You Sexy Thing," by Hot Chocolate
"Yeah!," by Usher
"Pump Up the Jam," by Technotronic's
"Crazy Love," by Brian Kennedy
"Home," by Michael Bublé
"I Was Born To Love You," by Queen
"Umbrella," by Rihanna
"S&M," by Rihanna
"A Symptom Of Being Human," by Shinedown
"At Your Worst," by Calum Scott
"Someone Like You," by Dina Carroll
"Turning Page," by Sleeping At Last
"Only Human," by Jonas Brothers

"Angel," by Sarah McLachlan
"My World," by Calum Scott
"Butterflies," by MAX
"Feel Again," by OneRepublic
"Wings," by Jonas Brothers
"Let's Get Loud," by Jennifer Lopez
"I'm Gonna Be (500 Miles)," by The Proclaimers
"Be My Lover," by La Bouche
"Gonna Make You Sweat," by C & C Music Factory
"I Grieve," by Peter Gabriel
"Señorita," by Camila Cabello & Shawn Mendes
"Footloose," by Kenny Loggins
"Low," by Flo Rida, T-Pain
"Don't Stop Me Now," by Queen

1

OLIVE

I stare out my misty car window, tapping my fingers on the steering wheel along to Queen's "Somebody to Love." The powerful words from Freddie Mercury make me wonder what I'd do if I actually found someone to love or if he found me. Some people probably think I'm not loveable, and right now, maybe I'm not. But I wasn't always like this. And I think unlovable is too harsh a description. Withdrawn, antisocial, unapproachable… those are probably better words to use.

I scan the lines of cars waiting for the ferry to Orcas Island—most likely people going to party for New Year's Eve. How many of them woke up a couple days ago and decided they needed to vanish for a week? How many decided they needed to celebrate their thirtieth birthday and New Year's Eve alone?

I'd guess the chance of that is about one percent. Me. I'm that one percent.

Am I out of my damn mind? No. But I will be if I don't do this.

Can I really do it, or should I go home? Before I second-guess myself out of this, I grab my phone and call my brother. He picks up after one ring, and I don't even let him say hello.

"You know Mom's going to say I'm selfish."

"Selfish, smelfish," Andy responds. "That's exactly what you need to be. Your life as a hermit is officially over. O. V. E. R. When you come home, I expect to see a happier, stronger, better you. I don't want to recognize you once that shell's off your back."

"The old me won't miraculously reappear, y'know."

"I don't expect you to be who you were in Los Angeles. You've experienced a lot since then. Try to let the good things burn through the clouds."

His constant enthusiasm and positive energy usually pump me up pretty quickly. But the only thing that can help me right now is the extra hot, triple espresso, one pump mocha resting in the middle console of my car. I really should cut down on the caffeine. New Year's resolution? No way!

"You won't even see me—you'll be back at your swanky new apartment in San Francisco, Mr. Amazon-Super-Bowl-Ad. How would you know?" Andy works for a well-known advertising agency and relocated to San Francisco around a year ago. He pitched an idea for Amazon's Super Bowl ad this year, and he's counting down the days till it airs on game day.

"What, you haven't heard of a video call? It's the only way I ever see you since you won't come visit. But you're coming to San Fran after this trip. ASAP."

"Annnnndy, I—"

He cuts me off. "Nope. Nuh-uh. No excuses."

I huff. "Pressure much? You make it sound like one week away will create a fucking miracle."

"Hey, I have faith. Now drive your ass onto that ferry and don't look back. I'll message you once Mom finds out you're gone. It'll probably be soon. And good luck with that. But I'll be here when she calls. I'll distract her when things get heated."

I bite my lower lip to prevent myself from shedding tears. Andy is my only sibling, my best friend, my biggest cheerleader, and right now, a lifesaver. He also loves shaking things up. He, along with my uncle Bruce, urged me to take off this week and suggested that we not tell Mom where I'm going either. But that's a whole other can of worms.

I'm going to Orcas Island. My parents always refused to vacation there or any of the San Juan Islands—they said they were just big tourist traps, not nice or nearly warm enough—but I found this beautiful hotel online, and that's where I'm going.

"Ugh, Andy. Remind me again why I'm going to this hotel alone? If I'm not supposed to be a hermit, shouldn't I have gone to a singles resort?" *Absolutely not.* "Why didn't you come with me?"

"Hell no," he snarks. "You need to get out of your usual surroundings and away from family. Hopefully, you'll meet some new people and find a new perspective on things. Maybe even a love interest." He clicks his tongue.

"Socializing hasn't been my thing for years. How do I jump back into the shark tank?"

"That's not for me to say. It's for you to figure out. You can do this! Take some chances, Olive. Something tells me this trip is going to change your life. If it doesn't, you didn't try hard enough." He releases a rough sigh. "We've already been over this last night and this morning before you left. It's a done deal."

"I know. I know. You're right," I grumble, straightening my spine.

"You're just figuring that out now? I'm always right… until I'm not."

"You make no sense." I grin. "But Andy, I can't tell you enough how much I appreciate you and Uncle Bruce doing this for me. And with me running, you're both in the hot seat with Mom."

"Don'tcha worry, Olive. We'll handle her with our charm. We probably could've executed this plan a little better, but desperate times call for desperate measures."

"Then charm the hell out of her. That's why you're the perfect ad exec. It doesn't hurt to live in another state either. Mom's not knocking on your door every damn day."

"True. Speaking of the door, I was so fucking proud of you this morning. Once you were out of your apartment, you drove away without hesitation. Everybody deserves a fresh start at least once in their life. I want my fun, courageous sister back. She's right at the surface. I can almost see her."

"So you say." Cars ease forward. "Okay, listen. I need to go."

"Fine," he says, "but don't forget to text like you promised. Me and Mom, every day."

"Yeah. She's going to flip out."

"She'll live. And so will you."

"I know. Okay. Talk to you soon." I disconnect the call.

I don't like who I am now, but do I want to go back to the old me? She wasn't perfect. Do I really expect perfection? I'm not sure what I want or need other than to be happy again. What will life be like when I return in a week? More of a disaster? Better than I expect?

The line moves forward again, still at a snail's pace. I

squeeze the steering wheel with sweaty hands—whether out of anticipation or dread, I can't tell. My jumpy stomach doesn't explain it either. I guess that could be the mocha not settling right, though.

I take a deep breath and say out loud, "It is time to be selfish, Olive!"

2

OLIVE

I walk through the automatic sliding glass doors of the Madrona Inn, stop short, and gasp. I thought the exterior was spectacular with its stunning brick-red siding and white shutters. White twinkle lights illuminated the trees and bushes around the entrance, and large wreaths accented the expansive picture windows, creating a warm welcome for guests. But this…this is spectacular. The spacious foyer is beautifully decorated for the holiday season, like something you'd see in a quaint country home magazine.

A wide, twelve- or thirteen-foot-tall balsam fir Christmas tree stands in the middle of the room, commanding attention with its abundance of white lights reflecting off delicate silver and crystal ornaments. Bushy red poinsettias fill the open space at the bottom of the tree. Evergreen garlands wrap around the wooden banisters of the staircase behind it and over the archways, adorned with silver balls, red ribbons, holly, and mistletoe. I'll need to enjoy the festive decorations while I'm here before they're taken down.

The smell of pine permeates the air. I take a deep breath and let it all sink in. It reminds me of my dad and his obsession with real Christmas trees. One glimpse of this place, and I'm sure he would've liked it here. I've been questioning my parents' refusal to visit these islands since I left the ferry. The quaint villages I drove through on the way here, the natural beauty of the surroundings—this place is incredible, and it's not summer or even sunny out. I don't get it.

My phone buzzes in my coat pocket, and I clench my jaw. Mom won't give up. Not that I expected anything different. I yank off my leather gloves and pull out the phone. The screen is blank. Strange.

The buzzing starts again, and I realize the noise is coming from the automatic sliding glass doors opening and closing behind me, almost clipping my big ass. I take a quick step forward and scan the area to see if anyone is around. The group of people at the far left in the reception area doesn't seem to have noticed. I straighten my coat and lift my chin high. Nope. My cheeks aren't sizzling from embarrassment. Not at all.

Great start.

I twitch when my phone actually vibrates in my hand. It's been off since I drove onto the ferry. The last thing I wanted to do was talk to Mom in the middle of a crowded deck. I turned the phone back on when I got here—only to find it flooded with missed calls and text messages. Some were from Andy warning me that Mom's going bat-shit crazy because I haven't answered her calls and angry messages. *Shit.*

Well, I'm here now, and there's nothing she can do about it. I guess I'll have to face her at some point. Check-in isn't for another hour, but sooner would be better for this. I can't wait until I'm in my room.

I stuff my gloves and my phone into my coat pockets and glance around for somewhere private. There's a lounge to the right. I go over and peek inside. I'm relieved to find it empty. Our conversation doesn't need an audience.

This room is as festive as the foyer with another gorgeous Christmas tree in front of a picture window. A plush, navy blue couch and matching armchairs, each adorned with cream-colored throw pillows, are arranged on an elegant blue and white oriental rug. The sitting area welcomes me to enjoy the warmth coming from the large, red-brick fireplace. Above the mantle, a mirror amplifies the size of the room. To the left, an expansive wooden bookcase, packed with colorful books, accents the wall.

Next to the doorway is a table with an assortment of teas and coffees for the guests to enjoy. *Caffeine.* My mouth waters, but I hold myself back. I might need something stronger than that after I talk to Mom. Is it too early for happy hour?

I park my large suitcase next to the couch and drape my forest green knit hat and black coat over the armrest. I drop my handbag on the couch and hold my hands out to the fire, absorbing the welcomed heat. I rise on my toes and catch my reflection in the mirror. *Shit!* My hair has formed an unruly halo around my head. Static crackles as I run my hand through it. Hoping to tame this disaster, I do it again, but the only thing that will help is water. With a closer look, I roll my eyes at the clear indentations on my forehead from my hat. Hey—it's wintertime. What do people expect? Who cares anyway? It's not like I'm trying to impress anybody here.

Once I'm warm enough, I sit on the cozy couch and let my body sink into the inviting cushions. I lift my phone out of the coat pocket and a call from Mom comes through. I take a deep breath and try to find my zone…wherever that is.

Swipe. "Hey, Mom," I say as naturally as I can, like nothing's out of the ordinary. But everything is different. So, so different.

"Don't 'hey Mom' me, Olivia." She only calls me Olivia when she's fuming. It's the same with Andy. "Where the hell are you? Our tracking system says you're offline, and Andrew won't tell me where you are. What is going on? I've been trying to get a hold of you for hours. For all I know, you're lying in a ditch somewhere." As dramatic as ever.

"I'm not home, and I'm obviously not dead." Good thing I turned my tracking off when I left the house. Knowing her, she'd have followed me here.

"Don't be smart with me. I'm sitting in your apartment with Andrew, and the only thing he'll tell me is that you left and you're fine."

"He's right."

Most of my life she's been a typical helicopter mom, even from a distance when I was in LA, but it's gotten excessive since my dad died. She doesn't know what to do with herself anymore and has latched onto me. I swear there's a steady thrumming sound whenever she's around.

But I am thirty as of today, not twelve. Weird, right? I do understand her need for control, but I've finally realized it's not healthy. Not only because of her smothering behavior, but because I let her do it. I was never like this. *Never.*

And she's still rambling. "Now that I know you aren't dead, where are you and what are you doing? When will you be back? I had to cancel the spa appointments I made for us as a surprise for your birthday."

Andy really hasn't told her anything! My stomach

churns with guilt. What was I thinking, just getting up and leaving?

There wasn't anything specific that pushed me over the edge. It was more an accumulation of things. But last night, the will to leave was so strong, I had to go. It was like two hands were on my back this morning, pushing me out the door. I was lucky to get a room at this hotel a couple of days ago.

"I'm at a hotel."

"W–wait, what? Where? And for how long?" she stammers.

"I'm not saying."

"Olivia…I don't understand. Did something happen? Is this code for being kidnapped? Should I call 911?"

I chuckle to myself at how insane this is.

"Nope. Not kidnapped, Mom. But I need some space, and I don't have that when I'm at home." A moment of silence follows.

I may live alone, but Mom shows up whenever she feels like it. Which happens a lot. She begs me to move back home all the time, but that's one thing I refuse to do. I drew the line with giving her a key too.

"We could've gone somewhere together," she finally whines. "A change of surroundings would've been good for the both of us."

"I want to be *alone*, Mom," I emphasize. "And your other child's visiting, don't forget. Tomorrow's his birthday. Focus on him for once." He's a year older than me, but we were born in the same year. Him in January and me in December.

"Yeah, Mom. What am I, chopped liver? I offered to go to the spa with you," Andy chimes in, laying it on thick.

"Oh please, Andrew. Like you want a mani-pedi."

"I'd do it. My dogs have been barking something fierce lately."

I crack a smile. Andy's such a wiseass. It's the way he deals with Mom's overbearing personality. He acts like a goofball when he's home, but he's one of the most intelligent guys I know.

"Don't you want to hang out with your awesome, successful son?" Andy adds. I can picture his pouty face and puppy dog eyes as he tries to distract her.

"Don't pretend you're innocent here. You know something about your sister's whereabouts and you aren't telling me," Mom retorts. Hints of anger are hard to ignore.

I tune out their bickering for a moment. I should hang up since she knows I'm not dead.

Too late.

"Now, Olive." Oh—it's Olive again. "You're being ridiculous. Tell me where you are, and I'll be there as soon as I can. It'll be fun." Her voice turns hopeful, as if I'm going to give in.

My guilt switches to full-blown anger. I hadn't realized how overbearing my mom has become until Uncle Bruce and Andy confronted me about it. They suggested an intervention. Hence my escape.

"Would you listen to me, Mom? I know it sounds harsh, but I don't want you here. I don't want *anybody* here. I need to deal with some stuff, and I can only do that when I'm far away from everyone and everything."

"Think about what things, honey? We've always been open with each other."

I don't need to see her face on the screen to know that her eyes are blinking faster than normal. A clear giveaway that she's out of her element and control. She only hears what she wants to hear.

"Not always. I haven't been happy for a long time."

Something she should've noticed, but as far as I can tell, hasn't.

"It's been rough since your dad died. It takes time."

"There's more to it, and you know that. Things changed for me long before Dad passed away."

"But did you really have to leave me on your birthday and New Year's Eve? It's selfish when we're supposed to go to your uncle's to celebrate."

There's the word. *Selfish.* It took longer than I thought.

"What am I supposed to do now," she wails. *Seriously?*

My heart rate spikes to a record high. "I'm being selfish? *Me?* Not everything is about you, Mom. Yeah, I could've told you sooner, but you would've done everything possible to convince me it was a bad idea. Like everything else I've tried to do to get me out of this funk. This is a birthday present to myself. Do something with Andy—he's right there with you!"

I'm no longer cold from the brisk, damp weather outside. I tug off the forest green scarf that's smothering me like a boa constrictor and toss it over my lap.

"Since when do you talk to me this way? Where did this come from? Did I do something wrong?"

Andy clears his throat in the background like he wants to say something, but I answer first. "No, Mom. Well, not directly," I mumble.

"And what is that supposed to mean?"

Before this gets really heated, I continue. "Listen, I'm done here. You heard what I had to say. I don't want to talk anymore. Give me the space I want and need. It'll be the best birthday present for me. I can't *think* with you hovering over me all the time. I'm not a child."

"Well, you're certainly acting like one," she fires back. "Running away like a little girl."

I grab the pillow next to me and squeeze it like a stress

ball. "No. If anyone's being a child, it's you. You can't handle me doing something without your knowledge. And what I'm doing is taking control of my life again. I'm thirty and not proud of who I've become or how I'm living. A milestone birthday and the start of a new year is perfect for making changes. It's time for me to live again."

"You go, girl," Andy cheers. Mom mutters something to him I can't distinguish. I hear a scuffle, then Andy whines, "*Ouch.* Olive, Mom hit me!" He lays it on thick. I love him to death.

"Stop playing games, Andrew," Mom warns.

Boisterous laughter in the lobby catches my attention. I turn my head to see what's going on and cover my mouth. How loud was I? I hope they didn't hear me. A woman and man are standing by the Christmas tree watching something on a phone. They guffaw again and slap their hands over their mouths. *When's the last time I laughed like that?*

Even from a distance, I'm drawn to the guy's beautiful hair. It's thick with loose, shoulder-length, ruffled curls. I try to avert my gaze, but I can't. Long hair on men is a weakness of mine. If only I could see his face. Quick glimpses of his profile are all I get from this angle. The man peeks around the Christmas tree, searching for someone or something near the front desk. He shakes his head and pulls on the woman's sleeve, then they sneak away, giggling.

Once they're out of sight, I drop my head back again. Sadness washes over my tired body, loneliness trailing behind.

"Olivia, are you listening to me?" And Olivia it is again.

"Not really."

"Well, I won't repeat myself other than your uncle is

going to be very disappointed in you." He won't care because he's part of the reason I left. There's going to be a handful of people there, mostly Uncle Bruce's friends and employees. Andy's only going to this party to ease the blow after my escape. I won't be missing anything.

"Uncle Bruce already knows."

She gasps. "Bruce knows? Wow…that hurts, Olivia. That really hurts." Her voice cracks.

"Don't cry, Mom. I'm not trying to upset you." A sniffle travels through the line. I clear my throat. *Stay strong.* Guilt loves to torture me. "It's time for you to live again too. I'm not the only one who needs a change. You need to find yourself, and it won't work if we're constantly together. It's time to stand on your own two feet. That hasn't happened since you married Dad over thirty-five years ago."

Someone enters the room. I glance over and catch my breath. It's the guy who was by the Christmas tree. His large friendly eyes are a unique shade of honey that complement his gorgeous wild hair. Hints of copper in the golden-brown mane shimmer under the overhead lighting like a regal lion's mane. I could admire him all day—

Well…as long as I don't look below his nose. What's with the horrendous mustache? I know they're trying to make a comeback, but this doesn't suit him at all. Granted, it's not dominant on his face because of the color, but still.

"Sorry to interrupt," he says with a velvety tone, then points to the fireplace. "This needs some attention." Ooh, his voice is sexy as sin, creating even more of a delicious distraction. I nod and watch him place a couple of logs on the fire. My attention's fully on him, not my mom blubbering on the phone. He grabs a poker and shifts the wood. Dislodged ashes fly up the chimney, and embers fall onto the marble hearth.

I prop my elbow on the armrest, cradle my head in my hand, and enjoy the delightfully unexpected view. "Hey, Mom, I need to go. I'm sorry again for escaping last minute on my birthday and New Year's, but I need to get checked in here."

She huffs. "All right. None of this sits well with me. I'm not even sure I'll go to the party tonight now. I don't like that you're alone and won't tell me where you are. Can you at least tell me when you'll be back?"

"In a week."

"A week?" she shouts. I pull the phone away from my ear. You'd think I said a month. "Seven days? What about your job?"

Lion Guy peeks over his shoulder at me, a subtle crease between his eyebrows. I guess he heard her too. Our eyes connect, and I think he's concerned. I look away quickly, embarrassed.

I give her a couple seconds to vent, then interrupt. "My job is not your concern, and yes—a week. Accept it. Can you please do that for me?"

I finished my last project a couple of days before Christmas. The next one starts in February. Free time is all I have, and I'm going to use it for more than sitting in sweatpants twenty-four hours a day, streaming romance movies, and fantasizing about some dream guy arriving at my apartment as if I'd ordered him from DoorDash.

"Fine. Fine. I'll try to respect your wishes," she says through gritted teeth. "Please promise you'll call me later. And remember—don't talk to strangers."

I can't listen to this shit anymore! I clench my jaw and take a calming breath. It's funny how she doesn't talk to Andy like this.

"No strangers. Got it."

I'm well aware of the irony as I continue to watch the

gorgeous stranger in front of me brush the fallen ashes into a pan. This may be the most interesting thing I've ever seen. It's not just his hair that allures me. It's his exposed toned forearms and the way his back muscles contract in his slim white button-down shirt when he sweeps up the mess. He turns his head, and the sharp curve of his jawline begs me to trace it with my finger. Is it me, or has it gotten hotter in here? I'm pretty sure it's not because of the crackling fire.

He's the first man to grab my attention in a long time. I'm talking years. Pheromones are practically pouring out of my skin, trying to latch on to him. They drop to the floor in defeat when he stands and leaves the room without another glance, taking the warmth with him.

Don't think I didn't ogle his delectable ass on the way out.

Mom's still talking about strangers, and I'm ready to pull my hair out. I cut her off again. "Okay. Got it, Mom. Say hi to everyone and have fun at Uncle Bruce's. Love you."

Before she or Andy can say anything else, I disconnect the call. I should turn it off for the entire stay or maybe throw it into the now blazing fire.

I rest my head back on the soft cushion and breathe deeply. Andy wanted me to text him after I talked to Mom, but there's no way in hell I'm doing that now. I'm drained of energy, and my caffeine boost has fizzled out. I glance at the coffee service in the corner but decide against it. Distant laughter catches my attention again, and I already know it's him.

He's probably the stranger I'm not supposed to talk to. But do I care? Nope! Do I have the nerve to talk to him? Not sure.

The old me wouldn't have hesitated.

3

OLIVE

I gather my belongings and head to the lobby, hoping to check in early. The older woman behind the front desk flashes me an inviting smile as I approach. "Welcome to the Madrona Inn. How can I help you?"

"I'd like to check in, please," I say, stacking my stuff on the suitcase.

"Great. What's your last name?" she asks, still smiling.

"Han—"

"Donna, I thought you were on your break. I'll take care of this guest for you." My heart skips a beat when Lion Guy approaches with a friendly demeanor. His voice is playful, not stern. He's even more striking close up.

"I'm fine, Leo." She waves him off. "I can check her in first."

Seriously? His name is Leo? Leo with the lion's mane. I smother a laugh but not fast enough. They both turn to me with round, curious eyes. "Sorry. Ignore me." Then I chuckle again. "Your name's really Leo?" *Olive! What has gotten into you?*

He grins. "*Pfft*. Like I haven't heard that before. Yep,

Leo it is." He points to his fluffy hair. "When I was born, I had an enormous head of hair like this. My mom said I looked like a lion and named me Leonardo. And when my eye color kicked in…" He shrugs.

My face sizzles like bacon. "I'm sorry. I didn't mean to be rude. It's—that's the first thing I thought of when I saw your hair. I hadn't seen your eyes yet, but when I did, wow, they're hard to ignore."

What's with the verbal vomit? Is there a rewind button I can press? Can he tell I haven't been social in a long time?

"You know what, Leo?" The Donna lady—or was it Dora?—pats his arm. "I think I will take my break. My back is acting up."

His lips split into a knowing grin. "That's what you said before that large group arrived. I'm on to you." He jerks his thumb behind him. "Now get going."

The woman giggles at the same time I do. "I'm going, but you be nice to this young lady." She points a finger at him.

Leo stretches out his arms. "When am I ever *not* nice?" he protests, pretending to be offended. "My middle name is nice."

Donna swats his arm lightly, then turns to me. "Sorry for the interruption." *Wait. Wasn't I the one who interrupted?* "Leo will take good care of you. Enjoy your time here. Happy New Year."

"Thank you and same to you," I reply, grinning. Their relaxed interaction has eased my embarrassment and seems to have slightly softened my usually guarded attitude.

My phone buzzes. Stiffly, I place it upside down on the counter, ignoring the call. It could be anybody at this point, but this is more important. Friends have been texting, wishing me a happy birthday, all day. Friends I've pushed away but who apparently still care about me.

"Again, sorry about that. She doesn't know when to take a break," Leo says, pushing a loose curl of hair behind his ear. There's a black hair band around his left veined wrist. Is it to put his hair back? I think I'd combust right now if he did. On top of that, he's wearing a thick black ring on his middle finger. Oh boy, don't get me started on his large, powerful hands. If I ever get married, I'd ask my husband to wear a black wedding band. I find them so attractive. How much hotter could he get? I glance at his mustache again. Funny, now it doesn't seem all that bad. Still not a fan, though.

I rest my elbows on the counter. His golden eyes suddenly capture mine, and I melt against the desk. I think he's saying something because his lips are moving. I don't respond because I'm still caught in his hypnotic stare. What does he see when he looks at me? Is my attraction to him obvious? Can he tell I'm struggling and ran out on my stagnant life today? How much did he hear from my conversation with Mom?

The ding of the elevator wakes me up, and I blink several times. "I'm sorry. Did you say something?" My languid voice is almost unrecognizable. A group of people file out of the elevator and head to the hotel entrance.

He shakes his head. "I don't know. We seemed to have both spaced out. I think I'm the one who needs a break. It's been a long day." He lets out a light laugh and focuses on the monitor. "Hmm. Right! I need your name to get things moving here." The humor's back in his voice.

"Olivia Hansen." I glance at the gold badge on his shirt. *Mr. Forrest, Manager.* Leo Forrest. Manager? He seems young for that role—probably in his early thirties. Then again, I don't know much about hotel management.

"Give me a sec to look you up."

I pull a blue folder out of the side pocket of my suitcase as he types away on the computer.

"Ahh, here you are, Ms. Hansen."

"Call me Olive, if you'd like." The words tumble out, surprising me. Why would I say that? The banter between us is easy. Calling him Mr. Forrest doesn't match the vibe between us.

He leans closer and lowers his voice. "It just so happens that I love olives."

My mouth goes dry, and I can hardly swallow. A pleasurable sensation pulses through me, catching me by surprise. I don't want it to stop. How can one man induce such a response? If I passed him while walking down the street, I'd probably stumble into a streetlamp and fall flat on my ass.

"Oh, do you? Lucky for me." I nod slightly while trying to smirk with confidence. It works in movies, but I'm not Scarlett Johansson.

"Okay, *Olive*. As long as you call me Leo."

"I'd like that."

"Great. Now that we've settled that, it looks like you've reserved a suite with a waterfront view for one week, correct?"

Oh no, don't do this to me.

"*Suite?* Um, no. I reserved a double room. Here's the confirmation." I retrieve a copy of the reservation from the folder. The information is on my phone, but I always carry a paper copy with me. I don't trust technology, and right now, I want to avoid my phone like the plague.

He scans it quickly, then his forehead wrinkles. "We seem to have a problem. There are no double rooms available. I apologize for the inconvenience. This happened the other day too. Our website has been acting up and caused some issues with the reservation system. With the holidays here, there's been a delay to get it fixed." Now he speaks like a professional. "Never mind."

It's probably a widget or plug-in issue, but I won't tell him that. I'm not here to work.

"Does that mean I don't have a room?" My voice rises an octave, and disappointment spikes my body temperature. I've come this far, and I refuse to go back home. Other hotels are probably full too.

"Because it's a problem on our end, we'll give you the suite for the price of a double room. How does that sound?"

A suite! Am I dreaming?

My eyebrows shoot up, and an odd sense of excitement takes over. "Are you serious?"

"Sure am," he says with a lopsided grin. "It's no problem. Oh, I didn't ask you if you're part of the Moore party?"

"No…it's only little ole me," I mumble, focusing on the wall behind him. This is the first time I've traveled alone. Who checks into a hotel on New Year's Eve and their thirtieth birthday by themselves? I guess people like me. Desperate and lost.

"Well, more space for you, right? You're going to love the suite. With its beautiful view and recent renovations, you won't want to leave."

The real question is, do you come with the room?

"Well, thank you. Happy New Year to me!" And birthday.

"Not a bad way to end the year or start a new one. Depending how you look at it," he says, focusing on the monitor again. "You did arrive a little early, so the suite isn't quite ready yet. It shouldn't be more than thirty minutes, though."

"No problem. I can wait in the other room by the fire again. It's warm and cozy in there."

He rests his bare forearms on the counter and tilts his head, a sparkle in his eye. How can someone be so utterly sexy? He doesn't even try! "Are you hungry?" he asks.

Huh? That's out of left field. "Um. Yes. Starving actually. Is there somewhere I can grab something to eat or a coffee?" I recall reading a review mentioning a café here. I really should've researched this place a little more.

"You bet. We have a great Parisian café here. You can wait there if you'd like." His eyes gleam. "Want to check it out?" He radiates happiness and confidence. If his aura were visible, I'm sure it'd shimmer like golden sunrays. It makes him even more appealing. Is it a facade because he has to greet customers at the front desk? Or is he that good of a salesman? Or maybe he feels bad about the reservation error or that I'm here alone? Probably all the above.

Or maybe he's a truly genuine, cheerful person, and you don't need to analyze everything. Say yes!

I shrug my shoulders. "Oh. Sure. Okay."

"Great. Donna should be back in a few minutes. Let's finish getting you set up, and I'll take you there myself."

Yes, please. "Oh, you don't have to do that. Point me in the right direction and—"

"It'd be my pleasure. I need my afternoon cappuccino and lemon tart, anyway." *Is he going to eat with me? In your dreams, Olive.* "They're like the ones I've eaten in Paris. I highly recommend them. Ever been to Paris?"

"Yes, but it was a long time ago." It feels like another lifetime. The old me backpacked through France, Germany, and Italy before I started nursing school. "I didn't try the tarts. However, I ate a lifetime's worth of chocolate éclairs."

He snickers. "Well, you're in for a treat. And if you

aren't a tart fan, there's a variety of éclairs and other pastries to choose from. And you definitely don't want to miss the croissants—especially the chocolate ones! There's something for everyone."

"Sounds delicious. I might have to try a few." Didn't I make a resolution to lose weight? Who cares? I still have today to eat what I want.

"That's the way to live," he encourages. "Now, let's finish this."

That's exactly what I came here to do.

To live.

4

LEO

What kind of bullshit was that? *I'll take you there myself...* Hundreds of beautiful women have stayed here before. When have I ever been this distracted by one? *Grr.* I need more sleep.

When we shared a look a moment ago, her large, cautious eyes expressed a history of sadness that made my heart clench. Something I can understand myself. She captivates me, and it throws me off kilter. How can a complete stranger—one I met a few minutes ago—do that to me?

We might have officially met right now, but I noticed her the moment she came into the hotel. She didn't see me because I was standing behind the Christmas tree fixing a couple of ornaments that were about to fall off a droopy, dry branch. I peeked around the tree when I heard the door open and froze. Her smile was breathtaking. Then I almost gave myself away by laughing when the automatic doors kept opening and closing behind her. I hunkered down behind the tree with my hand over my mouth and waited until she disappeared into the Blue Room instead of going to the front desk.

I got a glimpse of her eyes in the Blue Room, but nothing prepared me for their uniqueness. During my travels all over the world, I have never met another person with the lightest shade of brown like hers. It's the softest tone of a frothy cappuccino or light brown sugar.

It's not only her expressive eyes and their long, thick eyelashes that grab my attention. Her flawless ivory skin is free of makeup, and her soft, full cheeks seem to have a natural rosy hue. Her tempting, glossy lips create a hint of sensuality that distracts me even more.

Get your head out of your ass, Leo. You're working, remember?

"Are you familiar with Orcas Island?" I ask, trying to sound unaffected by her. She probably sees right through me.

She brushes her hands through her thick, shiny brunette hair, causing the ends to crackle and rise from static. "No. It's my first time. This trip was last minute and I didn't have the chance to look up what there is to do here. And if there's nothing to do, I'm fine with that too. I needed to get away." Her voice softens with a hint of vulnerability as she studies the counter.

Better than her staring at my hideous lip rug. Stupid bet. The countdown has begun until I can shave it off.

I wonder what happened to make her run away. I wanted to mention her birthday, which is none of my business, then I saw her face. Distant and troubled. The conversation she had with her mom in the Blue Room sounded intense. I wasn't eavesdropping, but Olive's firm tone and the sound of her mother yelling on the other end of the line caught my attention. It's different from the way she speaks to me; now she sounds weary and lost. Maybe even off guard.

I'm no stranger to escaping real life. I have my own reasons for never staying in one place for a long time, and they run deep. In fact, my next job assignment starts in two weeks. It's convenient that I'm filling in as manager today, because here we are, me and this intriguing woman.

"Most of the people who work here are locals. If you have questions, please ask. The hotel will be pretty quiet after today so I'll—*we'll* be begging to help you." I notice a slight curve of her lips. Is that a grin? I'll take it.

"Leo, I'm back. Let me finish that up for you," Donna says cheerfully behind me. Damn, that was a quick break.

I almost snap at her to say that Olive is my guest to take care of. This is fucking crazy. I don't obsess over people who stay here, but Olive? The draw to her is unexpected and happily accepted. Now that I know she's here alone, I want to make her stay here as pleasant as possible.

As the manager of the hotel, of course. Why does that feel like a lie?

Because it is, you ass.

"It's okay, Donna. I'm almost finished. Her room isn't ready yet. I'm going to show her the café."

"Would you like me to take her?"

I open my mouth to answer as a couple arrives. Olive moves to the side to make space, and I'm relieved by their perfect timing.

"Or maybe not," Donna adds, directing her focus to them.

"I'll take care of Ms. Hansen. Call me if you need anything." She nods and greets the couple.

Before I forget, I shove Olive's paperwork into an envelope. "Here's a copy of your invoice," I say, handing it to her.

"Thanks." She takes it, then slides it into the side pocket of her suitcase.

I round the counter. "Ready for the best tart of your life?" My enthusiasm might be over the top, but that's me.

A shy grin appears. "Sure. Lead the way." She reaches to gather her things.

"You can leave your luggage and coat here if you'd like. It'll be safe behind the counter. May I take them?"

She nods, and I secure them in the back. Then I motion for her to go down the long hallway to the right.

As we move along, I point out where breakfast is served, the bar area, mention room service, and tell her about the spa on the other side of the inn. She nods along but doesn't say much. Is she even listening?

To fill the silence that suffocates me, I say, "The café is a fairly recent addition to the inn. Tourists and locals from all over the island visit year-round. There's a separate entrance for those who are only visiting the café, but we have a direct entrance from the hotel." I motion for her to take a left. "This hallway connects the café to the inn so our guests don't have to worry about the weather. It's especially nice during the winter months."

"I'll be honest," she finally responds. "Your hotel was the first one that popped up when I searched for somewhere to stay. I liked the home page and the photos, read some reviews, then made the reservation. So far it's above and beyond my expectations."

"I'm glad it grabbed your attention." I'll have to thank the web designer again when she comes back from vacation.

I greet an elderly couple as they pass by. They stay at the hotel every year to celebrate their anniversary. They got married here fifty years ago on December 31.

"This hotel started out more than a hundred years ago as a small, simple inn on a sizable piece of land. Over time, the hotel expanded and added more amenities. It's much more than an inn now, but my mother's family, the Gable family, insisted on keeping the word in the name. Despite its size, we're committed to maintaining the same cozy, welcoming atmosphere it's had from the beginning. If you're interested, you'll find a little booklet about the inn's transformation over the years in your suite."

Great. I sound like a tour guide, narrating the hotel's history into a microphone for a group of tourists. *Really sexy, Leo.*

The café comes into view, but Olive doesn't notice because she's busy looking out the windows. It's an ugly, gray day, but the grounds are beautiful even during the winter months.

She finally looks my way. "I'll have a lot of time on my hands during my stay. I look forward to exploring the area."

"Well, if you want to have a coffee with me while you wait for your room, I can give you some tips." Her eyes widen. *Shit.* I'm totally screwing this up. I raise my hands. "No pressure, of course."

What am I doing? She's a guest at the hotel, and my behavior is bordering on unprofessional. I might be over-the-top friendly—my sister calls me a golden retriever— but it's not my norm to ask guests to have a coffee with me upon arrival. She probably thinks I'm hitting on her.

Well, I am, aren't I—in a way?

Yes, you are.

5

OLIVE

Leo wants to have coffee with me. *Me!* But he's the manager! Do managers have coffee with their guests to be hospitable? Is that ethical? Do I care? No.

"Sure. I'd love to," I say, ignoring my conflicted thoughts. I shove my hands in my pockets. "If it doesn't take away from your job, of course."

A handsome, bald man in a black and red checkered flannel, dirty jeans, and work boots walks toward us with a coffee in hand. And is that—I squint—a kitten cradled in his other arm? When he passes us, he scowls at Leo and, wait, did he grunt too? Leo snickers.

"Friend of yours?" I whisper once the guy disappears around a corner.

"That was my brother, Sully. My sister and I played a joke on him a couple of hours ago, and he's still pissed at us."

"When I was sitting by the fireplace, I saw you with a woman in the lobby by the Christmas tree. Was that your sister?"

"Was she short with shoulder-length brown hair?" I

nod. "Yes, that was Tonya. Unfortunately, Sully's one big grump and we try to lighten him up. Sometimes we go too far. I'm sure I'd be like him too if I were in his situation." He waves it off. "Enough of that. Let's eat."

It sounds like his entire family works here. At least his sister and brother do. I'm intrigued and want to ask him a ton of questions, but I'll start with the important one.

"Okay, but first—was he holding a gray kitten with blue eyes, or am I delusional from lack of sugar?"

"Nope, not delusional. He found her a couple weeks ago. That kitten hasn't left his side ever since. Don't they say pets pick their owners?"

"Couldn't tell ya. I never had one."

"Doesn't matter. Sully's sweet and gentle with her, and he only grunts at us."

That's a lot to take in. It's a reminder that everyone's dealing with their own struggles, some more visible than others. Do I look miserable? Andy usually tells me when I do, which is pretty often. But since I arrived here, I haven't felt that way. This is exactly what I needed—to get out of my head and to forget, even if it's only for a little while, what I left behind.

The tempting fragrances of roasted coffee beans and baked goods reach out and surround us like a blanket. My stomach wakes up and grumbles. I don't know the last time I've been this hungry.

I raise my chin and take a deep breath. "Something smells delicious."

"Yep, and it's right ahead through those doors." Leo presses lightly on my lower back with his hand, urging me to go first, sending delectable tingles up my spine. Then his hand is gone. I glance at him and, with a flicker of surprise, see that he's rubbing his neck and grinning. Did he feel it too, or is his neck stiff?

We enter the café, and my mouth drops open. "This place is amazing. It's like we walked off a street in Paris into a fancy conservatory full of people."

The glass walls and roof offer a view outside. An elegant gold chandelier with dangling crystals illuminates the room. To the left is a long white counter with gold accents and large, pastel-pink floral arrangements. Behind it are floor-to-ceiling glass display cabinets and a refrigerator filled with colorful delights. White tables with lit candles and pink-fabric wingback chairs fill the rest of the open space. French music plays softly in the background. Lively chatter from guests and the grinding of coffee beans adds to the charm. You'd never know that Christmas was a week ago.

"Hi, Mr. Leo," a young boy says, running up to us with a big toothless grin. He raises his hand, and Leo high-fives him.

Leo kneels down to be eye level with him. "Hey, Mr. Cody. Aren't you a happy camper this afternoon?" He waves to a couple at a table nearby. I'm assuming the boy's parents.

"Guess what I saw yesterday?" Cody bounces on the tips of his toes, his eyes lit up with glee.

Leo tilts his head. "Hmm. A dinosaur?" Cody shakes his head and giggles. "Oh, I know. A clown?" The boy's nose crinkles with disgust. Leo lifts his hands up in front of him. "Okay, someone doesn't like clowns." *Who does?* "I give up. Let me hear it."

The boy's eyes grow wide. "I saw a big fat whale," he says, loud enough that other customers look in our direction.

"No way! That's fantastic." Leo messes with Cody's hair. "You're lucky to have seen one this time of year."

"And look, I got this." He dashes over to where the

man and woman are getting up from their table. With an amused face, the woman hands Cody a large stuffed-animal whale. He runs back and shakes it in the air at Leo, handing it to him. "Mommy bought me this after we saw it."

Leo turns the whale side to side, pretending he's never seen anything like it. "This is awesome." He hands it back to the boy. "Take good care of it."

Leo urges me to come closer, then introduces me to Cody and his parents. Cody pulls on Leo's shirt for him to bend over again.

"She's pretty," he mutters to Leo behind his hand, loud enough that I can hear him.

"She is, isn't she?" Leo mutters back.

I don't know where to look or what to do. I'm completely out of my element, it's bizarre. Don't get me wrong, I'm flattered. Is this how Dorothy felt when she walked out of her house in Munchkinland? Leo peeks at me, grins, and high-fives Cody again. His parents say their goodbyes and urge Cody out of the café.

I haven't been around this many people in months, and I'm in major overload. My hands are cold and clammy, and a slight headache throbs behind my eyes. I'm tempted to leave, but I can't quite yet. I'm enjoying watching Leo interact with the guests. His warm, cheerful expressions give him a friendly, approachable look that would give anybody a sense of comfort. I thought I'd be alone in my room by this time, not out socializing. I take a deep breath to calm my jittery nerves.

Leo notices and quickly says, "I'm sorry, Olive. It's good for me to interact with the guests and make them feel at home. They're a nice family."

"No need to apologize. You're working. I'm the one who should—I'm keeping you from your job."

"No, you aren't. My work's here in this café right now. That's my excuse, and I'm sticking to it." He combs his fingers through his wavy hair and turns toward the counter. I wonder if it feels as soft as it looks. "Now, didn't we come here to get something to eat?"

I give a subtle nod with my hands clasped in front of me.

"Then let's do it," he says. "This afternoon calls for an extra shot of espresso in my cappuccino."

A glass case at the end of the counter catches my eye. It's filled with artistically decorated cakes, tarts, éclairs, and a large assortment of macarons. *Yum.* I forgot about those. Why can't my stomach be big enough to sample everything?

Leo greets someone behind the counter. Does he *like* to socialize this much? Doesn't his mouth get dry? Apparently, the girl's name is Laureen, and her flirty giggles irk me somehow. *Jealous, Olive?* I ignore myself. Refusing to check what she looks like, I continue drooling over the confections on display.

Seconds later, Leo comes back to me. He's close enough that his body heat seeps into mine, warming me up. It's been a while since I've been this close to a man. A light cloud of his enticing cologne catches my attention. It exudes a unique softness and warmth with a dab of spice. His shoulder grazes mine, inducing an unexpected, heavenly spark. We split apart, chuckling.

"Sorry. I've been full of static today. My hair alone could provide enough electricity to run this place."

"Don't I know it?" he comments, pointing at his own wild hair. "So, what do you think? Find something you want to try?"

"Everything looks tempting," I say, then turn around to admire the room. "I love it here."

Leo's face beams once again, and he nods. "Thanks. It took a lot of convincing and planning. I've spent more time than I can count in cafés like this during my travels, and I thought it'd be a great addition for the hotel." *Hmm. During his travels. Business or pleasure?* "My brother took the lead, and the rest followed."

"The one who grunted in the hallway?"

"You heard that, huh?"

"I wasn't sure. But your reaction gave it away."

"Yep, it's him. An old friend of his owns a construction company, and he agreed to build it since everything was shut down during the beginning of the pandemic. You know what it was like then."

"Oh, I remember." Too well. It shattered my life. It's what made me abandon Los Angeles and move back home. I shiver and lock the memories of death back into their little box to make them disappear.

"This is the perfect place to relax and enjoy the view. All the natural light through the glass roof and the windows…" Leo peers outside for a moment. "You can't really appreciate it now, but wait till tomorrow. I think the weather's supposed to be better. You'll see. There's an outdoor terrace too, for the warmer months."

"Hey, Leo! Are you here for your daily sugar intake? It's late for you." Someone with a smooth French accent approaches us from behind. It fits perfectly with the atmosphere. Leo and I turn to face a stylishly dressed, handsome silver fox whose black button-down shirt is dusted with flour. He does a double take when he sees Leo, then guffaws, holding his stomach. "What the hell is on your lip?"

Leo side-eyes me as he smooths the mustache, then looks at the goofy man.

"Well, I didn't miss that snarky attitude of yours while

you were away in France, Louis. Your accent got worse, I can hardly understand you." With a wide grin, he gives the man a bear hug. "Good to see you, old man. Welcome back. Happy New Year."

The man squeezes him and lifts him off the ground. Their greeting is almost like a father and son. It's sweet to witness. It makes me miss my dad more because he gave me the biggest and tightest hugs—sometimes I could hardly breathe. But those good times are out of reach and long gone.

"Please tell me that caterpillar is fake. It's so not you!" he laughs again, and I join in.

Leo strokes it and huffs. "Come on, it's not that bad." He turns to me and his gaze lingers, searching my face. "Is it?"

I raise my hands in mock surrender and utter, "I plead the fifth."

Leo braces his hands on his hips. "Seriously?"

Damn. Now I feel bad. "Sorry. I'm not a fan of facial hair."

"Listen to her. She knows what she's talking about," the silver fox says, then winks at me.

I'm getting a kick out of this show. I left my boring life behind to get out of my funk, and now I'm talking about mustaches, of all things. My face hurts from smiling so much.

Leo crosses his arms over his chest. "Well, I'm not a fan either. I actually hate it. I cringe every time I look in a mirror. I lost a bet to Tonya and Sully. A stupid challenge I found on TikTok. I'm not getting into it right now. It's too embarrassing because I really thought I'd win. But—when the clock strikes twelve tonight, it's coming off. A little scruff is okay, but full beards or mustaches...no thanks."

Phew. Only temporary. I can't wait to see his face

without it. Then again, Leo with a five o'clock shadow emphasizing his perfect jawline would probably make me combust. *Stop fantasizing!* I scratch my neck and discreetly clear my throat. Unfortunately it grabs the older man's attention anyway.

"We're being rude, Leo. Who is this lovely lady?" he purrs. "New girlfriend? I haven't seen her here before."

If my face wasn't already bright red, I'm sure it is now. I want to crawl out of the room. Where's the closest emergency exit when I need one?

We both respond, "No." But, without a second passing, Leo continues. "Louis, this is Olive. She's a guest. Her room isn't ready, and I thought I'd introduce her to some of your specialties."

"Ooh. That's very nice of you to accompany your guests. Is that a new service?" He elbows Leo playfully. Leo's cheeks turn a sweet shade of pink. Is he really blushing? I don't see him as the type to be easily embarrassed.

A customer approaches the counter we're partially blocking. I tap Leo's arm and point behind him. Leo apologizes to the person, then maneuvers us to the side, away from traffic.

Louis isn't deterred. "Hi, Olive," he says. "It's nice to meet you. Welcome to the Café Charmant. I hope you have a sweet tooth." If I were into older men, I'd be putty in his hands because of his accent and ocean-blue eyes. He offers me his hand, and I shake it gently. So this is what happens when I'm around cheerful people in a unique setting. I should've tried this sooner.

"Leo can't seem to stop talking about your tarts," I inform him.

"You're already on a first-name basis. Interesting." There's an undeniable twinkle in his eye.

"Louis," Leo warns with a light growl.

Louis ignores him. "He sure does love it here. That's why he spends hours at the gym."

Leo slaps him in the gut with the back of his hand. "Speak for yourself, old man. You're there just as much as I am."

Nodding with a grin, he grasps Leo's shoulder. "This guy's the reason I work here. He's the best man I know. After spending a couple days here, you'll understand why."

I'm catching on, and it's only been, what, an hour? I've lost track of time.

"All right. If you are trying to embarrass me, it's not working," Leo jokes, pushing Louis toward the end of the counter. "Don't you have some cakes to bake back there for the party tonight or something?"

"Okay. I'm going." Then he stops and turns around. "But first—how long will you be here this time?"

"You'll see me plenty. I have two more weeks to annoy you and steal food. Now let us order something."

Louis lets out a hearty laugh again.

Two more weeks. Interesting. I wonder what else he does.

"He's funny," I say.

"He's always like that." Leo takes a deep breath and places his hands on the counter. "Olive, I'm sorry about the constant interruptions. Your room is probably ready, and I've taken up too much of your time. Do you still want to order something? You can take it to your room if you want, and I'll get out of your staticky hair." He plays with me, but I know he's serious too. Not about my hair, of course.

I should go to my room, but why? What's there waiting for me? Nothing and nobody. And I don't want the time with him to end, and I'm starving. I don't feel lonely either, not having the chance to be since Leo appeared.

"I really do need to eat something, and there's no time pressure."

"Cool. Then let's finally order so we can take a sea—"

"Leo, there you are," someone else calls out behind us. Jeez, he's popular.

"Or not. It's never ending," he mumbles, pinching the bridge of his nose.

I turn to find perhaps the most beautiful woman I've ever seen. Tall and thin, with big green eyes and curly auburn hair. It's pulled up in a messy bun with a pencil sticking out of it. Loosened ringlets dangle around her face and neck. Basically the opposite of me. "I finally tracked you down. I haven't seen you all day. Have you been hiding from me?"

She waves to Louis behind the counter, then calls out to him, "Everything ready for tonight?"

"Oui. What kind of question is that? I have a rep to protect."

She blows him a kiss. "Thanks. Just double-checking." He winks at her, then turns away.

The redhead glances at me, then back to Leo. I can't read her expression. "Sorry to interrupt," she says.

Leo gives her a quick hug, more like a friendly one, not romantic. Something like jealousy creeps in again, which is absurd. Or is it envy? I'll stick with envy because who wouldn't want to look like her? In case I have to shake her hand too, I nonchalantly wipe my hands on my jeans. Or better yet, it's time to order a coffee. I turn toward the counter, and of course, no one is there. I pretend to read the menu that's on the wall opposite me as I eavesdrop.

Leo continues. "Nope, not hiding. Several of your demanding party guests kept me busy with their special requests," he jabs, humor clear in his voice.

I take a quick glance over my shoulder to see their interaction.

She cocks her hip. "You're such a liar."

"Maybe, maybe not. You could've called me if you needed something. Or did you want to see my handsome face?"

"Right." She rolls her eyes. "I was missing that fiesta fuzz too much."

Fiesta fuzz? I swallow my laugh and pull my eyes away before I draw attention to myself.

He scoffs. "Come on. Admit it. You want Sam to grow one. It adds character."

"Not on your life," she declares. "Anyway, just to confirm again, you aren't bringing anyone to the party tonight, correct? Bethany asked to sit next to you."

Who's Bethany, and why do I care? My nosiness makes me take a casual mini step closer along the counter to hear them better.

"I know she's your friend, but no. Not interested. Sorry, but not sorry."

Relief washes over me, which again is fucking absurd. I want to peek at them to see her face, but it'd be too obvious that I'm listening in.

Then Leo's voice changes as he adds, "Ya know what? Leave an empty seat next to me—*not* for Bethany. Who knows what might happen between now and midnight."

How does someone like him not have a date?

"Whatever you say, funny guy. Gotta go. I'm off to see your sister. See you tonight."

Melancholy washes over me. *Where is the damn barista?* I'm so out of place here while they talk about a party I'm not invited to and a woman who's interested in Leo. While they're partying tonight, celebrating the new year, I'll be in my room watching TV. Or sleeping before the clock strikes twelve.

"I'm back, Olive," Leo says from behind me.

I take a deep breath, slip on my happy face, and turn around. *Oof.* I collide with Leo's hard chest. When did he get this close? And why? He stumbles back and grabs my arms to balance us.

"I'm sorry. Did I hurt you?" His anxious gaze sweeps over my face.

I rub my nose. "Not really. It was more of a shock than anything else. I'm fine."

Leo places his hands on his hips and shakes his head. "Olive, I'm really sorry." His phone rings in his pocket, and he takes it out, checking the screen. "Damn it. I need to take this call." He groans. "Please order whatever you want. It's on the house since I keep making you wait. I really thought it'd be a lot quieter."

I wave him off. "No problem. Do what you have to do. I'm fine." He doesn't owe me anything. He gives me a thumbs-up, then quickly mentions to the barista that I don't have to pay. Of course she shows up now.

Along with a large cappuccino, I order a lemon tart and a chocolate macaron. "You can take a seat wherever you want. I'll bring your order to you," the barista says. I make my way over to a table in the corner.

A minute later, Leo returns. "Olive, I hate to say this, but I need to get back to the front desk. There are some fires to put out. Do you want to come back with me to see if your room is ready? I'm sure it is."

As he says this, my order arrives. I thank the woman, and she leaves.

"My room can wait. I'm going to enjoy this first." My stomach rumbles in anticipation.

"Good. Either I'll come by with your key or Donna

will. Or come to the front desk when you're done. Okay?" He's babbling, almost like it physically pains him to leave me.

"Leo, go. You're working. No need to babysit me."

He frowns. "That's not what I'm doing. I really wanted to sit with you. Hopefully, we'll get a chance some other time or later." His phone rings again, and he shuffles backward toward the door, almost tripping over a chair. "Okay, gotta go before someone comes looking for me. I really don't want that." He spins around and is out the door in a flash.

I deflate in my chair. From the second I arrived at this hotel, it's been nonstop. What an unexpected and perfect distraction. To prevent myself from crashing, I take a few sips of my cappuccino, then pull out my AirPods, a little notebook, and a pen from my handbag. Searching Spotify, I click a favorite movie soundtrack.

Opening to the first blank page of the notebook, I scrawl, *New Year Resolutions*.

It's time to make some changes.

6

LEO

"Thanks for helping me out, Leo," Donna says, wiping her brow with the back of her hand. "This website business is getting ridiculous. As far as I know, all our guests have arrived today. Why do things always go wrong around the holidays when we're short on staff? And then the bathroom faucet issue in room twenty-five. Sully saved the day on that one." She picks up a stray pen from the floor and drops it into the penholder on the counter.

"You know the Forrest boys. We get things done!" I flex my biceps like Superman.

"Your mom was looking for you," Donna says, unfazed by my antics. "She said you should go see her in her office when you're done flexing or whatever it is you're doing." Her mouth twitches with mirth.

I drop my arms and pat down my shirt. For some reason, I don't want to know what she wants. "Yeah… She's sent me a couple of messages." I look at my watch, then toward Mom's office in the back.

Donna moves away, then quickly turns back. "Oh! Ms. Hansen's room is ready. Is she still in the café? I can go get

42

her." She glances at the clock on the opposite wall. "Oh dear, she's been waiting a long time."

"Nope, I'll take care of it. The conversation with Mom will be quick." I know I'm being a selfish asshole and unprofessional. I should give Olive her key immediately instead of making her wait any longer. At this rate, we'll be lucky if she doesn't leave a scathing one-star review about the delay in getting her room. However, I have another idea in mind. *Hmm.* I decide to take my chances and make her wait.

"Hey, Donna, can you please do me a quick favor?" I search the area to make sure no one's around. "It's a secret."

Her face lights up. She loves secrets, and she's good at keeping them. "Sure. What do you need?" She lowers her voice like we're undercover.

I whisper in her ear what I'd like her to do. "I'll pay for it. And wait…one more thing." I grab a sheet of stationery and write a quick note. Donna clears her throat and taps her fingers on the counter. I fold the paper and slip it into a red envelope, then give it to her. "Can you please have someone put the bottle in her room with this envelope?"

Donna takes it from me and taps her hand with it. "Don't worry. I'm on the case. She's going to love it. Unless she doesn't drink." *Shit, I didn't think about that.* Donna squeezes my left cheek. "You're the sweetest. There's hope for you yet."

"Thanks… I guess." I'm not sure what she means by that. "Anyway, you know where I am if you need anything." I wouldn't mind if she interrupted my conversation with Mom.

She rolls her eyes. "I know how to do my job, young man. To quote you from before, 'get goin'.'"

I salute, then spin on my heel and head for Mom's

office. I catch her staring at the laptop on her desk, her red glasses perched on the tip of her nose. She looks up and flashes me a perfect, welcoming smile—the same one everyone says I inherited. She removes her glasses and places them on the desk.

"Hiya, Ma."

"Hi, honey. Come in and shut the door, please."

Oh, man. Interrogation time. What did I do now that the door needs to be closed? When Mom's mad, she's super calm. All the anger is in her voice. Her body language and facial features stay cool as a cucumber. It's scary as fuck. But I'm not seeing any of that right now. So far, it doesn't seem like I'm in trouble.

"Sure, but I don't have a lot of time." *Olive's waiting!* The woman who's probably glad I left after the constant chaos that followed in my wake, not to mention my almost breaking her nose.

I close the door, then take the chair opposite my mother's desk, propping my ankle on my knee. "So, what's up?"

Mom rests her forearms on the desk and clasps her hands. "I saw you charged a guest the double-room price for a suite. Did the system screw up again, was it a mistake, or was she cute?" She cocks an eyebrow, and the corner of her mouth ticks up with amusement.

Olive's beautiful, not cute.

"It's the system." I explain what happened with Olive's reservation. "Who knows how many more times it's going to screw up?" ·

She leans back in her seat, crosses her arms, and rocks gently. "Let me see what I can do. I swear I hate technology. It was much easier when I was younger."

"We'll figure it out. Anything else?"

"There is." She gives me a firm look, and I shift in my

seat. "I know it's been a busy day, and it's not the best time to bring this up. But—" *Here it comes.* "Your aunt Betty called me this afternoon." Yep, just what I thought. "Betty's been trying to get hold of you. Why haven't you returned her calls?"

"Been busy. I'll call her back when it's slower." *Liar.* I smooth my mustache. Hey, this caterpillar is a good stress reliever. Maybe I'll wait to shave it off.

Mom eyes me, knowing I'm full of shit. "You know what's coming up. It's been five years. Betty and Mason want to have a little family gathering in memory of Corey in March. Possibly go to the cemetery first, then have lunch here. Tonya's going to plan it. She and Tonya want to discuss your travel plans to narrow down a date."

I look away and focus on a leaf in the potted plant on Mom's desk.

"Honey," she continues. "I know it'll be hard for you, but you have to attend. If not for yourself, then for Corey and his parents."

I glare at her. "We've been over this a million times. You have no clue how hard it is for me, even after five years. It still feels like yesterday. And why would she want to have a party to celebrate his death?" My voice sounds colder than I intended. "No, thanks. I'll pass."

"Okay, that's enough. I'm sorry. I shouldn't have brought it up right now." She stands and comes around the desk, then rests on the edge near me. "You need to let it go, Leo. Traveling around the world hasn't changed a thing. Everyone grieves in their own way, but I don't think you've stopped long enough to do so."

Pulling on the hairband around my wrist, I say, "Why did you bring it up then?"

"A new year is upon us, and I'm hoping it'll be a year of change for you. You don't have to keep running.

Herbert retires in March. The manager position will be open April first."

"I'm not running." I know she's right, but I say this anyway. "I'm living the life that we wanted to have. To keep traveling."

She sighs. "And you always do it alone. Don't you get lonely? Aren't you tired of being on the go all the time? When you're here with us, you seem happy. Is it not enough to keep you here for the long run?"

Mom's talking to me like we've never had this conversation before, but the topic comes up often. Yeah, I'm tired. I feel stuck, waiting for something to push me in a new direction or show me there's more to life than writing hotel reviews.

Don't get me wrong, I love what I do. And I'm a cheerful person by nature, but my chest feels hollow. It has since the day my cousin got sick. Then one day, he closed his eyes and…never opened them again. There was no chance to say goodbye. He was my best friend. How am I supposed to get over that?

I lean over and rest my head in my hands. "What do you want me to say that I haven't already said the hundred other times we've talked about this, Ma?"

"I wish I knew." She pushes away from the desk and comes over to pat my shoulder. "Why don't you take off? Or go back to the café to tell that woman her room is ready. We don't want complaints from our guests, do we?"

My head shoots up. How does she know about that? *Donna? Louis?*

She smirks. "Word travels."

"As always. I was being nice." If that were true, why did I ask Donna to put something in her room for her birthday? To extend my niceness?

"Whatever you say, honey. I'm not sure I've ever seen

you take someone to the café. She's here alone, and you have time on your hands. Why not show her around while she's here?"

"Forget it, Ma. Whatever you have concocted in your head, it won't happen." Since when do I lie like this?

She throws up her hands and shrugs. "A mother can only hope."

I stand to leave, and Mom surprises me with a bear hug. "Leo…honey. Make this the best year you've ever had. Let that spark of life ignite again. You don't need Corey to do that. It's always been inside you. It's just dormant right now." She lays her hand on my heart. "You're a good man already. Think of where that power could take you if you let it out again."

"Impressive. That was pretty poetic. You should write that down or make a T-shirt."

She shakes her head and sighs. "There's no getting through to you."

I poke her side. "I'm playing with you, Ma. I heard every word, and I'll think about it. And I'll call Aunt Betty in a couple of days."

"Good. Oh!" she yells, making me flinch. "And stop pestering your brother."

"What?" She's going to give me a severe case of whiplash.

"Don't deny it. I already gave your sister a mouthful. I shouldn't have to say this when you're all adults. Sully's having a rough time, and you two don't seem to under-stand that. Nothing sucks more than getting your heart trampled on. It's like watching my life on repeat when I look at him."

Recently, Sully caught his best friend and business partner screwing his fiancée in his own office at work. When Mom was twenty years old, her best friend stole the man she thought she was going to marry. That was almost forty years ago. She met my dad a couple of years later. Now she says she regrets losing her best friend, but she'll be forever grateful to her because if she hadn't taken him away, Mom would've married the wrong man.

But Sully's still dealing with the pain of betrayal and rejection.

"We thought it was funny. I'll apologize when I see him. Are you coming to the party tonight? The bartender can make you one of those fruity drinks you like." I drape my arm over her shoulders and squeeze, knowing she'll say no.

She sighs. "I think I'll head home and celebrate alone."

"Shocker." I squeeze her again.

"You know I have the best view of the fireworks. And you know how I love my pjs." She shimmies her hips.

I head for the door, then turn around again at the last second. "If you change your mind, we'd love to see you. This could be your year too."

"Yeah, wouldn't that be a hoot?" She stuffs her hands in her pockets, not looking convinced. "Now get out of here. Take that woman the key for her room. And enjoy the party tonight."

My dad died when I was eighteen. He lived with severe diabetes most of his life. He had a kidney transplant and due to complications, he died shortly after.

Mom grieved, but kept on swimming. We're kind of alike in that way. We let out all of our pent-up emotions once or twice to get it out of our systems, and then we move on, grieving in silence for no one else to see. We have to, because life goes on. But our systems, mainly our hearts, are changed forever.

Enough of this depressing shit.

Go get your damn coffee and the girl!

7

OLIVE

I reapply my clear lip gloss, keeping a steady eye on the door. It's been a good thirty minutes since Leo left. What should I do? He said I could go to the desk to check for myself. Most people would've done that by now.

Please let me see his gorgeous face one more time today.

I can only procrastinate for so long. My table's been cleared, and they've asked me twice if I wanted anything else. A chocolate tart found its way over here, and I ate it. Don't tell anyone.

Just as I admit Leo's not coming back, he bursts through the entrance almost plowing over a customer who's leaving. Relief floods my body. He scans the open space, gathering his unruly hair into a bun. Then his frantic eyes meet mine, and his face transforms, creating the most beautiful smile…and it's aimed at me. Me, of all people. I glance over my shoulder nonchalantly to make sure.

"Yes, I'm looking at you," he says, loud enough I can hear him. A warm, tingling sensation swims through my blood. I look around, but everyone else is absorbed in their own lives. How can you ignore someone as vibrant as Leo?

He reaches my table, and I look up as he towers over me. Before I can catch myself, I blurt, "You have an amazing smile. It's contagious." It's true because my lips are about to split from stretching to my ears in response. "I'm sure you've heard that before."

If a guy I hardly knew said that to me, I'd write him off because it's a typical pickup line. Why stop embarrassing myself now? I'll be gone in a week and quickly forgotten. It's better than sulking in my room and dreaming about him.

Leo loosens his light blue tie, which looks a lot sexier than it should. "Oh, I've been told a time or two, but it's nicer hearing it from you. Thanks. And don't let it fool you. It causes mixed reactions." He chuckles dismissively.

I lean away in disbelief. "What do you mean?"

"Oh, you know. Bitter humans can't handle cheerful people. I've been around a bit, and let me tell you, I've had my fair share of negativity thrown my way."

"That's horrible. What do you do when that happens?"

He shrugs. "I keep smiling. Gotta know when to bow out."

"Screw those people. I mean, I might be a little envious of someone's obvious happiness sometimes, but not enough to be mean to them. I'm miserable most of the time, and I'd much rather be around someone who's more exciting."

He grimaces, and I regret my words as soon as they come out of my mouth. *Can I sound anymore depressing?* Time to change the subject.

"So, you ran out of here pretty fast before. Everything okay?"

Leo leans forward, resting his hands on the back of the

chair across from me. "Yes, the fires have been put out. I'm really sorry I've wasted your time."

Oh, Leo. The time I've spent with you is above and beyond what I had planned for this trip.

"It wasn't wasted. I got to drink caffeine and eat pastries to my heart's content," I mutter, gesturing with three fingers up.

He nods, then whispers back, "Told ya. They're addictive."

"They are. And I started a list of things to do around here. You'll have to help me…or maybe someone at the front desk could," I add quickly.

I suck at flirting. Time to add *Flirting 101* to my resolutions list. He did offer to give me some pointers. No, not on flirting. But I'm sure he has other plans.

Like a party with that beautiful redhead.

The corner of his mouth lifts. "I know I offered to help you before, and I still want to, but you've waited long enough to get your room. I'm the worst hotel manager for not coming sooner. Let me take you to get your luggage and give you your key."

"Don't be crazy. If anything, you're preventing me from being alone in my room, which is a good thing." Two tarts and a macaron in, and I'm bold like an eagle. No, that's bald like an eagle. Or is it bold like a lion? *Whatever.* Was there whiskey in my coffee?

"Well, I'm done with work for the day," he says with a sly grin. "And I didn't have my afternoon coffee. Want to keep me company while I inhale some much needed caffeine and sugar?" He checks his watch. "They close in about thirty minutes. That should be enough time."

A barista approaches and Leo requests his usual and some water for me. My kidneys will thank me after my coffee intake.

He pulls out the chair across from me and drops onto it. "This is going to be good. I've hardly eaten anything today. Too many issues to untangle."

"More website problems?" I ask, fiddling with my pen.

"Unfortunately, yes. But I don't want to bother you with boring computer shit."

I wave it off. "Believe me, I know how boring it is. I probably shouldn't say that since I'm a web designer." This was a backup plan that should've been temporary. Years later, and nothing has changed—I'm working from home for my uncle with little human interaction. "I could help you if you don't find someone to fix it."

"Our IT employee is on a safari in Africa with little to no Wi-Fi connection. Whatever's going on hasn't happened before. She doesn't come back until the end of next week. We were stupid not to have a backup plan."

"Well, the offer's there."

"Thanks. I'll think about it."

My water, along with his cappuccino and tart, arrive. His eyes light up when they're placed in front of him. He's like a child on Christmas morning. I glance at his cappuccino.

"Aww, look at you, getting hearts in your foam. I got a pretty leaf."

"It's almost too nice to drink. I don't want to ruin it. But I'm dying over here. Please tell me I can drink it," he pleads, licking his lips.

"Maybe you should wait a few more minutes," I tease.

"Wait? You're nuts," he exclaims. I just want to see him lick his lips again. "Haven't I done that enough?" He pretends to hug his food.

"Oh, like you'd really listen to me."

He looks around to see if anybody is nearby, then leans in. "Maybe I like being told what to do."

I can't take him seriously. "Okay, funny guy. I'll keep that in mind."

He points at me. "I made you smile, though."

I put my elbows on the table and rest my chin on my bridged hands. "More than anyone has in a long time."

Leo's heated gaze traces my face and lands on my lips. "Good, and I'll keep doing it as long as you let me," he says, his voice soft and sincere. I love the way words roll off his tongue.

"Keep it coming. Now drink your coffee before it gets cold."

"Yes, ma'am." He sprinkles some sugar on the top, takes a sip, then sighs. His eyes close like he's in heaven. If we all could enjoy something so simple.

Instead of making a list of things to do around here, he tells me more about the hotel and how his family runs it. His mom is the overall owner, his sister's the event manager, and his brother's a temporary member of the maintenance staff. He doesn't talk about his own job. The longer we chat about random things, the more relaxed I become. He's easy to talk to, funny, and animated when telling his stories.

Half an hour comes and goes too fast. Everything about this afternoon has been like a defibrillator to the heart. I've rediscovered a world I once knew but chose to forget. Now we're headed back to the front desk to pick up my things. He stops suddenly and turns to me.

"Oh, I forgot to mention—the town sets off fireworks at midnight. There's a perfect view from the hotel. Our guests can watch from their rooms or head down to the little beach area to enjoy the show by the water. You can check out the hotel map in your room for more details."

"Ooh, that sounds nice. I'll definitely do that." *Probably not.*

We approach the front desk, and Leo retrieves my things.

"Here you go. Safe and sound."

I grab my coat and hang it over my arm, then reach for my bag. He's too fast and rolls the suitcase toward the elevator, saying over his shoulder, "Follow me."

We stop in front of the elevator, and I reach again for the handle but end up grasping the warm hand that's wrapped around it. The contact shoots tingling sparks straight into my heart. I gasp, enjoying it way too much. *Did the fireworks start early?* I roll my eyes to myself. That was pretty cheesy.

I try to pull my hand away, but he grabs it before I can. "Olive, do you want to go to a party tonight? As my guest? There'll be great food, an open bar, music…"

Could I picture myself at a party where I don't know anyone? My social battery is close to zero. I bite on my inner cheek and don't know what to say. Is this the party the redhead was talking about? Of course it is. Being in a room with a bunch of drunken strangers doesn't sound like a good time. Not tonight.

I hardly know Leo, though I'm sure he's pretty harmless. Still, it's New Year's Eve—who knows how he behaves when he drinks. I could, however, go sing "Auld Lang Syne," steal a drink, and leave if I don't feel comfortable. Do people sing that song anymore? They probably do if they're drunk enough. *Forget the stupid song!*

No, the awkwardness is already setting in. I scratch the back of my neck.

"I'm not sure, Leo. Those are your friends. Socializing isn't my best strength."

He holds my hand in both of his. "You've been fine with me."

"I know, but that's because you're…*you*. And we're one

on one. Not in a group. I'm not sure I'd be the best company for you. What's the dress code, anyway? I didn't plan for a party when I packed."

"Okay. I get it. Let me think for a second." He lets go of my hand and looks up at the ceiling, tapping his chin.

And…I smile *again*.

"Okay. I've got it. How about this? When you're standing on your room balcony, and you look out at the water, you'll see a huge madrone tree with several large lanterns hanging from it that look like big sparkling snow-balls. Or maybe it's mistletoe." His eyebrows squeeze together as he considers. "I think it's mistletoe. Anyway, you get the gist. There's a white bench there under the branches. You can't miss it with the amount of damn lights my sister put on that tree.

"At eleven, I'll be waiting there for you. Meet me there if you change your mind. You'll miss the good food, but you won't have to sit at a table full of strangers for dinner. Then, we'll go to the party for the open bar and dancing." His babbling is adorable and very convincing.

"Eating isn't the issue. I was planning on calling room service, anyway."

"I promise you, you won't regret it. This is a fun group of people and there's no dress code. Some will wear suits or dresses, but the rest will opt for jeans. I'll be dressed casually. My friends hosting the party are laid back and love to have fun."

I did bring a white button-down top that I could wear with these jeans. My black boots would add a little extra zing to the outfit. *Wait a second! Am I really thinking about going?*

"My sister, Tonya, will be there too. I think you two would get along great. You came here to get away. Maybe a party or doing something different could help you forget for a little while. And I can be your p…partner in crime."

There was a tiny hesitation before those last three words. And they came out stifled, as if it pained him to say them. Strange.

I'm already a jittery mess thinking about it, but how can I say no to him? I picture myself standing there all awkward and alone while Mr. Social bounces around the room. It's not for dinner, though. Only drinks later on. Kind of like a party crasher. That's much more appealing.

Fuck, this is annoying. One side is ready to jump in and say, "Hell yes," while the other side firmly responds, "Fuck no."

"Anyway," he says, "think about it. There's plenty of time to decide. I can give you my number if you have questions."

I take my phone out of my pocket and turn it on without hesitation. Seconds later, tons of messages and voicemails pop up on my screen. Gritting my teeth, I ignore them. I open my contacts and hand him the phone. He adds his info, then gives it back.

"I won't ring myself, in case you don't want me to have your number. I'll leave it all up to you."

Is he real or only a dream?

He pushes the elevator button and the door slides open. "You're on the fourth floor and your suite is the last door on the left when you exit out of the elevator. I'd take you there myself, but I'd probably talk your ear off again."

"And I wouldn't stop you," I say with flirty humor. I step in, then turn to face him. "Thank you for everything, Leo. It was a perfect afternoon."

"It'll be even better if you meet me tonight." He wiggles his eyebrows.

I burst out laughing. "I'm sure everything with you would be better. Now let me go." I'm not lying.

He puts his hands up and retreats. "All right. I've only

known you for a hot minute and I'm already craving more. Now hit the fourth floor before it's too late and I jump in there with you."

Don't press it! My shaky finger lingers over the button. *Stay with him!* No.

The need to go to my room outweighs the desire to stay. *Click.* "I promise I'll think about it," is the last thing I say before the door closes.

I rest against the metal wall and squeeze my eyes shut. Did this miraculous afternoon really happen, or am I still on the ferry, fast asleep in my car? He was flirting with me, right? I'd rather not overanalyze it only for it to blow up in my face. Because, crazy as it sounds, he's not the only one who craves more.

The bell rings, and the door slides open. I step out and look to the left. I approach the wooden door bearing the correct room number. Opening it, I flick on the lights, and my jaw drops. This is definitely not a double room.

I enter, scan the spacious layout, and am instantly captivated by the charming country appeal. Directly ahead is a homey sitting area nestled near impressive windows and a glass door leading to the balcony. To the left is a separate bedroom with a luxurious king-sized bed. Exposed wooden beams run along the ceiling, and romantic decor featuring shades of crimson and ivory fills the entire suite. A week in this exquisite hotel won't be enough.

I peruse the lavish bedroom and bathroom, then wander over to the balcony door. The occasional squeak of the hardwood floor travels behind me. I step outside into the blustery air to find the tree Leo was talking about. I see its brilliance before I get to the balcony's edge. It's a towering tree, decorated with glistening balls of white lights swaying in the wind. Because of the distance, I squint and vaguely see a bench.

A gust of frigid wind passes by, making me shiver. I hug myself and slip back into the room. My eyes wander the room again, and I do a double take when I discover a bottle of champagne on the rustic coffee table. How did I miss that when I came in? A red envelope with my name on it rests against the bottle. It's probably from Andy. He's the only one who knows where I am. Or it's a generous welcome from the hotel.

I sit on the edge of the couch and eye the envelope like it's a precious diamond. Finally, I pluck it off the table and rip it open. Pure excitement transforms my mood. It's not from my brother or the hotel.

> *Dear Olive,*
>
> *I couldn't help overhearing that it's your birthday today. Here's a little something to kick off another year of your life. If you want to share the bottle with someone, you know who to ask. Happy birthday and happy New Year!*
> *Leo*

The words blur, and I realize I'm crying. There's no doubt in my mind what I'll be doing tonight.

And it's not drinking this alone in this suite.

8

LEO

Damn, it's cold. It's not raining but the air is damp, making it feel colder. I pace in front of my favorite tree and blow into my hands to warm them up. I should've hit the gym to burn off some of the buzzing energy that's been building since Olive went to her room. I tried to sleep for a little while before the party started, but my brain wouldn't shut down. It swirled like cotton candy.

Olive should've found the champagne already. I was hoping she'd send me a text, but there's been dead silence. Was it a bad idea? Now I feel like a complete idiot because I brought two flutes in case she comes with the bottle. I even brought a blanket to keep us warm if we sit on the bench.

How long should I wait for her? *You made her wait a long time for her room.* I glance at my watch again. Only five minutes to go. What if she can't find the tree? No, that's stupid. It's huge and lit up like a beacon. *Chill the fuck out!*

Why did I change my plans for her tonight? What is it about Olive that compels me to be impulsive? She's a stranger…but from the moment she arrived, I haven't wanted her out of my sight. I imagine myself following Olive everywhere, tugging on her shirt for attention. I chuckle to myself.

Since my cousin Corey died, I really haven't formed any meaningful connections with new people. Well, no, that's not true. The couple throwing the party tonight are the only ones. They don't know everything about my past, though. When I met them, their unparalleled love story sucked me in, and I adore their relationship.

It's been a while since I've been genuinely interested in a woman beyond sex. The closest I ever came to love was with my high school girlfriend. That was a joke, since it fizzled out right after graduation. Nothing's come close to it since.

But with Olive, somehow I feel a connection that's... fucking indescribable. I'm not saying it's love because that would be bullshit. Right? Then why does talking to her make my heart race, as if I'm being chased? And why does her intoxicating scent arouse me to the point I might embarrass myself? And why the hell do I feel like I'll burst if I don't see her tonight?

Because I'm borderline obsessed.

"Hi, Leo," Olive says softly behind me.

She's here! I stiffen from surprise and my pulse skyrockets, sending warm tingles to my icy fingers and toes. I turn around, unable to hide my excitement. Olive stands a few feet away from me with her arms behind her back. Her hair is pulled into a low side bun, and her lips are a glistening shade of pink.

"Hi! I'm really glad you came. You look beautiful." My cheeks are going to hurt tomorrow from my wide perma grin.

"Thanks. You look handsome yourself," she says, her

eyes cast down. "It wasn't a simple decision. My nerves were getting the best of me."

I lower myself to encourage her to look at me. When she does, I ask with anticipation, "What changed your mind?"

"This." She lifts the bottle of champagne in front of her. "I felt so special. Thank you, Leo. I knew you overheard some of the conversation with my mom. But I didn't think I mentioned my birthday."

"It was my pleasure. I hope you don't think I was eavesdropping."

"No. Not at all. I wasn't very discreet. I'm sure you've heard worse things while on the job."

I nod. "Unfortunately, yes." We gaze at each other for a few seconds. Every exhale from us produces shimmering clouds that blend together and dance toward the sky. "Can I ask how old you are?"

She looks away like she's embarrassed or something. "Thirty."

"Really? The big three-oh!" I exclaim with more excitement in my voice than hers. "We definitely have to party then. Let's pop this baby open. We can celebrate your big day for the next hour"—I check my watch—"no, fifty minutes. Then we can bring in the new year. How does that sound?"

"Pretty perfect, actually," she replies, with a shaky voice. "And how old are you?"

"Thirty. Thirty-one in September." I pick up the flutes from the bench. "Because I had high hopes that you'd show up, I brought these."

"What, you don't want to drink straight from the bottle?"

I raise an eyebrow, not sure if she's being serious. "I'm

game if you are. After our chat in the café, I think we've moved up a level. BFFs maybe?"

Olive purses her lips. "I don't know. Do best friends share bottles? It might be too fast, and then we'll be talking about dating, marriage and kids." She grins, unwraps the foil from the cork with gloved hands, and shoves it in her pocket.

I'm loving this playful side. Do I bring it out of her? I'll have to get used to her change of moods. She's like a yo-yo, going up and down, up and down. "Yeah, we don't want that, do we? But to be honest, I can't stand when people share glasses, bottles, whatever." I shiver. "You probably think I'm weird."

"Nope. Not at all. It is pretty gross when you think about it…and I've seen some pretty disgusting things." She stops, then quirks an eyebrow. "But what about kissing?"

"No problem there. That's different. I want to kiss that person."

She tilts her head, the bottle hanging from her hand. "So you wouldn't share this bottle"—she raises it between us—"with me, even if you wanted to kiss me?"

"Uh…um." My face heats up because kissing her has been on my mind since she arrived. Has she noticed? If I say I want to kiss her, will that turn her off? "This is the weirdest conversation I've ever had. Where are you going with this?"

"No idea. Forget I brought it up," she mutters, her shoulders curling forward. I hope I didn't upset her. She releases a long breath, then removes the muselet protecting the cork. "I've had the bottle sitting on ice. It should be cold enough by now."

Great diversion. "Good thinking."

Grunting because the cork won't budge, she gives up

and passes me the bottle. I hand her one flute and then the other when I have the bottle in my hands.

"You didn't shake this before you got here, did you? I don't want it to explode and cover us. It's a little cold for that," I joke.

"Now that we're BFFs, you can trust me." Her humor is back. She's too damn adorable for her own good.

"Weirdly, I do trust you." I twist the cork and it loosens. "Here we go." I extend my arms and aim the bottle away from us. A loud pop follows, and the cork shoots out into the darkness. Condensation billows outward, but the golden liquid stays in the bottle.

Olive holds up the flutes, and I pour in the bubbly, careful not to overflow. I place the bottle on the corner of the bench, then lift my glass. "Happy birthday, Olive."

Her soft gaze meets mine. "Thank you. It's been a hell of a lot better than I expected, but somehow, exactly what I wished for." Hearing that fills my chest with pride.

We clink the glasses and drink some. "I hope you like it. It's a favorite here."

Olive licks her lips, and I have to bite my tongue. She doesn't have a fucking clue how sexy she is from that one movement alone.

"It's crisp, and I love the fizz against my tongue." *Now I'm thinking about her tongue. It's going to be a long night.* "I'm a big champagne fan. Not that I drink it often. Not much to —" She stops and looks down at the grass.

I can guess what she was going to say. *Not much to celebrate.* Well, I'm going to make sure she does exactly that tonight, if it's the last thing I do. I take another sip, then sit on the bench and pat the empty spot next to me. She sits down, but not too close. I nestle the bottle between us.

Olive looks up at the tree. "I love madrone trees. Especially their pretty rust-colored bark and that they have leaves year-round."

"Me too. And now you know why it's called Madrona Inn."

"Is there a significance?"

"Someone planted this tree a long time ago. It's a symbol of resilience, survival, and strength. This hotel is over a hundred years old. It really is resilient." I snort. "And now I sound like a tour guide, reciting facts again." I take a quick sip from my glass to shut myself up.

"Tour guides can be boring. You're far from that. However, I *am* a tourist for the week. You're just doing your job." She plays with a button on her coat.

"Olive." She glances at me, and I look directly into her eyes. They're sparkling from the lanterns. "Sitting here with you has absolutely nothing to do with my job. I choose to be here. I *want* to be here. Okay?"

"Okay," she says with relief in her voice. "Now tell me something else."

"One more thing about this tree. When I was a kid, I'd sit on the grass underneath it. One day, I came out and this bench was here. After that, I figured it was meant for me because whenever I'd come out here to relax or think, it was always empty. Nobody would be in sight. And tonight it happened again. It's such a busy night with people wandering around. Someone could've easily stolen our seats."

"But they didn't."

"Nope."

"Lucky for us. I can't wait to explore the area this week."

I stretch my arm along the bench, my hand slightly touching her back. She doesn't move away. "Do you like to hike?"

She shifts to face me. "I used to love it." *Used to.*

"There are some great trails here with spectacular views. Since it's off season, you'll be able to enjoy them more."

"I should add hiking to my list of resolutions. You'll have to tell me which trails are the best."

Ask me to go with you and I'll show you everything.

"Did you make a birthday list too?" I ask.

"Huh?" Her eyebrows furrow. "Haven't thought about it. I guess the only thing I wish for is to be happy again."

Olive doesn't hide the fact that she's been through something that shaped who she is today and brought her to Orcas Island. Unlike me, she's an open book. I hide behind my personality. No one would believe the inner pain and struggles I carry around every day.

"When's the last time you were happy? Like truly happy," I ask.

The air suddenly shifts. *Too deep, Leo.*

"Other than arriving here? Years." She gulps the rest of her drink.

"Broken heart?"

"I guess you could say that, but not in a romantic sense." There's a finality in her voice, and I won't push it.

"Are you admitting you're happy here?" I brush her shoulder with my hand.

"Maybe, maybe not. It's too early to say." She nudges my thigh, avoiding eye contact.

"But you've been smiling a lot since you got here. It's a pretty one and it lights up your face." *And it shows off your fucking sexy lips that I want to nibble on.* "I hope you do it all night long. In fact, I'll make sure of it."

"You're doing very well so far." The side of her mouth quirks up, and she points a finger at me. "See, I'm doing it again, and it's all your fault."

"Since my job is done, I'm outta here. Adios." I stand and step away.

She yelps and springs from the bench. We watch in slo-mo as the bubbly pours out of the toppled bottle, through the bench seat, and puddles on the grass. Then, with catlike reflexes, she grabs it and lifts it in the air.

"I saved it…I think." She swirls the bottle slowly, then tries to look inside. "There's some left. Woo-hoo. Let's finish this. Give me your glass."

I hold it up. "Well, shit. That was a joke gone fucking wrong and a waste of some excellent champagne. I must be losing my touch. Sorry about that." God, my game needs a lot of help. That was so bad.

"Good try anyway." Olive fills my glass, then says, "There's not much left." She brings the bottle to her lips and tips her head back. I swallow deeply as she exposes her sensual neck and drinks down the remaining golden liquid.

I could do this all night. No need for a party or fireworks. Watching her enjoy herself is worth every second. This aspect of her personality lies right beneath the surface, begging to be unleashed. I have found my mission, not just for tonight but for the week.

She pulls the bottle away, then licks her lips. "Damn, that was good. Now it's empty." Burping lightly, she covers her mouth. "Oops. Shit. That was rude, right? Sorry."

I crack up. "Not at all. I love it. You're having fun."

"More than fun. I came here to figure out my life because it looks nothing like I dreamed of." Her voice drifts off. "You know what? I want to forget my problems this week. Want to help me with that?"

"I'll do anything for you." We both startle when a firework goes off in the distance, followed by a loud boom. "Damn, that scared me. They should've warned us beforehand," I quip. Olive shivers next to me. "You're cold. Should we go inside where the party is?"

She shakes her head. "I'm a little chilly, but I'd rather stay out here. If that's okay."

"Sure. I'm not going anywhere. When I celebrate New Year's here, I sit on this bench to watch." I place the empty bottle alongside our glasses on the grass.

"It's so romantic out here with the lanterns in the tree and the fireworks over the water." A loud bang goes off, and white sizzling stars burst in the air, cascading down until they disappear. Olive shivers again.

From my coat pocket, I retrieve tissues. "I've brought a blanket. Let me clean the bench first."

Olive offers to help. I hand her a tissue and, together, we dry it off as much as possible.

"That should be good enough," I declare, collecting the used tissues. She passes me one more, and I stuff the bundle into a glass.

"I don't care if my coat gets a little dirty." She plops down on the seat and crosses her legs. I follow suit, sitting closer to her than before.

I pull the blanket off the arm of the bench. "I'm getting a little cold too. Can we share?"

"Of course. We're BFFs, don't forget."

I drape the woolen blanket over our laps. She tucks herself under it almost like a barrier. "Afraid I'll make a move on you?"

"Don't lions pounce? I have to protect myself from wild animals." She covers her mouth and simpers.

"See, you do have a sense of humor. It might be a little rusty, but it's not too late. Oh! Let me check the time." I swat my thigh, and she twitches.

"Jeez, Leo. What's the matter?"

"Less than thirty minutes until twelve! Then we can

slam the door on this year and I can shave this damn mustache off."

She lets out a belly laugh. "You're freaking crazy."

"That I can confirm, but I think you secretly love it." She shrugs, but I see her lips twitching. "Come on. Admit it."

A grin breaks through. "Fine. I love it."

"See, that wasn't too hard."

She motions toward my mouth. "Are you really going to shave it off?"

"Yep. Right after the fireworks, I'll head over to my place and chop off this lip sweater."

She elbows me. "Lip sweater. Another good one. I think I like it better than fiesta fuzz." She must have over-heard my conversation with Ellie at the café. "Anyway, do you live nearby?"

"I live in a private cottage over there." I point to the left of the main part of the hotel. "We have four, and they're fully equipped. I stay in one, and my brother's in another. I travel a lot, so it suits my needs."

"I overheard you say you're leaving in two weeks. Aren't you the manager here?"

"I'm a hotel critic. I write articles for travel magazines and websites. When I'm not out on an assignment, I come home. Then if the actual manager of the hotel wants to take a vacation, I fill in."

More fireworks go off, and guests trickle down from the hotel and party. I study Olive's perfect profile as she observes the people passing by and how her face lights up like this is the first time she's seeing fireworks. I've seen the show from this spot for years, but I won't ever forget this one.

"Only a few minutes to go," I say. "Ready?"

"Yes. Good thing—you're quite boring," she jabs. "I need a little more entertainment."

I huff. "Oh really. I'll show y—"

"There you are! I've been looking all over for you!" Bethany jumps out from behind the tree. Olive and I jump off the bench like it's boiling hot, and Bethany snorts. The blanket lands on the damp ground, and Olive scoops it up quickly.

"Fucking hell, Bethany!"

She comes forward like it's an invitation and pulls me in for a hug lasting much longer than wanted. When she retreats, she drags her hands through my hair, creating a nest on top of my head since it was in a half bun. "I love your mustache. It's so *sexy*."

Ugh. A whiff of alcohol and cigarettes blows in my face. She has to be drunk—she's never come on to me like this before. Shocking me further, she comes at me like she's going to kiss me. I turn my head in time and her sloppy lips press hard on my cheek.

I pull away, wiping my face with the back of my hand. Then I shake my hair out, careful not to lose the band. I roll it onto my wrist and step closer to Olive. She tosses the blanket on the bench.

I put my arm around Olive's waist and squeeze gently. She stiffens, then quickly relaxes into my side. I trace my nose along her neck and inhale, then whisper in her ear, "Please, please follow my lead."

This is going to be hard to fake.

9

OLIVE

eo towers over me, and I melt into the side of his warm body. My eyes flutter shut when a hint of his cologne teases my nose, stirring something deep inside. *Dangerous*. The tip of his nose traces up my neck, and I can't control the desperate need for more of his touch.

"Please, please follow my lead," he whispers softly in my ear. It's hard to focus when his voice is smooth like velvet. I think I know what he's going to do. I've read it a thousand times in romance books. Time to turn on my acting skills. If I have any.

I simper, then say, "That tickles, babe. You're feisty tonight." I brush my lips across his soft cheek. Only for acting purposes! *Yeah, right.*

Leo's big hand squeezes my waist again, pulling me closer. "I can't help it. You're so damn beautiful and you smell amazing," he murmurs against my neck, his lips and mustache tickling my skin. Flames ignite inside me. Damn, he's good at this. Too bad it's fake. *Is it, though?*

Bethany's scowl is hard to miss. My lips quirk. What do we do now? It doesn't matter because the surrounding crowd starts to count down. "Three, two, one…Happy New Year!" Total chaos follows. People are hugging, kissing, dancing, and, of course, drinking. I'm in awe of my surroundings, and with the fireworks above us, it's magical.

"Happy New Year, Olive," Leo says, pulling my attention to him.

I gaze into his golden eyes and find it hard to breathe. He rests his hand on the back of my neck, leans down, and I close my eyes to let the moment sink in. His lips tease mine with the lightest touch. So warm. So soft. So gentle. So perfect.

"Leo!"

That isn't Bethany's voice. We break apart abruptly, putting some distance between us. I touch my mouth, shocked that we did that. Lost in a fake moment. I search for Bethany, and she's out of sight. Good.

"Leo! Woo-hoo!" A short woman runs up and jumps into his arms. I take a few steps back. "Happy New Year, brother." *Ah ha, his sister.*

Leo whispers something in her ear, and she punches him in the arm. He inches closer to me and places his hand on my lower back. "Tonya, this is Olive. She's staying at the hotel."

She grabs my hand and shakes it vigorously. It's comical. "Hi, Olive. Are you the one Leo took to the café?"

I regain my hand, then look at Leo. He clenches his jaw.

"Um, yes?" *Why is it such a big deal?*

"It's nice to meet you. Are you coming back to the party? I planned everything, and the room looks *fab-u-lous*!" She singsongs the word.

"Leo invited me, but I'd feel like a party crasher. Are you sure it's okay for me to be there?"

"No worries. You know Leo and me. Ellie and Sam are

the sweetest. Any friend of Leo's is a friend of theirs." Tonya turns to her brother, hands on her hips. "And you— Bethany was looking for you again. She's a little out of control tonight."

"A little?" Sarcasm oozes from his voice. "She was just here in her drunken glory. You should've seen the shit she pulled. She was all over me, even tried to kiss me."

Leo takes the elastic band off his wrist and puts half his hair up in a fashionable, messy bun. I watch every movement. It was up earlier, but—call me weird—witnessing him do that one simple thing unleashes something wild in me, catching me by surprise. He has great style, and he moves with confidence. I could go on and on.

"I cuddled up to poor Olive, hoping Bethany would get the point I'm not interested. It seems to have worked because she disappeared. If you see her, pretend Olive's my girlfriend."

No "poor Olive" over here. I'm enjoying every minute of this.

"You need to be firm with her," Tonya says, arms crossed over her chest.

"Tried that already. I even told Ellie I'm not interested in her. And now I've taken the situation into my own hands." He erases the space between us. "Olive has become my fake girlfriend tonight."

I elbow him. "Maybe you should ask me first. What if I don't want to be your…fake anything?" I sass.

"Then that gives me no choice." He gets down on one knee and kisses my hand. Tonya's mouth drops open. I hold my breath. His poor pants. Thankfully, they're black.

"Olive," Leo says. "Would you be my fake girlfriend for the rest of the evening?"

I rock my head from side to side. "Hmm. This is a

tough decision. You don't get asked this every day. What do I get out of it?" *More kissing, perhaps.*

"Something very special for you. You won't be able to resist." His eyes sparkle with mischief. "Are you ready?" Tonya and I both lean in with anticipation. "You can watch me shave off my mustache." I cackle, and she follows.

Once I catch my breath, I place my hand over my heart. "How can I resist that? It'd be an honor." I lay it on thick. "I'll be honest—even though that lip sweater was growing on me, I can't wait to see your adorable face without it. And I want to know what bet you lost."

"He bet—"

"Tonya!" Leo stands abruptly, cutting off her response.

She sticks her tongue out at him. "What? It was a dumb challenge you found on TikTok."

"Then it can't be all that bad," I say, my eyes ping-ponging between them.

"I'll tell you another time," Tonya says with an evil smirk. I like her.

"Not gonna happen," he says.

"Sore loser," she coughs out behind her hand.

When Leo looks at me, all joking disappears from his expression. "As for the fake thing, Olive, I know it's a lot to ask. If I were in your shoes, I'd think it's weird since we met only hours ago."

"*Pfft.* You're easy to say yes to. Obviously, since I'm not running for my life."

He lets out a light sigh of relief. Next thing I know, we're surrounded by some of Leo's friends. Hugging and cheerful chatter spread through the group. No hugging from my side. Again, my insecurities make an appearance because I'm an outsider. Leo stays close by and introduces me to some people. Half of them are drunk and won't remember me tomorrow. I've already forgotten a lot of their names too.

Regardless of my nerves, this is exactly what I needed. To be thrown headfirst into another world, where I have no option but to let loose.

10

LEO

Olive is the first woman I've taken to my little cottage off the beaten path. No one has captured my attention enough to care, especially since I don't live here year-round.

"Holy cow! This is adorable," Olive compliments. "It's like a large she shed. And look at this little porch and the rocking chairs. I want one!"

"I hope it isn't a mess, Leo," Tonya warns. "No underwear lying around, dirty dishes in the sink…"

The cleaning crew came today. Everything sparkles. I don't even know why Tonya's with us right now. Strike that. Yes, I do. She's nosy about me and Olive. Nothing to see here. Remembering my lips against hers and the surge of desire through my body tells a different story. It's probably a good thing that Tonya interrupted us.

"Shouldn't you be at the party keeping things in order?" I say to change the subject.

She props her hands on her hips and scoffs. "Are you challenging my party-planning abilities? Like all others, it's a well-oiled machine. The guests are drinking and dancing at this point. But you're right, we should get things moving."

I unlock the door and push it open. "Ladies first."

Olive enters and spins in the center of the room while unbuttoning her coat. Tonya and I follow her inside.

"Yep," she crows. "I'm moving in tomorrow. Too bad your reservation system didn't make a worse mistake. Don't get me wrong. I love the suite, but this is incredible."

The cottage has an open concept. The kitchen and living room run along the right wall. There's enough space for a kitchen table for two, a couch, and a coffee table. Stairs near the spacious bathroom lead to a cozy loft where the bedroom is. It's compact and airy; perfect for a getaway. I have all I need.

Olive's coat slips from her shoulders and I take it from her, then hang it on a hook near the door. She's wearing a fitted, white button-down shirt that fans out at the bottom over her blue jeans. The top three buttons are unfastened, giving me a glimpse of her full chest. With her hair twisted in a low bun on the side, her exposed neck makes me ache for one more trace of her silky skin. Her jeans hug her curvy hips and ass as if they were custom-made for her. To explore a woman's generous curves is incredibly beautiful and the ultimate turn-on for me.

My eyes trail her every move until I'm rudely interrupted by Tonya clearing her throat. I glance at her, and she gives me a knowing nod. I scratch my forehead with my middle finger, and she laughs. Olive inspects the small kitchen area, tracing the black countertop with her fingertips. Next, she heads into the living room and sits on the couch like she belongs here. She perks up and points at the opposite wall. "And you have a fireplace. I'm so jealous. I didn't need one when I lived in LA, and the apartment I live in now doesn't have one." Interesting piece of information. Several guests at the party are from LA.

I wait for Tonya to ask her a million questions about living there, but she doesn't. I look behind me, and I'm not surprised to see her putting away the plate and glass that were sitting out to dry. She's such a neat freak. You can eat off her counters and floors.

Once Olive finishes checking out the upstairs, which doesn't take long because the house is small, I usher them into the bathroom. I'm glad it's big enough for three.

I clap my hands. "Let's get this show on the road. The party's going to be over before we get back."

"And look at this bathroom," Olive says with delight when she enters. "The bathtub and shower are huge. How many people are supposed to use that shower at a time?" I'd tell her what I'd like to do with her in there, but I'm sure that'd win me a left hook to the face. Still, I can fantasize, right?

I put my shaving items and washcloth near the sink before I left. Tonya's already rearranging and polishing my toiletries, lining them up from tallest to shortest. I don't bother commenting anymore. If it makes her happy, why say anything?

"Need a hand?" Olive asks. "I kinda feel useless."

"Have you ever shaved off a mustache? Did another fake boyfriend have one too?"

She swats my shoulder playfully. "Whatever. Actually, I do have some experience. I used to help my dad. He couldn't decide. At random times during the year, he'd grow one. Mom hated it with a passion." She says it as if it were in the past. Did her father die, or did her parents divorce?

"Go for it then." I point to the things on the counter. "Are these what you need?"

She scrutinizes them. "Yep. We're good to go."

I could do it myself, but this might be the last time she puts her hands on me. I take my phone out of my pocket. "Let me get a before picture first."

"Wait, I want to be in it," Tonya exclaims, finished with her military lineup of toiletries.

She presses into my side, making kissy lips. I pull Olive into the picture. She hesitates, then gives in. I take a couple pics, then turn off the screen.

"Let me see them," Tonya whines, yanking on my arm.

"Nope. Later." I tap on my watch.

"How should we do this? You're much taller than me," Olive inquires. Without responding, I pick her up and sit her on the counter. She squeals. "I'm too heavy to sit here." She shimmies to get off. I hold her in place and put my hands on the counter, barricading her in.

"*You are not.*" Face-to-face, we stare at each other, hardly blinking. We're close enough that I could easily steal a kiss from her, but I refrain like a gentleman. Her chest rises and falls at a faster pace as her eyes drop to my lips. Is this having the same enticing effect on her as it is on me? She swallows, then looks away.

I grab the used towel hanging to dry and place it over my shoulders. Then I push the loose strands of hair out of my face.

Olive takes my chin between her fingers and asks, "Are you sure? I'm a little rusty. Speak now or forever hold your peace."

"No bleeding allowed. And you can't use these white towels," Tonya orders. I look over, and she's refolding the freshly folded towels on the shelf. Whatever floats her boat.

"That's what bleach is for," I counter. I look at Olive. "Ignore Tonya. She's like Monica on the TV show, *Friends*. Constantly organizing and cleaning." I hide behind my hand and whisper, "She irons her towels and sheets. Probably her underwear too."

"I heard that," Tonya says over her shoulder.

Olive's lips quirk with amusement. "Ah. One of *those* people, huh?"

"Heard that too," Tonya says, cracking a smile this time.

"Want to come and organize my apartment?" Olive asks.

While Tonya babbles about turning it into a job, I fill the sink with hot water and wait until their chatter dies down.

"Hello. My 'stache is waiting to die." I push out my furry upper lip to encourage attention. "Olive, I trust you, so…get movin'." I place the clippers in her hand, and she gets down to business.

"Come a little closer," she says, tugging on my shirt. I slide between her parted legs, placing my hands lightly on her lower thighs.

"This okay?" I ask softly, my gaze trained on hers, praying that it is.

Her fiery gaze travels down my arm to my hand. I give her thigh a gentle squeeze. When she looks up again, her pupils are dilated, and I'm sure mine reflect hers. "Yes," she responds with a shaky breath. Will we be able to leave this bathroom without mauling each other?

Ignore the twitch in your pants. I force my mind to go blank when she starts trimming, trying to prevent my dick from getting hard. It's been a long time since I've been with a woman. Olive is different because I want more than sex.

She turns off the clippers a few minutes later, wipes the trimmed hair with a damp washcloth, and inspects her work. Nodding in approval, she says, "Not bad. Next step, shaving cream." I watch her squirt a large blob of it in her hand. More than probably necessary. "Ready? It's going to be cold."

"Bring it on. I'm kind of warm anyway." More like hot.

She nods and cautiously smears the cream over my upper lip. It's refreshing. When she continues, I keep my eyes on her exquisite face and the glimmer in her eyes. A little crease forms between her eyebrows, and she nibbles on her lower lip in full concentration. Being this close to her, I notice a tiny crescent-shaped mark under her left eye. A scar maybe?

"I love the color of your eyes," I murmur.

Her hand with the razor pauses. "We have something in common then. I love yours too." She gives me a stern look. "Now no more talking or moving."

Ignoring her, I ask, "And they're not contacts?"

She swirls the razor in the hot water, then shakes it out. "I have my dad's eyes. It's my only similarity to him." I press the part where my lip is bare, and it feels cool. "You're fiddling," she says. "Don't touch. I don't want to cut you." I suppress my smile and happily follow her orders like a little dog.

Moments later, she places the razor on the counter and wipes my mouth with a corner of the towel that's around my shoulders. I wiggle my lip. It feels weird and cold. Naked.

I inspect my face in the mirror over her shoulder until she cups my cheeks and looks me directly in the eyes, all joking set aside.

"Don't hide yourself behind facial hair again." The words flow from her lips as she gently swipes my upper lip with her thumb. Did she miss some whipped cream? Oops, I mean *shaving* cream. My thoughts are in the gutter.

"Why?" My voice is raspy.

Her hands drop from my face, then cover mine, which are still on her thighs. "Because the world deserves to see all of you. So handsome. And when you smile…you take breathtaking to a whole new level."

Whoa. I'm rendered speechless. Not a simple thing to do. Nobody has ever spoken to me that way. I squeeze her thighs gently again and relish the warmth her words have created in my heart.

I squint. "Is that my fake girlfriend talking, or just you?"

She nods toward the door. "Your fake one is outside smoking a cigarette. I am the only one in this bathroom with you." The corners of her lips curve upward.

The urge to kiss her is worse than before. Not a fake kiss and not an innocent peck on the lips either. A powerful one where I can taste her on my tongue for hours. I want to hold her voluptuous body in my arms and make fucking sure that no other man compares. It almost happened at the strike of twelve.

I know I'm getting way ahead of myself, but I feel it in my bones. Olive's special, and for once, I don't want to walk away. My gut says I need to take it slow, though. There's something fragile about her. I can't forget that she came here to deal with some personal issues. Mixing in romance might not be what she wants or needs. I'll follow her lead. Anyway, I kind of like this push-pull attraction.

I step back reluctantly, giving her space. She slides off the counter and drains the sink. I wipe it down when it's empty and clean up the counter.

"Good job," I remark, gently spreading a drop of lotion over the freshly shaven area. "I forgot what my upper lip looked like."

She pokes my side with her finger. "See what I'm saying? Whole new level."

I turn my face back and forth in the mirror. "Hmm. Are we talking sexy or more like hot tamale?" I joke with her reflection, moving my hips like Magic Mike would. Chills run up and down my spine. Where the hell did that come from? I haven't danced since Corey got sick. *Mind blown*. Shake it off and analyze it later.

"White hot. Smoldering. Ten out of ten," she flirts, flashing ten with her hands. "You better keep an eye out for Bethany. She might attack you on the dance floor."

"Only my gorgeous, fake girlfriend is allowed to do that." I move closer, seducing her with my dance moves.

Olive yelps, then runs out of the bathroom. I zone in on her bouncing, gorgeous ass. Did I mention how much I love her curves? Oh. Yeah. Sorry.

"Really? And what else is a fake girlfriend allowed to do?" she questions over her shoulder, catching me red-handed, admiring her ass.

My gaze drifts to hers. "Let's make a list as we go to the party. It's getting late. Almost to the point of why bother, but I promised you a good time. I hope you aren't too tired."

"If I slow down, I will be. Can you give me a sec? I'd like to freshen up if that's okay."

"Good idea. I want to change since I kneeled in the grass. I'll do that while you're in the bathroom."

I step off the bottom stair just as she's coming out. She looks exactly the same because she didn't need to freshen up. I'll always think she looks perfect. I head to the bathroom and redo my hair, this time pulling it all up. Next comes a fresh spray of cologne and a quick gargle of mouthwash. I look at my reflection and see a different me. People might think I'm crazy for saying that, but they don't know how much I've been holding back. Sometimes I've almost felt like I'm cursed. Well, if I am, maybe she's the one who'll break it.

My phone pings in my pocket. I pull it out and read it. It's Ellie, wondering where I am. I step out of the bathroom and finally realize something. "Where the hell is Tonya?"

"Didn't you hear her? She got a text and needed to go back to the party."

"That's crazy. You had me in some kind of trance, you beautiful mustache shaver." Only a couple hours with her, and she's all I see and hear.

"It's my magical fingers." She wiggles them playfully.

I slide the coat up her arms and over her shoulders, then grab mine. "You're trouble, aren't you? I'm not believing this innocent, antisocial act anymore."

"As a fake girlfriend, I can be whoever I want." Her eyes sparkle mischievously.

"Well, time's a-wastin'. Let's go play pretend and see what kind of trouble we can get into."

Little by little, she's bringing me back.

11

———

OLIVE

"What about holding hands?" Leo asks.

I lift one. "Sure."

He intertwines his warm fingers with my icy ones, and I can't understand why it feels completely right. Why do they fit perfectly, like his hands were made for mine? I groan inwardly. What a cliché. I'm deleting my romance TBR, TV series, and movies, replacing them with thrillers full of blood and gore. No more love stories making me believe I'll find my person. My soulmate.

I'd rather not go to the party. I'd be perfectly happy having him to myself. It's not about sex, though my hormones are losing their patience. *You're here to be social.*

"Your hand's nice and warm. Thank you. Mine get cold when I'm nervous."

"Once you spend more time with my friends tonight, I think you'll relax. They're good people. Most of them, anyway. I don't know everyone here. Some of them live in LA. You mentioned you lived there, right?"

"Yeah, but it feels like ages ago." Another lifetime.

"It'd be funny if you recognized somebody."

"Highly doubt it. LA is a massive city." I say nothing else, hoping he catches on that I don't want to talk about it.

As we get closer to the party, I squeeze Leo's hand like a stress ball. My heart beats to the bass coming from down the hall. We reach the door, and he opens it and motions for me to go in first. I step into an intimate ballroom with cocktail tables adorned with silver tablecloths scattered about. Strings of twinkling white lights drape from the ceiling, casting a canopy-like illusion. Guests fill the black-and-white checkered dance floor in the center of the room, swaying to the beat. Glasses, streamers, confetti, silver and black balloons, party hats, and other items cover the tables and floor. I wouldn't want to be the one cleaning this mess after the party is over.

Technotronic's "Pump Up the Jam" plays, and I'm whisked back to LA when I used to go clubbing with my friends. Those are the happy moments I want to remember. If only they were all like that.

"I love this song," Leo and I say in unison.

"Jinx." I blurt it a millisecond faster than Leo does, then form my index finger and thumb into an L and press them against my forehead. "Loser," I sing. We burst out laughing as I bounce lightly on my toes. "I'm a huge fan of eighties and nineties music."

"Same here. Match made in heaven," he says, with a megawatt smile. "Want a drink?"

"Yes. I'm dying of thirst." He guides me to a connected room away from the dance area. The atmosphere is quieter, making it easier to talk. To the left is a lengthy bar with small clusters of people drinking and chatting, some already looking drunk and others on their way. Large circular tables stand to the right, likely where they had dinner tonight before the clock struck twelve.

We approach the bar, and a woman yells, "Leo, where

the hell have you been?" The redhead from the café runs up to us. The crowd behind her turns and watches. "Ah, the mustache is gone. Yay! We can see your cute face again," she says, squeezing his cheeks. "Happy New Year."

A stunning man appears and wraps his arm around her. My stomach makes a loop, and I freeze in place. *No fucking way.* It can't be him.

"Olive, this is Ellie Moore and her husband, Sam. This is their party."

I put my hands on my cheeks. "No way. *The* Samuel Moore? The soccer player from the LA Galaxy?"

Sam nods with a relaxed smile. "That's me, the *retired* soccer player from the LA Galaxy."

"Yes, sorry. That's right. I can't believe it. My brother's going to die. We're huge fans. We used to go to the games when he'd visit me in LA. It's really great to meet you both." I realize I'm shaking their hands with too much enthusiasm. I let them go. "Sorry. This is a bit much for me. It's been a crazy day." I'm totally starstruck, and my face and ears are on fire.

"So you live in LA?" Sam asks. "What area?"

My excitement dies. *It's your fault—you mentioned LA.* "Uh, I went to nursing school there. Now I live in a small town north of Seattle."

"Do you miss it?" Sam asks.

"Nope," I say, not open for discussion.

"Me neither," Sam agrees, sipping his beer.

"We live in Seattle. Sam's the coach for the soccer team at Seattle University…who won the championship this year!" Ellie throws her hands in the air, and the group around us chants the team's name as if they're in the stadium. Once it quiets down, she continues, "I'd tell you to come to a game with your brother and Leo, but the season is over. Come in the fall!"

"I'll have to make sure I still know Leo then." Everyone laughs. "Without his mustache, it might be difficult." *Who the fuck am I?*

"Hey." He nudges me with his hip. "You said you didn't like it."

"Just kidding." I caress his cheek with the back of my fingers. "You know I love your freshly shaven lip." Leo throws his head back and laughs. It lights me up when I can make him do that. Ellie assesses us with a slight, knowing nod.

"Hey, Sam, can I take a picture of you and Olive for her brother?" Leo asks, motioning for me to go stand by Sam.

"Sure. But let's all get in," he responds, his arms open wide for all of us to squeeze in.

"Really?" I squeal like an annoying fan, then bite on my lip to shut up. "I'm sure you're bothered all the time."

"Those days are long gone. Most people don't recognize me anymore." He doesn't sound annoyed at all.

"Which is nice for me," Ellie chimes in, kissing his cheek. "I get him all to myself." Can they be any more beautiful together? With her red hair and green eyes and his wavy brown hair and deep blue eyes, I can just imagine what their kids would look like.

I pat my pockets. "Shit, I left my phone in my room." I didn't want to deal with calls or messages tonight.

"I'll take the picture with mine. Let's do a selfie," Leo suggests. Everyone agrees and squeezes in together. I'm standing between Leo and Sam like a sandwich, and I won't complain. He takes several pictures because half of them were hilarious. I thank Sam profusely.

I wring my hands as adrenaline pumps through my body. "Leo, can you send me those pictures?"

"I would, but I can't," he replies. My eyebrows shoot

up. "I mean, I'm your fake boyfriend, and I don't even have your fake phone number. What the hell is that all about?" he whispers comically.

"At that time, you hadn't earned it. Now that you got me a picture with my favorite soccer player, I'll give it to you."

He hands me his phone, and I add my number under Fake Girlfriend. He chuckles when he sees it.

The thrill of meeting Sam dies down and the guests resume chatting in their circles. I wave my shirt away from my body, trying to cool off. Leo brings me some champagne and a bottle of water like he's read my mind. I down the water in seconds, surprised at how thirsty I am. Then I sip the bubbly. My mouth fizzes with the dry sweetness dancing on my tongue.

Once my glass is empty, I go to the bar to get another while Leo talks to Ellie. The DJ is playing great dance music, and I tap my fingers to the rhythm on my thigh. Sam comes up alongside me at the bar. I berate myself mentally for leaving my phone behind. I'd send a picture to Andy right now. I turn my head and smile at him. *Act normal!*

"So Olive, how do you know Leo?"

The bartender places my drink in front of me, and Sam orders another beer. I take a long sip to delay my response because I'm not sure what to say. Since it doesn't feel right to lie, I give him a broad answer instead.

"Funny story… We met today and hit it off. I'm a guest at the hotel."

His eyebrows soar. "No shit. Well, that fills in the blanks." The bartender slides his beer to him. He doesn't drink it right away.

I lift my glass to my lips again to hide behind it. "What do you mean?"

"Ellie and I were pretty shocked to see him enter the room holding hands with you. He told Ellie he wasn't bringing a date. I'm pretty sure we would've known if he had a girlfriend."

"Nope, just fast friends." *Maybe one day we could be more.* "How did you meet Leo?" Time to switch the focus to him.

"Funny story," he mocks me. I raise an eyebrow. He smirks and takes a pull of his beer. "Ellie and I were celebrating our anniversary in the Cayman Islands. Leo was there to review the resort. We met at the hotel bar and have been friends ever since. He's one of the best men I know." Funny how that's the second time I've heard that today.

"He lures you in with that incredible smile and those amazing eyes." I look over at Leo, and my heart thumps. "And then when he speaks, there's no going back." I turn back to Sam and shrug. "At least that's what happened to me today."

He eyes his glass while he traces circles on the rim with his index finger. "I get it. Ellie and I joke that if she weren't married to me, she'd be married to him." He chuckles, then looks back at me. "She loves him to death. He could put a smile on anybody's face, and he's a blast to be around. Ellie hates that he's always on his own. Of course she wants to play matchmaker."

I want to say, *someone like Bethany*, but I refrain. I'm suddenly feeling quite possessive and my claws are ready to pop out. This is a side of me I didn't know I had.

Jennifer Lopez's "Let's Get Loud" comes on, and some guests whistle and clap, then filter out toward the dance floor. I itch to dance too.

"Having fun?" Leo surprises me from behind.

I turn around and notice Sam is gone. "Hell yes." I shimmy my hips, then drink some more. At this rate I'll be drunk soon, since I ate hours ago. "I had a nice chat with Sam. He asked about us."

"Ellie asked too. I was honest and told her what happened with Bethany. And about the fake girlfriend thing to keep Bethany away. She asked me how we met, but I couldn't answer because her cousin interrupted us."

"*Phew*. I didn't want to lie to Sam, but I didn't mention the fake girlfriend thing. What did she say? Is she mad?"

"Opposite. She said she'll go along with it. And that she'll talk to Bethany. Ellie's cool."

"I Gotta Feeling" from the Black Eyed Peas comes on next, and I turn to face the dance floor in the other room. Perfect song for how my night is going.

"Want to dance?" Leo says next to my ear, his chest skimming my back. I fight the urge to lean against him, hoping he'll wrap his arms around me.

I glance over my shoulder. His face is close enough to kiss. "I do, but I haven't danced in years."

"Who cares? It's like riding a bike, right? I'm a little rusty too. Let's go."

I down the rest of my drink and put the empty glass on the bar. He grabs my hand and leads me to the other room.

We weave between people until Leo stops us in the middle of the dance floor. *Must we be in the center of everyone?* When I used to go clubbing, I thought I danced pretty well and confidently. I dig deep to find that piece of me again, hoping I won't make a fool out of myself.

Leo and I start off slow, and then it's as if someone flipped a switch on him. He unleashes a dance that electrifies the room. I'm frozen in place because I can't believe what I'm seeing. Rusty, my ass! Maybe I shouldn't be that surprised after he showed off some moves when we were at his cottage. Now I'm out of rhythm because my focus is on him. He's awesome, and it's like he's a totally different person. His eyes are closed and the look on his face is different—almost distant but elated. Other guests are watching him too. I'm waiting for the crowd to split like the Red Sea and for a big spotlight to shine down on him.

His golden eyes flutter open and zone in on me. He shimmies over with a wicked grin, grabs my hand, and spins me around twice. I squeal with surprise and try to keep my balance.

"Come on, FG. Let your hair down," he murmurs in my ear. He pulls off the hair band he was wearing and shakes his head, making his hair wild and untamed.

He's the most captivating man I've ever met. I can't take my eyes off him. The top four buttons are open on his snug black shirt, and I can see smooth skin, shiny with sweat. He's rolled up his sleeves, revealing his toned forearms again. His dark jeans sit low on his hips, and accentuate his muscular ass. The constant buzz of arousal pumping through me since I met him roars.

Leo points to my bun. I hesitate, then unravel my hair, letting it cascade over my shoulder. He motions for me to keep going. With a burst of confidence, I bend over, shake my hair out with my hands, then stand up again. Not the best idea because my head's spinning. I push my hair to the side, hoping to look as wild as he does. His heated eyes trace the curves of my body, and I think my pants will melt off.

Leo stalks up and pulls me into his arms. "You're so fucking sexy, Olive. *Own it.* Now dance." His voice has a deep commanding rumble to it that turns me on even more. Maybe I like to be told what to do too. The dance music changes to a Rihanna song that I don't know the name of, and he performs like a *Magic Mike* dancer. What other surprises is he hiding?

He takes my hand again, and we dance like our lives depend on it, disregarding those around us. I surrender myself to the addictive rhythm as the music seizes control of my body. The pulsating bass propels my heart into a faster cadence, and, exhilarated, I release all inhibitions. My stomach hurts from laughing, and I'm sweating profusely. It's the best I've felt in a long time. Free of worry. Free of negative thoughts. Free of guilt. I hope it doesn't end.

After a while, I know I need to stop and drink some water before I pass out from dehydration. On the other hand, if I don't go to the bathroom soon, I'm going to have an accident. I grab Leo's arm and yell into his ear that I need a break. He nods and keeps dancing like he's the Energizer Bunny.

I drag myself away and find the ladies' room. I open the stall door when I'm done and almost trip over Tonya, who watches me with glassy eyes. Is she drunk or—wait! Is she *crying*? I look around to see if anyone else is with her, but we're alone.

When I look at her again, a tear rolls down her face. I reach for her. "Tonya, are you okay? Did something happen? Are you sick or did you hurt yourself? Should I get Leo?"

"No. Please don't." She wraps her arms around me and squeezes me tightly. I freeze, knowing I'm a sweaty mess and we're in the bathroom, no less. Awkwardly, I hug her back. What else am I going to do?

"Thank you," she says, her voice cracking.

"For what? Want to go outside and talk somewhere else? Maybe get some fresh air." Her arms drop, and I put distance between us.

"No. I don't want Leo to see me like this." She takes several deep breaths, then wipes the wetness away from under her eyes, smearing the running mascara. She glances at her reflection in the mirror and gasps. "Oh, God, I'm a mess."

I grab a couple of tissues from a fancy dispenser and hand them to her.

"Are your eyelashes fake?" She asks it like it's a normal question to throw out there after she just broke down in tears. Is she drunk?

"Nope. They're all mine. I don't even have to wear mascara. I lucked out in that department," I say to her reflection in the mirror.

"If we could all be that lucky," she mumbles, pointing at her mascara-streaked cheeks.

While she wipes under her eyes, I wash and dry my hands. I catch a glimpse of myself in the mirror and draw back. My hair! Sweat-slicked strands stick to my neck, while the rest is a wild mess. I push the hair back with one hand and wave the other one to cool off.

Finally, because the silence is killing me, I ask, "Are you going to tell me what happened?"

She tosses the dirty tissues in the garbage, then grabs a couple more. "I'm sorry, Olive. I know I'm acting crazy and we don't know each other. It's, I—Leo was *dancing*." Her eyes well up with tears again. "Dancing!"

"And…?"

"He hasn't danced in, like, five years." She blows her nose like a trumpet, then wads up the tissue.

Five years? Still not getting it. "I need more than that. Why?"

"I can't tell you. It's his story to tell." She props herself against the counter and crosses her arms.

Then why bring it up?

"Y'know, Leo is a cheerful guy. Always Mr. Social. People can't help loving him. But they don't see him like our family does. Most don't know him the way we do. And what I saw tonight was nothing like how he's been. He used to love to dance, and he was fucking good at it."

"He's amazing. I didn't expect it at all. I felt like I was watching a TikTok reel."

"Exactly. Out on that dance floor, he looked more alive than I've seen him in a long time. There's fire that's locked up inside him, and I finally saw a glimpse of it again. That's what made me cry." She shakes her head, pointing to the wet streaks lining her face. "And now I can't stop. No more alcohol for me."

"But why thank me? I didn't do anything."

"Believe me, you did. You lit that flame again. I saw it a little back at his place, but I didn't want to get my hopes up. He meets hundreds of people every year, and not one has accomplished what you have in less than a day. And the way he looks at you? It's like you're the only girl in the room. Fake girlfriend or not, there's something sizzling between you two. Don't think I didn't see you almost kiss at midnight."

The kiss she interrupted. My face tingles, and I shrug. "Heat of the moment, I guess. *Fake* moment."

"Yeah, sure. Keep telling yourself that." She grins. I prevent myself from laughing while she begins straightening the tissue dispensers and the basket of travel toiletries. Then she rearranges the stuff in the basket and wipes down the counter.

"All I can say is, he's been the best distraction since I arrived. It's impossible to be in a shitty mood when he's around. I don't know anybody who throws off such intense positive energy like Leo does. It's hard to believe he's not who he portrays himself to be."

"Don't you worry. It's not an act. He's just holding back."

Holding back? What would he be like when he's in full force? Now I'm really curious. And confused. But is it really any of my business?

The bathroom door swings open, and a couple of women stumble in. They look as wrecked as we do. Tonya introduces me to them, and I politely slip out of the bathroom. That conversation took longer than I thought. Leo has to be wondering where I am. I'm going to pretend that chat didn't happen. It seemed too private for me to know.

Like he'd volunteer that information to a complete stranger.

But are we really strangers at this point?

12

LEO

I spin around one more time and open my eyes to scan the room. Olive is nowhere to be seen. When Bethany sways toward me, I hightail it off the dance floor.

I step over to a dark corner where I can catch my breath. Sweat drips down my temples, and my shirt sticks to my back and chest. I rake my fingers through my messy, wet hair. I can't stop smiling. It's been ages since I've felt the blood pump through my veins this way. Nothing matters when I get lost like that. No drug could ever accomplish the adrenaline rush and stress relief I experience after dancing.

It was always my happy place…until it wasn't.

I became a different person on that dance floor—someone I miss every day. Dancing was an integral part of my life, but when Corey died, the energy and thrill died with him. I packed up my memories of dancing—and everything else Corey and I loved to do—and stored them all in Mom's and Aunt Betty's attics. I haven't touched them since I put them there. But tonight—

Tonight is Olive's fault. She zapped me with lightning

and ignited that dormant part of me. She's troubled, inse-cure, innocent, caring, and gorgeous. Mix them all together, and she's the perfect storm. It's like, all the walls I've built up since Corey died came crashing down with that one brush of her lips against mine. The reaction is snowballing. What'll happen when I spend more time with her? Because I promise you, I will be seeing her again after tonight.

I roll my arms and shoulders, then head to the bar where Ellie and Sam are. I ask for some water and scan the room again. Still no Olive. I hope she's okay. She didn't leave, did she?

"Are you sure you're my friend Leo?" Ellie threads her arm through mine and gently pulls me away from the crowd. I grab the water bottle off the bar. "I didn't know you could dance like that. What else are you hiding?"

I shrug. "It's been a while. I took classes when I was a kid." And in college.

"I'd guess you took a lot of classes. Those weren't basic dance moves."

I shrug again because I don't want to talk to Ellie about this. Not now. "It's not a big deal," I say, hoping to sound like I don't care, even though I do. I swig my water to stop myself from saying anything else until the bottle is empty.

Silence ensues, which doesn't often happen when I'm with her. My good mood is plummeting. I scrape off part of the bottle label to busy myself.

Ellie frowns and rests her hand on my arm again. "I talked to Sam about Bethany's behavior and how you felt pressured to pretend you had a girlfriend. It's partly my fault; I was hoping you two would hit it off. You haven't dated anyone since I met you. I promise I'll talk to her and set it straight."

"Thanks. With my travel schedule, you know I'm not boyfriend material. Can we drop it?"

"Well, I do have to wonder," she says, tapping her chin. "Are you sure it's fake with Olive? You were holding hands when you came to the party and smiling at her the way Sam does me. That look suits you. And she was doing the same. Even Sam noticed."

"It was because of him. Not me," I joke.

"Don't try to divert the conversation, mister." She punches my arm.

I explain to Ellie how I met Olive and how she's here alone. "I've felt this deep connection with her since the moment we met. It's weird. I don't know what it means or what I'm doing, but fighting it seems pointless."

"Then don't."

I sigh. It's not that easy.

She rolls her eyes. "I know I sound like a hopeless romantic, but anything is possible. Look at how Sam and I met and how most people think we're lying about it. I fought against my attraction to him, but our lust turned to love within what felt like seconds. Every couple has their own unique love story. Who knows what yours could be? If you like her, don't pretend it's fake. Life's too short for that shit."

Don't I know it.

As she finishes that sentence, Olive comes into view. She scans the room, perhaps searching for me. When she finally sees me, the smile I think Ellie mentioned transforms her face, and I respond the same. I wave her over.

Ellie pokes me. "See—that's what I'm talking about. She's around here somewhere, isn't she?" She giggles in excitement. "Yep, I hear wedding bells."

I snort. "I've had enough of you. Go back to your perfect husband."

Ellie sneaks away, singing, "*Daa dum da dum.*"

Wedding bells. No way. That's fucking insane.

Then why does my heart skip a beat and my chest fill with warmth when I hear them too?

13

———

OLIVE

I flip over onto my back and stretch, then let my gloriously sore, exhausted body melt into the cloudlike mattress. I replay every amazing moment since I met Leo yesterday. How his mesmerizing honey gaze ignited a sultry heat that coursed through my veins the whole night. Pleasure pulses through my blood, making me ache between my legs. *Nope, not going there.*

Leo and I partied until we were almost the last ones to leave. As we strolled to my suite, we joked about Bethany and her antics to get Leo's attention on the dance floor. Of course, my duties as his fake girlfriend ended as soon as we said goodbye and I closed the door. I could've asked him to stay, but my gut told me not to. Not because I had a bad feeling—the undeniable sexual tension was there and welcomed. But I want to take my time. I don't want us to be a one-and-done type of thing. Leo is special.

The last thing I remember is Leo's exuberance when he hugged and kissed me on the cheek goodbye. Yes, only the cheek. That moment was more intimate to me than the kiss at midnight. I think we both got something unexpected from meeting each other yesterday.

I think about what Tonya said. *He's holding back.* Seriously, what would he be like in full force? As the entire conversation repeats in my head, I get emotional too. It breaks my heart knowing that he's been through something that changed him so drastically.

Just like me.

We're more alike than I thought. I'm only here for a week, though. He probably won't tell me what happened.

I still can't believe I met Samuel Moore. Before we left, Ellie and I exchanged phone numbers and as soon as I got back, I looked her up on Instagram. She'd already followed me. What alternate universe did I get thrown into?

Oh, shit. What kind of sister am I? It's Andy's birthday! I should've messaged him last night, but I fell asleep as soon as I got into bed. Hopefully Leo sent me the pictures like he said he would.

I throw off the comforter and shiver. *Brr.* It's damn cold in here. I put on the fluffy white robe that came with the suite, turn up the heat, then head to the other room to get my phone. The red single-serve coffee machine near the sitting area catches my eye. Coffee before phone! While my favorite beverage brews, I enjoy the beautiful view outside.

Sunrays poke through heavy clouds. The lanterns in our tree sway gently in the breeze. Our tiny bench is visible in the daylight. I laugh. *Our tree. Our bench.* Different footpaths lead in various directions. I can't wait to walk around and take pictures, maybe find Leo's cottage.

I prepare my coffee, grab my phone, and return to bed. Stacking the pillows, I rest against them and get comfortable. After a few delicious sips of steaming rich coffee, I'm ready to deal with what's on my phone.

I unlock it. WhatsApp shows forty-five messages—not

bad. I expected more. Friends, old coworkers from the LA hospital, Mom, Andy, Uncle Bruce, and Leo. My stomach flips. Of course, I open Leo's message first.

> Leo: Thanks for a great time last night. Here are the pictures. Hope to see you soon.

Hope to see you soon? That's a good sign, right?

I scroll through the photos. We look plastered in some of them, but we weren't. Then I find the bathroom selfies he took. I zoom in and touch the screen, wishing he were here with me, cuddled up in my bed. He's like sunshine on a rainy day.

Whoa, I have such a crush. It's a foreign feeling and concept for me. If I looked in the mirror right now, I'd probably see hearts floating above my head. It's kind of pathetic, but I grin and download the pictures for safe-keeping.

Next, I open Andy's messages. They include new year greetings, complaints about me not responding to him or Mom, and a three-minute accidental video of him moving around. I attach some pictures with Sam to a new message.

> Me: Happy birthday and New Year! Yes, I'm alive, and check out who I partied with last night.

I send it, then watch eagerly for his reaction. My hand twitches when the phone rings. We agreed to only text this week, but I need to rub this in his face.

"Hello, this is Samuel Moore's fan club. How can I help you?" I bite back a laugh.

"I call bullshit. There's no fucking way that's really him," Andy challenges. "That has to be a look-alike or a life-size cardboard statue."

"Sorry to disappoint you, brother, but he was in the flesh in front of me. I crashed his party. Kind of."

"Crashed a party? This is my sister Olive, right?"

"Yes, and it was the best night ever!"

"Too loud. Hungover," he moans.

"Sorry." Not really. "If you made it back to my place, go to my medicine cabinet and take some painkillers and drink lots of water."

"At Uncle Bruce's." He grunts. "There I was, stuck listening to Mom complaining about your escape and not hearing from you—and you were hanging out with our favorite soccer player!"

When I hear him describe his night like that, I feel a twinge of guilt. "Hey, you pushed me to meet new people. That's exactly what happened. And I didn't even have to try. I met a guy who works here and the rest is history."

"Oh, ho, *really*? You work fast. What's his name? Is he in any of the pictures?"

"His name is Leo. He's the guy with golden-brown, curly hair. Half of it is up in a bun."

He huffs. "You and your long-hair obsession. And—wait a second. Olive! Your smile! I can see your teeth and it's reaching your ears. It's amazing how happy you look. Now tell me *everything*. Leave nothing out. Does he have a sister?"

For the next half hour, I share all the juicy details.

"How did that all happen since yesterday? It sounds like you've been there for days."

"I know, right? Anyway, I haven't danced like that since LA. It's like I let out all my frustrations on the dance floor."

"It sounds like it."

I tell him what Tonya said in the bathroom. "If he wants to tell me about his past, then I'll listen. It's not like I'm going to dump all my baggage on him."

"Don't tell him too much about your issues. You need to stay his *fake friend* until next soccer season."

"That ended when he left my room. Sam and his wife were really cool to hang out with. But get this. They said you and I should go to one of Sam's home games with Leo."

"Fuck yes. Work it, girl. But all jokes aside, are you going to see Leo again?"

"I really hope so." I huff. "What am I saying? I could see him today and he could act like a different person. That would be mortifying."

I pull my legs up to my chest and rest my chin on my knees. My insecurities shoot to the surface again. Ugh! What if that happens? *It won't, Olive. It isn't high school.* He was too sweet when we said goodnight, and he sent me the pictures not long after he left. I can't imagine him acting like it meant nothing; there was too much electricity sparking between us for that to happen.

"Worry about it when you see him next. Promise me you'll keep an open mind. I know how easily you shut down and hide from people. Now's not the time."

"I promise I'll try."

"No matter what, I'm proud of you. Living it up with a celebrity on the first night already."

"Whatever. I'm glad I didn't get drunk. Oh, and it's total bullshit what Mom and Dad said about this island. So far, everything I've seen is beautiful. Not that I've seen much. They don't know what the hell they're talking about."

"Send me some pictures," he says through a yawn.

I sink further under the covers. "Will do."

"Anyway, I have to show my face downstairs since I'm the birthday boy. Maybe I'll get a toy truck this year."

Gotta love him. "You're crazy. Sorry I'm not there to celebrate or to give you a present."

"I'm not. You're doing exactly what you needed to do, and that's enough. Hanging out with me wouldn't help you. Anyway, go have fun. Don't forget to drop Mom a message."

"I don't want to," I grumble.

"You have to. Keep taking the new year by the balls. And don't send Mom the picture of you with a bunch of strangers. She'll have a heart attack. I don't have the energy to deal with that shit right now."

I wish him a happy birthday again before we hang up, then I write Mom a quick message. Before she responds, I lay my phone on the nightstand and force myself out of bed. Time to get this day started.

Where's the ibuprofen when you need it? My legs were already killing me *before* I tortured myself on the exercise bike for twenty minutes. What was I thinking? Stupid resolutions.

Now I'm sitting in my underwear in the empty locker room, an oversized towel wrapped around me, trying to find the courage to go into the sauna. What if there are people in there from the party? What if I can't handle the heat and steam?

I am naturally a bashful person, and my self-confidence has plummeted since leaving LA. I'm overweight with an hourglass figure—if a man likes big butts, I'm his gal. Despite Leo making me feel like the most desirable woman last night, sitting around in a towel with other people has the opposite effect. It doesn't help that the sauna is co-ed, and some people go naked. Or is that only true outside the

US? I don't know. The thought alone makes me want to chicken out.

But I won't. It's now or never.

I resecure my towel over my chest and dangle the locker key band from my wrist. I make my way out of the locker room and head to the sauna. As I approach, someone leaves. Before the door closes, I peek inside and spot one other person. Okay, I can do this. Just open the door and find a seat as quickly as possible without looking at them.

Here I go. I'm vaguely aware of the other person as I drag myself to the far corner. I cast my eyes down and breathe through the steamy heat. Immediately, I cough in the thick, humid air. Yeah, I won't last long in here.

Out of the corner of my eye, I watch the other person leave. *Phew.* I lift my head, roll my shoulders, and stretch my neck. This wooden bank is smooth but hard and uncomfortable to sit on. And I'll be honest, it grosses me out that others have been sitting in the same place, sweating their asses off. Where are the disinfectant wipes when you need them? I'm glad my towel is long enough that it covers where I'm sitting.

Before I can fully relax and enjoy having this place to myself, the door squeaks open and someone enters. I readjust my towel to ensure I'm still covered, including my upper thighs. Sweat drips down my neck, and I wipe my brow with my forearm. This is brutal. How can it be healthy?

"Fancy meeting you here," a familiar voice says. "The one person I can't seem to get out of my mind."

My heart leaps, and I quickly raise my head, a smile already on my face. I can't hold back with him. I'm an open book.

Oh, for the love of everything good and holy. Another surge of warmth envelops my body. Is it possible to burst into flames in a sauna? I don't know if it's from the stifling temperature in the room or the delicious sight before me.

Leo stands near the closed door, a towel wrapped low around his narrow waist, revealing his sun-kissed, sculpted shoulders, broad chest, chiseled arms, and lightly defined abs. His build is lean and athletic, not bulky. There's a faint dusting of hair across his chest and around his belly button. His unruly hair is pulled back in a bun, with stray tendrils framing his face and neck.

He might not be perfect to anyone else, but he's perfection in my eyes. This image is going into my memory bank. It's only the second day here, and I get to see this much of his bare skin? Go me!

Suffering in this steam cooker is worth it.

"Didn't mean to scare you," he says with a wide grin, resting his hands on his hips.

"I'm a little jumpy," I admit. "Sauna virgin over here. I don't usually hang out with half-naked strangers." *Don't make this awkward, Olive.*

"Well, I'm no stranger. Just imagine that we're wearing bathing suits. They cover less than our towels, and we don't find that uncomfortable."

"That's debatable," I mutter, fiddling with the edge of the towel.

How is he this relaxed? It's no different from how he acted yesterday. It's me who's being awkward. I can't help it. He's standing there like a top model shooting a sauna ad, and I'm wrapped up so tightly that I'm going to turn blue soon. This is far out of my comfort zone, which is a good thing, but...but...but...

I'm so exposed.

"Can I sit by you instead of talking across the room? Or would you like me to leave you alone?"

My heart pounds rapidly, and it's hard to inhale deeply. *Loosen up, Olive.* I pat the bench next to me and smirk. "Come on over, BFF." *See, that was easy.*

His face lights up, and he sits down about two feet away. I try not to peruse his body, but I'm no saint. I can't help but wonder where that light patch of brown hair below his belly button leads. Of course I know, but you know what I mean. Don't think I didn't see the large bulge behind the towel. *Eyes above the collarbone, Olive. Focus on your breathing.*

"Is this your first time in a sauna?"

"Yes. I'm pushing myself to try new things this year. And here I am, thinking I'd be alone." His face falls. "No. No. Sorry, that came out wrong. I was really hoping I'd see you again. Though not necessarily in a sweatbox." I'm rambling.

"But we're BFFs, and I saw you sweating last night when you were tearing up the dance floor."

I snicker. "You know this is different."

"I know. Just trying to help you relax."

"You seem to be good at that." Not right now, though. My skin has a heartbeat, and I'm slightly woozy. *Keep talking.* "Thanks again for last night and the pictures. My brother was uber jealous when he saw them. Ellie, Sam, and Tonya are really nice."

"I had a quick breakfast with Ellie and Sam before they checked out. They told me to say goodbye to you. Then I worked for a couple of hours and went for a run. Now I'm here."

"Perfect timing."

"I was going to call to see if you wanted to join us for breakfast, but I didn't want to wake you up or monopolize your time."

I almost reach out to nudge his bare leg. "Don't be

crazy. Monopolize as much as you want while I'm here. I'll turn back into a pumpkin at the end of the week."

"Be careful what you ask for, Cinderella. I might do that." He casually leans back on his forearms. The heat doesn't seem to bother him at all. His sweaty skin glistens like he rubbed oil all over his body.

I watch as a solitary drop of sweat cascades leisurely along his temple, gliding over his cheek, making its journey down his throat, trailing along the contours of his chest. I tilt my head, then lightly trail my hand down my neck and chest. He follows my every move and focuses on where my hand is. My body yearns for him to touch me the way he rubbed against me on the dance floor when "Señorita" and other erotic songs were playing. I lick my lips and blink the sweat out of my eyes. The room sways.

"Are you okay, Olive?" he asks, leaning toward me. "Your face is beet red, and you're breathing heavily. Is the heat too much for you?"

I push my damp hair away from my face, thankful that he can't tell I'm lusting over him. "I'd love nothing more than to stay and talk with you, but I'm feeling a little dizzy." His closeness is making it worse, and he needs to put some damn clothes on. My heart can only take so much heat. "I think I'm going to have to cut this short."

I stand abruptly and lose my balance. My knees are seconds away from giving out, but I manage to grab the bench. I breathe in, but the steam is too much. My air passages feel obstructed, and I gasp. Panic sets in when I can't inhale. Memories of my time in the hospital, watching people drown from the fluid in their lungs, flash through my mind like a slideshow.

"I can't bre—"

Leo is quickly at my side and wraps his arm around my

waist. "Small steps forward. We're almost at the door. You'll be fine once we're outside."

I inhale again and again, but nothing is going in. *Click. Click. Click.* This time I'm part of the slideshow, gasping for air that never comes. Fear rattles my body, and I hold on to Leo with a death grip. I'm going to die like the others.

My butt hits a hard surface, then a cool breeze tickles my upper half. I hear a gasp. Something covers my shoulders and breasts, then someone captures my quivering hands. What's happening?

"Olive, look at me. You're in the locker room now."

I force my eyes open and meet Leo's concerned gaze and realize his lips are pressed against my clenched hands.

"Should I take you to the hospital?"

I shake my head wildly and try to move, gulping for air.

"Okay, okay. I need you to calm down and catch your breath. Keep your eyes on me and focus on your breathing. I'll do it with you." He puts my hand on his chest and inhales deeply. I follow. "Come on. Relax with me. In and out."

Slowly the panic dissipates, my heart rate decreases, and my breathing evens out. Leo cups my cheek with one hand. "There you go. Keep breathing. You need to drink some water."

"I have a bottle in my locker," I say, my voice weak. Leo pulls the key chain off my wrist and fetches the bottle quickly.

He opens it, then places it in my hand. "Here you go." I guzzle the refreshing liquid. He takes the empty bottle and hurries out of the room. Seconds later, he comes back with it refilled and hands it to me again. "Drink as much as you can."

He takes a fresh hand towel, kneels before me, and gently wipes my face.

"I'm sorry." A tear slides down my cheek.

He wipes it away with his thumb. "Why?"

"I didn't want you to see me like that."

"I won't lie. You scared me, Olive. Did you have a panic attack?"

I nod. "That and I couldn't handle the heat. Thank you for not calling anyone and for taking care of me. I despise hospitals." I take several careful, measured breaths. "I think I'm okay now."

He kisses my forehead, then stands up. It finally hits me we're in the ladies' locker room. I look down to see a towel draped over my shoulders and chest. The other one is pooled at my waist.

I tighten the one around my shoulders. "You saw me naked?"

He winces. "When you sat down, the towel broke loose. My focus wasn't on your body, Olive. I covered you up again as fast as I could. Don't be embarrassed."

I huff. "This is not how I imagined you seeing me naked."

"If it'll make you feel any better, my towel dropped at one point too."

"Well, that's not fair. Not sure that would've calmed me down."

"I didn't see you completely naked. But let's focus on the fact you were thinking about it. And when was that?"

"I'll never tell." I look up at him innocently. "And I'm glad we can joke about this."

His goofy grin is on full display. How can he make me laugh at a moment like this? Can I take him home with me when the week is up? I already dread the moment I drive off the ferry and return home.

"I told you last night you were gorgeous. It's up to you to believe it."

I nod, then take another sip of water. "Shit, that was intense," I mutter a few moments later. Leo sits next to me, his muscular thigh visible where the towel parts. Can this day be anymore torturous? "I knew the potential side effects, but—"

"You either love it or you hate it," he finishes my sentence.

"Hate's an understatement. I should've been more careful, but someone was *monopolizing* my quality time and I didn't want to leave." I nudge him lightly with my elbow.

"Sorry." He places his hand on mine, intertwining our fingers. My inhibitions fly out the window from that one simple movement. "You must be feeling better if you can joke like that."

I ensure my body is covered, then I stand. "I'm much better. Thank you. All I need is more water and a cool shower back in my room." I reluctantly let go of his hand and take a step toward my locker.

"Can I walk you back? I'd feel better knowing you're okay." He looks up at me, his eyes pleading.

"Don't you have more sweating to do in the sauna or work?"

"I'm done with the sauna today, and unfortunately, have to work again tonight." He stands, then steps closer to me. "I'd much rather be with you."

I cock an eyebrow. "Even when I'm a sweaty mess."

His eyes trace up and down my body, then catch mine. "I'll take you any way I can have you." *Whoosh!* There's that fire again.

With my finger, I trace a line from his collarbone down to his chest. Goose bumps follow the trail, and his breathing increases. He quickly clasps his hands in front of his groin. My eyes stay trained on his. "You keep sweet-talking me like that, and I'll be whoever you want me to be."

This is way too much fun. I'm seconds away from letting these towels slip to the floor! I'm never this bold! And to think, just a few minutes ago, I was on the brink of death.

Leo wags his finger. "No acting. I want the real you."

His undeniable interest in me is such an unexpected surprise, I can hardly resist touching him. I don't think one week with Leo will be long enough.

14

LEO

Heavy raindrops pelt my head as I sprint from my cottage to the hotel. I should've grabbed an umbrella. Olive and I agreed to meet in the lobby after our showers to check out the hotel grounds she hasn't seen today. With this unexpected weather swooping in, I'm not sure that's going to happen.

What Olive experienced in the sauna terrified me. I thought I might need to take her to the hospital or perform CPR if she stopped breathing. Then she mentioned hating hospitals, which confused me since I'm sure she said she was in nursing school in LA. What made her not follow through? The pandemic hit LA hard—that might have played a role. But guessing doesn't get me anywhere.

I want to ask her a slew of questions, but she doesn't need me prying into her business. I don't want her to ask me certain questions either. This week will fly by, and I fear I won't have the chance to get to know her as much as I desire.

Once I'm inside, I take off my jacket and shake off the rain. Boxes line the walls for the staff to pack up the

Christmas decorations this week. Approaching the front desk, I find Olive staring out the picture window, unaware of my presence. Her profile catches my eye from where I stand, and I take a moment to admire her. From her slightly upturned nose to the tiny crinkles at the corner of her eyes and mouth from grinning, she's beautiful from every angle. And she looks…happy and relaxed. It takes a huge load off my chest after what happened before. She turns toward me and her beaming smile is instantaneous, then her gaze turns sultry. Warmth fills my stomach and my body quivers as she walks toward me.

"What's that look for?" I ask, my voice huskier than normal.

I feel the heat of her stare as her light brown eyes trace my face and my hair. "I have a weakness for men with hair like yours. Especially when it's up. Even wet with rain, it gives you an edge. And the light scruff along your jawline does it for me too. I said don't hide behind facial hair, but I think I was wrong." I remember what she said to me in my bathroom last night. My ego can't take this many compliments.

It would take hours for me to list all the things I find attractive about her. Like now. Her glossy hair is tightly pulled back into a ponytail, highlighting her sparkling eyes. Her heart-shaped lips glisten, and her endless curves evoke something deep within me. I want to touch her all the time. My reactions to her are addictive. I'm not sure I'll be able to give her up when she leaves in less than a week. Why couldn't we see each other again?

You're looking too far ahead, buddy. Slow down.

"Thanks," I reply. "I really can't believe that you're shy. What you say and do has proven the opposite. Not that I mind. Everyone loves compliments."

"When I see you, the words fly out with no effort.

Maybe someone slipped a truth serum in my drink last night."

"I'll have to keep that in mind when I ask you questions."

"Oh no. Now I'm in trouble." She steps to the side and pulls me with her as a couple passes us.

"Don't worry. I'll go easy on you." I point at the window where the rain is splashing against the glass. "Still want to head outside?"

"Not really. Another time?" she says, with a hopeful glint in her eyes.

"I'm sure I can squeeze something in for you between my work hours."

"I hope so. Since you've been good to me, how about I check out your website before you work again tonight? Or has the problem been resolved?"

"It doesn't matter. You're not here to work."

Olive places her hands on her hips. "Come on, show me."

"All right. Let's go. We can use my mom's office." I lead her there, greeting my coworker manning the front desk along the way.

I unlock the door, and we slip inside. Olive looks around, then says, "Tonya must take after your mom. There's nothing out of place in here. Sticky notes, empty coffee cups, half empty dishes of candy, and wrappers cover my desk."

"Oh yeah? What's your favorite candy?" I ask.

"I love sour gummy things. Such a weakness."

My mouth tingles thinking about it. "Sour gummy things…like bears, worms, and how about tongues?"

She crinkles her nose. "*Tongues?* Where do you get those?"

I wave it off. "Sorry. I forgot that you can't find them

here. In Germany, you find gummy everything. I load up whenever I'm there."

"You'll have to share some with me one day." She licks her lips, pulling my attention to her mouth.

Fuck me sideways.

I clench my jaw. Now I'm thinking about her petal-pink tongue and what it tastes like. Definitely not sour. Tingling heat spreads all over my body, landing below the belt. "We're already getting off topic."

"You asked," she says coyly.

I quickly sit in the desk chair, hoping to hide the obvious bulge in my pants. "I know," I mutter, "and I regret it now." She covers her mouth, attempting to suppress her laugh. "Give me a second to find the login information." *And to calm down certain body parts.*

She stands behind me, her hands resting on the back of the chair. I search through the pile of colorful folders that are stacked in the order of the rainbow. Tonya must've been in here. Mom's a neat freak, but not to this extent. I find the green one and pull it out. Once I've logged into everything and Olive tells me what she needs, we switch places.

"This is like a foreign language to me. Go for it, but please be careful."

"My dad owned a hosting company. I've been creating websites for clients since high school. Your website's in expert hands." She cracks her knuckles and wiggles her fingers for fun.

I peer over her shoulder, trying to follow what she's doing. Click here, click there at a rapid speed. Windows pop up and close, making my eyes cross.

Several minutes later, she says, "Okay, I think I figured it out. A widget didn't update properly."

"A widget what?"

She giggles. "Forget it. Let's see how it goes."

We both look up when there's knocking on the office door. Tonya pokes her head through. "Hey, guys. Whatcha doing?"

I point to Olive. "I think this website master fixed the reservation system."

Tonya cocks her hip and crosses her arms. "You only met her yesterday, and you have her working here already? *Tsk. Tsk.* Don't you want her to come back?"

"He's a slave driver." Olive pouts. "Said he'd never talk to me again if I didn't do it. He's so mean."

I guffaw. "What the hell?" She smirks as Tonya approaches us and gives her a high five. "Two against one. That's what you call mean."

"Olive, why don't you come to dinner at Mom's tomorrow night? She's making her famous pot roast," Tonya says. "One section of the hotel is her house, so you won't need to go too far. I know she'll want to meet the person who's fixed our woes."

Smooth, Tonya. Meddling always was her thing.

"Oh. Um…I'm not sure." Olive's worried eyes bounce to mine. "Um. Well…I don't know your mom. Isn't it rude to show up without warning?" She lets out a nervous giggle. "Then again, I did the same at the party last night."

All I want to do is kiss her worries away.

"Give me a second." Tonya pulls her phone from her pocket and leaves the office.

"Leo, I don't know if I'd feel comfortable. We only met yesterday, and then to go to dinner at your *mom's*…" Olive continues to babble.

"It's a done deal." Tonya comes back in with the phone up in the air. "Mom would love to meet you. It's a way of saying thank you for your help."

"Well, I'm pretty sure I fixed it, but shouldn't we wait for proof?"

I place my hand on her back. "Olive, please. It'd be perfect because we'll be starving after our hike tomorrow." When we walked back to her room, she agreed to go hiking with me. "I promise you, my mom's awesome. You already know Tonya, you're aware of Sully and his kitten. Donna will be there too. You met her yesterday. Believe me, Mom's pot roast is amazing."

This is perfect. I was already going to invite Olive to dinner before she offered to help. I know it might seem strange, but it feels completely right to have her with us. With me.

"You're not a vegetarian, are you?" Tonya asks, her nose scrunching up.

"Not that there's anything wrong with that if you are." I eye Tonya.

"Opposite. I love any type of meat. There's nothing like a good ole steak." Olive kisses her fingers.

"Good," Tonya says. "Well, I'm off then. See you at Mom's. Have a good hike."

"Wait, Tonya. Why did you come here to begin with? I thought you were at Mom's helping her cook something."

"Good point." She goes to the printer and pulls some pages off it. She checks each page, then waves them at us. "I came to pick these up. And you know everything has been meticulously prepared already. Mom's working on the last dish right now. Don't you know us at all? Jeez. Later, gators." She straightens the tape dispenser and stapler before she's out the door.

I stand in front of Olive and place my hands on her shoulders. "There's no pressure to go with me. If you want, think about it tonight and let me know in the morning."

"I want to go, but the thought of meeting more new people… My job is mostly virtual now. I hardly ever have to interact with anyone in person. You know, I think I've met more people in the last twenty-four hours than I have in the past six months."

"Well, Mom's the only person who'll be there tomorrow that you haven't met." That's not quite right. She hasn't formally met Sully, but I'm not going to say anything.

"That's true," she concedes.

"Besides…" I scrutinize her playfully. "You said you had fun last night. Was that only because you met Sam?"

She taps her chin. "Hmm. He was a highlight. But there was this other guy…danced like Magic Mike. He caught my eye way more than Samuel Moore did. We even exchanged numbers. Can you believe he hasn't asked me out yet? I'm one hell of a catch."

I whip out my phone and type a quick text. A chuckle slips out when I realize she's still listed in my phone as FG. Her phone pings. I change her name quickly in my contacts.

She glances at it. "Oh, look at that. He sent me a message. Took him long enough. Let's see what he wrote."

> Me: Hey beautiful. Remember me? I'm the guy who couldn't keep his eyes off you last night. Or right now.

She types back.

> Olive: Was that you? I didn't recognize you without your '70s mustache.

I'm going to hear this for the rest of my life. Not complaining, though.

She looks up from her phone and says, "I'm not sure it'll beat my mom's. I guess I'll have to go to compare."

I slide my phone back into my pocket after I switch her name in my phone. "Good. You won't regret it." I straighten the green folder and place it back exactly where it was to avoid Mom's or Tonya's stink eye.

"Can I ask you a question?" she says.

Shit. Her tone is serious now. What if I don't want to answer?

I rest my hip against the desk and cross my arms. "Shoot."

"I didn't hear you mention your dad."

"Oh." I tap my upper lip, wishing I'd kept that stupid 'stache. "He died when I was eighteen. He had a kidney transplant, but his body rejected it. He passed away the next day."

She frowns. "Oh, Leo! That's horrible. Your poor father and family. Transplants are always dangerous."

I massage the back of my neck. "We got through it somehow."

I regret a lot of things, not the least of which was my strained relationship with Dad. I'm ashamed to admit that losing my cousin was harder for me.

"I lost my dad too, a year and a half ago, to a bee sting. He was highly allergic and was never without his EpiPen—until that day. He went outside to do something in the yard while Mom and I were out grocery shopping. He didn't make it to the house in time to get it. We usually shopped on Fridays, but that week, Mom switched it to Saturday. When she got home, she found him lying on the grass—it was already too late. I can't imagine what she went through in that moment, dealing with it all alone. She doesn't talk about it much, but I know she blames herself because she wasn't there. If she had stayed home with him, he might still be here today. It's brutal when guilt and grief collide."

This conversation has taken a sharp nose dive, but I can definitely empathize. "It's still hard, especially for my mom. After all this time, she has no interest in meeting other men. The pain doesn't go away, but I've had more time to deal with it than you have."

"Yeah, it feels like yesterday." Her voice cracks and her eyes brim with sadness. "A life event that contributed to the way I am now." She turns her back to me, and I hear her sniff. "I'm sorry. That ruined the mood. And now I've embarrassed myself two times in front of you today."

I step in front of her and pull her into my arms. She rests her cheek on my chest and wraps her arms around my lower back. Her warm, soft body fits perfectly against mine. I kiss the top of her head like I've been doing it forever, smelling her floral shampoo.

"No need to be sorry, Olive. Sometimes it's good to talk to a stranger. Someone who's removed from the situation."

"Why do you want to deal with someone who's such a mess?"

"I like messes." *Because I'm one too.*

"Sure you do. And you don't feel like a stranger." She looks up at me, then drops her chin to my chest. "It's funny. The last thing my mother said to me yesterday was not to talk to strangers. What did I do? I came in here and started talking to you. Haven't stopped yet. And don't plan on it anytime soon."

I arch an eyebrow, and she rolls her eyes.

"Yes, I know I'm thirty. It doesn't matter to her. She probably thinks I'm still twelve. Another reason I ended up here." *Sniff.*

"Even more of a reason you should come with me to Ma's then. Hiking, pot roast, and apple crumble to take your mind off things."

She strokes my back, then drops her arms. "I think you're right." *Sniff.*

I reach across the desk and snag a tissue box. She takes one from it and blows her nose like a bugle. Now I know I really have it bad because I find it adorable.

"Why don't we go have a drink at the bar before I have to work again? No alcohol for me, though."

"Okay. And you can tell me where we're hiking tomorrow and other things I can do."

"We never got to do that, did we? I'm horrible at my job."

"Far from it. But is this how you treat all your female guests?" She smirks, but her eyes reflect uncertainty.

"Olive, you're the first." *And the last.* "No one's caught my eye until you came through our doors yesterday."

She covers her face. "Please tell me you didn't see my butt triggering the door sensors when I first arrived."

I throw my arm around her shoulders and steer her toward the door. "Let's go to the bar first, then I'll tell you."

15

<hr>

OLIVE

I relax in the seat as we drive up the steep mountain, my sleepy eyes ready to close. My legs and feet ache from our four-mile hike around parts of Mountain Lake. Maybe it's not strenuous for most people because it was fairly flat terrain, but I woke up this morning with sore muscles from dancing at the party and yesterday's exercise. Have you ever heard the phrase "second day burn"? Enough said.

Despite the pain, I couldn't be happier or feel more alive. As we hiked leisurely along the dirt trails, we chatted about little things and goofed around a lot. I miss letting loose and not having a care in the world, and Leo seems to be the perfect person to do that with. My favorite part was how we couldn't stop touching each other. Holding hands, his arm draped over my shoulders, my arm wrapped around his lower back. My soul is at ease with him, as if I've known him my entire life. If only this could last longer than a week.

Why can't it?

"We're almost there." Leo nudges my thigh. My stomach swooshes as we round another curve. I'm

124

surprised I'm not nauseous from the winding roads. Leo turns on his left signal and drives into a parking lot where a small group of people are getting into a minivan.

"This is my favorite viewpoint in this area," he says. "What I want to show you is a few minutes' walk from here." He gets out of the car, runs around to my side, and opens the door for me.

I turn to get out of the car, and my legs and feet scream. Wincing, I stand up and pretend everything's fine, but it's obviously not true when I move like an old lady. Leo chuckles behind me when he closes the door. I stretch one thigh at a time.

"Man, I'm out of shape. My body's not used to this much exercise anymore."

"Most of the hotels I stay in have great fitness studios. I have no excuse." He strolls toward a path and I follow.

Since he's not facing me, I take the chance to be bold. "Well, it's working, whatever you're doing. It was hard not to notice before I almost passed out yesterday." *Look at you flirting! You go, girl.* "Maybe that's why I was breathless."

He turns around with a cocky grin that I want to kiss off his gorgeous face. "Miss Olive, are you admitting to have looked below my chin yesterday in the sauna?" He places his hand over his chest. "I feel violated."

"*Excuse* me. Don't forget, you saw my boobs up front and center." How am I talking to him about my boobs like we're talking about the weather?

He taps his temple. "Something I won't forget. But, Olive, it was only for a few seconds. I told you, I was a perfect gentleman. I wrapped them up with care." He wiggles his eyebrows.

I tip my head back and laugh. I can't with this guy. Now I'm picturing him tying a red ribbon around my bare breasts. Besides my legs aching, my cheeks are too. I can't stop smiling—simply being close to him brightens my day.

"Too bad I didn't get to witness the disappearance of your itty-bitty towel. Then we could call it even."

"I'd be lying if I said I was sorry. And I ain't no liar, beautiful."

He stops and turns around near a bench. He's such a distraction that I haven't been paying attention to where we're going. I guess I'd follow him right over a cliff. *Nice visual, Olive.*

He points to the view in front of us. I gasp. "Worth the drive, isn't it? Saved the best for last."

I pull out my phone and take several pictures. Definitely some framers among them.

"We're at the top of Mount Constitution. It's one of the best views of the San Juan Islands," he explains, motioning again to the spectacular outlook. "It's been a while since I came up here with someone."

In the far distance, a snowy mountain peak emerges out of billowy clouds. "What mountain is that?"

"That's Mount Baker over on Lummi Island." He wanders over to the bench and sits. I do the same, and he automatically puts his arm around me, pulling me closer to him. *Swoon.* "I like coming up here to think and relax. We're lucky that we're the only ones here. Gotta love off season."

We both take a deep breath at the same time. The crisp, clean air tingles in my lungs. We're still for a few minutes, enjoying the peace and quiet. This is the place to be to clear your mind. I wish I knew what he's thinking about.

"We couldn't get any better with the view. I didn't expect everything to look this clear today." He squeezes my shoulder. "You're lucky. Somebody must be watching over us."

I rub my cold hands between my legs. It's chillier here than I expected. I didn't notice when I got out of the car. Slowly, the day is catching up with me, and a cloud of gloom storms around me.

"Have you ever seen the movie *City of Angels* with Meg Ryan and Nicolas Cage?" I ask, my voice barely above a whisper.

Leo shakes his head. "I've heard of it, but haven't seen it. Why? Is it good?"

"A favorite of mine. Especially the soundtrack. I haven't seen it in a long time." I observe a bird near us, hopping around, searching for something to eat. "Do you believe in angels?"

He clears his throat. "I don't know. Sometimes. Maybe. Wait…City of Angels. Los Angeles?"

I nod. "It takes place in LA. Nicolas Cage is an angel, and he falls in love with a mortal, Meg Ryan. He stands alongside people who are facing death. When they die, he guides them to the afterlife. Other times, he protects people in need. A guardian angel."

He shifts toward me, and I look at him. "Olive, why are you telling me this? Does it have to do with why you left LA?" His concern wraps around my heart.

"A little. It makes me wonder what's out there that we can't see. I used to be an ICU nurse in a major hospital in LA. I witnessed devastating things every day, but I saw unbelievable miracles too."

"I'm sure you did. Were you good at it?"

I pull my hat down on my head, like it'll hide my humiliation. "I thought so. It came naturally to me and I really loved working in the medical field. But if I was, why did I just…leave…one day and move back home like a quitter?"

"You quit?" he says, surprise obvious in his voice.

"Yep. I thought I could handle anything. That I was invincible. Turns out I was wrong. Angels were sparse for the patients when I was there, but there always seemed to be one around me." I'm mumbling more to myself than to him.

"Olive, I don't understand."

I look up at him again and admire the way the sun reflects in his curious and sympathetic golden eyes. Right then, I know I can tell him anything, and he won't judge me.

He caresses my cheek with his thumb. "Tell me. We're safe up here. No one can hear you. I won't tell a living soul anything you say."

I lean into his soft touch. "I worked in that hospital during the pandemic. I witnessed firsthand how people were dying left and right. So much death." I close my eyes briefly and breathe through the chills that rack my body. "Old, young, healthy, sick—it didn't matter who. That damn virus latched on, and too many times, it didn't let go. The smell of illness and death, the horrifying noises of people choking and gasping for air, machines beeping, and dead bodies not being taken away fast enough… They're all part of my nightmares.

"We were covered head to toe to protect us. My face and around my eyes were cut and bruised from the goggles we wore." I point to a tiny scar beneath my left eye. Most people wouldn't notice it, but I do every time I look in the mirror. "No matter how much you saw on the TV, it didn't capture how truly helpless we felt or were."

Leo touches the mark softly. "I noticed it when you were shaving me. I wondered what it was from."

"Now you know."

He embraces me, his cheek resting against the side of my head. "I'm sorry, Olive. Nothing I say can change anything, but I truly am."

I lay my head on his shoulder. "It does help, believe me. But I think I'm a coward."

"What? Why? You helped all of those people."

I pull back and narrow my eyes. "Did I?"

"That's why you asked me if I believed in angels?"

"Yeah. You'll have to watch the movie to understand what I mean. I know it's only a movie, but it really resonates with me. I haven't seen it since I left LA."

"We'll watch it. Together." He kisses my temple. "Keep talking."

"Were there angels roaming around the hospital? A few of my close coworkers and friends died. To this day, I still haven't contracted the virus. Has an angel been by my side the entire time to protect me? Why didn't it protect the ones who suffered? Why was I allowed to live?" I look to my right. "Is there an angel sitting on this bench with us right now or standing over there by the edge of the cliff? Was an angel with my dad when he died? Or with your dad?"

Leo keeps quiet because he knows I don't need an answer. I'm just throwing my thoughts out there.

"One day, a…another coworker lost her life, and I…I couldn't deal with it anymore. I was physically and mentally depleted and devastated. The nonstop pace and sixteen-hour days were impossible. Death was all around me. I couldn't stand being in my own skin."

"You were in survival mode. Anybody would understand your decision. And I'm sure you weren't the only one. I can't fathom what you went through."

"Healthcare professionals were desperately needed, but

I left. I gave up, returned to my parents a quitter, hid in bed for a few months, and then moved out. Since then, I've spent my life sitting in my apartment in front of the TV or computer screen. What kind of person does that make me?"

"Human. It makes you human. Everybody reacts to situations differently. You were working in extreme conditions, and you didn't have as much experience as others."

It's sweet that he tries to make excuses for me, but I hate it as well. I let people down, and I'm mortified.

"I'm not sure I'll ever forgive myself. I stopped talking to the people I knew in LA. They try to contact me once in a while. Some sent me birthday messages the other day, and I was too chickenshit to respond."

"Have you been back to LA?"

I shake my head, looking at my hands folded in my lap. "Nope. Out of fear, of course. I don't know how I'd mentally react."

"Is that why you freaked out yesterday when you couldn't breathe? Why you hate hospitals?"

I nod, biting on my lip to stop it from quivering.

"Maybe going there is something you need to do to put it behind you. Have you gone to therapy?"

"No. I thought I could deal with it on my own… Boy, was I wrong. Lately I've been thinking about finding a therapist. I should've gone a long time ago. Not only because of the pandemic, but because of the way I am. Things got worse when my dad died. I don't think my mom or I have fully dealt with his death. All the energy she once devoted to loving him has shifted toward me now, and it's stifling. My brother and uncle confronted me about my mom's codependence and my misery. It was a huge wake-up call, and I knew I needed to do something. Coming here was the first step."

"Has it helped?"

I rest my head on his shoulder again and sigh. "More than you know. I still have a ways to go, though. This is the most I've spoken about it in a long time. It felt good to let all that out."

He caresses my arm. "I've been dealing with my own issues for a long time too. Maybe we can help each other."

I pull my head back. "What problems do you have, Mr. Sunshine?"

He toys with my hair. "We all have things we're dealing with, beautiful. Some show it more than others or differently."

"Like what?"

He taps my nose. "Nope. Don't even try it. We aren't talking about me. Today is about you."

"You're not fair." I pout.

"Life isn't always fair," he says, his voice losing its cheerfulness. Vulnerability takes over. "I learned that a long time ago."

"Hey, you can't be sad. You said this was *my* day." I didn't mean to drag him down with me.

His face brightens. "You're right. Sorry. There's something about you that makes me want to open up and dissect my past. Anyway, back to you. Would you ever consider working in a doctor's office? It's not a hospital, and you could use your nursing background. Or the pharmaceutical industry? Or teach?"

"I don't know if I'm ready. Another reason to go to therapy." I stand and take in the beauty in the distance, my hands stuffed in my coat pockets. "I'm sorry, Leo. I know I'm a fucking mess. I shouldn't have dumped my shit on you. We were having such a great day."

Seconds pass, then his arms embrace me from behind. I sigh in relief and relax against him like he's my boyfriend. It's amazing what a hug can do for someone. At this moment, I realize how touch starved I am.

"You're not a mess, Olive. You're grieving both the life you had and the loss of your father. Regardless of your problems, mood swings, whatever, I want to be around you. I need to be. The intensity of it is insane, but it doesn't scare me."

I turn in his arms and look into his loving eyes. "It's crazy, but I'm the same. And I wouldn't change it. I love being here with you."

"Me too," he says. "Me too. And I'm at the end of my rope trying to resist you. But I want to do this right and take it slow."

Cold wind whips around us, and I shiver. Leo's embrace tightens around me. My eyes drift to his mouth, and I wish I could feel his tempting lips against mine. He dips his head until our mouths are almost touching. My heart pounds like I'm running a marathon. Magical energy crackles around us. I close my eyes, waiting for his lips to brush mine. *Kiss me, please.* I'm desperate for his touch.

"Look at that view," a person says in the distance, ruining the moment. My body goes rigid, and we break apart.

Interrupted again! I want to scream for them to leave, but it's useless. Leo's clenched jaw shows he's not happy either. He said he wanted to take it slow. This is taking it at a snail's pace.

Leo glances at his watch. "I didn't realize how late it is. We need to get going if we want to get to Ma's on time. Ma and Tonya are like drill sergeants with their schedules." I like how he said *Ma's* instead of *my ma's*. There's something more personal about it.

"That doesn't surprise me. I can't wait to eat," I say.

"You won't be disappointed."

"I know that. I'll be with you, and I have a feeling I'd be happy when I'm with you, regardless of where we are."

"Such pressure. But I'll take that challenge while you're here. You'll never want to leave."

"But I will…because you won't be here anymore. You'll be off luxury hotel hopping, and I'll be a distant memory." During our hike, Leo told me about his job as a hotel critic. Who wouldn't want to travel the world, stay in the best hotels, and make money doing it? I noticed something when he talked about it though—his enthusiasm diminished. I get the feeling he doesn't really enjoy his job. But what do I know?

"Yeah, see. That's where you're wrong. There'll be no forgetting you."

I love it when he says things like this, but can I believe it? What could I offer him when I have too much baggage weighing me down? Maybe it wasn't such a good idea for me to come here to Orcas Island. Now I'm thinking I might go home with a much bigger problem.

A broken heart.

16

OLIVE

Man, this is nerve-racking. It's not a date or a meet-the-parents kind of thing. It's nothing more than a home-cooked meal. *Are you sure about that?* But when Leo opens the front door to his mom's house, I straighten my jeans and smooth down my shirt as best I can with one hand. The other one has a death grip on a bouquet I insisted on buying. Once we're inside, we remove our shoes and leave them lined up at the door, next to the others.

"We're here," Leo calls as he leads me down a long hallway with powder-gray walls, white chair rails, and beautiful hardwood flooring. The delicious scent of pot roast wraps around me like a blanket. For a second, it's like I'm home having Mom's traditional Sunday pot roast dinner with Andy and my parents. It was Dad's favorite meal. This smells similar and familiar, my heart fills with warmth and maybe ease.

I'm pulled away from the visit down memory lane when Tonya appears in front of us wearing a cute strawberry-patterned apron and holding a pink martini in one hand. Cosmo maybe? I wouldn't mind one right now.

"Hey, Leo. Hi, Olive. Welcome! You're just in time for a drink before dinner." She turns around and says, "Follow me."

Leo gently ushers me forward with his hand on my lower back, a calming little gesture. Really, any touch from him keeps me grounded. Tonya leads us to a gorgeous country kitchen with floor-to-ceiling white cabinetry and a massive center island. A muted gray, blue, and green mosaic backsplash adds color to the room. High-back stools line one side of the island. Far to the right side of the kitchen is a long wooden table with five place settings. Mom would love it here.

"Ma, stop hiding in the pantry," Tonya calls, smirking. "Olive doesn't bite."

"Tonya," Leo warns.

"I'm not hiding. I'm getting the cornstarch you didn't put out for me. You're losing your touch, Cosmo Girl," his mom says as she appears with a box in her hand. Her apron matches Tonya's. She's a couple inches taller than me with light brown, shoulder-length hair.

Tonya's face turns pink. "Blasphemy!" she cries. "My ears are burning." She's a hoot.

Leo's mom turns toward us, a welcoming smile on her face. It falters for a second when she looks at me, and her hazel eyes flash. I correct my posture, suddenly uncomfortable. Does she not want me here? Did Leo see it, or is this my usual insecurity? Maybe she's protective of her son? She's already intimidating, and I just met her!

"Ma, this is Olive." Leo gestures toward me as he introduces us.

She extends her hand. "Hi, Olive. I'm Marla. It's nice to meet the woman who's caught my son's eye." Her eyebrows tip up. "And look at your pretty ones. What a unique shade of brown."

"Here we go," Leo grumbles, scratching his neck like he has hives. My mom would be the same if I brought him home with me. Probably worse. "Let's not lay it on too thick tonight."

"And look at her thick eyelashes, Ma. They're real! Isn't she lucky?" Tonya says, finishing her martini.

Be brave, talkative, and polite. "Nice to meet you, Marla. Thanks for having me. Happy New Year too. It smells delicious in here." I hand her the flowers. "Leo says you love yellow roses."

She puts the cornstarch on the island and takes the flowers from me. "I really do. Thank you. A woman can never get too many flowers." Her smile reaches her eyes this time. *Phew.* "Leo, will you please get my favorite vase from the other room? You know which one."

"Sure." Leo leaves the kitchen.

"I hope you're hungry and like pot roast. The gravy is almost finished," she says, heading for the stove.

"We hiked most of the day. We're starving."

Marla lifts a lid off a steaming pot and stirs the contents. "Good. That's what I want to hear because we have plenty of food."

"Who wants a drink?" Tonya interrupts. Then she looks beyond me at something over my head. I startle when I realize someone's behind me. *Holy hell.*

"Hey, Sully," she says. "We didn't hear you come in."

I step to the side to let him pass and melt when I see his kitten curled up on his shoulder. I wonder if he'd let me hold it. Tonya clips the stems of the roses in a snap and takes the vase from Leo, who's back. She arranges them perfectly, then places the vase on the table.

Leo formally introduces me to Sully. He remains silent but nods and shakes my hand. Then he kisses Marla's cheek. Now that I have a better look at him, I can see his resemblance to Leo. His eyes are slightly more brown than golden, perhaps due to the black cloud around him. He's about two inches taller and wider too. He's handsome in that angry, don't-fuck-with-me kind of way. It gives him an edge that some women find attractive. He's the dark force in the room, and Leo is the light from what I've witnessed so far.

Tonya stands out in her own way because her hair is brunette, not as dark as mine, and straight. It's styled in a bob right below her chin. Her eyes are hazel, like her mom's. She's short, petite, friendly, fiery, and seems to have good business sense, but no one outshines Leo.

Tonya asks again what we'd like to drink, then orders us to sit at the kitchen table and relax. I offer to help, but both she and Marla say no. Message received.

"Where's Donna?" Leo asks, taking his beer from Tonya a few minutes later. She hands me a cosmopolitan garnished with an orange peel and Sully a beer. I sip mine and go cross-eyed. *Holy shit, that's strong.*

Marla wipes her hands on a dishtowel, then continues to stir the gravy. "She's having problems with her back again. Didn't she send you a message? She wanted to see if you could fill in for her tomorrow afternoon, hoping she'll get a doctor's appointment."

Leo's eyebrows furrow. "Olive and I wanted to do something together."

I nudge him with my elbow. "Don't worry, Leo. I can wander around by myself. I'd like to go in to town and visit the shops I saw this morning while getting my hiking shoes. Maybe buy some new clothes."

"I'm going in to town tomorrow to check out the sales and to run a couple of errands. Want to come along? I can show you all the good stores," Tonya offers. "It'll be fun to have some company."

When was the last time I went shopping with a friend? Years! "I'd love to. Are you sure?" I mentally pat myself on the shoulder with pride. One more step out of my comfort zone.

"Positive," she responds, polishing her fork and knife. I grin as she places them perfectly next to her plate like we're at a formal affair.

To my surprise, Sully sits next to me at the table. The kitty is on the shoulder next to me. "Can I pet her?" I ask. "Is she a he?"

"Sure. She." Okay, one-word answers. At least I didn't get a grunt or a growl.

I lift my arm and gently stroke her soft fur. Light purring vibrates my fingers. I gush at the cuteness. I'd love to get a cat, but it's not allowed in my apartment complex.

"What's her name?"

"Smokey," he responds.

"That's cute. It fits her." I push my luck. "Can I hold her?"

Grunt. Okay, I guess not.

"Come on, Sully. Be nice," Leo urges.

"Don't worry. I understand." If he's going through a hard time and that little kitten is the one thing that's keeping him together, he doesn't have to share. I'd be the same way.

Like Leo's helping me. If another woman, like Bethany, tried to get his attention right now, I'd probably do more than grunt. Hell, I didn't think I was the jealous type. But Leo's unique. He's a keeper.

Marla places steaming dishes of meat, green beans, mashed potatoes, and gravy on the table, and we pass them around. As we devour the food, conversation ranges from the hotel's reservation system to hiking and even stories from when they were kids. I thought Tonya might bring up

Leo's dancing, but she remained quiet. Marla asked about the whole fake girlfriend business, and Leo took charge of that discussion. Overall, it's been easier than I thought because the focus hasn't been directly on me.

"*Mmm,* delicious," I praise. "This pot roast tastes similar to my mom's. And I love that I'm not the only one who eats it with mustard." I raise my chin to Marla because she has a large dollop of mustard on her plate.

"Thank you," Marla says. "I picked up the habit a long time ago. So, Olive, tell us a little about yourself. Have you ever been to Orcas Island before?"

"No. My family's always vacationed in places like Southern California, Mexico, or Hawaii. My parents preferred more tropical destinations. Because of them, I never really considered coming here. Habit, I guess. Before I was born, they came here, but said it's too touristy and didn't like the weather."

I cross my legs and accidentally kick Leo. "Sorry," I whisper. Before I can move away, he presses his leg against mine and leaves it there. Adorable.

Tonya passes the platter of pot roast to Sully and he stabs two large slices, then drops them on his plate. He offers me some, but I decline before he puts the platter back on the table. I'm only halfway through my plate, and he's on his second serving. Then again, I'm talking a lot more than he is.

"Do you agree with them now that you've seen the island?" Tonya asks.

"Not at all, but it's not tourist season. Hiking was spectacular today, and the view from Mount Constitution was breathtaking. I'd love to come back in the summer and do it again."

Marla adds more green beans to her dish, then asks, "Are you from Washington?"

I wipe my mouth with a napkin and place it next to my plate. "I live in a small town north of Seattle called Aston Springs."

Marla drops her fork. It hits her plate with a clang and topples to the floor. Smokey wigs out and hangs by her claws off Sully's shirt. "Boy, do I have butterfingers today. I also dropped two glasses this morning, and they shattered all over the kitchen floor."

Tonya gets up and fetches a new fork for her and throws the dirty one in the sink. Smokey climbs Sully's shirt again and cuddles up where his shoulder meets his neck. My heart melts.

"Do you live alone or with your parents?" Marla asks with a strange twang in her voice. I can't tell if this is her personality or something else. All I know is that I'm catching a vibe. I hate that I'm paranoid.

"I live alone. My mom lives nearby in the house where she grew up. When my grandma died, my parents moved in right before my brother was born and never left."

"No father? How many siblings do you have?" she questions further, cutting up her second slice of pot roast into equal-sized pieces. She focuses on her plate, not me.

"Ma, what's with the questions?" Leo interrupts with an annoyed edge to his tone.

"It's okay, Leo." If I'm going to stop hiding in my apartment, I have to get used to people asking me personal questions. "I have an older brother who lives in San Francisco. And my dad died a year and a half ago."

"Oh, I'm really sorry to hear that." Marla's sudden warmth and sympathy makes her sound like she really cares. She blinks her glassy eyes, then grabs her napkin to dab the corners of them. "How's your mom handling it?"

"As best as she can in her situation. My parents were happily married. They were inseparable. Always affectionate, even after being together over thirty-five years. It's something I—well, anyone—would be lucky to find." I keep my eyes from seeking Leo's, sensing what my heart already knows. Something ridiculous, but maybe not. "Because he's gone," I finish, "she's kind of attached herself to me. It's been hard for her."

"Over thirty-five years… That's a long time," Marla sympathizes.

"They got married after college and had kids later when my dad's business finally took off. My brother and I were born in the same year." *Like Leo's family really cares about that.*

"Our parents were happy like that too," Tonya mentions, glancing at Marla. "Right?" Marla blinks several times.

"Ma? Are you okay?" Sully says, startling me.

Marla tilts her head back. "I think I might have gotten a little mustard in my eye. It stings. Excuse me for a second."

"Do you need help?" I ask, quickly standing. "If you have eye solution, like eye drops, you need to flush the eye immediately. If you don't, a lot of water. It can damage your eye if it isn't treated right away. I can help you if you'd like."

Unbelievable! That came out of nowhere and it felt unbelievable. I didn't have to think about it, I knew what she should do. I had patients in the ICU with horrific eye injuries. *Nurse Hansen is in the house!*

"Thanks for the advice. I'll be fine. Please finish your food." She pushes away from the table and leaves the room, sniffling along the way.

Was it really mustard or is she crying? If it were mustard, she'd be in a lot more pain. Something doesn't seem right. Did I remind her of her late husband when I mentioned that my dad died? Now I feel bad. But she's the one who asked.

I sit and pull my chair in, ignoring my personal revelation and that I may have made a spectacle of myself.

Leo leans closer and whispers, "That was impressive. It gave me a little glimpse of you as a nurse. You've still got it."

I give a slight nod and grin, then I glance at Tonya and Sully to see if they heard Leo. This is not the time or place to talk about it.

Tonya gets up and refills the water carafe, then brings it back to the table. "Don't worry, Olive. I'm sure Mom's fine. Anybody want more water?" I push my empty glass forward for her to refill.

Leo strokes my back gently. "I'm sorry. I didn't think Mom would grill you like that."

"Well, it's rare that you show interest in our hotel guests or any woman at all when you're home," Tonya points out, scooping up another serving of mashed potatoes. "Of course she's going to ask questions. And I'm sure you're curious too."

Sully nods, agreeing with her.

Leo glances at me and squeezes my hand under the table. Without pause, he says, "I'm definitely interested."

Me too.

17

LEO

Mom's acting weird—not at all like I thought she would. I know the excuse we gave Olive to come to dinner was because she helped us, but Tonya, Mom, and I all had ulterior motives. Because of that, I thought Mom would fall all over Olive to make her feel welcome and to embarrass me with baby stories. None of that has happened yet.

My family knows not to discuss certain topics such as Corey, my dancing, and other talents I haven't practiced in a while. But why Tonya hasn't brought up my dancing the other night draws a big blank. I thought for sure she'd have told Mom and Mom would be asking me a million questions instead of grilling Olive. Was it not as monumental to Tonya as it was to me? I'm glad they're smart enough not to go there with me tonight. I want Olive to get to know that part of me when the time is right.

Mom's usually super warm and welcoming to guests, but I haven't seen that side of her since we arrived. It's like she's skeptical about something. And for her to get emotional—that's way out of left field. The whole mustard thing had to have been an act to hide it. I haven't seen her get upset about Dad in a long time. I wonder what triggered it.

And to see Olive immediately offer to help her and instruct her on what to do was surprising. I think it was for Olive too. I pictured her in a hospital room dressed in scrubs, full of confidence and experience. It's sexy as hell. She could be my nurse anytime.

"So, Olive, did you make any resolutions this year?" Tonya asks between sips of her drink. "One of mine was always to be less obsessive or anal about everything. Never happened." Sully and I nod in agreement. There's no stopping her. "I don't bother anymore."

Olive relaxes in her chair. "I have a mixture of resolutions and things I want to do this year. I guess they're considered the same."

I nudge her foot with mine. "Any you care to share with us?"

"Oh, you know the typical lose weight, exercise…blah blah blah." She rolls her eyes. "And to get out of my apartment and socialize more. I've accomplished those two already in the last forty-eight hours." She glances my way with a sweet smile and wraps her pinky finger around mine under the table.

"What else?" Sully speaks up, shocking all of us. We aren't used to hearing his voice anymore.

Olive looks up at him like God spoke to her. "Let's see. A random one is to sing at a karaoke bar. I can't sing for the life of me and then to do it in front of people…horrible. But this year, I'm going to face some of my fears. Starting with the little ones."

Tonya's face beams. *Not good.* "Clover Bar has karaoke night tomorrow. We should all go. Then you could cross that off your list. What do you say, Leo? Sully? You in?"

She's got a lot of nerve. I ball my hands at my sides and shoot Tonya a dirty look. Olive notices and frowns. My gaze pivots back to Tonya, whose smile is as big as ever. *Traitor*.

"Come on, Leo. We haven't gone there in ages. Thorsten would love to see you."

"I'm in," Sully says, pushing his empty plate away. Of course, he wants to be social now. Well, they're going to be highly disappointed.

"Really?" Tonya perks up in her chair with excitement.

Sully's shrug wakes Smokey, who's been snoozing on and off since we got here. He picks her up and kisses her nose. "Want to hold her for a minute? I want to go check on Ma."

It takes a second to realize he's talking to Olive. Tonya pouts. "How come she's allowed to hold her?"

"She's the guest, and I'm still pissed about the video you two did. And…she always swats at you." He hands the kitten carefully to Olive, and my heart melts because of the wide grin on her face.

Olive lays Smokey on the crook of her arm and cuddles her to her side. When she scratches behind Smokey's ears, I hear the gentle sound of purring.

"Whatever. She swatted only a couple of times. And I'm your sister," Tonya complains, staring at his back as he leaves the room without another word. "It's not our fault you can't take a joke."

"What did you guys do to him?" Olive lowers her voice.

"Have you seen those scare prank reels on TikTok or Insta where people pretend to be scared and freak out others around them?" Tonya asks.

Olive snickers. "Yes. I saw one where a woman was leaving the house with a man, then the woman started screaming and running around the front lawn like a lunatic. The guy completely freaked out. It was hysterical." She presses her lips together, but her bouncing shoulders give her hilarity away. She looks behind me, then whispers, "I love those videos."

"Well, we did something like that to Sully and, as you can see, it didn't go over well. Especially because we scared Smokey. Leo can show you later. It was all good fun. We tried to scare the anger and sadness out of him."

"Major fail." Tonya and I cackle. Mom comes back into the room, and we straighten up. "Ma, are you okay?" I ask. "Your eyes are bloodshot."

She waves it off as she sits at the table again, but won't look at me. "Never get mustard in your eye. It's a horror. I tried to rinse them out, but it wasn't easy. I'll be fine." Olive observes her intently, but doesn't say anything. Mom picks up her fork. "So what did I miss?"

"We're going to take Olive to Clover's tomorrow night for karaoke," Tonya answers. "And Sully agreed to go."

Mom's hand freezes right before she puts a fork full of potatoes in her mouth. "Really? I must've been gone longer than I thought."

"I did," Sully confirms as he walks back into the kitchen. He gets himself another beer from the refrigerator and returns to his chair. Olive hands him Smokey. He leans back slightly and lays the kitten on his chest, where she instantly starts making biscuits. It's amazing how tame she is now. When he found her she was starving, skittish, and wouldn't let anyone near her. Within a week, she was the opposite. To him anyway. I guess he's got the magic touch.

Mom's brows shoot up to her hairline. "I must be in another universe." *Say nothing about me.* "Did you agree on a time? Maybe I'll come too." *Great.* How am I going to get out of this?

"Hey, if karaoke isn't your thing, you don't have to go," Olive whispers to me. "You don't have to sing."

Suck it up, tough guy. I need to get my mood in check. This isn't about me. It's for Olive to cross one more thing off her list. With a wicked grin, I say, "I wouldn't miss hearing you sing for the world."

Her eyes narrow. "And what about you? Can you sing? Maybe we could have a competition? You know, like what Tom Holland did against Zendaya. You could definitely pull it off with your dance moves."

I grit my teeth, waiting for someone to use this as an opening.

"I'd love to see that," Tonya exclaims, clapping her hands. "But that was lip-syncing, and I'm not sure Thorsten wants a dance off." She sighs with hearts in her eyes. "I love that video of Tom Holland lip-syncing 'Umbrella.'"

"Right?" Olive confirms. It's nice to see them hitting it off. "I never heard of him until I saw that video." She turns to me. "So? You gonna sing too, and make a fool out of yourself with me?"

I shake my head. "No can do. I'll be going to hear you or them. It's not about me." There's a finality in my voice that not only shocks me but the others too. Olive must think I'm being a dick. I'm the funny guy, not the downer.

But everything I've been avoiding for years is closing in on me.

Maybe Mom was right.

Maybe it's time to stop running.

18

OLIVE

I turn around one more time in front of Tonya's bedroom mirror. "Are you sure this outfit looks okay? Should I wear the dark green shirt instead?" It's only the millionth time I've asked.

"No to the green one. The outfit you're wearing now is perfect. If Leo isn't in love with you already, he will be by the end of the night. His tongue will hang out like a little doggy's," she says, folding and stacking my new clothes on the bed.

An unattractive snort slips from my lips. "Whatever."

I look over my shoulder into the mirror. My ass looks perky in these black pants that hug my curves. Tonya noticed when we were shopping how uncomfortable I am with my body, and she suggested I wear a bodysuit that smooths everything out. It's a big hype right now. I thought it was silly till I tried it on. I ended up buying a black lace one with a nude underlay and two others.

All I can say is, wow! I feel a whole size smaller. My boobs look amazing in the low-cut burgundy shirt I'm wearing, and I can see my waistline again. To top it off, this thing is sexy *and* comfortable. Whoever came up with this design deserves the amount of money I spent on it. And don't get me started on the sexy black boots I bought for 50 percent off. It'll be nice to have a little more height tonight when I'm standing next to Leo.

What was supposed to be a shopping day turned into an afternoon makeover session. I never made it back to the hotel. After brunch, we stopped at Tonya's hairstylist to reschedule an appointment. Once she had a new one, the conversation veered off course, and I found myself sitting in the chair with wet hair, discussing hairstyles I liked.

I'm not a flashy person by nature. I don't wear a lot of makeup, don't dye my hair, and don't wear nail polish. Bright lipstick is an absolute no. Other people can wear it all they want; I don't like how it looks on me. But I let them do a makeover.

The stylist turned me away from the mirror so I couldn't see what she was doing. Tonya stayed the entire time, and her approving animated facial expressions during the process decreased my reluctance. Not completely—I gripped the chair handles with sweaty hands the entire time.

All that gripping was for no reason. When the stylist turned me around, I froze in my seat. It wasn't a drastic change, but a needed one. My hair is still dark, but there's an extra shine to it, and the color transitions to a chestnut tone toward the ends. It's subtle enough that it looks natural, like the sun kissed it.

She also trimmed my hair, added some long layers, and put loose curls in it. It's a style I've tried to do myself at home, but the curls flopped seconds later. The only makeup I'm wearing is a soft pink blush and some reddish-pink shimmery lip gloss.

With this new outfit, shoes, hair, and makeup, my

confidence level has gone through the roof. Hopefully, I'll feel more comfortable singing in front of Leo and a bunch of strangers tonight. I've made a mental list of songs to choose from, and I'll decide at the last minute based on the mood. I'm hoping Leo will be in a good one, considering he didn't seem thrilled about going.

I turn toward Tonya and find it hard to speak. "Thank you for keeping me company today. I knew I needed a change, but never realized how much. I feel like a new woman."

"Right back at you," she says as she shuts her closet door. "It's too bad you don't live here. We'd do it all the time."

"Don't worry, I'll be back. One day in Eastsound and a day of hiking have me hooked." Leo and his siblings have already convinced me to come back. I'm not sure about Marla, though. The jury's still out on that one.

I don't want to think about going back home. My mom has sent me hundreds of texts and voice messages. Some were frantic because I didn't respond fast enough. She doesn't seem to understand what one text a day means and that I want to be left alone. I dread the talk I'm going to have with her when I get home.

Don't get me wrong. I love my mom very much. She's always showered us with love and comfort. But she's changed a lot since Dad died. She's lost and doesn't know how to live without him. I want to be patient and understanding, but it's getting harder every day.

Time's flying by, and before I know it, I'll be back in my car watching the island disappear into nothing. And Leo will be farther and farther away from me.

～

I flex my hands, trying to calm down. I'm nervous and excited at the same time. Tonya told everyone we'd meet them at Clover's because she wants me to make a big entrance. Now I'm on edge because what if Leo doesn't like how I look? Yes, I know I shouldn't care, but I do. As for excited, I'm about to do something way out of my norm. In front of a crowd, no less.

Once we're through the bar's entrance, I remove my coat and drape it over my arm. This place is fuller than I expected for a Thursday, and it's loud like a typical pub. I follow Tonya as she weaves through tables, saying quick hellos to several people. It was the same way when we were shopping. It's obvious that Leo's family is well known and respected on the island.

Leo and Sully are already here and are supposed to be holding a table near the stage. We're both looking for them. Finally, Tonya nudges me and points to where they are. My stomach flutters. There's no need for lights in here because Leo radiates his own. He's standing next to a big, old burly guy.

As I get closer, the guy bumps fists with him, then moves away to greet customers at a table nearby. Leo turns and sees Tonya first. When he sees me, his mesmerizing smile takes my breath away. We stand there watching each other. His golden-brown locks are up again, revealing the long, smooth line of his neck and his chiseled jaw. The black Henley he's sporting fits him like a glove, reminding me of what's underneath. Dark blue jeans finish this perfect vision in front of me. I vaguely notice Tonya taking my coat.

His eyes take a slow, torturous tour of my body, and I swear I can feel the heat tracing my every curve. Instead of feeling uneasy, I stand up straight and let him get an eyeful. A sexy smirk graces his kissable lips. I'm on fire, and he hasn't even touched me yet. He approaches and kisses my cheek, his soft lips lingering there longer than usual. One inhale of his alluring scent makes me want him even more.

"You look stunning," he whispers. "I'm going to have to fight off all the men for you tonight."

I lean into him. "No you won't."

"Oh, really. Why is that?" He brushes his knuckles over my burning cheek. By the end of this night, if he doesn't kiss me—a genuine kiss—I'm going to attack him myself. A lightbulb turns on in my head. Now I know what song I'm going to sing. And he better get the damn point.

"I'm not interested in anyone else," I say. He cocks an eyebrow. "I must be doing an awful job if you didn't know that already."

"Okay, lovebirds. Stop with the whispering and come sit. I'm hungry and need a drink. Since I'm not driving tonight, I can indulge a little, even if I do have to work tomorrow," Tonya says. Lucky for her, she lives walking distance from this place. "Olive, you need to register the song you're going to sing. Did you finally make a decision?"

"Yep. It just came to me when I walked into the pub."

Leo pulls out the chair for me that has my coat resting over the back. I sit and he follows, sliding his chair closer to mine.

"So lay it on me. Which one did you choose?" Leo's eyes twinkle with interest.

I trace my finger along his jaw. "It's a surprise. You're just gonna have to wait. I thought of three songs, but when I arrived, I got inspired. Now how do I sign up?" While Leo tells me what to do, we order drinks and some food. I'm starving, but my stomach is in knots. No alcohol for me tonight.

Several people approach the table to say hello. I'm

surprised at how shocked some are to see Leo and even more by the sympathy they express. I don't understand what's going on. It's hard to hear everything with the loud chatter around us, but I catch an older woman saying she's missed seeing Leo up on stage, and another one asks if he's blogging again. *He used to sing karaoke? Blogging what?* He told me he travels for his job. Was that all bullshit? I'm missing something.

What do you expect, Olive? You've known him for less than a week.

"Where's Smokey tonight?" I ask Sully to bring him into the conversation and to distract myself. He's hardly interacting with anybody. It's no surprise, given that he's sitting with his arms crossed and has a resting dick face. Can you say that for a guy? Either way, his demeanor screams unapproachable. Still, his presence here tonight seems to be a big deal to his family.

"She's at home, probably sleeping on my pillow." I can imagine him strolling through town with a kitten in tow. Women would flock to him.

Time passes quickly as we eat, drink, and chat. I submitted my form for the song I want to sing. No one else from our group submitted one. I guess I'm the only one embarrassing themselves tonight.

"Is your mom coming?" I ask.

"She said she'd try." Tonya rolls her eyes. "Ma doesn't go out much. We try to encourage her to do things outside the hotel, but she rarely does."

"Same with my mom. They should meet since they're both widowers and loners."

"Well, maybe Ma would be up for that. I told her this should be her year to do something different. Let's see what her life looks like in December," Leo adds.

I rest my chin on my hand. "My life better be a lot

more interesting by then. I'll hate myself if I fall back into my usual boring routine when I get back home."

"I won't let you," Leo says close to my ear, making me shiver.

"Oh yeah? Want to be my accountability person or whatever they call it? Call me every day to keep me on track?"

"Sure," he simply offers. "I'm gonna talk to you every day anyway. It won't change after you leave." His blatant honesty and determination have now been added to the long list of things I find so damn attractive about him.

"And what can I do for you, then?"

His honey gaze locks on mine with sincerity. "That's simple. Stay in my life." My heart swells to the point I think it's going to pop.

"Hey, Sully," a guy slurs, bursting our bubble. He acknowledges Tonya and Leo with a lift of his chin, then grasps Sully's shoulder. "How's it going? I haven't seen you in ages."

Other than shoving his hand off his shoulder, Sully doesn't respond. The tension in the air, however, thickens by the second.

"Oh, that's right. Your fiancée dumped you for your business partner. That shit hurts, doesn't it? It's funny how what goes around comes around. Been there done that, haven't we? Or should I say you?" Sully's stone face turns crimson, and his jaw clenches.

Engaged? That's why Sully's miserable. And he had a business, or still does. Leo mentioned he was between jobs.

Tonya gasps and Leo stands, his chair almost falling backward. Sully lifts his hand to stop Leo from doing something he'll probably regret. Leo sits back down and takes a pull of his beer. I rest my hand on his thigh, and he surprises me by placing his hand on mine and giving it a subtle squeeze.

The troublemaker mutters something else and grabs Sully's shoulder again. Sully pushes him back hard enough to make his point. The asshole straightens his shirt, then staggers away with a drunken smirk. Grade A asshole. Tonya reaches out to Sully. He dodges her hand. Then swigs his beer, his face revealing nothing.

Leo must see my concern. "An enemy from high school. Total dick. He's always accused Sully of stealing his high school girlfriend. Never happened. Talk about living in the past."

I want to go over to Sully, give him a hug, and then drive back to his place to pick up Smokey. It annoys me that I've wasted so much time feeling sorry for myself when everyone has their own shit to deal with. We're all human, striving to get through each day.

Time flies as the scheduled performers do their thing. Some are excellent while others are more funny than anything else. Every time a name is announced, I'm on the verge of peeing myself. Speaking of which, I should've gone to the bathroom.

"Next up, Olive Hansen. This is her first time here, folks, so let's give her a big round of applause."

Leo shouts over the crowd, "Good luck!" Tonya hoots, and Sully lifts his beer with a nod. I think he's warming to me.

Reluctantly, I get up and step onto the stage. *Why am I doing this?* A man hands me a microphone. It's now or never. "She'll be singing Prince's 'Kiss.'"

My grip on the microphone is like a vice. The music starts abruptly, and the words begin to roll. I mess up the first lines, but then I get into the rhythm and let loose.

Some people in the crowd sing along, while others dance between the tables and cheer me on.

Every time the lyrics mention "my girl," I swap them with "my boy" and gesture toward Leo. His face lights up, exactly as I hoped. There are points in the song where Prince's voice rises an octave. I try to do the same, but it's a big fat fail. The scene of Julia Roberts singing in the movie *Pretty Woman* keeps replaying in my mind. My sweaty body moves autonomously as I shake my booty, unconcerned about looking ridiculous. All of my inhibitions vanish like they did the other night on the dance floor. I'm having a blast singing my heart out for the guy who's charmed his way into my life.

The song's over too quickly, and I'm shooed off the stage. The crowd claps until I reach our table. Leo stands and waits for me with open arms. I jump into them and he wraps them around me tightly. Shouting above the noise, he enthuses, "You nailed it. I'm damn proud of you." I don't get a kiss, but what is he going to do—kiss me in front of a crowd?

Be patient, Olive. You'll get what you want.

19

LEO

I sit here in awe. I'm going to marry this woman. Yep, you heard me. Call me crazy, but I don't fucking care.

I knew from the moment I laid eyes on Olive—I've never felt such intense attraction before, and the constant desire to be with her bewilders me. Watching her perform on stage, singing "Kiss" directly to me—yes, I could sense her eyes penetrating me, inviting me to kiss her. There's no doubt it'll happen tonight if I have anything to say about it.

Mom described it as love at first sight when she met Dad on a blind date. She almost canceled because she had little faith in relationships after what her best friend did to her. While she was walking to the restaurant where they were supposed to meet, she spotted a man standing next to his car. She knew right away he was the one. They soon discovered they were each other's blind date.

So why couldn't it happen to me? Would life be so cruel as to dangle Olive in front of me, only to take her away?

Olive has become my muse without either of us realizing it. First she got me dancing, and now I'm ready to do something else I haven't done in years either.

She trots off the stage and hurries toward me. A blinding smile spreads across her face and I open my arms wide for her. She hops into them like she belongs here—which she does—and I lift her off the ground.

"You nailed it. I'm damn proud of you," I say into the crook of her neck. Her light, floral scent assaults my senses. I want to kiss her now, but I refrain, squeezing her affectionately instead. It's not because of the crowd—I don't care about that. It's because I have a plan.

We have fun with Tonya and Sully, our bodies constantly connected in some way. She's not the same person who checked into the hotel days ago. For Olive's sake, I hope she stays like this. Seeing her confront her problems this way has made me realize I need to do the same. I've been a coward for far too long.

When the coast is clear, I excuse myself to go to the bathroom. Once I'm out of sight, I search for Thorsten, the owner, and find him near the bar. He nods with a sly grin after I tell him what I want to do. This is going to be good. Or really bad.

When I return, we order another round of drinks and listen to a few more singers. I'm so fucking charged I could detonate any second now, and I've only had one beer. A war of emotions rages within me, and I have only three ways to release this energy. Sex, but that's not happening here. Neither is dancing. As for the third, you'll have to wait and see.

Then I hear it. "Next up, Leo Forrest. It's been a while since he's sung for us."

Three heads whip in my direction, their mouths wide open. I try not to laugh at the comical sight, but it sneaks out anyway. Tonya's eyes already shimmer with emotion. I see Sully's teeth because he's smiling, not scowling, and Olive looks like a deer in headlights.

Before they can say anything, I rush to the stage, determined not to chicken out. I'm going to sing Queen's "I Was Born to Love You." I used to cover Queen's songs all the time, but I don't know how my voice will sound now.

I psych myself up and pray to Corey to help me out. We learned to dance and sing together as kids, and we planned how to use our talents. It all went to shit when he fell sick and died. I haven't sung since. Not even in the shower or the car. The music starts.

Here goes nothing.

I belt out the lyrics, and it's as if no one else is here except Olive and me. Every word belongs to her. Tonya probably thought coming here would inspire me, but the lively atmosphere isn't what's done it. It's that beautiful woman in the crowd with the soft brown eyes and glowing smile who touches my soul. She's gazing at me the way I look at her. Like I'm her future and she's mine. It's time to make significant changes to become worthy of her love. If she'll have me.

Am I really using the word *love*? Yes. All the pain and suffering I've been through has led me to this moment. I've been traveling around the world to avoid my home. Too many memories haunt me when I'm here. But things are changing within me, and for once, I'm excited about it and don't want to leave.

The song ends, and I ignore the people standing and clapping. My sole focus is on kissing Olive's fucking sexy mouth. When I finally stand in front of her, I claim her mouth with mine. She wraps her arms around me, parting her lips, teasing me with the tip of her tongue. And then I taste her. Pure elation pulses through me. I pour all my energy, love, fear, and desire into this kiss. She'll never have to wonder about my feelings for her.

Loud whistling surrounds us as someone pulls on my arm, separating us. "I enjoy a hot kiss as much as anyone," Tonya says playfully, "but you're getting a little out of control. You should continue this elsewhere."

Olive cuddles up to my side and rests her head on my chest, clutching the front of my shirt.

"Want to get out of here?" I ask, rubbing my nose gently behind her ear.

She nods and whispers, "Yes."

I turn to Tonya and Sully and mention leaving. We all came separately, but they're ready to go too. Together, we weave through the tables toward the exit, and that's when I see her.

Mom's standing at the end of the bar with Thorsten's arm around her, and her eyes are fixed on me. She came. Will Thorsten finally make a move on her? He's been in love with her for years. Of course, that's a whole other story.

I release Olive's hand, then stride to Mom and embrace her. We don't need words. I've finally achieved what she hoped I would—I've found my voice again. She was my greatest supporter when I sang and danced. It broke her heart when I stopped. Tonight, Mom caught a glimpse of the old me. I'm not that person anymore, though. I'm more, I think.

Hell, I'll be honest. I have no clue who I am right now, but this is the best I've felt in a long, long time. I feel alive again.

As we part, her watery eyes shimmer with happiness. "I love you, Leo. Welcome back."

I kiss her cheek. "Love you too, Ma. Thanks for being patient."

She smiles at Olive, who's waiting several feet away from us. Then she looks back at me and grins. "Take the rest of the week off," she says.

I lean back, ready to say no, but she lifts her finger, then shakes her head. I salute her and acknowledge Thorsten. She giggles because it's been a habit of mine to salute her when she wins a dispute. Tonight, she's won in more ways than one.

I give Mom a last, quick hug and stride over to Olive. She looks confused. I can understand why. "I bet you're wondering what's going on, huh?"

"Ya think?"

I peck her lips. "Let's go home. I'll answer any questions you have."

I'm ready to tell my story.

20

LEO

We take Tonya home, since we have to get Olive's stuff from their girls' day out anyway. I'm not sure what to expect from my sister right now. My entire family's been urging me to move on since Corey's death. Tonya's got to have something to say, but so far she's been holding it together. Sully affectionately smacked me on the back before heading to his car, but didn't say anything. With him, actions speak louder than words.

While Olive gathers her things, Tonya gives me a big hug. "I'm really proud of you," she whispers. "And fucking jealous too. I want a guy to kiss me like that again."

I pull back. "*Again?*"

She shakes her head. "What? Did I say that? Ignore me." *Okay.*

"Don't worry. It'll happen," I assure her, not wanting to get into it. I love my sister, but my mind is somewhere else.

She releases a deep sigh of doubt. "Maybe. Someday." Olive walks into the room then, and Tonya smacks my arm and pushes me toward the door. "Anyway…this was a great night. You two go have fun."

We're quiet on the drive to the hotel. The sexual tension and pulsing electricity between us is so thick not even a Katana sword could slice through it. My heartbeat pounds in my ears like an amplified drum. If we aren't on the same page right now, my rock-hard dick will shrivel up and fall off.

Once we reach her door, she retrieves her card and waits for what feels like an eternity. Is it intentional? *I will not pounce. I will not look desperate.* Finally, she opens the door, enters, and switches on the light. She doesn't glance back as I close and lock the door. The only movement is when she drops the bags and her purse to the floor beside her. She then removes her jacket and tosses it onto the bags. I follow suit.

My chest heaves as I await her next move, like a lion stalking his prey. Olive saunters to the bedroom, then turns around at the door, bracing her hands on the frame. Her glimmering eyes capture mine. She lures me with a smoldering grin, beckoning me with the curl of her index finger. She's the most desirable woman I've ever met.

Without a word, I close the gap between us. As I approach, she steps back with a smirk. Such a tease, and I love it. Then the air shifts. We move simultaneously, barriers crumbling. Our mouths hunger for each other, ablaze with fire and passion.

Kissing her reignites me, erasing all my doubts and fears.

"Please tell me this isn't a dream," she says, gasping for air. I trail open-mouth kisses down her silken neck. "Do you feel it too?"

I don't have to ask what she means. "Every cell in my body. I want you. All of you. Let me..."

"Yes," she breathes.

With the speed of a cheetah, I pull her shirt over her

head, revealing a sexy black bodysuit underneath. Her overflowing, perky breasts tantalize me, and my mouth waters. I relish the delicate salty and sweet taste as I kiss from her neck to her collarbone and on to the gentle curve of her chest.

I hook the straps of the bodysuit with my fingers and pull them down, watching as her tempting breasts spill out. She gasps when I pull one of her pebbled nipples into my mouth while I massage the other one. Her hand presses the back of my head, encouraging me to keep going.

"I love the way you taste, how you feel like silk against my tongue. Everything. I need to see all of you."

I get down on my knees and unzip her boots. She places her hands on my shoulders as I take them off and then the socks, one by one. Her feet are cute too. I look up at her with my hands on her soft, round hips, making sure she's with me. Lust fills her gorgeous eyes, and her wet, parted lips reveal her desire. I take off her pants, and she finishes by removing the bodysuit. I trail soft kisses from one hip bone to the other, then stand up and step back.

"Gorgeous…every single curve. You are perfect, and I'm going to make sure you know that, right now."

"Then what are you waiting for?" Her velvety whisper goes straight to my head. Her eyes trace a heated path down my body, flashing when she notices my obvious hard-on. She sucks on her lower lip.

I love how she stands in front of me, completely exposed, without inhibition. There's something insanely arousing about it—her completely bare and me fully clothed.

Her hand traces down between her breasts, then rests on her stomach. The other moves over her shapely hip.

"Take my jeans off," I command to see her reaction after I pull off my shirt. "I won't last long if you keep teasing me like that." I kick off my shoes to speed things up.

"We don't want that now, do we?" She approaches me with a seductive curve of her mouth. A tremor of desire travels through my body when she kisses the valley between my pecs, and tickles my skin with her fingertips around the rim of my jeans. "Ah, you like that, huh?"

I nod, speechless because I'm painfully hard and my pants are cutting off my circulation. I groan when she pops the button open, lowers the zipper, and grazes her knuckles along my dick. This is downright fucking torture.

She continues her seductive game and slides her hands into the back of my jeans, caresses my ass, then gently squeezes. "So sexy," she purrs. Her hungry eyes assess my face for a response to her audacious touch, ending on my lips. I capture her mouth to urge her to keep going. She pushes my jeans and boxer briefs down, and my hardness springs free. Relief! I kick the clothes away, then pull her body against mine. We moan in unison when our bare skin touches each other.

I move us backward until her legs meet the mattress. Seizing the initiative, she pulls herself onto the bed and poses like a Greek goddess, her hair spread around her head and her creamy skin exposed, inviting me to explore it all night.

I kneel beside her, and my pulse speeds up as she peruses my body. I crawl closer, then hover over her with my hands on either side of her head.

"Was that song for me?" I lean in close, my lips almost brushing hers. Her back bows, and her hard nipples scrape along my chest, making me tremble.

"Ever since I met you," she breathes, "I've dreamed of you doing more than kissing me."

"Your dream is my command, beautiful."

Where shall I begin?

21

OLIVE

Possessed. That's what I am. Never have I ever been this bold in bed. I can't stand looking at myself naked in the mirror, but right now with Leo, I am completely comfortable in my skin. He embraces all my exaggerated, unwanted curves and insecurities, lifting me to new heights.

I've always loved kissing, but kissing him takes it to a whole new level. If I had my way, we'd never separate. I know it's not logical, but a woman can dream when the man of her hottest fantasies hovers above her and devours her mouth.

Goose bumps bloom on his skin as I stroke his muscular back. He hums in delight as he slowly lowers himself between my legs, blanketing my body. His arousal presses against my inner thigh, and I ache for more. I break away from his seductive lips and nibble on his neck. His hair tickles my face.

My hands travel farther down and grab his perfect ass, rocking him against my throbbing core. "I want you so much. Touch me more."

Leo pushes up and rests on one arm as he hooks his other arm under my right leg and opens me wide, exposing my wet center. His eyes travel downward, stopping where our lower bodies connect. Every synapse in my body goes off.

"I wish you could see what I see. So sexy, so hot," he says, his voice rough and strained.

I arch my back, and he captures my nipple with his demanding lips. Slowly, he begins rubbing his length against me, and I moan. I'm so sensitive, I could come undone like this.

He unhooks my leg and drags his hand down to my slick folds. Before he can ask, I say, "Yes. I want to feel you."

"You're going to kill me." I capture his mouth with mine. While I taste his tongue, he inserts one finger, and I almost see stars. "You're so wet, so warm. I can't get enough," he says between kisses. It's been so long, and it feels amazing.

His rock-hard length moves against my thigh in the same rhythm as his finger.

"Leo, I want you inside me. Please."

He looks into my eyes with passion and tenderness, still teasing me. My eyelids flutter from the exquisite pleasure. "I want that more than anything, but are you sure? There's no pressure. I don't have a condom with me."

"Completely. I don't want to waste time and regret not being with you. I'm negative and on the pill."

"I'm negative too, and it's been a long time since I've been with a woman. Not sure how long I'll last." He grins.

I push curls behind his ears. "It's been years for me. I don't care how long it'll last. Just give me all of you."

He devours my lips and lifts his slick lower body off mine. I wrap my hand around his hard shaft, pulling a delicious groan from him. His hips move back and forth as I increase the surrounding pressure.

When he stops and lowers himself to my entrance, I guide him, and we watch as his length slides into me. I don't know who moans louder. He stops to let me adjust. I nod when I'm ready and wrap my legs around him, encouraging him to move. When he rocks into me, I embrace him and follow his motions.

"I could live like this for the rest of our lives. Buried inside you. We were made for each other," he mumbles into my neck, one hand cupping my breast.

Our movements quicken and become erratic, signaling we're both close. He rests his hands on the sides of my head and locks his beautiful eyes with mine. His pace picks up, and he hits that special spot in me. I detonate without warning. That's a first. Every nerve lights up and electricity pulses through my entire body, pushing him over the edge. Our blissed-out eyes don't stray as we watch each other's expressions of pleasure. The sounds we're making are animalistic, and I hope the room on the other side of this wall is empty.

As our bodies come down from the euphoric high, we kiss with tender passion. He whispers my name. Our sweaty bodies cling tightly to each other, unwilling to let go.

Once our breathing slows down, our lips separate and our bodies' tight grip relaxes. He caresses my cheek. "Olive, this changes everything."

On the verge of tears, I say, "I hope so."

As of this moment or since I got here, my life will never be the same.

And I'm so damn happy about it.

22

LEO

Olive steps out of the shower, her gorgeous body glistening with water droplets dripping from the ends of her hair onto her luscious curves. I hand her a fresh towel. My pulse spikes and blood rushes below when I see the marks I left near her collarbone. I couldn't help myself. I want to mark her for the entire world to see that she's mine. If someone asked me yesterday what word describes me, possessive wouldn't have been one of them. I guess that has changed. But I was nice, and they're out of sight.

I can't get enough of her—I don't think I ever will. The towel cinched around my waist doesn't hide her effect on me. Not that I want to keep things from her anymore.

Her eyes give me an appreciative once-over, focusing on the tent under my towel. "Again? Seriously. You're like a machine. Not that I mind." She snickers, drying herself off. I wish I were that towel. Finished, she wraps it around and tucks the edge in the side to anchor it over her chest, showcasing her cleavage.

It's almost embarrassing how desperate I am for her.

"I can't help it. You rev me up. You turn me on like a light switch. You melt my butta, woman! I thought we were doing the no-pants dance." I tease while shaking my hips, holding onto my towel. She tosses her head back and laughs. I love the sound.

"You're too much," she says, "but I love it."

I lean against the doorframe and gaze at her intently as she towel-dries her beautiful hair, then brushes it. I realize I might look like a creeper. "Do you want some privacy?"

"No way. You stay right there, mister. I don't want you out of my sight," she demands with a wicked gleam in her eyes. "You'll be sick of me by the time I leave."

Not possible. My chest swells with an emotion I won't reveal until the time is right. That could be today or two months from now. Yes, I'm confident that this is only the beginning for us. It's an amazing feeling, but how will I handle being away from her for weeks on end?

She catches my eye in the mirror. "Not that I mind you looking all dreamy at me like I'm your favorite candy, but you have to stop. At least for now. You promised me we'd talk." There's a serious edge to her voice now.

"I know." I resign with a sigh. "We will."

"Good. I need to blow-dry my hair a little first." She unwraps the towel hugging her body, flashing more of her beautiful skin, and puts on a white robe from the hotel. She pulls the dryer off the hook on the wall.

"Can…Can I do it for you?" The need to take care of her almost knocks me out. It's unfamiliar but thrilling all the same.

"Um." She pauses, staring at the hairdryer, then at me. "Sure. As long as I can do yours. Even trade."

I usually let my hair air-dry because blow-drying it makes me look like a poodle instead of a lion. But hell, I'm up for some laughs. "Anything you want."

"I'll remember that later on."

I take the dryer from her and let her brush her hair out one more time. This is mind-boggling, and it's hard to mask my emotions. I can't keep my eyes off her natural beauty.

She pulls out the wide cushioned stool from under the counter and sits on it, facing the mirror. "I'm ready. It doesn't have to be completely dry."

I stand behind the stool and turn the dryer on low. She drops her head back slightly, closes her eyes, and relaxes her shoulders. As the air blows the strands around, I inhale deeply, smiling when the familiar floral scent of her shampoo overpowers the bathroom.

Her hair dries faster than I would've liked, and I turn off the dryer. Her eyes flutter open. "That was nice. I was ready to fall asleep."

"Want me to brush it again?" I'm going to get on her nerves.

Her face lights up. "Yes. It's so relaxing."

I brush through the knots, and she doesn't complain. "I love what you did to your hair. Did Tonya push you to do it? She has the power of persuasion."

"Not really. We were talking to her hairdresser, and I had an impulse. She encouraged me, too. It worked out that she had time. New hair, new clothes...it works wonders."

"I'm glad you had fun and it wasn't awkward."

"Not at all. Tonya is a force to be reckoned with, though."

"You've got that right." I place the brush on the counter. "My turn."

She stands and points to the other robe hanging on the wall. "Put that on. You must be cold."

I wave it off. "Nah. I'm good. I run warm most of the time."

She raises her hand close to my shoulder, then gently glides her fingertips down my arm. "I can confirm. Hot to touch."

She taps the seat, and I sit in front of her. It feels incredible as she brushes through my curls and the warm heat from the blow-dryer swirls over my shoulders. If I had a tail, it'd be wagging, and my tongue would be hanging out the side.

When she turns off the hairdryer a few minutes later, she says, "I'm jealous of your curls. Never cut your hair. It's too sexy." Her fingers tickle my scalp as she runs them through.

"Even when I look like a poodle on a humid day?" I point to the fluff ball on my head.

She wraps her arms around my shoulders from behind and kisses my cheek. "Should I call you Fluffy now?"

Our eyes lock in the mirror, and without warning, bolts of electricity consume the oxygen in the air. Every molecule and cell in my body vibrates. I turn my head and our mouths collide, our tongues and lips fight for dominance. She releases her hold and I push the stool back, then loop my arm around her waist and pull her between my legs. The robe opens and I push the material to the sides, exposing her delectable skin. My hands skim up her ribs, my thumbs trace under her breasts, then blaze a trail down her hips to her generous ass.

A contented hum escapes her lips. "Our talk can wait a few more minutes." She bends over and flicks my towel open, exposing how hard I am again. "This won't take long."

I'm all for it. No more words need to be spoken. There is

no tenderness with our kissing, only pure, unadulterated lust. Sucking. Biting. I guide her onto my lap, and she sinks down onto me, her heat almost unbearable. Grunts and gasps echo off the walls. For a moment, we don't move, enjoying the feeling of our bodies connected again. Her robe slips off her shoulders and hangs from the crook of her arms. She moves up and down, and we catch sight of ourselves in the mirror. I've never done this before, and it's the most erotic thing I've ever seen. It's the best kind of torture.

"You bring out a side of me I didn't know I had," she says with a shuddering breath. "You being inside of me is indescribable."

I wrap one arm around her lower back and rock her against me while I massage her breast with my other hand. She pushes her chest forward, urging me on.

She tilts her head back and looks toward the mirror. I'm captivated by her hungry gaze reflected in the glass as she watches us. "Kiss me," I beg. "I need to taste you again."

She grabs fistfuls of my hair, angles my head to where she wants me, and claims my lips with a searing kiss I know I'll feel for days. Our breaths quicken and the sounds of passion fill the room. I don't know if they're coming from me or her or both of us. Her hands land on my shoulders, squeezing them like a vise.

"I'm almost there, baby," I whisper against her swollen lips.

The mix of her body vibrating against mine and her sexy moans set me off. The pain turns to pleasure. I jerk my hips one more time and scream her name as her insides contract around me. Our exquisite moans blend as we hold each other in a gripping hug.

"Holy shit," I mumble, trying to catch my breath. "That just happened."

"It sure did." She rests her forehead on mine.

We burst out laughing.

~

We clean up *again*, then Olive goes to the left side of the bed, still naked—no complaints here—and I go to the right, also naked as a jaybird, like this is our norm.

She slides under the comforter. "Get in the bed, sexy." She flings my side of the blanket open for me, then smooths her hand over it.

I shuffle under the blanket and shiver. "It's cold. Come and warm me up."

"Yeah, okay, Mr. I-Run-Hot. Excuses to invade my space," she quips. "Already so needy."

Out of pure instinct, we wrap our arms and legs around each other, our warm bodies not helping with my problem below. If I had my way, we'd stay in this bed wrapped up like this until the second she has to leave.

"Something hard is digging into my hip." Olive looks under the covers and then at me with a playful grin. "Oh, it's you. I thought it was a steel pipe or something."

I narrow my eyes and grab her ass. "You think you're funny, don't you? I know a way to get rid of it. Should I show you and put our pillow talk on the back burner?"

She gasps. "No way. How are you able to go another round?"

"It's your fault."

She huffs. "Whatever. I'm spent. Only cuddles from now on."

"All right. I'll behave."

She kisses my nose. "Good. Now start talking."

I readjust under the thick comforter, stuff a pillow

under my head, and face her. She does the same, then hooks her leg over my hip. *That doesn't help either.*

I trace my finger over her bottom lip. "Y'know, you didn't have to sing me a song to make me kiss you. You could've smacked those plump lips of yours on mine at any time. I don't mind when a woman takes charge sometimes, like you did before. Remind me how it's done." I run my hand up her outer thigh.

Olive shakes her head in amusement, then nudges my chest, keeping me from getting closer. "Leo, I'd love to 'show you how it's done' later. Stop deflecting. My questions are piling up. I don't know where to start. First, Tonya told me you haven't danced in years but wouldn't tell me why." *News to me.* "Then you sang tonight like you were fucking Freddie Mercury himself. And according to what the people were saying around us, you haven't done *that* in a while either. Are you famous and I'm the only one who didn't get the memo?"

I crack up. "No. Far from it. I've lived here forever, remember? It's a small island—everyone knows everyone."

"Hmm. Makes sense. And here, I thought I'd hit the jackpot. Would've been cool if you were famous." She shrugs, the corner of her mouth tilting upward. "Too bad."

"Oh, so that's how it is?" I peck her lips.

She pulls her head back and pins me with her stare. "I do wonder—are you the same person I met on my birthday?"

"Oh, I guarantee I am. There are layers I keep hidden from everyone, but I'm not going to hide anymore. Not from you."

"Good." She caresses my cheek. "Start talking when you're ready, and let's see where it leads. We've got all night."

I can't believe I'm going to spill my guts to Olive. It'll bring up a lot of painful memories, but maybe this is where my healing will finally begin. I like that she'll be the one I tell my past to and how it has shaped me. I'm not proud of everything I've done since Corey died, but I did it to survive.

Here it goes. Time to walk down memory lane.

"I had a cousin. His name was Corey. We were born a couple weeks apart and were inseparable. It was like we were twins. We basically grew up in this hotel because our moms worked here. Corey's mom, my aunt Betty, is married to my uncle Mason, Ma's brother.

"Anyway, you can probably figure it out. We were best friends and did everything together. We had fun, we got in trouble, we annoyed the shit out of our parents." I relax into the bed while I think about the stupid things we used to do. "Because we fed off each other and I did more crazy shit than him, our parents put us in a hip-hop dance class when we were ten years old to keep us occupied and to burn off the excess energy we had. It pissed us off in the beginning until we realized we were pretty damn good at it and it was fun. We took lessons all through school."

I massage my forehead, trying to get the past in order. Sometimes I forget when things happened.

"Corey heard me singing in the shower a couple of times without me knowing it. Things snowballed, and my parents urged me to try out for the school musical, *Footloose*, in tenth grade. Corey tried out too. He could dance, but he didn't like to sing as much. We both got parts in the play. I was Ren, and he was Willard." Her eyes widen and a relaxed smile curves her lips. "You know *Footloose*, right?"

"Yes. Of course. Great soundtrack. I would've loved to have seen it."

"Maybe you will. I have video clips of it somewhere." I

wiggle out of bed. "Be right back." I wander into the other room to grab some water bottles from the fridge.

"Don't you dare put clothes on. I want you naked and back in this bed," she yells. I snicker.

"See…showing me how it is," I say, holding up the bottles when I return. I hand her one, then climb back under the covers. "Damn, girl! You wore me out. I need to hydrate—my throat's killing me from screaming your name." We drink some water, then place our bottles on the nightstand.

She nods and her mouth ticks up on the side. "I should pat myself on the back. Making a guy scream like that is new for me."

"I don't want to hear about other guys. I'm your only guy from now on. Got it?"

She smiles brightly and nods in agreement.

"Now let me see, where'd I leave off? Oh, okay. Fast-forward through high school, we became a hit with our performances. Puberty made an appearance, my voice improved, yada yada."

"Am I the only one who says you sound like Freddie Mercury?"

I chuckle. "No. It's all I've heard."

"Did you become famous? Maybe try out for *American Idol* or some other talent show?"

"Nah. Not really. Word did get around though. People encouraged me to pursue acting and all that. I loved singing and dancing, but I didn't need to be famous to do it. Corey and I started to street perform during tourist season. We made a shitload of money," I admit, feeling nostalgic.

"Did you go to the same college?"

"Yep. Seattle University, but we didn't go for performing arts. I went for hotel management, for obvious reasons, and he went for marketing." I stop and am quiet for a minute. Then I take a big breath and continue. "Unfortunately, my dad died right before we left for college. Corey got me through that tough time. Hmmm, that was so long ago."

She runs a hand down my arm, compassion oozing out of her. I close my eyes.

"He was my best friend, Olive. My ride or die, my partner in crime, whatever you want to call him. We did everything together. Anyway, during college, we kept up the dancing lessons and street performances. We did competitions and all that, but not to become famous. We made good enough money at it that we traveled between semesters and during the summer.

"We came up with the idea to blog and then moved on to vlogging our adventures too. It was wild, how it took off. We had thousands of followers and it kept growing. Social media was fucking crazy." I shake my head and grin. "We had so much fun."

Memories surge forward in my head, things I've refused to think about for way too long. Smiling and laughing comes naturally when I think of the best times of my life. Olive props her head on her hand and watches me as if she can see them too.

She traces my lips. "There's that smile I love. It's my new favorite thing—"

"What?" I protest. "In the shower, you said your favorite thing was my love stick."

"You're ridiculous. *Love stick*? I'd never call your cherry-flavored lollipop that."

I crack up. "It doesn't taste like cherries."

Before I can say anything else, she covers my mouth with her hand and says, "We can discuss names and flavors later. Keep talking."

"Right. Before long, we decided we should be professional travelers on a budget. Our parents said they'd back us as long as we finished college." I grab my bottle from the nightstand and twist the cap, then down the rest of the water. "I'm babbling, I know." I toss the empty bottle to the floor.

She kisses me. "It's okay. Babble, laugh, scream, cry…I want to know everything."

"Okay. Fast-forward to after we became successful professional travelers. It sounds fancy, but we were just two guys in our twenties, having the time of our lives and traveling the world for work. And then…Corey got sick. Literally—one day he was fine, and the next he wasn't. We had no idea what was going on. After tons of tests, he was diagnosed with acute myeloid leukemia. It's the deadliest kind."

She releases a breath. "Shit, Leo. I've seen how people suffer from that during my training. I'm really sorry."

I memorize the freckles on Olive's shoulder, remembering that horrible day and everything that followed. She takes my hand and laces our fingers together, then holds them against her chest. Her heartbeat taps my skin.

"I remember when the doctor told us the diagnosis. I refused to believe it was true, especially when they said the survival rate to live past five years was maybe twenty-five percent. The entire time Corey was sick, he was the tough, positive one." My voice cracks and my eyes well up. "And all for what? He didn't live past a year."

Olive gets up, slips into the bathroom, and comes back with tissues. She quickly jumps under the covers to stay warm. I look at her with bleary eyes. She captures the tears running down my face with a tissue. "I hate seeing you cry. I wish I could take the pain away."

I pull her close to me again. Her body heat warms me after recalling the bitter memories.

"He died five years ago in March. Right before the lockdown. When he did, a part of me died too. I can seriously understand how twins feel when the other one dies. Lost? It's a fucking understatement for what I was. It ripped my heart out to watch him turn into a different person, to see the cancer eat away and suck the life out of my best friend. I dropped everything to be by his side the entire time. I thought I could help him through it and then we'd continue pursuing our dreams. I didn't think I could live without him, but he made me promise to keep doing what we started."

This is just as hard as it was then. I pull in a shaky breath.

"The real shitty thing is that I wasn't there when he took his last breath. He was under hospice care at home. That day, I went out to pick up something for my aunt at the pharmacy. The doctor said he still had some time, but by the time I got back, Corey was gone."

A giant sob surprises me. The painful ache in my chest returns, stealing my breath as if I've walked into his house again, where he took his last breath without me.

Olive embraces me, her grip tight. I bury my face in her hair and inhale her beautiful scent.

While stroking the back of my head, she says, "So, let me guess. You haven't danced or sung since that day."

"Even before that. I didn't want to if he couldn't do it with me. We were a team. It didn't feel right without him."

"What did you do after? What happened to your job, the blog…?"

"I gave it all up. I was stuck here on the island because the pandemic hit, and everything reminded me of him. The hotel was empty. I had way too much time to think—there was nothing else to do. As soon as the lockdowns were lifted and travel resumed, I contacted travel magazines. I offered to be a journalist since that was my minor in college and I had experience with traveling. As soon as I got an offer, I jumped on it and left. That's how I got my current job as a hotel critic."

"And it became your escape. But how do you deal with the traveling? That was part of what you and Corey did too. Doesn't that hurt?"

"Yep. It's different, though. I only critique fancy hotels, not cheap ones or hostels. Corey and I showed people how to travel on a budget. Now I visit stunning locations, but I don't get the same pleasure from them as I did the crazy places we went to. I do my job and go to the next hotel." I shrug. "It provides a distraction from this place and all the pity I get here. Over time, I guess it's gotten easier. Either that or I've grown accustomed to the heavy burden on my chest."

"I know that feeling. My dad's death is still fresh for me. Sometimes it feels like someone put a cinderblock on my chest. Especially when I think about things my dad will never experience—walking me down the aisle on my wedding day or holding his grandchildren."

My heart swells as I realize that, not only is she dealing with her past in LA, she lost her dad not long ago too. She hasn't had as much time to grieve as I have, yet her empathy shines through.

"It's hard to believe it's only been a few days since we met." She plays with a strand of my hair. "I had no idea you were dealing with so much. You're like the sun. Happy, goofy, social. Everyone gravitates to you... Is that all an act?"

"No. I've always been like this. It's the side of me that I show. The dark part I keep hidden deep down here." I point at my heart.

"I'm not sure that's good, Leo."

"No, I know. I don't let it rule me like I used to. It's easier to come home now, but I always need to leave again after a while. I don't like talking about Corey much. It brings everything back, and it seems everywhere I go around here, someone mentions him. I mean, it's great that people remember him, but—"

"He must've really been special," Olive says.

"He was." I rake my hand through my hair and switch gears. "Anyway, all the things that were ours from traveling, blogging…I packed them up and stored them at Mom's and in Aunt Betty's attic. I don't want to look at that stuff. And I'm embarrassed to admit this—" I stop, tears stinging my eyes and choking my throat.

"You can tell me anything," she assures me.

"The last time I was at his grave was at his funeral. I couldn't go again."

"Leo, look at me."

My cloudy gaze locks on hers.

"That doesn't make you a bad person. It makes you human. Everyone deals with death differently. Didn't you say something like that to me?"

"I know, but I still feel like shit because of it. He deserves better than that. Guilt wears me down every day. Especially when I'm here. I could go visit him any time, but I don't. I'll drive out of my way to avoid going near the cemetery."

"Okay, so what's different about this week," she asks. "Why the change? Dancing, singing?"

"Isn't it obvious?"

Her eyebrows furrow.

"You arrived."

23

OLIVE

"Me?" His heart melting words are going to kill me. With him, it's no holds barred. It takes a while for me to express what's in my mind and heart.

I shake my head because of how crazy this is. "I'm no shining light like you are. If anything, I dim your brightness."

"You're too hard on yourself. I've watched you become happier every day. From the second you arrived, you've blossomed. You fascinate me."

"Are you sure you're talking about me? Is there someone else in this bed?" I check under the covers. "Nope. Only me. I haven't changed that much."

"You don't think so?"

I already know the answer, but I hesitate. "Well, yes. Maybe. But I'm in a different environment right now. Who knows what will happen when I get back home. My issues aren't going to magically disappear after a couple of days here. I have, however, had some excellent influence. Some great guy burst my protective bubble and nothing's been the same since." I poke his side playfully with the rhythm of the words.

"*Uh huh*. Some guy? Who?" He squints his red-rimmed eyes at me. "Oh, I know! It was Louis from the café."

I laugh, then use the worst accent to reply. "*Non*. It was his friend with the crazy hair and awful lip blanket."

He arches an eyebrow and squeezes my hip. "Sure it wasn't the tarts?"

"Actually, it was the champagne. I can't turn down a bottle of bubbly. Louis's friend must have known somehow." I lean in and kiss his lips, long and soft. "Did you plan on singing tonight before you got there?"

"Nope. But when you sang, you put all your heart and soul into it. It was amazing. It reminded me of the adrenaline rush I got every time I sang or danced. Seeing you dance the other night and sing tonight flipped a switch in me. You inspire me and give me the courage to stop running. I've been doing it for so long, and I'm tired, Olive." His body deflates, and his eyes glisten. "But I watch you, and I think, here is a woman breaking free and having a blast. Why have I waited all these years to do the same? Then it hit me."

"What?" My eyes search his for answers. "Tell me."

He presses his lips together, drawing my eyes to his kissable mouth. Such a temptation. Finally, he says, tapping my chest, "I had to wait for you to show me how exciting life could be again."

I'm speechless.

He continues. "I pushed you, and you did the same to me without knowing it. We're opposites in some ways. You show your issues openly, while I conceal mine. When we come together, we connect in the middle, gradually blending into one."

I melt into him. How is this my life right now? It feels

like a dream. Is it too much, too soon? Is it smart to get involved with someone when I'm trying to improve myself? I'm only here for a couple more days, and then he'll be away at some hotel in whatever country.

"I can see my future, Olive, and there's one constant."

"What's that?" Somehow, I know what he's going to say, and it both excites and terrifies me.

"Not a what. A who."

I stop breathing. *Will he say it? No, I don't think so.*

"You."

I'm stunned into silence again.

"That's why I sang that song," he whispers, looking away.

Now who's being shy? *I was born to love you.* Does he mean it literally? Is he trying to say he loves me? No, he couldn't.

My chest warms as I melt into the bed. When Mom and Dad met, they fell hard and fast. They knew right away that they'd get married. *Why am I thinking about this?* I know why, but I'd tell someone else how crazy it was if they were in the same situation. My brain is buzzing like a beehive.

"Leo, I don't know what to say."

"It's all right. I realize how irrational this sounds, but I can't ignore it. If it turns out that I'm an idiot, I'll always remember you and what you've done for me in such a short amount of time. The rush and the depth of emotions I have for you have blindsided me. How could they be misleading when they feel beyond amazing?"

I toy with the unruly curls that have fallen around his face. "It scares me," I admit. "When I decided to take off this week, ending up in bed with the most attractive man I know was not even remotely a part of it. This is like a dream I don't want to wake up from."

"That's a good thing, isn't it?"

"You have no idea."

He cocks an eyebrow at me.

I laugh. "Right. What am I saying? Of course you do."

"So?"

"It's a lot to take in. I'm extremely attracted to you. It'd be easy to dive in headfirst and not look back. But is it smart to get involved when I'm only here for a couple more days, and then you're off into the world somewhere? I can't imagine how hard it's gonna be to say goodbye to you now. If we add more to it—"

I flip onto my back and groan. I'm already somewhat attached. And we're both experiencing major life changes. We lie there in silence for a few minutes, then Leo moves to hover over me, his warm eyes locked on mine. How could I not fall in love with him?

"Whatcha thinking about?" he asks.

"About…why do I have to be an adult? We could probably have wild sex every minute until I leave."

"Mom gave me the rest of the week off." He waggles his eyebrows.

"Oh, really? Whatever shall we do?" I envision our naked bodies entwined, reflected in the mirror. Him pinning me to the mattress, teasing me until I fall apart in his arms. Damn! I'm turned on every second I'm with him.

"Ooo, you're blushing. Someone has a naughty mind." He squeezes my butt, and his hard love stick presses against my leg. "Tell me."

A giggle slips out, then I give him a stern look. "Nope, not happening. I won't be able to walk tomorrow. Focus."

He composes himself. "All right, I'll be serious again. Just because you're leaving soon and I'll be traveling doesn't mean we can't visit each other in between. We also have video calls and text messaging. I'll do everything in my power to see your beautiful face in person and to kiss your addictive lips."

"These lips?" I tease him by tracing my bottom lip with the tip of my tongue.

"I'll take whatever I can get."

If things work out the way he predicts, he'll end up with everything.

And so will I.

24

OLIVE

I step out of the elevator on the first floor by the front desk. Looking around, I try to absorb all the details of this special place before I leave tomorrow. Almost all the Christmas decorations are gone, but even bare, the lobby still reflects beauty, charm, and history. I gaze ahead at the entrance, unable to believe it was only one week ago that I arrived.

I wander over to the crackling fireplace in the Blue Room. The holiday atmosphere is gone here too, but the coziness remains. I glance at myself in the mirror over the mantle and remember what I looked like inside and out on the first day. Mentally and physically drained, lost, shy, insecure…the list goes on. I'm still that woman, but I'm an improved version now. My issues won't disappear in a week, but the confidence and inner strength I've gained here will help me confront them when I return home.

I ease onto the couch where I first saw Leo. The cushions feel different, firmer somehow. I remember wanting to lose myself and vanish. How silly that was. If that's all I wanted, I could've easily gotten lost on my couch at home.

From my first conversation with Leo, he encouraged me to accomplish what I came here to do. His support was subtle, never imposing. Well, maybe a little. He pushed me to tap into an auxiliary power I didn't realize I had. He's become my biggest cheerleader and positive influence.

A light tapping sound jolts me out of my thoughts. I focus my eyes and find Marla coming toward me, exuding professionalism in a perfectly pressed white button-down and navy blue pants. "I'm sorry. Would you prefer to be alone?" she asks, stopping behind an armchair on the other side of the coffee table.

With confidence and determination, I wave her over. "Not at all. Feel free to stay. Just walking down memory lane. The first time I saw Leo was in this room, and I wondered if I'd ever have the courage to talk to him."

With a kind expression on her face, she says. "Let me guess, he took care of that for you."

"Yep. He said one word, and I fell right into his universe." I can't hold back the lovesick smile spreading across my face.

"Hmm," is all she says, then roams over to the tea and coffee service in the room's corner. I can't read her at all, which is annoying as shit. While we spent time with her last night, I caught her observing me with a facial expression I couldn't figure out. And the constant questions, like she was screening me for a job! Leo had to interject at one point again.

Would my mom act like that when or if I introduce her to Leo? I'm not sure I'll tell her about him. Not until I know we truly have a future, anyway.

"Would you like a coffee or tea?" Marla asks.

"No, thanks. I'm meeting Tonya at the café in a little while. It's a farewell since she won't be around tomorrow when I leave."

Marla *hmm*'s again, and my hackles shoot up. I hope I'm misreading her. She's so confusing. She opens a yellow packet and places the teabag in a cup. I wait as she pours the steaming water and dips the tea bag in it. Maybe she'll leave the room without another word. I almost wish she would.

Finally, she comes over and places her cup on the coffee table, then sits down across from me. *Sure. Make yourself comfortable.* "We've had an eventful week since you arrived. Usually, we don't encourage the staff to get involved with our guests. Leo has always taken that seriously until you came along."

And your point would be? Her tone isn't malicious, but it's hard to identify otherwise. That's okay—I'll wait her out. One thing's for sure, I won't apologize for getting involved with her son.

She glances my way. "That's when I knew something was different. His actions spoke louder than words. He tried to hide it at first, but…I hadn't even met you yet, and I could see how he felt about you. And let me mention he's never brought a woman home before to meet the family. Well, you're staying here, but you get my gist."

I nod, but school my emotions. Is she annoyed that I caught his attention? This little convo's obviously leading up to something.

Marla cradles the cup in her hands and blows on it. "Tonya came to me flooded with tears when she saw Leo dancing, and when he sang to you, I was the one crying." She takes a sip, then rests the cup back on the table.

"He didn't sing to me." Why am I protesting when he said the song was for me?

Her eyes narrow. "We both know that's not true."

"Okay, if he did sing to me, what are you trying to

say?" That came out more defensive than I wanted it to, and she picks up on it.

"I'm sorry, Olive. I'm doing this all wrong. This is very new for me. Let me try again." She rubs her hands down her pressed pants. "Seeing parts of Leo that have been missing for a long time makes me hopeful. I can't thank you enough. It's a mother's dream to see her children truly happy, and that's what I see when he's with you. If you think he lights up the room now, you should've seen him before…" She frowns and her shoulders droop, her tough woman act disappearing.

"It's okay. He told me about Corey, their plans…"

"Good. I'm glad he's opened up to you. That's not easy for him. It's been awful, watching him grieve and suffer for years. We were all still grieving, but I've never seen Leo break down the way he did. Not even when his father died. I can't imagine what he was going through, losing his best friend and only cousin." She gasps, then straightens and covers her mouth. What the hell?

I push to the edge of the seat and reach out my hand. "Are you okay, Marla?"

"Yes, yes." She wipes her forehead. "I just remembered something. Anyway, where was I?" She takes a moment to gather herself. "Time has helped. We've seen bits of him come back over the years. But the parts of him I've seen this week have made me ecstatic, and he doesn't even realize it."

That has me smiling.

"But—" Her eyes harden with concern. "I'm also worried. Will he disappear again once you leave?"

"You should probably talk to him about this. I don't think he'll relapse. He's not the only one who's changed this week. We plan to keep in touch. We feel strongly about each other, but we both know—I can't solve his problems and he can't solve mine. We can only help each other along the way. Logistics and jobs are also an issue. We have a lot to talk about. I won't take Leo for granted. I consider myself very lucky, and I hope my future includes him in some shape or form." I hesitate, and then my own doubts sneak out. "Of course, we've only known each other a week. There are no guarantees."

Enough, Olive. You've said more than you intended. Zip it now.

"Time doesn't matter when it comes to finding your soulmate. When you know, you know." Marla shifts in her chair and shrugs. "It happened to me and my husband. Our parents were skeptical because we jumped in head-first. Best decision of our lives." A soft smile appears on her face. I can imagine what she's thinking about.

"Same thing happened with my mom and dad," I say. "I think they had issues in the beginning, too, but they didn't really talk about them to me or my brother. Seems like you and she were lucky to find great men." It's sad to think that both Marla and Mom have lost their husbands. "It's strange though. I mean, to think that every event in my life has been steering me toward Leo all this time? That I got up one day and made a crazy decision that I thought was random, but it's ultimately changed my life for the better?"

"Now you sound like Leo…and I guess me when I met my husband. Love hits you when you least expect it. When it does, grab onto it and don't let go," she encourages. "Life's too short to say it's too soon or it's not possible. I promise you, *it can happen*. And I think deep down inside, you both know that. You can deny it if you want, but all you're doing is wasting precious time. I don't know your personal story, but it seems you've been dealt a shitty hand, much like Leo, and it's shaped your outlook on life."

She hit the nail right on the head. Why am I so skeptical and denying my feelings? Hopefully, it's not out of fear of what my family will say. Their opinions shouldn't matter. I'm thirty, for fuck's sake.

Marla continues. "Even Sully talks more when he's around you. You've got a magical touch, and you don't realize it. I guess we needed an outside force to shake things up a bit."

She's talking like I'm the answer to their prayers. "You give me way too much credit. You all do, but I'll take it."

She glances at her watch. "Oops, I have a conference call in ten minutes. I've gotta cut this short."

"No problem. Tonya's probably already at the café. I'll head over there now." I stand and step away from the couch. She does the same.

"I don't know if I'll see you before you leave tomorrow." She pulls me in for an unexpected hug. "Don't be a stranger. You're *always* welcome here." She leans back and braces her hands on my upper arms. "Bring your mom for a visit. Let's prove to her it's a beautiful place to be even when it's cold."

When she lets go, I step back. "That's a good idea. I might have to drag her off the ferry kicking and screaming."

She grins. "She sounds like an interesting character."

"Oh, she is, but I love her anyway. She's had it tough too. Maybe this hotel will miraculously change her like it has me."

"I'd love to see that. Oh, and don't forget to give us a five-star rating on the internet."

I guffaw with shock, and she cracks up.

"Oh my gosh, Olive. Of course, I'm just kidding!"

"Sure. Sure." I play along.

We leave the room in silence, but the tension is gone. I understand her better now. A sense of relief seeps in because I think I received approval without asking for it. We all seem clueless here.

"Have a safe trip home, Olive," Marla says, then turns toward her office. I head to the café with a pep in my step.

~

I walk into Café Charmant and scan the room for Tonya. I spot her in the corner, sitting at the same table I used on my first day here. She's writing on her tablet, deep in thought, her tongue peeking out the corner of her mouth. I wave to Louis and the barista, then move toward Tonya.

A week ago, I would've never gone into a café alone and waved to people like I own the place. Instead, my head would've been down, and I'd have searched for the closest empty table. Now I'm excited to come here to meet a friend.

Friends. I have had no close ones in a long time. That was my doing. The ones who live near me are married with kids or single and partying. I couldn't relate to any of them. Being cooped up at home was all that I knew. It's time to change that and reach out to my old friends. Not only the ones in the Seattle area, but also in LA. I shiver just thinking about stepping a foot back in that city.

"Hey, Olive," Tonya exclaims when she sees me. She stands and gives me a hug.

"How's it going?" I ask. "You seemed kind of pissy yesterday when we saw you."

She sits and rearranges her things on the other side of the table. "Yeah, sorry about that. You guys caught me right after I got off the phone with a bridezilla. Nothing I couldn't handle, though. I guess it keeps my job entertaining and pays the bills." Her smile doesn't reach her eyes.

The barista comes and takes our orders. "I hate that you're leaving tomorrow." Tonya touches my hand. "You've added some excitement here this week. It'll be weird after you're gone."

"I'm not sure about that."

She huffs. "Oh, *please.* Sully let you hold Smokey. And Mom's friends are calling, asking about Leo's *girlfriend.* The"—she makes quote marks with her fingers—"woman he kissed at Clover's."

I wince. "Oh shit, half the town witnessed that, didn't they? We were caught up in the moment." And many other moments since then. Every chance we've had, we've been naked. "But *girlfriend?* That's kind of weird, isn't it?"

This denial shit is getting really boring, Olive. That kiss wasn't a simple gesture, and you know it. You felt that thing down to your bones. Not to mention the rest of the week.

But he hasn't introduced me as his girlfriend. I know we talked about it, but it's still hard to believe the connection we have. Is it too good to be true? Then I think about what Marla said. My brain is on the verge of exploding, and I'm ready to scream. Welcome to my world, where I overthink every fucking thing.

Tonya shrugs. "It's my family. We've been here forever, and Leo has always stood out. That's why it's a big deal. Which girl finally captured Leo's heart?" she gushes with playful sarcasm. "Too many people think they know our personal business. It's a small island and they gossip, whether it's good or bad. I know it happens in the city, too, but you can hide there. Here, not so much."

"Have you ever thought about leaving the island?"

She props her chin on her hand. "Like everyone else in this area, I attended Seattle University and lived there for a while. I got tired of the city life and came back here. Eventually, I took over as the event manager. Will I do this forever? Who knows."

"Do you get lonely?"

"During this time of year, *yes*. It's frustrating." She fists her hair and groans. "Business picks up again in April. But there aren't many eligible men at the hotel. The ones who come here are usually taken. It's a romantic hotel, not a party place for people our age. There's been some discussions about expanding or advertising to attract more business functions. Maybe that'll increase my options. Oh, hell, what am I talking about? It doesn't matter because we aren't allowed to fraternize with the guests. You're the only exception." She grins.

I roll my eyes. "Well, what about in town? You've got karaoke," I tease.

"*Pfft*. I go out, but I'm tired of the singles scene. Why can't I meet someone and click instantly, like you and Leo did? Or when my mom met my dad. It looks easy for others, but not me. Be honest, do you think it's my analities?"

We both inspect the table space next to us. Her tablet and papers sit neatly stacked with rainbow stickies poking out. Three different colored pens line up in a row like soldiers next to the stack. The spacing between them is precise, like she measured it herself with a ruler.

I burst out laughing, then instantly feel bad. "No. I don't think so. Your *analities*, as you call them, make you unique. So your 'instant click' is out there somewhere."

"Instant click," she repeats, nodding. "I like that. Well, my Mr. Instant Click better get here soon. I'm losing my patience."

"Why do you have to click right away? It doesn't happen like that for everyone. Have you ever had a serious relationship?"

"Not really," she mumbles. She inspects the surrounding area, then leans in. "I can't believe I'm considering telling you this. Can you keep a secret?"

I lean in closer and whisper, "Of course." One thing I'm good at is doing that. My head is a vault, and people seem to pick up on it somehow. Random strangers have spilled their guts to me, like on the bus or standing in line at the DMV. I don't miss that because it felt like some were confessing their sins to a priest. And don't get me started on what people lying on their deathbeds have told me.

"Did you ever have hate sex before?"

My eyebrows hit my hairline. *Say what now?*

"I guess not." She looks away and doesn't continue. There's an awkward silence and I'm not sure if she's waiting for me to say something.

"And…? You can't stop there."

She takes a deep breath. "Okay, about a year and a half ago, I stayed at a friend's apartment in San Francisco because I had an internship at a convention center. My friend didn't mention that she'd sublet the other bedroom to a guy until he ended up at the door. Long story short, he was a total slob, took nothing seriously, and drove me absolutely batty. What he called organized chaos was more like a tornado went through the place."

She would hate my brother.

"Oh no. I can see where this is going." I lean in. This is like listening to an audio romance. Who cares about food?

"And what annoyed the shit out of me most was that he was *gorgeous*," she snarks. "Like *GQ* model, drool fest, light-my-body-on-fire gorgeous. If he wasn't wearing a designer suit, he was strutting around shirtless. The chemistry between us was off the charts from the moment we met. We bickered nonstop, and that added to the sexual tension." She fans her flushed face with her hand. "Damn, I'm getting worked up thinking about it again."

"Me too," I admit, blood rushing to my cheeks. Where's Leo when I need him? Now I'm really looking forward to tonight.

She nods with amusement. "Right? It gets better. The tension built until it exploded. Fireworks galore! We attacked each other. Clothes flying, knocking things over and breaking them, pawing each other—raw and intense, nothing soft about it. He threw me around like a rag doll because he was so big and bulky." Her lips quirk up and she stares into space. "I loved that."

I chuckle, then snap my fingers in front of her dazed face. "Hello, fireworks galore?"

She shakes herself out of her stupor. "Oops. Sorry. We went at it for hours. No talking at all. Just pure lust. When I woke up magnificently sore, sated, and covered in hickeys, he was gone with all his belongings."

"No way!" I say, my voice carrying through the café. I look around and whisper, "Sorry." Then I want to shrivel up. What if people are listening to our conversation? I hope the old couple two tables over can't hear about Tonya's sexcapades.

"Yep. Gone. Not a word. Not even to my friend. She didn't care because he'd paid everything in advance."

I sit back and cross my arms. "Well, that's bullshit. You didn't know where he was from or anything to help you find him?"

"Nope. I was okay with that. We didn't discuss that kind of stuff. He's the one who left. I wasn't about to go chasing him. No regrets. Hands down, the best sex of my life. There were no feelings involved besides hate. The downside, I've never felt that fire again since."

Our coffees and pastries arrive, and we spend a few

minutes enjoying them, putting a welcomed pause on the subject. Tonya finishes the last bite of her vanilla éclair and cleans up her little mess, ensuring every crumb is off the table. I do the same with the remnants from my chocolate tart.

Finally, she looks up at me and says, "I'm still sad that you're leaving tomorrow."

"Me too. If you ever leave the island, come visit me. Or I could meet you in Seattle."

"Sure! I'd love that."

I slide out of my chair. "Listen, I need to go pack so I don't have to do it tomorrow morning. Leo has something special planned for us tonight."

She stands and braces her hands on the table. "Know what I think? I bet you and Leo are married by this time next year."

I'll play along, but she's crazy. Who knows if we'll stay in contact after I leave tomorrow. "You're on. What's the wager?"

She taps her chin a few times, then suggests, "How about a spa weekend away?" Her face lights up. "Leo would know the best places to go. Or we can think about something else. We have time. Let's shake on it." She extends her hand, and I shake it.

"You're on, girl."

If fate is on my side, she'll win.

With a sad face, she announces she has to go—she has to call a florist for the bridezilla's wedding. I watch as she places her stuff meticulously into a black computer bag, then we hug and she leaves. Before I follow, I say goodbye to Louis and his team.

This time tomorrow, I'll be at my apartment.

The thought tugs at my heartstrings, and a strong sense of sadness rushes through me.

25

LEO

Tonight is our first actual date. I can't wait to see what Olive thinks when she gets here. I stand in the middle of the small cottage with my hands on my hips to assess my work. To make the place more cozy and romantic, I wrapped some white Christmas lights around the railing going up the stairs to the bedroom. Tea light candles will add a soft glow to the open space. As well as the small fire burning in the fireplace.

Originally, I planned to order out for dinner, but I am feeling inspired. I'm probably out of my damn mind because this is the first time I'm cooking for a woman. Olive likes steak, and I thought I'd give it a go. I'll follow some cooking videos I found and have the iPad ready on the counter. Maybe she'd like to help.

I bought another bottle of the champagne we drank on her birthday. For dessert or snacks, I bought gummy bears and worms. I couldn't resist.

If it weren't her last night here, I'd try to persuade her to stay with me tonight. Not that I think it'd be difficult, but I know she needs to pack. I've spent the last two nights in her room. Okay, I'll confess, we've spent every second possible together since karaoke night.

It messes with my head how much I want to be around her. And the need to touch her all the time is such a foreign feeling. Yes, I'm affectionate with my family, but with Olive it's different. Being intimate with her, skin to skin, is something I didn't know I was missing. How am I supposed to turn off that feeling when she leaves? Or when I'm traveling around the world? As far as I'm concerned, I'm taken. There will be no other woman warming my bed.

When we were in town yesterday, we were always kissing, holding hands, hugging, and joking around. You know, the annoying things new couples do. But can I call us a couple? I know we're all over each other and having amazing sex, but that doesn't mean we're *together*, together. Does it? We've been making it up as we go along, but tonight we have to make some decisions.

The clock is ticking. There are no small steps in this budding relationship, only giant leaps. Go big or go home, right? Okay, enough of the motivational bullshit. I want her, she wants me—what's the problem?

I glance at my phone. She should arrive soon. I light the candles, then head to the bathroom for a quick once-over, smoothing out my casual clothes. Then I rinse my mouth with mouthwash and spray some cologne.

As I step out of the bathroom, there's light knocking on the door. My smile returns and my pulse picks up. I open the door, and there's Olive, gorgeous as ever, her suitcase beside her. Her twinkling eyes scan my body from head to toe. And mine do the same with her.

"Hi, handsome. I like your outfit," she purrs. "There's something yummy about a man in a Henley. Are you up for another sleepover before I'm ferried off tomorrow?"

"You read my mind, beautiful. I need to get my fill of

you." I grab the suitcase and roll it inside with marvelous speed. Before she can move, I wrap her in my arms. "Mmm. If I had my way, we'd be having sleepovers for the rest of our lives."

I don't give her a second to respond before my lips connect with hers. Without separating, I guide us into the open space and kick the door shut. Her arms wrap around my neck. I'm thirsty for her taste and seek her tongue with mine. She tastes like mint and smells like blooming spring flowers. My hands slide under her coat and I embrace her back, pulling her closer to me. She moans into my mouth and I growl, forcing myself to stop because we'll end up naked all night. It's enticing, but that's not what this night is about.

"I missed you," I say in between heavy breaths, relaxing my arms around her but not letting go.

She kisses my pulse point while gripping the back of my shirt. "Missed you too. I want to live in a cloud of your cologne. I love it."

"Just sprayed some. I hope it's not too much."

"Nope. Not possible." Her eyes wander behind me and her mouth drops open. She steps to the side and I take her coat. "Look at this place. I love it."

"It's all for you. I thought we could make this our first official date, ending with a sleepover."

She rests her hand over her heart, and her expression softens. "You're too good to be true. I'd love that."

I hug her again because I can. Because after tomorrow, I won't be able to. "And it's not our last date either."

She traces her finger along my collarbone. "Promise?"

I press a soft kiss to her nose. "Yep."

"Good. So, what did you plan for our first date?"

I take her hand and guide her toward the small kitchen

counter. "When you're hungry, I want to make you steak for dinner."

Her face lights up. "Really? You can sing and dance like a professional, and now you're telling me you can cook too?"

"Sorry to disappoint you. I'll possibly burn the kitchen down. Traveling year-round doesn't give me much time to experiment in the kitchen. I can make a mean tomato sauce and that's about it."

"No worries. It's sweet that you want to try. I'll help you, but I don't have much of a clue on how to make a steak."

She'll help! "*Phew*." I wipe my brow. "Disaster averted."

"Don't speak too soon. Now what else is on the agenda?" She taps her fingers on the counter.

"I didn't think that far because I don't care what we do, as long as I can spend every second with you. We can watch a movie or play strip poker. Sorry, I meant play poker." I kiss her neck, smiling against her skin. "I vote for stripping, by the way."

"And I volunteer as tribute. Nakedness all the way." She swirls her hips, rubbing against my crotch, igniting me at the wrong time.

Ignore it. "I knew I liked you for a reason. You need to behave now. Any movement like that gets me going."

With hands in the air, she snickers. "Sorry. And you're right—no matter how much I want to strip out of my clothes for you, I want to do this right." She presses her index finger against my lips. "Not a word about you showing off your sexy moves. I already find it hard to concentrate when you have clothes on. Now, let's make dinner."

"Got it. Clothes stay on," I quip. "So this is what I was

thinking." And I tell her how I want to make the steak, potatoes, and veggies, then we divvy up the tasks and get to work.

Dinner takes a little longer to make because Sully stopped by with Smokey to say goodbye to Olive. It meant a lot to her and to me. He stayed and had a quick beer while Olive played with the kitten. Smokey bit me several times, making it clear she wanted nothing to do with me. Then Sully took off when we asked him to stay for dinner. We didn't want to be rude and kick him out.

An hour or two later, I'm drying a pot. "I'm surprised we didn't set off the smoke detectors."

"That's because we work well together," Olive says, flicking a lot of water at me. She gasps. "Sorry, that was more than I intended."

I look down at my wet shirt and the floor, then flash a wicked grin. "Now you're in trouble."

She shrieks and runs out of the kitchen, dripping more water on the floor. I trail behind her, smacking her gorgeous ass, making her yelp. This place is small, so she won't get far. She stops behind the coffee table because there's nowhere else to go.

"Come and get me," she taunts, hopping from one leg to the other.

To trick her, I move to my left, and she tries to make her escape. Too late. I tackle her onto the couch with a big *oof*. We're both laughing so hard we can hardly speak. Somehow I finagle us so I'm lying on my back and she's on top of me. I thrust a couple of pillows behind me to prop myself up.

She pushes up on her hands, and her shirt hangs open, flashing me her mouthwatering breasts. "*Ick*," she says, "our shirts are all wet."

I'm not going to let that distract me from the perfect

view. "Feel free to take it off and hang it by the fire. I know a way to keep you warm." I squeeze her hips.

"You wish." She lowers herself till we're chest to chest.

"I do," I agree, not ashamed. I push her hair behind her ears and study her flushed, cheerful face. My chest bursts with emotion, and I say the one thing I know I truly am at this moment. "You make me so happy, Olive. Happier than I've felt in years."

It's time to execute my new plan. I'm calling it *Operation Make Olive Fall in Love with Me*.

Maybe she already is.

Because I know I'm in love with her.

26

OLIVE

I drape myself over Leo like a cat, hardly believing how comfortable I am with him. I want to stay in this little cottage forever. Who am I going to have fun with when I get home? Or cuddle with? Help shave?

He pushes my hair out of my face, gazing at me with the sweetest grin, and all I can do is melt into him. Could it be love I see shimmering in his dreamy eyes?

"You make me so happy, Olive. Happier than I've felt in years," he murmurs. My heart hammers against my chest. "You were so unexpected. I thought New Year's Eve was going to be the same old thing. Then you appeared, and I knew my life would *never* be the same."

I caress his smooth cheek. "Me too. You broke the chains that were preventing me from moving on, and you've reminded me what happiness feels like. You're dealing with your own traumatic past, yet you remain positive. I'm a different and better person now because of you, because of this hotel… I couldn't have asked for a better gift for my thirtieth birthday."

"That makes me even happier and strokes my ego."

I tickle his ribs. "I'm sure it does."

One smoldering kiss later, he continues. "What are we going to do after you leave tomorrow? I'm not giving up on us. This isn't a fling for me."

I rest my cheek on his chest and let out a long sigh.

He massages my back with firm, relaxing strokes. "What are you afraid of? Talk to me."

"Pretty much everything."

"I need a little more than that, beautiful."

"If we're going to have this discussion now, let's sit first," I suggest.

I slide off him and onto my knees next to the couch, then stand. He sits up and twirls on his butt until he's facing forward. Once he's comfortable, I turn to sit next to him, but he pulls me onto his lap. Of course, I'm hesitant because of my weight, but I know he likes it.

"That's better." He pulls me in for a gentle kiss. I love how he spoils me with affection. I rest my forehead against his and breathe in his soft scent. "Now, what are you worried about? Tell me…specifically. Let's get it out in the open and see what we can do."

Always Mr. Positive. I wish I could be like that. "I love the way I feel here. Happy, relaxed, and mentally stronger. I've been more outgoing—with your help, of course. I've challenged myself, and I have a better outlook for my future now. I love who we are together, as a pair. This attraction is more than physical. It warms me up from the inside and pours into my veins. I was drawn to you the second I heard your laugh."

"It wasn't my awesome ass?" I eye him, and he squeezes my hips. "Okay. I'm sorry. I'll be quiet." He zips his lips.

I scratch my head. "Hmm. Where was I before I was rudely interrupted?" I grin, but then I get serious. "I'm afraid that once I drive onto that ferry tomorrow morning, everything I've gained will disappear. I'm afraid that what we have will fizzle out. I want to be a better person, a better partner, but I have to figure out my own issues first." I groan. "And I have to deal with my mom."

"How are things going? Has she chilled with the messages?"

"Somewhat. I got a text from my uncle saying he had a long talk with her and hopes it'll defuse some of the lingering tension."

"I don't know your mom, which makes it difficult for me to give advice. But once she sees that you're happier, maybe she'll give you the space you need. Or she'll reevaluate how she's treating you."

"I don't want her to be the one who brings me down. She's not a terrible mom, Leo. I know that. She's dealing with her own grief. We deal with things differently all the time."

"What about your living arrangements? Do you want to start over again somewhere new? You can build websites from anywhere."

Should I tell him? I purse my lips and hesitate for a few seconds. "Want to know a secret?"

"Sure. Secrets can be fun," he says, his eyes sparkling.

"I don't need to work. Dad left me a lot of money in his will. And then, when Mom sold his half of the company to my uncle, I inherited money from that too. I'm only working for him to occupy my time."

"D'you mean I've met the woman of my dreams, and she's a sugar mommy? I hit the jackpot!"

I click my tongue. "*You know it.* Well, I might be sweet, but I'm not that rich. Anyway, my point in telling you this is that I could've done whatever I wanted. But because of Mom and because of my mental health, I wasn't brave enough to make a fresh start—not till I was at the end of my rope. And it led me here to you."

He squeezes my backside and pulls me closer to him. Slowly, he peppers kisses down one side of my neck and up the other. Then he asks, "Do you have a plan?"

"I think so. My next project is supposed to start in February. I've decided to take a leave of absence and transfer that project to another team."

"Hmmm." He purrs against my skin. "Can I be part of that plan?"

I wrap my arms around his neck and kiss his sweet lips. "I hope so. But how, when you'll be traveling everywhere and hardly have a permanent residence? How can we build something when we can't see each other?"

"You're right. It'll be a challenge, but I love a challenge here and there."

I blow a strand of hair out of my face. "I can see that."

"I don't think I'll be able to go a day without talking to you. We can text, call, or video-call. We can get to know each other without the physical being involved. It's also a way to share our daily routines." I pull on my lower lip considering what he just said. "Please say that'll be enough for now until we figure everything else out."

I run my hands down his chest. "Yes, that's what I want too. I guess I'm hesitant because I don't want to bring you down when I have bad days."

Oh God, I'm such a pessimist. Why the hell would he want to be with someone like me? We aren't perfect people. But maybe we're close to perfect as a pair.

He grabs my hand and presses his lips to my palm, making me quiver. "When you have bad days, I'll help pick you up. Do you think I don't have days like that too? I do, and I'll need you even more then. I'm all in, Olive. You won't get rid of me without a fight. Deep in my soul, you're who I want."

That warmth in my heart ignites again, reminding me how cherished he makes me feel. How could I not fall in love with him? I'm not only going to fight for me, I'm going to fight for *us*. We'll figure it out.

"You know what else, sweet thang? I have a secret too." Sweet *thang*? He pulls a chuckle from me. "If I say yes to it, it will be a huge game changer for me. And it might be the answer to our living arrangements."

I tap playfully on his chest with my fingers. "You've been holding out on me. Spill it."

An earnest expression transforms his cheerful face, piquing my curiosity.

"The current manager of the hotel is retiring soon. Mom asked me to take over when he leaves. And in the future, I'm probably in line to take over the hotel when Mom can't do it anymore. Sully has already said he doesn't want to do it. Tonya isn't sure, but I have the feeling she doesn't want to either."

My eyes widen with surprise and hope. "Holy shit. That's awesome. Well, I think it is. Does that interest you?"

He flashes me a lopsided grin. "Well, I met this woman who's compelling me to rethink everything. Especially about settling down. It could be here…or maybe not. Not sure where it would be, actually, but as long as we end up there together, I don't care."

I rest my forehead against his. "I want that too. So much. Are you willing to wait for me?"

"Look at me, Olive." I pull back and gaze at his serious face. "I'd wait for you forever. I want you to get into a place where you feel you can give yourself freely, not because I want you to. Find your way. You need to do what's best for you. Not for your mom, not for me, not for anyone except yourself."

I wrap my hands around his and bring them to my lips. "Okay, but that goes both ways, Leo. It's not all about me. I want what's best for you too. You're also your own priority."

I'll ask it a million times—how did I end up here in this amazing man's arms, being treated like a priceless diamond? Do I deserve him? Maybe. Maybe not. He gives me the encouragement to bust my ass for what I want. And at the end of the day, he's who I want standing by my side.

Leo sits back and looks concerned. "I didn't tell you this before, but my aunt and uncle want to have a memorial for Corey to mark five years in March. All the things I've avoided are coming to a head. When you leave tomorrow, I have to start facing them. And it's something I have to do by myself. We're kind of in the same boat."

I caress his cheek with my finger. "When you put it that way, I guess we are."

He lightly grips my thighs and gazes at me intently. "When *we* are ready, Olive, I'll be waiting for you with open arms."

There are plenty of things I've done that I'm not proud of, but I must've done something right to find someone as special as he is. "I guess me leaving is a good thing in the long run," I conclude. "We both need time to make things right."

"Yes. And when we achieve what we want, the endgame is you and me, baby."

"You and me. I like that." I comb my fingers through his soft hair, and his eyes sparkle like he knows what I'm going to say. "Can we take a break from all this serious talk and move on to kissing and—what did you call it the other day? Do the naked dance?"

"I'm all for that," he says with a heated gaze. "I need an extra-large dose of you to hold me over until we see each other again. It could take all night."

Without warning, I push off of him and dash for the stairs. Leo growls. I run up the steps while pulling off my shirt. Not as easy as I thought it'd be. I'm already breathless. Leo's footsteps aren't far behind me, making me move faster. Once I reach the top, my bra goes next. I gasp when he wraps his arms around me from behind.

"Caught ya!" he purrs close to my ear. "Ready to put in an all-nighter?

I twist around in his arms. "Bring it on, tough guy. You've met your match."

It's time to seal the deal. There's no going back.

27

LEO

This is a completely different kind of loss. I press my hand to my aching chest and take a few calming breaths. Yep, half of my heart is missing. The other half is now on the ferry with Olive, stuck to her like glue. Loss comes in all shapes and sizes. It tortures your soul until it becomes unbearable.

After a night full of laughter, conversation, and sex, we had hoped for a quiet breakfast together before she left. Didn't happen. Olive's alarm didn't go off, so we had a quick goodbye in the hotel parking lot. She tried to get a ticket for the next ferry, but that one was canceled. I offered to drive with her to the ferry, but she declined, saying it'd make leaving even harder. I understood because I would've ridden it to the mainland and back to spend more time with her. *Desperate much?*

I have to keep telling myself this is only a temporary separation. Am I experiencing separation anxiety? Maybe. I lost my dad first, then Corey, and perhaps I'm scared I'll lose her too. *It's temporary!* When the time is right, we'll be together again. But how long will we have to wait for us to be ready for forever?

This week went too fast, and I became attached to her without effort. She slipped right into my life, finding a permanent, cozy spot in my heart. Isn't that how it should be when your soul finds its perfect match? A lot of others have tried to penetrate and mend it over the years. Not only women, family and friends did too. My heart wasn't ready to love or open up again until Olive unexpectedly appeared. Then it screamed at me, *"There she is. Finally!"*

Olive's absence differs from what I felt when Corey died. Corey and I had a connection since birth. He was a constant in my life, and I didn't know any different. He was the closest thing to having a twin brother in every way except for different parents. Our connection was indescribable on a completely emotional, platonic level. How do you sever an invisible line to someone after twenty-five years without feeling like a piece of your soul has been torn away?

My connection with Olive is mending my broken soul and filling it with a love I never knew existed. A love that is not only emotional but physical. When she's near, an all-consuming wave of passionate desire thrums beneath my skin. From day one, I saw my future with her in it as my wife, best friend, mother of our children, and the woman whose hand I'll be holding until we're old and gray.

And now I'm sitting alone on our bench planning how to execute *Operation Make Olive Fall in Love with Me*. I only got a few hours of sleep last night, though, and yawns keep slipping from my mouth. I startle when a hand grips my right shoulder.

"Sorry," Sully says, walking around the bench. "Late night?"

I eye him wearily. "What do you think?"

"I hope so. Up for some company?"

"Um. Yeah. Sure." I move over to give him some room. "Did you leave Smokey at home?"

He sits next to me and unzips his jacket a couple of inches. Smokey's little head peeks out, and she releases a light meow as if she's saying hi or complaining it's too cold. I scratch behind her ears, regardless of whether she or Sully like it or not. No complaints from either. A win for me.

Looking out at the water and enjoying the view, we sit in comfortable silence. I'm used to that when I'm with him, but this is a different quiet. He shocked me last night when he stopped to say goodbye to Olive. I'll wait him out until he says something.

"Figured I'd find you out here. Maybe I should claim a tree and a bench to sulk under."

"I'm not sulking."

"Oh, sorry. I guess that's only my job."

"*Pfft*. You don't sulk. You scowl."

He shrugs while petting Smokey. "Not gonna deny it."

I turn to see him better. "Thanks for coming over last night. It meant a lot to Olive…and me."

Another shrug. "She's good for you."

I pretend to almost fall off the bench. "Holy shit. Was that a compliment from you, Mr. Grouch?"

Sully smacks me upside the head. "Don't be a dick." I smooth out my hair, and Smokey hisses at Sully. Is she telling him to behave? "You probably think I don't pay attention to anything except my shitshow of a life."

I rest my elbow on the bench. "Basically. But it's understandable."

And another shrug. His muscles are going to cramp one day, and his shoulders are going to get stuck to his ears.

"My eyes are always open. Remember how pissed off

you and Corey would get because I knew your secrets or whatever shit you got up to? I'm observant." Then he shakes his head and scoffs. "Not that it did shit for me with my current situation. How could I have been that blind? How did I not notice my best friend and business partner screwing around with my fiancée?" He growls. "Sorry, I'm not here to talk about me."

"You know, it's okay to talk about what happened, Sul. I mean, I don't have room to talk"—I roll my eyes at myself—"but please, promise me you won't be as stupid as me to waste so much time feeling sorry for yourself. You won't get that time back. It's okay to mourn what you've lost and mend your heart along the way. But I've wasted too much time, lost too many friendships, drove my family batty—and what did I get out of it?"

"Olive," he says with finality. I didn't expect that from him. Neither did he. He looks as surprised as me that he said it.

"Since when did you become such a wise fucker?" I punch his arm. "You're right, though. But I wish I had met her earlier. I could've spent that time with her instead of alone at some hotel, avoiding my past like a selfish shit."

"You can't change it now. I can't either. I've seen a difference in you and it makes me happy to see my little brother coming back. You're kind of a mixture of the old and new, which is a pretty good deal. Gives me hope that my life won't be like this forever." He waves his hand in front of himself. "That *I* won't always be like this. Stuck in a big black fucking hole."

Smokey licks the back of Sully's hand to comfort him. Maybe I should get a cat. *Negative.* In a couple of months, things will get better. I hope.

"I promise you won't. My issues haven't disappeared, but I'm on the right track now. One day you're going to wake up and find yourself in a life that's better than you could've imagined. And you're going to be thankful. And it doesn't have to be because of a woman. It could be a job decision. Or you could win the lottery." He narrows his eyes at me. "Come on, you know what I mean."

"Fine. Let's stop talking about my problems. Don't let Olive go. Fight for her. Is that where I went wrong? Maybe I didn't focus enough on our relationship. On her."

"Don't blame yourself. There were others involved. I'm glad you found out before you got married."

"Me too." He crosses his ankles in front of him. "So what are you going to do now?"

"I have an idea. I threw a bunch of stuff in Mom's attic after Corey died. Aunt Betty's too. Want to go look through it with me? It'll be tough, but I think it's about time. What do you say? Do you have work to do?"

"Ehhh. There's always shit to be done here, but we know the owner. We can skip work for a little while. I think we could all use a good dose of the past. Want to ask Tonya too? Maybe she'll whip up some martinis. I wouldn't care if they're the fucking pink ones either. And then she can fulfill her daily quota of organizing shit." He chokes on a laugh.

I cover my gasp with a cough, hoping he didn't notice. It's amazing that he's joking around and talking this much. Sully was known for his boisterous laugh. I look forward to the day he finds it again. I look away and blink to keep my emotions in check. Then it hits me. This is how everyone else felt when they saw me dance and sing again.

"Sounds like a plan. Thanks, Sully. I feel a hell of a lot better."

"Anytime. Maybe you can return the favor one day."

I stand and wipe off the back of my jeans. "You can

count on it. But it better be under your own tree and bench."

He adjusts Smokey in his jacket and zips it up. Then he stands and pulls me in for a hug, keeping enough space between us so we don't crush her.

"Love you, bro," I say, patting him once on the back.

"Love you too." He pushes me away and I balance myself. "Now, enough of this shit. Let's go down memory lane, get drunk in the middle of the day, and forget about everything else."

"You're on."

I've missed this.

I'll never take a second for granted again.

28

OLIVE

Saying goodbye was tougher than I expected. But it was also easier because my damn alarm didn't go off. I had a whole half hour to gather my things and check out of the hotel. Our goodbye was short and sweet. Too short, but that was probably better for the both of us. I didn't break down until I was on the ferry. That wasn't the best situation because I had to leave my car and go up to the deck, but I found a seat in a corner by a window and faced outside.

There's a weird emptiness inside me, yet a bubbling anticipation too. And I'm overflowing with motivation. I accomplished quite a few goals this week. Of course, I didn't expect to add a new one to the list. Still, I'll do anything to prepare for a life with Leo.

The first thing to do is find a therapist. It's time to confront the aftermath of working in a hospital during the pandemic, the guilt that latched on to me when I quit, the hole that was left when Dad died, and my relationship with Mom. I need to find coping mechanisms for when things get out of hand.

And deep down, I know I have to go to LA to confront my demons.

I turn on my blinker as my apartment complex comes into view. It's white but looks gray from years of neglect. It has three levels with four apartments on each floor. It looks the same as it did a week ago, I know, but somehow, it's more depressing and ugly. The damp, cloudy weather doesn't help. It's hard to come back to reality after staying in a beautiful hotel for a week.

I park, then sit there in silence, delaying the inevitable. I'm afraid that when I step through the door into that familiar but disheartening atmosphere, the weight of my past will come rushing back.

I lift my wrist to my nose, sniff, and relax. Before I left Leo's cottage, I sprayed myself with his cologne. (Don't tell anyone this, but I ordered a travel-sized bottle for myself too. It should get here tomorrow. If that's the one thing I can have of him until I see him again, I'll take it.)

Now that I think of it, I should have stolen a T-shirt to sleep in too. Damn.

I grab my phone and send Leo a message, letting him know I'm home. He responds seconds later with a picture of him, Sully, and Tonya. They're surrounded by boxes and holding up martini glasses. What are they doing?

Too bad Andy moved away. It'd be nice to—no, I'm not sad that nobody's waiting for me in my apartment. I start to respond to Leo, then decide not to. We'd keep texting, and I'd end up staying in my car the whole time. I'll respond once I'm settled.

A few minutes later, I unlock my door on the third floor and trudge inside, fatigue kicking in. I look around my two-bedroom apartment and…it feels different. The air is stuffy from being closed up for a week. An extra layer of dust has settled on the furniture and everything is stock-still. I hear nothing, not even the neighbors. Normally, I prefer quiet and seclusion, but this feels eerie after having been surrounded by people all week.

Leaving the suitcase in the middle of the living room, I carry the bag of food I bought on the way home to the kitchen. If I want to stay awake, I need some strong coffee. I start a pot while I put the groceries away and sort out my suitcase. When it's ready, I pour a steaming cup and sit on my comfy recliner. The one piece of furniture I really like.

I text Andy before I do Mom. I need his positivity right now. A video call comes through seconds later. Someone's curious. Let's see if he notices my new hair color. I've hardly told him anything in our text exchanges this week.

I can't hide my smile when I see his familiar face. *Why can't he be here?* "Hey there, big brother!"

"Shh. Wait a second, Ol. I was in a meeting and called for a fifteen-minute break because I had to make an important call. Let me close my office door." No matter how busy he is, his family comes first. It's amazing how he can change from tough businessman to goofy brother in just a few seconds.

While he moves around, his jumpy phone screen makes my head spin. I stop watching and grab the blanket from the back of the recliner and drape it over my lap. Finally, he settles in his office chair and props the phone against something.

"Okay, I'm ready. Welcome back!" His enthusiasm to see me brightens my mood. It's nice to know you're loved.

I flash a bright smile and fluff my hair. "What do you think? Do I look different?"

"You're much happier than last time. Show me your back. Did you lose the shell?"

"I'm proud to report it's gone, and it's never coming back."

He leans closer. "Wait a sec. Did you dye your hair?"

I pull my hair forward to show him the dyed ends. "I had a little makeover while I was there. Bought some new clothes and shoes too. You're looking at the new, improved me. You'd be proud."

"I want details because it's obvious you were holding out on me with your 'I'm fine' texts. You're more than fine, sis. So was it worth it?"

"Above and beyond. It was the best week of my life, Andy. I'm so thankful I went." I sound lovesick. I might as well be throwing flowers in the air.

His eyes bug out of his head. "Holy shit! You met someone, didn't you?" He snaps his fingers. "Oh, the guy in the picture, right? What was his name again?"

"Yes," I squeal. "His name's Leo, and he's amazing."

"Sounds like someone's in luuurve. Your face is as bright as a lightbulb."

I wiggle in my seat, finding it hard to contain my excitement.

"How? When? What? Give me the details. And again, does he have a sister?"

"You're a freak. Yes, he does, and no, she's not your type. She'd eat you alive."

He growls. "I kinda like that."

I grimace. "I don't want to know." He flashes me a shit-eating grin. "Anyway, there's a lot to tell you, but I'll wait until you have more time. Just know that I feel amazing, and the decision to run away has changed my life."

"That's what I wanted to hear." He glances at his watch. "I hate living in San Fran sometimes. I'd love to show up at your apartment whenever I wanted. I'm going to have to wait to get the dirty details because I have to go back to the stupid meeting. I'm happy for you, Olive. I told you something amazing was going to happen. You deserve it."

I twist a strand of hair around my finger. "Thanks. Call me when you can."

"Quick question. Have you called Mom?"

"Not yet. I was waiting until I spoke to you. Any advice?" I ask, dreading his response.

He smooths out his hair and adjusts his navy blue paisley tie. "Umm…be honest with her and don't let her bring you down. Personally, I think she needs therapy or some kind of support group, but what do I know? Maybe she'll surprise us."

"If you talk to her, don't mention Leo unless she does. I'm not sure what I'm going to tell her yet. I think I should keep him a secret for now," I say, nibbling on my thumb.

He picks up the phone and hurries to the door. "Nuh-uh. Back up. No secrets. This is your *life*. You're happy, and you shouldn't have to hold back your excitement. Moms should be uplifting and want to see their kids thriving and happy." Marla said something similar.

"Listen to you! Have you been reading self-help books or something?"

His brows furrow. "I have no clue where that came from, but it's true. Okay, I really gotta run. Talk soon. Love ya."

"Love you too," I say, too late. He's already gone.

No secrets. Andy's right. If Mom can't be happy for me, then that's her problem.

Maybe I'm being too hard on her.

I call her an hour later, but it's the shortest call in history. Fifteen minutes later, my doorbell rings as I'm wiping down the kitchen counter. I take a deep breath and pray for help and patience…and then I swing open the door, a smile plastered on my face.

"Hey, Mom. How are—"

She cuts me off with a bone-crushing hug. Wow, she's thrilled to see me. That makes me hug her even longer. Maybe this won't be as bad as I thought.

But when she finally lets go of me and steps back, her eyes are shooting daggers. "Never do that to me again! Running off like that and then not talking to me for a week? I was worried sick. And then only getting brief messages from you. And you ignoring mine. God forbid you picked up the phone." She rages on and on.

I touch my cheek like she slapped my face and close the door. My neighbors don't need to hear this. Here I thought she was happy to see me. When she grabbed me in that hug, I even thought maybe she understood why I left. Nope.

You knew she'd be this way. I think quickly about how to respond to her. "Mom," I finally say, "I don't want to fight with you as soon as you come through the door. And I'm sorry I upset you, but I did what I had to do to save myself."

With her chin held high, she sniffs. "You're forgiven."

My eyebrows cling to my hairline, and my blood begins to boil. It's *always* about her—everything. She doesn't care how I'm doing. Yeah, she was worried, but about what? Obviously, the talks with Uncle Bruce and Andy did nothing.

I need to stay level-headed. Look at the situation from both sides. At least, that's what I try to do. *Think of Leo and how you feel at peace when you're with him. And stand up for yourself!*

"I don't need your forgiveness."

Her eyes flash with something, but it's hard to tell what. I keep going.

"This week away was a real eye-opener, and I'm

beyond happy I went. And nobody—not even you—is gonna take that away from me. I'm a different person now."

"Someone who is disrespectful to her mother."

Okay. That's it. The gloves are off.

"Do you hear yourself? If someone's being disrespectful, it's you. Everything is always about you. Did you hear anything about why I left? Did you not see how I was hiding in my apartment most of the time, miserable and antisocial? On the verge of depression? I just turned thirty, Mom, and I was living like I was sixty. I should be having the time of my life. Instead, I hid and let you feed into my misery. Thankfully, Andy confronted me and convinced me to snap out of it."

"You think I want to see you miserable?"

"If you don't, then what is this? Ever since Dad died, you've attached yourself to me. All your focus went to me, and I liked it at the time. But eventually, others saw how unhealthy it was, the way you hung on me. Pampering me but not trying to lift me up. Could you not see how miserable I was? That I had no life? Or did you enjoy my reliance on you because you couldn't focus all your energy on Dad?"

Her head snaps back. "That's not fair."

"You know what's not fair? That the first thing you did when you saw me is treat me like I'm a teenager who stayed out all night and didn't call. How hard is it for you to ask me how I'm doing, how my week was?" My voice cracks.

She props one hand on her hip and points at me with the other, her eyes piercing mine. "Did you ever stop to think that I was as miserable as you? It wasn't just your dad who died. My husband and soulmate died! He's the only man I ever loved and he was by my side every second of every day—until suddenly, he wasn't. Because I wasn't there."

"I know that, Mom. You were grieving. And you still are. But you can't do that by smothering me and making me feel bad for wanting a life of my own. That won't bring him back, and it won't make you happy again. You have to deal with his absence and learn to stand on your own two feet."

"So I'm supposed to forget about my dead husband." She turns away, her nose held high. "I can't turn off my feelings like you did."

"You know what, Mom, you can throw anything you want at me right now. I didn't tell you to forget about Dad because I haven't either. But you need to move on. It's time to find yourself—the woman who's now on her own. Make yourself the priority."

She shakes her head manically. "Fine. You don't want me around, I'll go. I got your message loud and clear. I won't bother you again."

I stand frozen in the middle of my living room as she storms out, slamming the door behind her. *What the fuck was that?* She pinned everything on me. Again. She's in denial. I need to read up on the stages of grief.

Exhaustion overwhelms me. I drop into the recliner and bury my head in my hands. I probably should've gone after her, but what would I have said that I didn't already? Maybe I'll call Uncle Bruce to find out what he discussed with her and how she reacted. Not now though.

This is exactly why I didn't want to come home.

I grab my phone and type a text to Andy on the way to my bedroom. He's probably out to dinner or entertaining someone.

Me: Catastrophe! Stormed out of my place. Didn't tell her about Leo. No chance.

I toss the phone on my bed and collapse face down beside it. A couple of seconds later, it chirps.

Andy: Don't let it get you down. We'll figure out what to do. Can't call because I'm at a business dinner with potential clients.

I respond with a thumbs-up and stuff a pillow under my head. Sleep is out of the question; it's only dinnertime. Instead of getting up, I flip through the pictures I took this week. I grin ear to ear even as my eyes blur. One teardrop slips out and slides down the side of my face into my hair. How can I miss someone so much who I've only known for one week? How will I survive several weeks without seeing or touching him? Another text comes in from Andy, interrupting my pity party.

Andy: Before I forget. Super Bowl party at my place. You're coming!

What? Watch the Super Bowl at his place in San Francisco? I huff. Then realization dawns. Of course—he wants everyone to watch his commercial the first time with him. A week ago, I would've said no. Times are changing. An idea strikes, and I sit up on my bed. Maybe Leo can meet me there between his trips. I know he's supposed to be in California at some point.

Me: Count me in.

Andy: Bring lover boy.

Me: Already thinking about it.

Even if Leo can't go, I will anyway. I have to keep my high going somehow.

Even if Leo can't go, I will anyway. I have to keep my high going somehow.

29

LEO

I place the heavy box on the coffee table, and Sully puts another one next to it. Then he pats me on the shoulder and turns to leave.

"Thanks for the support today," I say, hoping I'm not slurring. We had a few too many martinis, and it doesn't help how exhausted I am. "You and Tonya were a big help. It was a blast hanging out like old times."

He turns and fixes his intense gaze on me. "I know it was hard for you to look at all that stuff, but it was hard for us too. We all have great memories of Corey. They shouldn't be forgotten and placed in a box somewhere gathering dust." He's out the door before I can respond.

Ouch. As quiet as Sully is, when he does speak, it hits deep. And he's absolutely right. Corey deserves to be remembered. It wasn't my intention to forget him. It was too difficult to look at things we worked nonstop for. A constant reminder of what could've been. Where would we be now? Would I have met Olive?

Like Sully said, it was great looking through the boxes with him and Tonya. Somewhere along the way, I'd forgotten that they were close to him too. We laughed until we cried and cried until we laughed. I found the hard drive where I'd downloaded all our videos, blog entries, and pictures. Tonya ran to her office and brought back her computer. Then she made us fresh cosmopolitans to give us strength to view what was on there. We didn't get through half of the stuff.

While watching videos of our travels, I got an idea of how I can show Olive who I used to be. It'll also give her the chance to know Corey. I'm not scheduled to leave for another five days, so I'll prepare what I need and take it with me. Sometimes technology really is your friend.

I drag myself upstairs and change into my sleep pants and T-shirt. My bed is calling, but I want to talk to Olive before I pass out. I'm dying to hear how things went with her mom. I huff as I realize I left my phone downstairs. I trot down and slide it off the table. The screen lights up with a message from Olive. She wants to talk too.

I make it back upstairs and sit on the bed with my back against the headboard. I press the video-call button, and she answers immediately. Her beautiful face fills the screen and my body buzzes with happiness and longing.

"Hey, beautiful," I purr. "It's good to see your face."

A sweet smile curves her lips. "Hi, handsome," she replies, moving around in what looks like the kitchen.

"Whatcha doing?"

"Making some chamomile tea. I'll need something to help me sleep since you won't be here to wrap around me like a koala bear." She pouts, making me want to suck on her lower lip.

"I want to see your apartment. Give me a tour." Her eyes narrow. "I'm serious."

She spends the next few minutes explaining the spacious place to me as she goes room to room. It's not what I expected. I thought it'd be cozier, but it seems cold in a way. Maybe it reflects her personality in the past. There are no bright colors or pictures on the walls. It's like she didn't care about her surroundings, except she's home most of the time. Maybe I'm wrong—I guess it could be the lighting.

"And that's it. Nothing special. I like your cottage better. I noticed how sad and boring my place is when I came back today. It's bland and impersonal. Almost like a furnished temporary apartment."

"Hmmm." *I was right.* "Maybe you can brighten it up with something. Maybe pictures on the walls?" My mind fast-forwards to the future I want right now, and I imagine buying pictures together for the walls in our new home.

"It looks like you're on your bed. I'll do the same, and then we can pretend we're in bed together. Let me grab my tea."

"Sounds good to me." I wait until she gets comfortable and props her phone up so she's hands free. She has cute powder-blue pajamas on, and her hair is in a messy bun like mine.

"Okay. I'm ready, Freddie." Her smile stretches across her face. "My very own Freddie Mercury. You can sing me to sleep."

"I would if you wanted me to."

Her face softens, and she looks fucking adorable. "Really? I'd love to hear your voice again. But only when you're ready."

"I need to practice a little first. How did it go with your mom?"

Her smile dims. "It ended with her leaving and slamming the door behind her. And she was only here maybe ten minutes."

I jerk my head back in shock. "I didn't expect that."

"It is what it is. It wasn't realistic to expect that she'd be happy to see me when I left the way I did." She sips her tea and lowers the cup.

"Tell me what happened and don't leave anything out." Anger toward her mother bubbles under the surface when she unloads everything. It's hard for me to be neutral since I've never met her.

"And that's how it ended. Her slamming the door. I don't know what my next move will be. I'm too exhausted to think about it right now. Some cutie kept me awake last night. Our sexy night has been on replay."

"It was fun, though." I wiggle my eyebrows. "Sleep would be nice, but I'd rather talk to you."

"Me too." We gaze at each other with lovesick grins. She perks up, pulling us from the moment. "Hey, what was with the martinis?"

I tell her about my short but heartfelt conversation with Sully and what led us to my mom's attic.

"I'm proud of you. Are you glad you did it?"

"Definitely. It hurt like hell, but we had fun reminiscing too, which helped balance the mood. We realized how long it had been since we really hung out together. Not hiding or holding anything back. I still have a ton of stuff to go through…lots more boxes at my aunt's. But enough of that for tonight. Tell me something good."

"Let's see. I ate junk for dinner. I'll resume my health kick tomorrow."

"Don't be losing your perfect curves. You know how much I love them." I'd do anything to glide my hands over her gorgeous body right now.

She points at the phone. "Don't be giving me that look. It's not fair when I'm not in the same room as you. Focus on me."

"That's what I'm doing. I can't help that I'm addicted to you," I whine. "I miss your lips."

She pretends to kiss the screen. "Poor baby. Anyway, I spoke to my brother. I can't wait till you meet him. I think you'll get along really well. Did I ever tell you he's the one who came up with Amazon's Super Bowl ad this year? He works for a popular ad agency."

"No. How cool is that?" I buzz.

"He's having a Super Bowl party in San Francisco and asked me to come."

"That's awesome. Did you say yes? I'd be all over that."

"I haven't visited him since he moved there. It seems like the perfect time to do it." She bites her lower lip and looks shy suddenly.

"What's up? Is there something else?"

"Um. Any chance you can sneak in a trip to watch the Super Bowl with us? I don't remember where you'll be in the world at that time. I think it's on the second Sunday in February this year."

"Very tempting." *Of course I'm going to go.* "Maybe I can switch things around. I'll let you know. If it works out, we'll get to see each other sooner than we planned. You're gone less than a day and I can't stand not physically seeing or touching you. It's fucking tough."

"I know, sexy. When it gets hard for us, we need to remember the endgame. The. End. Game."

I scratch my head. "Endgame. Hmm. And what is that again?"

"You and me. Together. Forever. Ring a bell?" she quips. "Or am I talking to someone else?"

"Ah, *that* endgame. My bad. I thought you were talking about the Avengers."

She gives me the stink eye. "Such a smart-ass. I think you could make me laugh while I sleep."

"I'd rather you scream my name instead. Wait. That sounds wrong. Screaming, but not while you're asleep. *Grr.* You know what I mean." My sexiness has gone out the window.

"You act like you're sex starved. Last night should've held you over for a little while." She moves her phone to a pillow next to her, then curls up under the covers, facing me. She fell asleep like this last night, and I stayed up a bit longer to watch her peaceful face. It hits me again how in love I am with her. It's mind-blowing.

I slip under the covers too. Once I'm comfortable on my side and my head is propped on my own pillow, I murmur, "I want to fall asleep with you on the phone. Can we do that? It's the closest thing to sleeping together."

Her eyes dance with elation. "I'll take whatever I can get. I might not feel you, but I can hear and see you. It's good enough for now."

My eyelids become heavy and sleep is about to take me over when she whispers, "You make it easy to fall in love with you." When darkness takes over, I'm grinning like I have a special secret.

I woke up a few minutes ago to find my phone dead. While the coffee brews and the phone charges on the table, I brainstorm a song to pair with the first video clip I'll send to Olive. It has to be motivational and also a song I love. The video clip will be part of our first dance recital. Olive will get a kick out of that.

I prepare my coffee and head over to the couch with my laptop. My eyes scan the cottage, and I want to smack myself. I criticized Olive's apartment for being bland and impersonal. My place doesn't lack color, but it looks exactly like what it is—a hotel cottage. I don't have personal items around either. If Mom said I couldn't stay here anymore, all I'd have to do is grab my suitcase and leave. There's nothing of mine here to pack up. Nobody would know I'd been there.

What a depressing way to live. No permanent residence, no personal items except for the clothes in my suitcase. That isn't living. It's past time for a change.

It took one person to make me disappear, and it took one person to bring me back to life.

I pick up my phone and see I have a message from Olive. And what does that make me do? Smile. Not an ordinary one. It's one that lights up not only my face but my entire body as if I've had several espressos. I click on the message.

Olive: Aren't you the cutest?

It's a video, and I snort when I see what it is. She's filmed me sleeping. I zoom in to check if I was drooling or talking in my sleep. It's hard to see because of the lighting. I chuckle again. I'd probably have done the same thing if she'd fallen asleep first.

Time to create my video clip and song.

30

OLIVE

Leo fell asleep faster than I did last night. I laid there like a psycho, watching him sleep. I don't know if he'll appreciate the video I made of him. He looked peaceful and kissable. I couldn't help whispering, "You make it easy to fall in love with you." If he heard me, he didn't react.

We haven't used the word *love* yet, but that's okay. I told my long-term boyfriend in college that I loved him, but after graduation, he went off to grad school on the East Coast and I stayed in Cali for nursing school. Our relationship fizzled out quickly. It made me realize the difference between *love* and *in love*. Leo's the first guy I've ever been *in love* with.

I didn't tell Leo because most people would find it absurd to make such a declaration after a few days. They'd say it's only lust, not love. Yes, I know, I shouldn't care what people say. A week ago, I would've been one of those judgmental people. I even doubted Mom and Dad's claim that it was love at first sight for them. I guess you have to experience it firsthand to believe it. And now, I'm a believer.

Anyway, when I woke up this morning, I sent Leo the video clip of him sleeping, then gave myself a pep talk to get things moving. I made a list of therapists, some gyms, and found a puppy yoga place. I'm not a big yoga fan, but who wouldn't want to lie around with puppies? Maybe Mom would go with me…if she ever talks to me again.

Just as my lips are about to kiss the rim of my coffee cup, my phone plays "I Was Born to Love You." A rush of excitement hits me—I set that song as Leo's ringtone and text message tone. I open the phone and find two messages with attachments. *Hmm.* Interesting. I click on the first one.

> Leo: Good morning, beautiful. Thanks for the awesome reminder of how good I look when I'm sleeping. I should be a model for pillows, mattresses, or melatonin supplements. Anywho, every day until I see you next, I'm going to send you a video or picture of me and Corey. This way, you can get to know us a little better. This one is a clip from our first dance recital. Check out my hair! Corey's the one standing to my right.

I click on the video and brace myself. A group of eight boys, all wearing white tank tops and big, baggy black pants, stand in a row. Leo's easy to find in the lineup with his frizzy hair. It's like he stepped into a rainforest. I pause the video and zoom in so I can see Corey better. He's slightly taller and thinner than Leo and has dark brown hair. It's hard to make out his face because it's an old video. I start it again and focus when a song begins. I think it's from Usher. Then it's go time.

My mouth drops open and I don't blink because I'm too enthralled. This is their *first* recital? When did he say he started lessons? Ten years old? The performance is amazing. My heart melts as young Leo dances around the stage with enough enthusiasm to grab anybody's attention. When the video ends, I restart it. The song has me pumped up now! I play it three more times, then put the phone down and massage my cramped jaw from my perma smile. I click on the next message.

Leo: I hope you enjoyed that. That one really makes me miss Corey, but I think watching them is the only way I'm going to move on. Speaking of healing, here's a song that can get anybody's motivation to kick in. No matter how hard it gets, we know what the endgame is. 😉

Let's see if I know the song he picked. I click on the YouTube link. It's perfect. The music video of Katy Perry's "Roar" plays. I love this freaking song. The first time I heard it was during a Super Bowl halftime show. I switch over to Spotify and create a new playlist to save all the songs he sends me. We already have a playlist created for us, but this one will be just for me.

Then I read the checklist I made this morning when I woke up.

It's time to roar.

The next morning, my doorbell rings. I'm hoping it's the cologne I ordered; the delivery was delayed. I whip open the door and freeze.

"Hi, sweetheart. Can we talk?" It's Mom, clutching her

crimson red purse. What a difference from how she greeted me last time.

"Of course, Mom. Come in." I want to hug her already, but refrain. Instead, I step aside to let her in. She stops in the living room with her arms crossed over her chest, her purse hanging from the crook of her arm. It's rare for her to look so insecure and uncomfortable.

"Let me take your coat." She places her purse on the coffee table and hands me her matching red peacoat. One thing to know about Mom, she has good fashion sense. "Do you want something to drink?"

She shakes her head. "No, thanks. I'd like to have a heart-to-heart with my daughter."

"Okay. Let's sit." Leo's song of the day, "Unstoppable" by Sia, is playing. I turn off the music and set the phone facedown on the table. I drape her jacket over the arm of the couch, then toss the scattered pillows aside. She sits down, her shoulders squared and tense, hands clasped in her lap. I join her, one leg folded under me on the couch and my back against the armrest.

"Talk to me, Mom. I want everything out in the open. This conversation is long overdue."

She nods wearily. I reach over and grab her hands to encourage her to speak. A few seconds later, she says, "I've been thinking a lot about what you said to me. And your uncle Bruce. And Andy. You were right—instead of me listening to anyone else, I only thought about myself.

"Your dad left us without warning. What began as a great day ended with him never coming home again. Never sleeping in our bed, never kissing me throughout the day, never saying 'I love you,' never teasing me about my baking skills—" Her voice cracks and she closes her eyes. I blink back the stubborn tears that want to make an appearance. She takes a few deep breaths and continues.

"Instead of dealing with his death, I put all my energy into you and Andy. Andy left without a second thought, and I shifted my focus to you. When I showed up on your birthday and Andy told me you'd left and wouldn't say where you were, I—"

Oh. "Mom—"

She raises her hand for me to stop. "It seems like everyone is leaving, and I'll be left here alone. Your dad was my best friend, but you're my only daughter and best girlfriend."

That's another thing I don't understand about Mom. She doesn't have her own friends. My parents had friends who were married or couples, and they only socialized in pairs. She was content with Dad.

She continues. "I'm ashamed that I didn't urge you to get help after LA and your father's death. Instead, I made sure you needed me because, without that, my life has no purpose. I'm sorry, honey. Caring for my family was my favorite role, and now it feels like no one needs me anymore. The house is cold and empty, and the silence is unbearable."

I move closer and rest my hand on her back. "Mom, I'll always need you, but we need boundaries. This was both of our faults. I hung on to you too. We've experienced traumatic events, and instead of dealing with them head-on, we gave up. At least I did, anyway."

"But what made you leave on your birthday?"

"Believe it or not, it's because I watched *Under the Tuscan Sun* right after Christmas. Do you remember that movie? We saw it together years ago."

She tugs on her lower lip while deep in thought. "I think so," she says. "With Diane Lane, right?"

"Mm hmm. Remember the part where her best friend was talking about her being at a crossroads?" When she nods, I continue. "Well, there was this quote that her friend said, something like, 'Someday, someone will look at you and wonder what happened to make you so miserable and closed off.' And I realized at that moment I was like that woman, and I was a few days away from turning thirty.

"I knew I had to do something, Mom. Uncle Bruce and Andy had been nagging me to get a life. And I'm sorry, but if I'd told you, you would've insisted on going with me."

She fiddles with her fingernails, then glances at me. "You're right."

"I needed to be in a new environment where I could find myself again. It was scary as hell to go to a hotel alone."

She places her hand on my knee. "You might not believe this, but I'm really proud of you. And envious. I don't know if I could do that."

"That's because you had Dad. You never had to do things alone. Now's your chance. Being alone can be awful, but it can be awesome too. Go make new friends, take advantage of your freedom, and try new things. Like me— I found a puppy yoga studio nearby and there's a class tomorrow morning. I'm gonna try it. Want to go with me?"

"Puppy yoga? I do love puppies." She crinkles her nose. "Not sure about the yoga thing. My body's not as flexible as it was in my twenties."

I snicker. "Who cares? It's something new. You might like it. You might even decide to get a dog. You've always said you wanted one but couldn't because of Dad's allergies."

"Hmm."

I wrap both of my hands around hers. "Promise me you'll think about it. I'm telling you, Mom—one week away has changed everything for me."

"You do seem happier or lighter. I like your new hair color." She lifts a strand.

"Thanks." I perk up. "While I was there, I had a little makeover and bought some new clothes."

The doorbell rings, and we both jump. I head to the door and open it eagerly. A mailman hands me a box. Leo's cologne. I want to tear it open and smell him again, but I'll wait until Mom leaves. I set the box on the kitchen counter and return to the couch.

"It's wonderful to see you smiling again." Mom's eyes fill with regret. "I'm such a terrible mother. I never imagined I'd become this kind of parent. Please forgive me, Olive. I promise I'll do better."

"I Was Born to Love You" pulses in the air, interrupting us again. "I'm sorry, Mom. Let me turn it off." I pick it up and beam when I see his name. I turn the volume off and rest it on the couch.

"You're glowing. What's going on?" Mom comments, her own smile growing.

Suddenly nervous, I stuff my hands between my legs. "Um. I met someone while I was on Orcas Island."

Her face drops, and rapid blinking follows. Not good. I can hear the buzzing of her thoughts. "Oh. Was…was that him calling?" She glances at my phone. "And you went to Orcas Island?"

"Yes. I loved it there and can't wait to go back."

Mom's eyebrows transform into a unibrow. "Why there, of all places? Especially at this time of year."

"Just because you prefer warmer weather doesn't mean I have to do the same. The island was gorgeous."

"You're right." She looks defeated again. I glance at my watch because I have to leave soon for my appointment.

She finally meets my gaze with a blank expression and

says, "Where did you stay?" *Jeez, Mom.* At least act interested in what I have to say.

"I stayed at the Madrona Inn. It was huge and truly romantic. They have the best French café."

"And who's the young man you met?"

My chest warms, thinking about how he charged into my life and changed everything. "His name's Leo. From the first time he spoke to me, he had me under a spell." My body feels warm and fuzzy. "He's gorgeous and so my type. We spent every second we could together."

"And you're still in contact? Does he live nearby? Will you see him again?"

"He's a hotel critic. He'll be traveling for the next six weeks. When he's not on the road, he lives at the hotel his family owns. The one I stayed at. We plan on getting together when he returns. Mom, I think he's the one. The *real thing*." I love being able to talk about him with someone.

"You think he's the one after one week?" Skepticism drips from her voice.

Seriously? Of all people to ask that. What a hypocrite!

"Yes." I say firmly. "He treats me like gold."

"And that's what I like to hear. My daughter deserves nothing but the best." She says the right words, but her voice is flat.

I tip my head to the side. "Right. You sound really convincing."

"Sweetheart, I'm simply trying to catch up with everything that's happened since you left. And now you're telling me you've met someone. It's—"

My alarm interrupts us. "Sorry, Mom." I turn it off and stand up. "I have to leave in a few minutes for an appointment." Good timing, because I'm concerned she might break down again or say something about Leo that'll piss me off.

"Okay." She stands too and reaches for her coat.

I intercept before she picks it up. "Mom, about before. I love you and I only want what's best for you. It takes time to embrace the changes in your life. It won't happen overnight. We're both going to have good and bad days. I want us to be there for each other. I have a long list of things I need to do and change. The most important is to go to a therapist. I got a last-minute appointment at one and that's where I'm going now. And I even want to go to LA."

Her eyes widen. "LA? Are you sure?"

"Yep. I want to see my old boss. If it doesn't help, at least I'll know I tried. Right now, the guilt is killing me and holding me back."

Mom suddenly hugs me with all her strength. "You're much braver than I am, Olive. I'm proud of you. You give me hope." We separate slowly and giggle because we're both slobbery messes.

She wipes the moisture from under her eyes. "Good luck with your appointment. I'm off to the cemetery to talk to your dad."

My heart clenches. "That's sweet, Mom." I remember that Leo hasn't gone to Corey's grave since his funeral.

"It makes me feel better. Want to come with me? I could wait until you're finished with your appointment."

I flash her a genuine smile. "I'd love to."

We visited Dad's grave that afternoon, and then we went to a café together. It felt good. I didn't want to talk about my therapy session yet, but the black cloud was no longer hanging over Mom and me. Somehow, we set aside the issues between us and simply savored a relaxed moment together. I listened to her tell stories about Dad, ones I've heard a hundred times before. It didn't matter; what counted was how happy it made her.

I know she's skeptical about Leo and his intentions, even though she didn't say anything out loud. Looking at it from her perspective, I understand her worries. I described the Madrona Inn to her and asked her to go back with me, but she wasn't interested. That's okay—I'll be going back either way.

And that's how the day went. I know it didn't solve all our problems, but it's a big step forward.

31

LEO

I've been sitting in my car for fifteen minutes, trying to find the nerve to get out. Corey's grave is close by, but it feels miles away. I fixate on the painted rock I found in a memory box, flipping it over in my hand.

When we were around eight or nine years old, this rock caused a massive paint fight between Corey and me. I close my eyes, replaying it in my mind. A rainbow of colors splashed the garage walls, including my dad's expensive tools and machines. Paint covered our hair, mouths, skin, and clothes. My throat constricts remembering the taste of it. Our parents grounded us for two weeks. They shouldn't have given us the paint to begin with.

It's been a few days since I brought the boxes back to my place, and I've come to realize that I've essentially been erasing the first twenty-five years of my life, because he was always with me. But forgetting Corey is impossible, and five years of this denial is an embarrassment.

There was a letter from Corey stuck between some books in one of the boxes. If I could, I'd fucking pummel my own ass right now. I packed those boxes, but I never saw it before.

Reading that letter was bittersweet. I cried, laughed, and threw some shit across the room. Don't worry, I didn't break anything important. If I did, I would've been in the dog house with Mom. But it made me drive to the cemetery.

Get out of the car. I count backward from five. On one, I open the door and step out, gripping the painted rock in my hand.

Someone told me once people leave rocks on headstones to show respect to the deceased and reflect their visit. Maybe Corey doesn't want me here. I can almost feel him pushing me away, yelling at me to leave. Anytime we ever fought, it only lasted a couple of minutes before we'd erupt into laughter. We never took anything seriously. Now, I'm not sure.

I inch forward, glancing at the other headstones as I pass them. Some have rocks on them too. As I draw closer, my heart pounds, and I take a trembling breath. I rub the surface of the rock with my thumb repeatedly.

I stop and read his name and the dates on his headstone. My legs tremble. *Too young.* Holly berries and pine cones adorn the fresh grass before it. Beside them stands a mini pine tree decorated with red bows. I'm sure Aunt Betty put it there. If she had her way, I bet his headstone would glow like the Griswold's house from *National Lampoon's Christmas Vacation.*

I step close beside the grave and place the colorful rock on the headstone, reminding myself again of what an asshole I've been for not visiting. I return to the front with a lump in my throat. The weight on my heart gets heavier and pulls me to the ground. I fall to my knees on the damp grass, then sit back on my heels.

Why is this so fucking hard?

I scan the surrounding area to ensure I'm alone.

"Hey, Cor," I mumble. Suddenly, all the words I've been holding back push their way out of my throat as I shatter into a million pieces. With my head in my hands, I apologize for not visiting, for not being there when he took his last breath. I tell him how much I miss him and how I've been stuck. Five years of sadness and anger flow out in streams, watering the grass before me.

"I know you've been watching me, and you're probably disappointed in how I've been living. I'm sure of it because of the letter you wrote. You remember? Well, like you predicted, I've met a woman. She's it for me, Cor. She's reignited my heart. Out of all the women I've met since you've been gone, Olive's the only one. She's brought back my love for dancing, singing, and the desire to live.

"I wish you two could meet… But you can't. Omigod, Corey. It fucking hurts that my two favorite people will never be in the same room together. You'll never see how much you mean to me and how much I love Olive." I sniff so hard it's disgusting. Why didn't I bring tissues?

There's a bare patch on the ground, and I realize I've been pulling out pieces of grass and tossing them to the side this whole time. I smooth the area as best I can.

"Anyway, I miss you more than I can express. Maybe my snot gives it away. You'd be the one to let me walk around with a big-ass booger hanging out of my nose and not tell me. Man, you were such a dick sometimes. We both were. That's what made us so funny. So awesome. To us anyway.

"Thanks for the letter. I'm sorry I didn't find it sooner. I'll keep it in a safe place now and read it often. Please watch over me, Olive, and our families. I'll bring her here with me someday.

"And I promise, I won't take one more day for granted. I'll live my life to the fullest for the both of us. We miss you, Cor. I love you, man."

I sit in silence for a moment with my eyes closed, letting the breeze ruffle my hair, the sun dry my face, and the wet ground seep through my jeans.

"Bye for now."

I get up and head for my car, watching the ground as I walk. When I look up, I'm shocked to see Aunt Betty standing next to my car, holding flowers.

Damn! I thought I was all dried up, but the tears come back, full force. We hug tightly, mumbling and crying together. Once we let up, she hands me a pack of tissues.

She tilts her head. "You okay?"

I nod, happy that it's the truth. "I'm getting there."

Her face radiates love and kindness. "Good. I'm glad I came when I did. I was going to wait for your uncle Mason to get home first before I came here."

"Um." I clear my throat. Not sure why I'm nervous. "So when should we plan Corey's memorial?"

"How about today?" she responds, her voice filled with excitement. "I'll call Tonya when I'm done here."

"Perfect."

Slowly—no, quickly—everything is falling into place.

I scratch my stubbly jaw. The universe wants to delay my trip. When I got home from planning the memorial, I found an email informing me that my flight from the island to Seattle had been canceled. I'll need to take the ferry to the mainland instead. An hour later, I get another email saying my flight to Japan's been canceled too. I do some research, but all the other direct flights are full. With connecting flights, it'll take me over twenty-four hours to get there. No, thanks.

Oh! I could ask Sam to fly me to Seattle with his helicopter. He loves to fly, but I don't want to bother him. I roll my neck from one shoulder to the other. Another idea pops into my head, and I quickly check flights for another day.

Yes. This could work. It's approaching five o'clock now, and I haven't heard from Olive. Is that good or bad? I rub my hands up and down my thighs. What should I do? I need to book these plane tickets now. My gut says to do it, so I click the purchase button. If it doesn't work out, I'll be home longer than expected. But if it does… I shoot Olive a text.

> Me: I haven't heard from you. I hope everything is okay. It's been a long day. I've got a surprise for you. I'm home for the rest of the night.

While I'm waiting for her to call, I double-check when the Super Bowl is and compare it to my work schedule. I really want to spend that weekend with her and meet her brother.

I also need to touch base with my boss. We talked before the holidays, and everything was on track for what they expect from me. Things are different now. My life is about to drastically change. This will be my final article for the magazine. I plan to tell Mom that I want the manager's position, but I have to make sure it works for Olive and aligns with our endgame first.

Me, making plans for a personal life? It's an anomaly. I've been in limbo, but this woman with cappuccino eyes and a heart the size of Texas has pulled me out. The life I envision with her makes me want to start it right now.

It's been an emotionally draining day. I'm antsy and

need something to do. I throw on some sweatpants and head over to the gym.

Twenty minutes in, I'm drenched and struggling to breathe. This is the hardest I've pushed myself on the treadmill. When Olive's name appears on my screen, I brace myself on the sides and pull the emergency cord.

I'll always stop what I'm doing for her.

32

OLIVE

I close my apartment door and lean against it, dropping my purse on the floor. I'm wrung out. Today's therapy session was heart-wrenching, and I didn't expect that. Our first session was introductory, but today, she dove right in and used every second of those forty-five minutes. And we only discussed my time in LA! Don't even ask me how I got two appointments a few days apart because I asked myself the same question. Fate?

I appreciated the therapist's soft, empathetic manner and how she didn't ask me "how I felt" about any of it. I also liked that she had a motherly presence. I'll stick with her for now and see how it goes.

I wish Leo could be here waiting for me. We'd cuddle up on the couch, enjoy a glass of wine together, and talk about our day. *Soon, Olive.*

I load the wash, then pour a large glass of white wine and settle in to rewatch the second season of *Bridgerton.* Before I start the show, I unpack and set up the cell phone stand I bought earlier today, propping my phone on it.

Messages from Leo and Andy appear on the screen. They're from hours ago.

I read Leo's message first, and my heart skips a beat. He has a surprise for me! I don't bother responding and video-call him instead as I get comfy on the recliner. After a few rings, he appears on the screen breathing heavily; his face is bright red. He lifts his finger for me to wait a minute. I watch closely as he drinks water from his bottle. His hair is in a sexy, sweaty, messy bun, with frizzy ringlets sticking out around his face. His biceps bulge and his light gray tank top clings to his body. I want to rip it off him. How can I wait weeks until I can touch him again?

I groan. "You're such a jerk. You're too damn attractive and I can't enjoy it in person. There better not be any women in there."

His mouth turns up into a comical, cocky grin. "Give me a second. I need to cool down and catch my breath, but when you look at me like that, it won't be possible."

"I'm trying to decide whether you look hotter now or when you were in the sauna. This is torture."

He dries his face and neck while walking slowly on the treadmill. "I aim to please. Let's keep this conversation PG in case someone comes in. I don't want any guests to see me with a raging hard-on."

I smirk. "We wouldn't want that now, would we? Do you want to call me back?"

"Nope. I was killing time and burning some lingering energy. Let's talk."

"I'm sorry I didn't respond to your message. I must've had network problems—I didn't see it until a couple minutes ago."

He steps off the treadmill, then sits on the closest workout bench, somehow maneuvering the phone so I can see him. "It's all good. We've both had busy days. It'll be worse when I'm traveling. Japan is a sixteen-hour time difference."

"Ugh, don't remind me. Now tell me what the surprise is?" I lift my wineglass to my mouth.

"Want company this weekend?" He smirks with a hint of insecurity.

I jump off the couch, spilling my drink on my hand and sweatshirt. "What? Really?" I set the glass on the table, relieved I hadn't had wine in my mouth. "Of course! How?" My heart's going to burst with excitement. "Hold on a sec!" I dash to the kitchen, rinse my hand under the faucet, shake off the excess water, and wipe it off on my sweatpants. "I'm back."

"Things got screwed up with my flights, and I can't fly out until Sunday."

I curl up on the recliner again. "Omigod, I'm ecstatic. It's getting harder and harder the longer we're apart. It feels like weeks, but it's only been a couple of days."

"I'll take a car from the ferry."

"Nope! The second you walk off that ferry, you are mine. I'll pick you up and take you to the airport when you leave. You're flying from Seattle, right?"

"Isn't that a pain for you? I have no problem finding my way."

I shake my head and point my finger at the phone. "I want to spend every second I can with you. Don't deny me this."

He shakes his head, smiling. "You're adorable when you get like this. Anything for you."

I blow him a kiss. "Now I'm not going to be able to sleep tonight."

"Me either." He yanks his shirt over his head, pulling

more hair out of his bun. Now he looks like a mad scientist. I giggle behind my hand as he pulls on a hoodie. "Can we stay on the phone while I walk home?"

"Of course. You said you had a busy day. What did you do?"

"I went to Corey's grave." My eyes widen, but I quickly relax when I see he's smiling as he heads outside into the dark night.

"And…how did it go? I love that you're happy."

During his trek back to the cottage, he tells me why he went and how he talked to Corey and released a ton of emotional baggage.

"And get this," he says. "When I went to leave, Corey's mom, my aunt Betty, was standing at my car. I let my wall down. All that heavy weight that was on my chest is gone. We went back to her house and helped plan his memorial with Tonya."

He unlocks his front door and walks in, turning on the lights. Homesickness—which is crazy—sweeps over me. I miss it there and want to curl up in his bed.

"That's definitely something to be proud of, Leo. Sometimes you gotta let it all out. It really helps. You wouldn't believe how much I cried during today's therapy session. I was surprised the floor wasn't wet."

His forehead crinkles. "That bad, huh? Do you like her?"

"So far, yes. I'll keep going to see what happens next. I understand how you feel, though, after visiting Corey. Tears are cleansing."

He downs half a bottle of water from the fridge, then sits at the kitchen table. "And you say you're proud of me? Look at the day you've had."

"And I didn't even tell you everything. Mom stopped by again."

"She did? Why didn't you say anything?"

"I wanted to hear about your day first."

"Shit. Did she yell at you again?" He growls like a lion. I love that he's so protective of me.

With a blank face, I say, "Only when I talked about you."

He scowls. "Seriously? What the hell? Why?"

Yikes. "Just kidding. Who can yell about you? You're sweeter than gummy worms."

"Those are sour," he points out, sounding annoyed. "Be serious. Tell me what happened."

"Okay, okay. I'm sorry. Don't be mad. I promise, there was no arguing about anything. However, she's skeptical, much like your mom, and didn't say much. But she commented again on how much I'm smiling. I think it made her feel better. This smiling thing will probably be an issue for the rest of my life. You make me so happy."

"Such a tragedy," he mocks. "I could stop if you want."

"You'd better not!"

"Listen, beautiful. I'm cold and hungry. Let me go shower and eat before you tell me more about your mom. We should have dinner with her when I'm there."

He pulls his sweatshirt off. *Perfection.* I lick my lips and ogle him with uncontrollable desire.

"Um, hey Olive."

I snap out of my fantasy world. "Yeah?"

"You might want to wipe the drool off your chin." He snickers.

"What?" I giggle, but wipe my chin surreptitiously anyway…just in case. "Go take your shower before I beg you to take the phone in there with you."

"Ooh. That's kinda kinky. I like it."

"Shut up and go before this conversation gets out of hand."

"Fine," he says, bending over. The phone doesn't go lower than his stomach, but he grins wolfishly at me as he stands back up. Something wings past the camera. "Oops," he says. "My sweats are gone. Gotta go. Pick a movie for us to watch together." He winks, then disconnects the phone.

He's evil, and I love it. Friday can't come fast enough.

33

LEO

This damn ferry better speed up, or I'll swim to the fucking docks myself. I can see Olive in the distance, bouncing on her toes. My stomach flips with excitement and my smile takes over my face.

I'm the first passenger off the boat. As soon as my feet touch the ground, I sprint toward her. Ignoring the chance of my stuff being stolen, I set my suitcase and computer bag to the side as she gets closer. With pure elation, she leaps into my outstretched arms where she belongs.

There's no time to speak. My mouth has more important things to do, like kiss her senseless. Her lips are petal-soft and taste like mint with a hint of coffee. I hold the back of her neck and deepen the kiss, disregarding the people passing by. Her body melts into mine, as if yearning to become part of me.

Someone clears their throat loudly as they pass us, and Olive releases my tingling lips. I chase her for one more peck.

We separate slowly, eyes locked on each other. "Hi," we say at the same time.

She gives me another quick hug. "I can't believe you're here."

"Well, believe it." I caress her cheek, then suck in a breath. "Shit, my luggage." I turn around, but my bags are right where I dropped them. I retrieve them, then extend my hand for her to hold.

She grabs it and pulls me toward the parking lot. "Let's get out of here. I need to be alone with you," she says. I toss my stuff into the trunk without even noticing what she drives.

Once we're inside, we kiss until we're breathless and the windows fog. "I don't want to stop kissing you, but this isn't the best place to be doing this," I say, panting as I adjust my increasingly tight jeans.

"You're right. Let's go home and resume there." We fasten our seatbelts.

Home. I love hearing that.

As we drive to her place, she points out different landmarks, cafés, or restaurants she likes. We pass by her old high school, and I try to imagine her at seventeen years old. "I want to see pictures of you when you were younger. You've seen some of mine."

"Sure."

She places her hand palm up on my leg, and I lace my fingers with hers. I sigh in relief. This is what makes sense. *We* make sense. I bring our clasped hands to my lips and kiss the back of hers. "This weekend is about having fun. At least tonight, anyway."

Olive glances at me from the corner of her eye. "It is. I've invited another person for dinner tomorrow night. I hope that's okay with you."

I twist in my seat to see her better. "Your brother?"

"I wish. I told my uncle Bruce how my trip went and

about you. He wants to meet you, so I asked him to come for dinner with Mom. I really want you to meet him. He helped me escape on my birthday."

"That's fine. Sounds good, actually. You've already met my family. Now it's my turn. Bring on the interrogations." I shake out my arms.

"I wish I could say there won't be any."

I notice her tense profile. "I don't have anything to hide, and nothing they say or do will scare me away."

"Good. I'm counting on that."

She asks about my family and little Smokey. I confess it was a hard goodbye. I hugged Mom the longest, thanking her for everything and for being supportive through my toughest times. It's not like I won't be going back. However, I think life will be very different when I return home.

The thought of living out of my suitcase for the next six weeks fills me with dread. I know I shouldn't complain —I'll be staying in five-star hotels, living like a king, surrounded by luxurious rooms, spas, and starred restaurants. But I'd rather be taking this trip with Olive. Exploring cities with her, showing her new places, and spoiling her with luxury would be amazing. *The time will come. Patience.*

The clicking of her turn signal grabs my attention.

"Here we are. It's not as beautiful as the hotel, but it's my home for now."

For now. That thrills me, knowing she doesn't plan to be here forever.

"Wherever you are is where I want to be. You're gonna have to pull me off you like a banana peel. *Eww.*" I cringe. "That was really bad."

She crinkles her nose. "Kind of. But I know what you

mean. I guess we have to do everything together, down to taking showers."

"I like the sound of that. Can we please go inside before I devour you in the parking lot?" That has her jumping out of the car like her ass is on fire.

Her apartment building is pretty standard. It could use a fresh coat of paint, but the grounds are well maintained. Reality hits me. I'm going to see how she lives. What if she's a messy person or a hoarder? What if she only has Twinkies in her refrigerator or stashes of canned kidney beans in the kitchen cabinets? Or has a collection of freaky porcelain dolls?

Chill the fuck out, Leo.

She's standing next to me, looking puzzled. "Does it look that bad?"

I dangle my arm over her shoulders. "Not at all. I'm trying to picture you living here. We aren't at the hotel anymore. This is real life now. I can't wait to see what makes you tick." I kiss her temple.

She pops the trunk, and we grab my stuff. Before I know it, we're in her living room. I scan the layout to see if anything looks different from the virtual tour she gave me the other day. With the sun shining through the windows, it feels warmer and more welcoming. Other than that, it looks the same. It's a spacious open-concept apartment. The kitchen, on the right, has a table and four chairs. A vase full of flowers on the counter adds color to the room. There's minimal clutter and not a doll in sight. The hallway on the left leads to the most important room. Her bedroom.

I put my things to the side and we take off our coats. Olive turns, and the atmosphere shifts. The need to touch her overwhelms me. I pull her into my arms.

"Show me your bedroom," I growl.

Her eyes glaze over with need. "Follow me."

Then she runs away, shaking her ass seductively, and I chase her like I always will.

34

———

LEO

I hold up a hand mirror, trying to see my reflection in the bathroom mirror behind me. The scratch marks on my back are blazing red. "Look at those babies," I say proudly.

Olive extends her hand to touch them, then hesitates. "Do they hurt?"

I check them out again. "A little bit. Don't worry about it."

She urges me to the side, then opens the cabinet under the sink and pulls out a plastic container overflowing with bandages, rubbing alcohol, cotton balls… You name it, it's in there. She sifts through and takes out a tube of Neosporin. "Let me put this on you."

I lay the mirror on the bathroom counter and talk to her reflection. "Olive, I'm fine. And why are you sorry? I loved it. You staking your claim on me, woman?"

"It's just… I've never done that before." She nibbles on the inside of her cheek, her face flushed. Her bashfulness is endearing. "I've only read about stuff like that in romance books. I didn't think it really happens."

"Olive"—I pull her into my arms—"I loved every second. My mission is to get to know you *inside* and *outside* the bedroom. I want to know everything you desire or fantasize about. Every. Little. Thing. Be open with me and show me what you like. And I'll do the same. Everything we've done so far makes me want to do it again, especially in front of the mirror." I kiss her neck.

She rests her chin on my chest and looks up at me. "I don't know what it is about you. When I'm with you, my inhibitions go out the window. My hormones rage nonstop. I love it, but I'm not usually vocal about it. And that mirror incident was a first and definitely a favorite of mine too." She teasingly bites my pec.

"Then let's put that on the list under *hell yes*."

She nudges me away and puts the container back under the sink. I get my suitcase and take it to her room. Something on the dresser catches my eye. I step closer to it as Olive joins me.

I point at the bottle with a grin. "That's my cologne."

She throws her arms up in surrender. "You caught me red-handed."

"Now, why would you have that?" I pick up the bottle and spray my neck with some.

Her eyes close when she inhales. "You know I love how you smell. I saw the name when I was in your bathroom."

I shake my head. "Sneaky. Good idea, though." I pull on a blue Henley and a pair of black sweats from my suitcase.

She opens the top drawer and pulls out a pair of black socks, then sits on the bed. "It was that or steal a T-shirt drenched in your cologne."

"You could've done that too. I'll leave something here before I go on Sunday."

She grabs my hand. "I'd rather you stay."

I bring her hand to my lips and kiss the top. "I'd love that, or you could come with me."

She falls back onto the bed. "In reality, I could, since I'm not working. But…no. You know I can't."

At that moment, my stomach roars like a lion. I haven't eaten since breakfast, and we've been busy since we arrived.

"Let's order something. Come with me." She gets up and leads me to the living room.

An hour later, with a full belly, I'm ready to fall asleep on the couch. Olive's in the kitchen making us coffee. Her phone buzzes on the coffee table. I pick it up and take it to her.

"Olive, your brother's video-calling you."

She puts the milk back into the refrigerator, then takes her phone and swipes the screen. "Hey, what's up?"

"Just checking on you and your *lover boy*. Making sure you're behaving," Andy teases.

She rolls her eyes and rests her elbows on the kitchen counter. "We're fine, weirdo. No complaints from the neighbors yet."

"Then you're doing something wrong."

I guffaw, and I show my face on the screen. "Hey, Andy. Nice to meet you." Is that his apartment in the background? Nice view of San Francisco.

"There's my man. My favorite soccer player's friend."

"*Andy*," Olive warns.

I rub her back to help her relax. "That's me."

"Are you coming to my Super Bowl party? I want to meet you. Olive needs my stamp of approval before she moves to that island."

"Shut up, Andy," Olive warns again. She looks at me hopefully and asks, "Does it work with your schedule?"

I nod with a grin. "Yes, I'll be there. If all goes well, I'll fly in on Saturday and leave on Monday. In and out. That's the best I can do." Olive claps her hands silently, then kisses my cheek.

"Awesome. Do you want to invite Sam too?"

"Andy!" Olive snaps. "Are you fucking crazy?" She glances at me. "You don't have to do that."

"And"—he continues as if Olive hasn't said a word—"if we're going to be one big happy family in the future, why don't you ask your sister and brother? The more the merrier."

He's hysterical. I like him already.

"Are you high or something?" Olive peers at her brother through the screen, then turns to me. "I apologize for my brother."

I rub the crease between her eyebrows until it relaxes. "Don't. I love this."

"See, Ol. He loves me already. But seriously, Leo, work it for me. You guys can stay here because I have a guest bedroom."

Olive leans away from the phone and frantically mouths, "No way!"

I wrap my arm around her waist and pull her into view again. "I'll do my best. Thanks for the invite."

Andy continues speaking while he styles his hair, using the video as a mirror.

"Focus on us, not your precious hair, Andy. Or hang up," Olive points out, obviously used to his behavior.

"I'm going out soon. Gotta look good." He's a trip. I can't tell if he's trying to be funny or is cocky. "My main reason for calling was to wish you luck tomorrow with Mom and Uncle Bruce. He'll be a good buffer. But, Leo, I think you'll hold your own." Someone calls his name in the background. "I gotta run. Call me on Sunday." The phone disconnects, and Olive deflates against me.

"Do you really think he's on something?" I ask, concerned.

She shakes her head, looking unfazed by him. "Nope. That's the way he is. You wouldn't recognize him at work, though. He's the complete opposite. Relentless competitor." She picks up our coffee cups and heads for the living room. I take mine from her and sit at the end of the couch.

"Don't worry about asking Sam to the party or Tonya and Sully. I can't believe he put you on the spot like that. I could kick his ass." She rests her back on the armrest and extends her legs toward me.

"The way he approached it makes me want to ask them." I can't stop grinning.

"What's putting that smile on your face?"

I place my hand on her leg and squeeze it. "This. You and me. The call with your brother. Making plans for the Super Bowl and our future. Why shouldn't I ask them? The worse they could do is say no."

"Or 'what the hell? We don't even know this guy,'" Olive says, thick with lighthearted sarcasm.

I put my cup down, take hers away too, then crawl over her and nuzzle her sexy neck. "Don't rain on my parade."

She caresses my face and holds my gaze. "I'd never do that. If you want to invite them, go for it. I'd love to see them again."

I slide off the couch and make some calls. Tonya is an instant yes. Sully will need convincing because of Smokey. Then we call Sam from my laptop. Talking to him is difficult because Ellie and Olive are chatting at the same time. Honestly, I didn't think Sam would have time, but he's all for it. Ellie is too. The call was chaotic, but I loved it anyway. This is the kind of shit I've been missing.

Olive sends Andy a message about Sam, then she plops next to me and gloats, "Andy's probably twitching in a corner right now. You are officially his new favorite person. I've been kicked to the curb."

I close my computer and pull her onto my lap, squeezing her perfect ass. "And you're officially mine."

"What do you want to do now? Stay in or go out?"

"Why don't we relax and watch a movie together…in one room this time?"

"Sure. It's your pick. I chose last time. Something funny." She slides off my lap and takes our empty coffee cups to the kitchen. She comes back with bottles of water and puts them on coasters.

"How about *Avengers: Endgame?*"

She puts her hand on her hip and looks down at me. "Seriously? Is that a funny movie?"

I place my hand over my heart in shock. "Are you telling me you haven't seen *Endgame?*" She shakes her head. "Any of the *Avenger* films?"

"Nope." She smirks with pride.

"You're killing me. I'm not sure we can continue this relationship."

She grabs a pillow and swats the side of my head. I grab the other one and do it to her. An all-out pillow war breaks out, and I learn she's vicious. "How dare you threaten our relationship," she yells between swings and our bouts of laughter.

"Come on, it's a rite of passage. You know who the Avengers are, right?" I duck before she can bop me again.

"What is it with you men?" she snarls, panting. "Of course I know the Avengers. Andy's a big Marvel fan. I may have been a hermit, but I have TV."

"I like him even more. I foresee a bromance in the future," I tease, then bop her one more time on the back. Her eyes dance with mischief, then she pushes me backward. I fall onto the couch, and she straddles my thighs.

With our arms around each other, we relax and catch our breaths.

She gives me a sweet kiss. "You make me feel like a kid again. I hope we always have this much fun together. Now that I feel this way, I won't be able to live without it. Without you."

"Well, that's good, because you're stuck with me."

I kiss her with sheer intensity to prove how in love I am with her.

Because that's exactly what this is. Love.

35

OLIVE

As you can probably imagine, we never watched that movie last night. Physical activities throughout the apartment proved more enticing. We're both insatiable. So much so, I insisted we leave the apartment for a late breakfast to give us a breather.

We leave my favorite bookstore with a small bag of books. Leo lifts it up. "I haven't bought a paperback in forever. I use my iPad for everything."

"Same here. I hate technology, but it's a modern world."

"I'm dying of hunger. Where are we eating brunch?" He drapes his arm over my shoulders.

I point to the large café next door. "They serve the best breakfast. I wish the bookstore and this place would knock down the connecting wall and make it one big venue. I'd bring my laptop here and work all day long."

Leo opens the door, then follows me inside. It's a busy Saturday, but fortunately we snag a table by the windows overlooking the street. A waitress hands us menus and takes our drink orders. When we're alone again, Leo and I hold hands above the table. He caresses my skin with his thumbs.

"Have you decided whether you'll quit your job?" he asks.

"I didn't tell you?" He shakes his head. "Yes. I already spoke to Uncle Bruce. He understood that I need time to work on myself and figure out what I really want to do."

"I hope you're considering the medical field again. Without you realizing it, you do subtle things that reflect your caring ways and enthusiasm."

I lean back and cross my arms. "What do you mean? Like what?"

"For example, the massive container you have of first-aid products under your sink. There's enough for the entire apartment building." The corner of her mouth lifts up. "You were eager to take care of the scratches on my back. Or how about when Ma got mustard in her eye. You were the first to offer to help and quickly told her what to do. And the other night when I opened up about Corey's cancer treatment, you talked about it like a medical professional, not some random person having a conversation. You were truly interested. These are little examples, but they add up. You deeply care about people and their wellbeing."

I'm quiet for a minute, digesting what he's said. "You're right, Leo. That is the way I am. And I do it without hesitation. But it's different from working in a hospital."

"I know, Olive. But promise you'll think about it."

I nod and break eye contact.

The waitress comes back with two cappuccinos and two glasses of freshly squeezed orange juice. I'm glad to let the topic drop as we order pancakes, scrambled eggs, bacon, and bagels to share to hold us over until dinner tonight.

"Hey, I didn't show you the video of the day yet." Leo pulls his phone out of his pocket. He loads something, then hands it to me. I hit play.

"Oh, my gosh. Where was this? A jungle?" The volume is on low, but I hear someone talking. It's not Leo. "Is that Corey?"

"This is from Corey's headset camera. We were in Costa Rica. It's probably my favorite place I've traveled. What you see in the video is Corcovado National Park. We were ziplining over the rainforest. It was incredible."

My heart sings as Leo describes the experience with animated gestures. Corey's riding above the trees. Then he looks down, and my stomach bottoms out.

"Guess he wasn't afraid of heights, huh?" I say, full of jealousy.

He spins the black ring around his middle finger. "Not really. I was when we did that, but it was such an adrenaline rush. Totally worth it."

"Did you guys ever bungee-jump or go skydiving?"

His glow dims a little. If someone didn't know him, they probably wouldn't have noticed. But I did. "Bungee-jumped. Skydiving was next on the list. Then he got sick, and we never got the chance. After that, I didn't want to anymore."

I'm going to change that. Somehow, somewhere, I'm going to make him jump. And I'll be right there with him…even if it kills me.

Our food comes, and we question how hungry we are because the table is almost too small for our several dishes. We're in our own little bubble, feeling like we're the only ones in the café. I love doing normal couple things with him. This weekend was beautifully unexpected.

"Olive?" Someone calls my name. I turn and am

surprised to see my friend, Dawn. Beside her is her husband, carrying their sleeping daughter.

I usually run the other direction when I see old friends, but this time I'm happy to see them. I jump up. "Oh my gosh, Dawn. Kain." I give her a hug. "How are you doing?"

"We're great. But how about you? You look amazing."

I press my hands to my warm cheeks. "Thank you." Dawn's eyes dart to Leo. Leo stands and comes to my side. "This is my boyfriend, Leo."

That's the first time I told someone he's my boyfriend… I couldn't be more proud.

He shakes their hands, and we make small talk. I haven't spoken to them this much in nearly a year. I'm not avoiding conversation this time.

Before they leave, Dawn leans close and says, "Keep up whatever you're doing. You look happy again. Don't be a stranger anymore. We miss you." That warms my heart and also breaks it.

We say goodbye, then drop into our seats. "That was unexpected," I say. "She's a high school friend. She tried to help me when I returned from LA, but I pushed her away. Like everyone else, she eventually gave up. I don't blame her."

"She was thrilled to see you. That's a true friend."

Tears threaten to spill over. "Leo, who am I? I was a stranger to myself, avoiding everyone I knew because I was miserable and embarrassed. I'm so ashamed—I treated people like Dawn horribly. But now, I'm a new person. Not completely healed, but I'm getting there." I dab beneath my eye with a napkin. "Am I making any sense?"

Leo slides his chair closer to me. "Perfectly."

I take a few cleansing breaths, but my thoughts remain tangled. My food is an afterthought. "The number of changes that I've had since my birthday is hitting me like a tidal wave."

He strokes my hair. "Olive, talk to me. Do you want to leave?"

I put my hands on the table and take a deep breath. "No. Give me a sec. I need to let everything sink in. Please don't worry. It's nothing bad. I'm sorry for acting weird."

I'm happy, healthy, and have an amazing boyfriend. I'm extremely grateful and lucky to have gotten a second chance to live again.

"Don't apologize for your emotions. Everyone deserves a chance at happiness regardless of their past. I believe that now," he murmurs as he tenderly holds the nape of my neck and draws me closer. Rubbing his nose against mine, he adds, "And you, Olive, are the reason I do."

If someone asked me now if I've ever been in love, I'd say yes. I am.

36

LEO

"Hey, girlfriend. Did you finish chopping the garlic? I need to add some to the tomato sauce." I peek over Olive's shoulder to check her progress, then brush her hair aside and kiss her neck instead. I can't get enough.

"Hey! Stop that before I cut off a finger," she says over her shoulder. "Would you still want me with only nine garlicky fingers?" I can hear the way her mouth lifts in the corner.

"Like I've told you a thousand times, I'll take you anyway I can, stinky and all." I steal a kiss, then resume my work at the stove.

I woke up this morning with Olive lying on me like a blanket, and I enjoyed every second. She's not a figment of my imagination or some woman I met last night. I've had my share of women over the years. Every encounter was to get off and leave right after. Sex and nothing more.

How different sex is when it's mixed with attraction, affection, and love for the other person! The connection Olive and I have is life-altering. What if she hadn't shown up under my tree...*our* tree...on her birthday? Would fate have found another way to push us together? The thought of going back to my mediocre life makes me break out in a sweat.

"Let's finish this up and let it simmer for a while," I suggest. She slides the cutting board over to me and I toss half the garlic into the pot. The rest is for the mushrooms. I turn the heat down.

We're making stuffed mushrooms for the appetizer and chicken parmesan for dinner. And for dessert, chocolate cake. Olive says it's Evelyn's favorite meal. I convinced her to let me make the sauce, and she's doing the rest.

"I'm going to scrub my hands in the bathroom to get the garlic smell off my fingers." She pecks me on the lips and jumps out of the way before I can smack her butt. I wipe down the counters and put dishes in the dishwasher. How domestic.

We went grocery shopping after brunch, and I noticed some differences between us. She's more frugal than I am and loves coupons. She hates peas, and I could eat them every day. I'm a Cap'n Crunch fan, and she'd rather have granola. I could devour a jar of Nutella, but the thought of it makes her sick. I told her she needs to try European Nutella. It tastes so much better. And yes, there is a difference. To me anyway.

I enjoy seeing her in her own element, like she's seen me at the hotel. I don't really have an established "element," but the hotel is pretty close. It's how I spend my time when I'm not traveling, anyway.

Olive comes back, wiggling her fingers. "I can still smell it, but it's almost gone."

I reach out and lead her to the couch. "Come sit with me. Let's look at our calendars." I open mine on my phone and click on the date of Corey's memorial. "What are you doing the first weekend of March?"

She scrolls her calendar. "As of now, nothing, because I haven't looked that far ahead. Why?"

"Corey's memorial is that weekend. March second. I'd like you to come."

"Really? It's a family affair, and I haven't met Corey's family. And—"

I press my finger to her lips. "Olive, you're part of the family now. Please come. They already know that I was going to ask you."

She considers with a smile. "Then, yes. I'd love to."

We square away the details for that weekend. I'll finish my assignment the weekend before the memorial. Olive will come out the Monday after and spend a week with me. We also discussed Super Bowl weekend. Since she doesn't want to stay at Andy's place when I'm there for obvious reasons, I told her I'd pick the hotel and surprise her. And she insists on picking me up when I arrive. No argument there. After a month apart, I want to see her face when I walk out of the airport.

They should be here any minute. I've been calm most of the day, but something has triggered my nerves. Now I can't stop fidgeting. Currently, my fingers are picking at my jeans.

Olive grabs my hand. "If you don't stop, you're going to wear a hole in your pants before they even get here. There's no need to be nervous. They're going to love you."

"What if—"

She cuts me off, wagging her finger. "Nope. It doesn't matter if they like you, anyway. What matters is that *I* do. More every second that passes. They can have an opinion, but it doesn't mean I'll agree with them. Hopefully any negative ones will stay in their heads and not come out of their mouths."

She wraps her arms around my neck and gives me a long, all-consuming kiss, convincing me that everything will be fine. That's shot to shit when the doorbell rings. Meeting new people has never been a problem for me. Until now.

"Let the games begin," she says, grinning as she goes to the door. I follow and open it for her. "Hi! Come in." Olive hugs her mom first and then her uncle.

"Mom, Uncle Bruce, this is Leo," she says with enthusiasm. Her mom gives me a once-over, focusing on my hair mostly. Not a long-hair fan? Her hands are clasped in front of her, giving me a closed-off vibe.

"Nice to meet you, Mrs. Hansen," I greet her as friendly as possible.

"It's nice to meet you, Leo. Thank you for entertaining my Olive, while she was gone. And please call me Evelyn." *My Olive? Entertaining?*

There's no chance to respond because Olive's big, jovial uncle jams himself between Evelyn and me. "Nice to meet you, Leo. Glad I could make it tonight. Call me Bruce." He shakes my hand and firmly squeezes my shoulder. "It smells delicious in here. I heard we're having chicken parm. Can't wait."

I whisper to Olive, "By any chance does Andy take after your uncle?"

The corner of her mouth tilts up. "That obvious, huh? You should've met my dad. He was definitely the life of the party."

I observe their interactions and watch Evelyn the most. Olive looks a lot like her. Similar height, same dark features, thick hair. Olive's eye color is unique. I remember her saying she has her dad's eyes. They are beautiful women.

Evelyn looks friendly enough, but is it fake? I know things have gotten slightly better since Olive returned, but I can't imagine her being all that welcoming to me. Call me insecure, I guess.

"I brought some champagne, and it's cold. I thought we could celebrate Olive's thirtieth birthday tonight, since we missed out." Evelyn takes the bottle out of a bag and hands it to Olive. Was that a jab at Olive? She doesn't seem to notice.

"Let's pop that baby open," Bruce says, rubbing his hands together. He'll definitely be the buffer tonight.

Olive takes the bottle to the kitchen, and I follow. She opens a cabinet and reaches up as far as she can, lifting her shirt, revealing her creamy, soft skin. I skim the soft patch with my hand. "I'll get them for you." I grab four flutes and place them on the counter near the bottle.

"Thanks," she says, brushing her lips against mine.

"Can I help with anything?" Evelyn interrupts us, her voice louder than necessary. We both jump.

"Sure, Mom," Olive answers, not bothered by it. She hands her mother two of the flutes. "Put these on the kitchen table. We'll bring the rest." She gives me the other two and the bottle. "I'll be there in a sec. I need to check the mushrooms."

"Come chat with us, Leo," Evelyn urges, then turns away.

I glance at Olive, and she shoos me away with her hands.

"They don't bite."

I'm not sure about that. I follow Evelyn and put the flutes and the bottle on the table. I look at the brand of champagne. At least she has great taste. Brownie point for her. I open the bottle and pour equal amounts. Olive arrives shortly after and takes a glass of the bubbly. Bruce jumps in and makes a hilarious toast, which convinces me he's harmless.

Evelyn stretches her arms out to hug Olive, but Olive hugs and kisses me first. Evelyn's cheerful expression fades, and when she glances at me, her eyes turn cold. It suddenly clicks. I'm a threat to her. What kind, I don't know. When Olive turns to hug her, the smile that returns to Evelyn's face looks forced. Of course, Bruce gets a hug too, and he lifts her off the ground.

When the mushrooms are ready, we sit in the living room, chatting and munching. Thankfully, the focus isn't on me yet. I sip my drink and observe some more. I notice how Evelyn watches my hand on Olive's thigh. Her expressions are hard to read. It's like looking into a kaleidoscope, something new revealed with every movement.

Because Bruce didn't know everything, Olive and I recap how we met, how my family owns the hotel, how my mom's a widower too, and how much Olive loves the island and the hotel. Evelyn has heard some of it already, so she stays quiet, but I can't forget she's told Olive more than once that she doesn't like the island. And I hate that I'm on the defensive. Everyone has the right to their own opinion.

"Mom, I forgot to show you these pictures," Olive blurts out, pulling me from my thoughts. She hands Evelyn the phone, and points at Sam. Bruce leans over to see too.

He snaps his fingers. "That's… What's his name? Oh, Samuel Moore…the soccer player," he acknowledges, addressing Olive. "Weren't you and Andy obsessed with him?"

"Yep," Olive says. "And there he was at the New Year's Eve party I almost didn't go to." She threads her arm through mine. "Leo, however, was more than convincing, and I gave in. What a night that was. No regrets there."

Evelyn leans over, props her arms on her knees, and clasps her hands. "Leo, it sounds like you pressured Olive into doing things she didn't want to do."

I pull my head back. "Come again?" Oops. A little attitude snuck out there.

Bruce coughs on a piece of mushroom, and Olive snaps, "Mom! He didn't force me to do anything. Give me a break. It was a party."

Evelyn's calm persona changes, and she throws up her hands. "Jeez. Sorry. I didn't know it's a sensitive subject."

The real Evelyn has arrived.

"Leo, tell us about your job. I heard you travel a lot," Bruce says, obviously trying to cut the tension. Olive squeezes my knee.

I explain what my job entails and where I'll be going. They begin questioning me about where I've been and what nightmares I've seen.

"Ugh. I've found things like half-eaten food in the minibar, used condoms under the bed, and something on the floor that looked like fresh blood. The hotel denied it, of course. Let me put it this way—just because a hotel has a five-star rating, doesn't necessarily mean it's the best quality."

"That's disgusting," Olive says, and the others nod in agreement.

"And have you reviewed your family's hotel?" Evelyn asks, shoveling a mushroom into her mouth. "Find anything that would keep us away? Is the hotel a two-star or three?"

Don't take the bait.

"It's a four-star hotel, actually. Because I know what to look for, probably better than most, I ensure the hotel is in order whenever I'm there. No hotel is perfect, but we're proud of the quality we provide for our guests."

"I couldn't complain about one thing during my visit. Other than the reservation system, but I lucked out in that situation." Olive grins, nudging me in the side.

"*Pfft.* Don't rub it in." I tap my elbow against hers. "Anyway, Evelyn, you should come stay for a couple of days and check it out for yourself."

"I don't know about Evelyn, but I sure will," Bruce interjects. "Do you have space for business meetings? I was thinking about doing an off-site team building event this year."

Evelyn gives her brother in-law the evil eye. "You can't be serious, Bruce."

"There's plenty of space, Uncle Bruce. Leo's sister is the event manager," Olive says through gritted teeth. At least I'm not the only one noticing Evelyn's negativity and rudeness.

"As Olive said, we do have the space. This year we want to focus on the hotel being more than a party venue. We hope to pull in more business for corporate meetings, training… Things like that. Let's try to chat later."

The timer for the chicken parm goes off, and I jump at the chance to help in the kitchen. I need a breather. Evelyn and Bruce make it over to the kitchen table and sit. Olive and I bring the feast over, interrupting the quiet bickering between Evelyn and Bruce. My mental eye-rolling is going to give me a migraine.

We open a bottle of wine and give Bruce a beer. I wouldn't mind one of Tonya's strong martinis right now. A pleasant peace fills the room while we enjoy the meal. Evelyn compliments Olive on her cooking.

"Leo helped. He made the sauce from scratch. It's delicious. I'll probably use his recipe from now on." She holds my hand up and kisses the back of it.

"It's delicious, Leo," Evelyn says dryly, her eyes focusing on Olive's hand entwined with mine.

"Thanks. My mom's recipe. She's a great cook," I respond.

"Yeah, she makes a mean pot roast too." Olive grins, then adds hastily, "Not as good as yours, though, Mom."

"And what are your plans tomorrow?" Evelyn asks us, abruptly changing the subject again.

"I'm driving him to the airport. He has an early flight," Olive says, then turns to me. "We need to make the most of our time tonight."

"I don't care what we do or how late we stay up. I can sleep on the flight."

"Do you think you'll stay in touch after this?" Evelyn asks. Bruce shakes his head, keeping his eyes down.

Evelyn's poking the bear. But you know what? I've got this.

37

OLIVE

Damn! What the hell has gotten into Mom tonight? What happened to being more open and understanding?

I haven't told her everything about my trip—she didn't ask for many details—but I'm pretty sure I made my feelings for Leo clear. Either she ignored me or she's in denial. This has to be about her fear of being left alone.

I've been trying to stay calm and ignore her little jabs here and there, but my patience is running thin. Leo's taking everything in stride. I wish I could read his mind. Uncle Bruce is joking around more than usual to lighten the mood. I'm so glad he's here. Leo's mom wasn't the warmest in the beginning, but she didn't manipulate her words to cause problems. Mom wants to know if we'll stay in contact? I open my mouth to respond with something that'll probably piss her off, but Leo beats me to it.

"I think the answer is obvious, don't you?" He looks at me with adoration. "Not a day will go by without us talking. It'll be difficult being apart, but we have our weekend in San Francisco to look forward to. And it gives us a chance to get to know each other without other things getting in the way."

Like you, Mom.

"Mmm hmm. And after that? You'll see each other every couple of months? How would that work while you're off having your fun?"

Oh, for all that is good and holy! I'm about to scream, but Leo keeps his calm and answers perfectly.

"What I failed to tell you is that this is my last assignment. I've been offered the manager position at the hotel. If I accept, and I most likely will, I'll start April first. If all goes according to plan, Olive and I will be able to see each other more frequently, and then we'll take it from there."

"And how does your family feel about that? How you're rushing into this?"

"Mom!" I snap, exasperated at this point. "Would you stop?"

Uncle Bruce huffs. "You mean like how you rushed into things with Pierce, Evelyn? Should I remind you of how you two talked about each other when you first met? Actually, this"—he points at us—"looks more than a little familiar."

Mom's mouth opens and closes like a fish out of water. I want to thank Uncle Bruce, but I don't get the chance.

"My mom and dad were supposedly like that too when they met on their blind date," Leo continues smoothly with a sweet grin. "Oh, and my family loves Olive. She hit it off with my brother and sister. Not only did I help Olive, she's helping me break through my own barriers. I'm a better person because of her, and my mom noticed right away. She wants me to be happy, the same way you want Olive to be."

Take that, Mom. I swear I could ravage him right now. I love him so much.

"Yes, well, I don't want to see her hurt a few months down the road." Mom's voice is oddly defensive.

Leo pulls me closer to him. "I can promise you this, Evelyn, Olive isn't getting rid of me. We're in it for the long haul."

I melt like an ice cube in the Sahara Desert and kiss his cheek. "You're not getting rid of me either."

My gaze shifts back to Mom. There's a flicker of emotion in her eyes—sadness…or anger maybe? I stare her down until she looks away. What is her game?

"What's for dessert?" Bruce intervenes abruptly, standing with his dirty dishes.

I need to send him a bottle of his favorite whiskey. Or maybe a case.

Mom's quiet while she picks at her piece of chocolate cake. Uncle Bruce takes over the conversation, telling us he's never been married and has no desire to be. *Maybe I should introduce him to Marla.* Then he chats with Leo about the different countries they've both visited. At least they're getting along, and Bruce is giving him a chance.

Mom stands from her chair. "It's getting late. I know you two would like to be alone. Bruce, why don't we head out?"

Bruce and I check our watches. It's only nine. Well, if she wants to leave, that's her prerogative. I'd rather be alone with Leo than stuck in this tense environment. Bruce gets up and follows Mom to the coats.

"Wait, don't forget your leftovers," I say, rushing to the fridge. "Let me wrap up some cake too."

"Not for me, dear. Keep everything for yourself."

I frown. "But you love chicken parm and this cake."

"I know." She pats her belly, then looks at mine. My jaw drops to the floor. "We need to watch our waistlines. No need for extra curves."

"Life's too short for that shit," Bruce quips, patting his round belly with pride. "Give me her leftovers."

Leo wraps his arms around me from behind. "I happen to love Olive's curves." I lean against him and pat his hands.

I catch Bruce scowling at Mom. If looks could kill. Leo drops his arms, and I hand the leftovers to Uncle Bruce.

I look at Leo. "I'm going to walk them out."

He kisses me on the forehead. "Good luck."

Uncle Bruce shakes Leo's hand. "It was great meeting you. Have a safe trip," he says sincerely.

Mom stands in the open doorway, showing no effort to shake Leo's hand or give him a friendly hug goodbye. "Have a safe trip, Leo." She slips out the door before Leo can respond.

Bruce glances at Leo. "I'm sorry. I don't know what has gotten into her. I tried."

Leo waves a dismissive hand. "No worries. She's being a protective mom."

I scoff, then follow Uncle Bruce out. When we get to the car, he gets in immediately. I face off with my mother. "Mom, what was that in there? You were downright rude and embarrassing."

"I'm trying to prevent you from making stupid mistakes. You met him a few weeks ago, and you act like you're getting married."

"What did you tell me the other day? You said you were going to be more supportive and happy for me. Insinuating that I need to diet isn't supportive, especially in front of Leo. That was humiliating and hurtful. Are you deliberately trying to sabotage my relationship with him?"

Since she treats me like a clueless teenager, I'm waiting for her to forbid me from seeing him again.

"I did what I had to do. He's not good enough for you.

You think he doesn't have a woman waiting for him at every hotel? He probably feeds them the same lines he does you."

"I—" I gasp and take a step back. It takes everything in my power not to show weakness or slap her across the face. "You have gone too far. Dad would be disappointed in you."

"Well, he's not here, is he?" She opens the car door and gets in, slamming it shut.

I'm so stunned, I don't even remember going back to the apartment. When I walk through the door, Leo takes one look at me and his face darkens with rage. "What the hell did she say to you?"

His unfamiliar protective tone triggers me, and I lose my composure. He leads me to the couch and pulls me into his arms, and I break down sobbing. Once I have no tears left, I tell him what happened.

"She's lucky she didn't say those things in front of me. It was tough staying calm the entire evening, but that would've tipped me over the edge," he says, kissing my temple. "I can't stand seeing you cry. Especially when you've done nothing wrong." His tone is firm, but his touch his gentle.

"You didn't deserve how she treated you either. I'm sorry. She's terrified of being left alone and she'd rather me be miserable than with someone who makes me happy. I've never seen her act so ruthless and cruel."

He palms my cheek. "Nothing will ever change my feelings for you. You understand that, right? Nothing. We don't have to defend our relationship to anyone."

"I know."

I wish it were that simple.

38

OLIVE

I rest my chin on my hand as I stir my first coffee of the day and revel in the early morning silence. The Golden Gate Bridge is in clear view through Andy's ceiling-to-floor apartment windows. His career is obviously booming more than he lets on. I can't imagine what this place must cost. And to top it off, it's spotless. Andy isn't known for his tidiness.

These past four weeks have been one big therapy session for me. If I wasn't baring my soul to my therapist or Leo, especially about Mom, I was either at the gym, in a yoga class (without puppies), or wondering what to do with my life. Puppy yoga was fun in the beginning, but I was peed on one too many times. I was surprised to find out that I like yoga in general. I'm becoming quite flexible… something I can't wait to show Leo. *Wink. Wink.*

I've also lost some weight. It's a subtle change. Let's see if he notices when I pick him up at the airport. I haven't mentioned it during our calls.

As Leo promised when I dropped him off at the airport, we have spoken every single day. We've shared our hopes, dreams, fantasies, favorite memories, and biggest fears. He still sends me old video clips of him or Corey and a new song every day too. Sometimes it's a video of the hotel he's staying at in whatever country at the time. My favorite was a short video of him eating a lemon tart with a cappuccino at his favorite café in Paris. The one he modeled Café Charmont after. I would've done anything to be there with him.

All these photos and video clips have made me feel like I practically grew up alongside Leo and Corey. I've seen how they changed over time and what they experienced. I'll always cherish this because, even though I'll never meet Corey, I feel like I know him at least a little now.

My relationship with Mom is still very strained. My therapist says she's grieving and afraid of being alone. I didn't need to pay anyone to tell me that. I already knew. It's not fair that Leo and I get the brunt of her pain. I'm glad she hasn't seen him again. I don't even talk about him with her. Last thing I said to her last week was to go to therapy. I haven't heard from her since.

The thing I'm most proud of is that I went to LA before I came to Andy's. With encouragement from my therapist, I finally felt it was time. It's the one step I needed to be ready for a future with Leo. He doesn't know I went. I'm going to tell him tonight.

I didn't know what to expect when I landed in LA. A couple of days before the trip, I sent a message to my old boss and mentor, Adele, asking if we could meet. Her response came back saying, "YES!" That made it easier to get on the plane.

We met in a park near the hospital that we frequented during our breaks. As soon as I saw her, I fell apart. We hugged each other like vices, then sat down under a tree.

My sadness, anger, and mostly guilt came out full force. I'll always remember what she said.

"Working in the medical field is challenging from day one. We hold people's lives in our hands. When someone who's in your care dies, the guilt hits you like a ton of bricks. You ask yourself nonstop what you could've done better or how could you have missed that diagnosis even when it wasn't your fault…" She shakes her head, and I know she understands.

"Does the guilt ever stop? I mean, I know it was the pandemic, but I got up and left all those suffering patients. I let my colleagues down. How do I forgive myself for that?"

"Everyone's different. Some people can turn off their emotions and not think twice about it. You and I aren't like that. And you were too young to experience death all around you. None of us had ever dealt with anything like it, even those with the longest careers. It was a very trying time. And you aren't the only medical professional who quit."

"How did you handle it?"

"Well, if you'd returned my calls, you'd know that I quit as soon as things settled down," she responds with her typical sass.

My eyes bug out, and my breath hitches. "What?"

"Yes. Me." She points at herself. "I quit."

"But you're much stronger than me, than a lot of our coworkers were."

"Maybe, but everyone has a breaking point. I almost left California altogether. I ended up staying to fight the guilt and find another way I could use my medical experience, but it wasn't easy."

"You're still working in the field?"

"I'm working at a small pharmaceutical company in their drug development area. I'm still a registered nurse, but I use my knowledge on clinical trials.

"Olive, you were an exceptional nurse with so much promise. Don't throw it away. Use your experience and find something that could fulfill you in other ways. It doesn't have to be in a hospital.

You'd be surprised how many options are out there. It's not too late. Let go of the guilt and move on before you end up old and crotchety like me."

When we said goodbye, I felt better than I had in years. Then I had the guts to go to the hospital where I worked. I wasn't strong enough to go inside, though. I rode the same bus I took from the hospital to where I used to live. My old apartment building looked unchanged, like nothing had happened, proving to me again that life goes on. Time may not heal all wounds, but it helps lessen the pain. I went to other places that I frequented too. The local grocery store that had my favorite smoothie, the hotdog stand I visited a couple times a week, and my nursing school campus. With my eyes closed, I searched through my memories and focused on the good times at each place.

When I finished in LA, I rented a car and drove to San Francisco. I left that city in a gorgeous Audi, feeling refreshed and excited to move on. Finally ready to be the new me. I can't wait to show Leo who I am now when I see him today.

Leo thinks we're going to the hotel after I pick him up at the airport. We will, but I have a special surprise for him first. I hope he'll be as excited as I am. As well as the others who'll be meeting us there.

He wasn't able to do it with Corey, but maybe he'll want to do it with me.

39

LEO

That last damn flight was excruciatingly long. Not to mention the whole last month. Every day, every hotel I was at, I wished Olive were with me. I was in gorgeous hotels, but I had no one to share them with. And for the first time, I couldn't stand it.

I did use the time wisely though. I needed the time alone to get myself to where I am now. I went through every single video and picture that was on the hard drive. To see Corey healthy, happy, dancing, goofing off, and being his crazy self…it ripped my heart out like he died all over again. Over time, I've realized I'm no longer the person in those videos and pictures. And I'm okay with that. It's time to start the next chapter in my life—with Olive by my side.

Ellie's texted me several times while I was away. Since she saw me dancing, she's tried to talk to me about it, knowing that I wasn't telling her something. One day, I called her and explained everything. That was also therapeutic, and it strengthened our friendship.

I zigzag around the other travelers, following the exit

signs quicker than most. The finish line is so close, I can almost touch it. People holding up signs with names come into view. I scan the crowd and spot Olive waving wildly. I swoop her up into my arms and squeeze her tightly. She's my home.

Gently, I lower her, then cradle her face. Her eyes shimmer from unshed tears. "I promise I won't leave you that long again," I mutter against her perfect, most delicious lips. I want to tell her I love her. It's pretty obvious. Right? But I'll hold off a bit longer. Reuniting like this is a significant moment, but I want something more monumental.

"I've missed you and your gorgeous face so much." Not sure how she managed to get all that out between my constant kisses.

Finally, I put space between us and reach for her hand. "Let's get out of here. I want you all to myself."

She rests her hand on my chest. "Slow down. I have a surprise for you." I push out my lower lip, and she pokes it. "No pouting. I promise we won't leave the hotel room until tomorrow…after your surprise."

I steal one more kiss. "Okay, beautiful. Wherever you go, I'll follow."

"We'll see if you'll still say that after your surprise." She pretends to bite her nails.

I tilt my head. "Now I'm really curious."

She winks and leads me to her car. My pulse kicks up when we approach the sleek, glossy black Audi she just unlocked. "That's what I call a fine piece of machinery. Whose car is this? Andy's?"

"Nope. I thought I'd splurge a little and rented it. It's easier and more flexible since we'll be going to the hotel, anyway."

I open the passenger side door and my mouth waters.

"Can I get turned on by a woman who drives a stick shift?" I learn something new about her every day.

"My dad taught me when I got my driver's license. Wait until you actually see me do it. And don't worry, that's not the only stick I'll play with today." She blows me a kiss.

I growl and sit in the car. "You're playing with fire." The engine roars to life, its powerful vibrations sending a shiver through the metal frame.

"I know," she murmurs, drawing closer. I passionately press my mouth against hers. The softness of her lips mixing with her signature scent sends a rush of warmth and desire through my body, making my heart thunder. Her eyes twinkle as she pulls away. "Okay, that's all you're getting, so you better calm down that party in your pants."

I guffaw and readjust myself. "Who are you? This month apart was good for you. And the time you spent at the gym is noticeable. Me likey." How the hell am I supposed to wait when she teases me like this? "You sure we can't go straight to the hotel?" I give her my best impression of puppy dog eyes.

She scratches under my chin. "Aww, sweet doggie. We're on a strict schedule, so no." Then she puts the car in gear and takes off, propelling my head back against the headrest. I can't help the crazed cackle that escapes me. This is awesome. I wonder if I could drive it too.

Music drifts through the speakers and I recognize it as a song I sent her, "I'm Gonna Be" by The Proclaimers.

"Is this the playlist you made of all the songs I sent you?"

She glances at me from the corner of her eye and nods. "It's on top of the list. I think my all-time favorite is "Someone Like You." And it's the version from a movie I love."

"Mine too. The lyrics reflect how I was feeling while a

thousand miles away." I massage the back of her neck. "I'll sing it to you one day with my own twist on it. How does that sound?" *At our wedding.*

"Perfect. But not now because I need to focus on driving."

I practiced singing when I was in the hotel rooms and showers. Lyrics flew out of me like I'd never stopped. My desire to sing and dance is overwhelming, but I don't know how to use these talents anymore.

As she concentrates on the road, I soak in her features like I'm seeing them the first time. Her glossy lips curve into a radiant smile, almost glowing. The wind from the open windows tosses her thick hair around like she's in a photoshoot. Her shoulders are relaxed, and she maneuvers the car like a professional. She exudes confidence, and I absolutely love it.

I break my gaze, noticing we're out of the city. What does she have up her sleeve? I'll play along with it because I love surprises. Plus, I'm kind of at her mercy here.

"I haven't heard from Tonya. Is her flight on time?" I ask, looking at my phone. Sully declined to come this weekend.

"Yep. Everything's going according to plan."

"I talked to Ellie and Sam. They arrived yesterday. I'm not sure what they're doing today." I glance at Olive and notice a smirk on her face, hinting at the secret she holds, perhaps more.

The GPS says we're two miles away. I see a small plane take off in the distance. As the destination gets closer on the screen, I notice a road sign up ahead. The word *skydiving* catches my attention. Olive puts on the left signal and turns into the parking lot.

No fucking way!

A tornado of emotions swirls around me as I stare out

the window. Corey and I were supposed to do this together. We'd even made reservations to go skydiving over the Grand Canyon. And then he got sick. I found the receipt in a box that was stored at Aunt Betty's house.

I think about the letter Corey wrote me, and my sadness turns to excitement. It's time to do this. My heart expands when I see anticipation, not fear, in her sparkling eyes and wide grin.

"What do you think? Want to jump with me?"

Without hesitation, I say, "Fuck yes," and scramble out of the car. "Let's go."

We grab our things and rush to the entrance. I skid to a stop when a group of familiar people start screaming my name and waving. Tonya, Ellie, Sam, Andy, and Sully approach us. *Sully* came? Everyone has skydiving gear on except Ellie. I'm not surprised because she's deathly afraid of heights.

"Surprise," they exclaim.

I have no chance to respond or breathe because there's constant chatter and hugging all around. Andy shakes my hand and mentions we'll talk later.

Once it quiets down, I ask, "What are we celebrating? It's not my birthday."

Olive wraps her arm around mine. "I told everyone that you were supposed to go skydiving with Corey but didn't get the chance. This year is about change and new beginnings. Why not do something crazy with the people who care about you most?"

"Let's do it for Corey!" Tonya shouts. Everyone agrees and follows her to the counter so Olive and I can check in. I have no chance to be alone with Olive because everything is set in motion. We're given our gear to wear and then thrown into training with our instructors for tandem skydiving.

Only two tandem pairs can go per plane. Since Andy and Sam are ecstatic, like teenagers eager for the front row on a rollercoaster, we agree they should go first. Tonya and Sully are next, then Olive and I will follow. Ellie will take pictures at the landing area.

Finally, as everyone waits to board their planes, I get the chance to hug Olive. "Did I ever tell you how amazing you are?"

"I think so, but you can tell me again," she jokes, gripping my jumpsuit.

"You, Olive, are *amazing*. Thank you. I can't express how much this means to me. Especially because you're afraid of heights. Are you sure you want to do this?"

"Absolutely. One more fear to face this year. You deserve nothing but the best. We all do." She pats my ass. "You look hot in this outfit, by the way."

I can't respond because we're ushered to our plane. As we take off and gain altitude, my skin prickles with spiking anxiety. Fear grips me like a vise, twisting my stomach into knots. I'm about to jump out of a fucking airplane and hope to God the parachute works. I've bungee-jumped and ziplined from high altitudes, and I've flown in hundreds of planes without a problem. Skydiving apparently tops the adrenaline junkie in me.

Olive will follow me after I jump. I feel slaphappy from the rush blasting through my body. I look back at her, and she yells something. I can't hear it, but I read her lips, "For Corey."

"For Corey," I yell back, punching the air as the plane door opens. *Fuck.*

My instructor and I shuffle toward the edge. Wind and frigid air whip me in the face and rattle my jumpsuit. *This is it. There's no going back.* With one last nudge, we fall out of the plane, and gravity's claws dig in, yanking us down instantly.

I whoop with elation until I can't breathe anymore. The powerful wind screams in my ears, celebrating with me. My cheeks flap in the wind as we plummet faster toward the beautiful landscape of the California coastline. Every ounce of bottled-up fear, pain, and grief flows freely from my fingertips and toes.

And Corey's laugh surrounds me as if he were right next to me.

The parachute deploys, jolting us out of the steep dive. The harsh wind subsides to a steady whisper as we glide through the clear blue sky. My heart rate slows, and the surge of intensity ebbs away, leaving my body wrapped in peace and tranquility. This experience was fucking out of this world.

I savor every second of the descent, watching the landscape below become clearer as my friends and family await. When my feet touch the ground, a wave of accomplishment and relief floods over me.

I fucking did it!

Once I'm stable and detached from my instructor, everyone crowds around, saying how incredible it was. Especially Sully, which shocks me. Tonya says she wants to do it again. I always knew she had a wild side.

"Here comes Olive," Andy says. Everyone turns around to watch her land.

With an unspoken agreement, the group stays back as I hurry toward her. The distance between us feels like miles. This is the moment. When I finally reach her and swoop her into my arms, I proclaim, "I love you."

40

OLIVE

When I land, I can't get my parachute off fast enough. That was the most exhilarating experience of my life. As I glided through the open sky, every negative thought and memory vanished from my body and mind. I feel liberated and excited about the new life that's waiting for me.

Leo marches toward me and I meet him halfway. Before I can say anything, he grabs me in a hug and whispers in my ear, "I love you."

"I love you too," I say. "So much."

My instructor taps me on the shoulder while we're hugging, telling us we need to leave. I thank him for everything, and Leo urges me along.

"Are we done here yet? I really need you naked." He doesn't care who hears him.

"You read my mind, but I'm way ahead of you. The gang knows that we're going straight to the hotel and won't see them until tomorrow." I feel bad leaving them, but they were cool about it when I explained everything to them. "Now tell me which hotel we're staying in."

~

I couldn't tell you what the hotel lobby looked like or what our room number was. Leo and I had one mission, and that was to get to our room as fast as possible.

With our mouths sealed in a kiss, he kicks the door shut behind us. I pull his shirt out of his pants and lift it. He removes it and tosses it to the side, his hair wild from before. My shirt and bra are the next to go. The rest of our clothes are off seconds later.

This will be quick because I need him now. We can take it slow after. As if he can read my mind, he sweeps me up like he has the strength of the Hulk, and I wrap my legs around him, his arousal obvious. I trail open-mouthed kisses down one side of his neck and then up the other, sucking gently under his ear. He marches us through a set of doors to a massive bedroom with a ginormous bed.

He lays me carefully onto it and is on top of me an instant later. "I want to take my time, but I can't wait," he says, nuzzling my neck.

"I don't want it slow." With all my strength, I flip us until I'm on top.

His eyes turn dark with lust, making my entrance throb. Then his hands trace my bare skin from my back all the way down, gripping my ass as I grind against him. I quiver from his bold touch and adjust my position. Spurred on by desire, I slowly lower myself onto his length. We both moan from the sweetest relief after waiting a month for this.

"You're so damn warm and tight. I've missed this. Missed *you*," he says, voice strained and rough.

I capture his mouth as I gyrate my hips. He grips my thighs, controlling the rhythm of our movements. Our breaths grow ragged and moaning fills the air around us.

He sucks my nipple, triggering an orgasm that floods my body with intense pleasure, leaving me breathless. Leo flips us over and thrusts deeper until his body tenses and he releases a throaty cry.

We wrap our arms around each other and catch our breath. Neither of us speaks as we bask in the afterglow. I already knew we had a future, but after today, he's the one I want to lie in bed with every day.

"I want to spend the rest of my life with you," I whisper against his cheek. "I love you so much."

He lifts his head, his face beaming. "Me too. You're the love of my life. I thought my chance to be this happy and excited was long gone. Thank you for today...for everything."

"I'd do anything for you."

"Like move to Orcas Island?" he says, hope in his voice.

Without hesitation, I say, "Yes."

His face lights up. "Seriously? I threw that out there, not expecting an answer."

We wiggle our way under the covers, then face each other. "I've had a lot of time to think about us, about our future. Before I came to San Francisco, I went to LA. That's where I rented the Audi."

He lifts onto his forearm. "Wait a second. You went to LA and then drove here by yourself?"

"Sure did, and I loved every minute of it. It was therapeutic."

"Damn, girl! You're full of surprises. I can picture you hot-rodding it down the highway. So sexy." He pecks my lips, then lies back down. God, I've missed this man. "With the way you've been acting today, is it safe to assume it went well?"

"It did, but it was difficult. I cried a lot, as usual." I tell him about seeing Adele and visiting the hospital and visiting where I'd lived. "I can put it behind me now. I won't work in a hospital again, but—" I tell him how Adele quit her job too and where she's working now. "It gives me hope that I can utilize my knowledge and experience somewhere else. Now if I could only figure out where."

"You'll find something, and I'll be at your side along the way."

I scoot closer to him. "Thank you for understanding and for being patient."

"If anybody should understand what you're going through, it's me. I've been wondering myself where or when I can sing and dance again. Change is good, but it's a mental game too. And since we're having this heart-to-heart, tell me what you really think. Should I take the manager's job at the hotel?"

"That's not for me to say. Deep down, only you know what you want." I tap the skin over his heart. "So you tell me what it is."

"I want to take it. It's time to be with my family again, and I love working at the hotel. I'll need to find another place to live. Can you picture yourself with me there? Would you be happy? There are things you need to think about. It's an island. You'll always have to take a ferry to the mainland. It's a lot quieter than LA or Seattle. You'll be far away from your family."

"I've gone through all the pros and cons with my therapist and Andy. And no matter what, everything leads me to you."

"How about I tell my mom I'll do it for two years? Then we can reevaluate the situation. What do you think?"

"That sounds perfect. You really don't know how you'll feel living there permanently again." He nods in agreement. "Other than your mom, though, let's keep it to ourselves for now, maybe until after Corey's memorial. I'm not ready to deal with my mom yet."

"Let's not talk about her. No time for negativity." He taps my thigh. "Let's get cleaned up and order some food. Then I want to hear how you got everyone there today. Especially Sully."

I didn't have to do much. As soon as I told them my idea, they were on board. Sully wasn't supposed to come, but when I told him the plan, he was in too. Everyone loves Leo and would do anything for him. It makes my heart burst with love, knowing how much they care.

Andy and Sam hit it off immediately when they met the night before Leo arrived in San Francisco. Andy and Tonya are another story. Tonya won't put up with his flirty bullshit, but that doesn't deter him in the least. If he's not flirting, they're arguing. At one point, their quiet bickering annoyed the hell out of us. Sully sat between them to shut them up. I'm curious how the Super Bowl party will go tomorrow.

Leo helps me out of the bed, and I actually stagger when my feet hit the floor. My legs feel like rubber. "I want to explore this gorgeous hotel room. Someone had me pretty occupied when we got here."

"Sorry, not sorry." He traces his fingers up my sides, giving me goosebumps. "It's the perks of my job."

"I'd give this bedroom a five out of five. Let's go test the shower. I want to clean you up and then make you dirty all over again." I pull him out of the room, not a care in the world.

"You are one sexy woman," Leo purrs. "Damn, I'm lucky!"

41

LEO

I stand in front of the Madrona Inn and consider it my new home, no longer a temporary spot to put down my bags and sleep. It's weird to think I won't be writing articles anymore or traveling nonstop. Soon I'll be doing the job I went to school for. Not long ago, I would've run back to the airport instead of agreeing to come back here permanently. Now I look forward to it because Olive will join me here one day. We're going to discuss that in more detail when she arrives on Monday.

I enter the hotel and breathe in the familiar scent of my surroundings. My eyes scan the area, recalling the one time Corey and I played basketball in the lobby. I threw the ball over Corey's shoulder, and it hit an expensive antique, shattering it. Per my usual punishment, I was grounded for two weeks.

Donna jumps up from behind the front desk when she sees me. I guess her back is doing better. "Leo, you're finally here." She hustles toward Mom's office. "Marla, Leo's back!"

I set my stuff aside, then give Donna a hug and a kiss

on the cheek. Mom runs out of her office, swerving around Donna. She wraps me in a warm, motherly hug. "Leo, we've really missed you around here. We're glad you're home. Come back to my office for a few minutes, or would you rather go home and freshen up?"

"Let me go take a shower first. It's been a long day."

"Go do that. Come over for dinner. I'll whip something up, and I'll tell Sully and Tonya to join us," Mom says, shooing me away.

"Sounds great. Thanks, Ma."

I walk through the halls, trying to imagine me and Olive living on Orcas Island. Finding a place we call home. I wonder how quickly I can convince her to move here.

The scent of fresh coffee brewing from Café Charmant tempts me to say hello to Louis and grab a tart, but I need to settle in. I stayed at two new hotels this week. The one in Las Vegas was phenomenal. I'll definitely take Olive there. The one in New York City was good, but nothing near the exceptional quality of the other. The flight from Vegas was delayed three times, making me miss the connection to Orcas Island. I've had it with traveling.

My little cottage comes into view, and all I want to do is face-plant onto my bed. Once I'm inside, I take a deep breath. It smells thoroughly sanitized from ceiling to floor. It's all wrong. It should smell like Olive. I leave my suitcase by the door and go straight to the bathroom.

It's time to tell Mom I'm staying.

"Ma, it's me," I shout out as I close the front door. Instantly, I smell the tomato sauce recipe I made at Olive's apartment. My stomach rumbles loudly. All I want is a home-cooked meal.

"In the kitchen," Mom hollers.

As I enter, she drops a large spoon of sauce on the counter, red liquid shooting everywhere. I grab some paper towels and help her clean up the mess.

"Well, shit. That spoon's a slippery little sucker. Thankfully, I'm wearing black."

"Butterfingers again?" I kneel and wipe up a couple drops off the floor. "Are Sully and Tonya coming?"

"Yes, but later. They'd rather eat at home," she says, cleaning her shirt.

Good. I was hoping to chat with her alone. I purposely didn't call her during the week because I wanted to speak face-to-face.

We finish cleaning up, and she puts the lid on the sauce. I refill her wine glass, pour myself some water, then sit at the kitchen table.

She tosses a dishtowel on the counter. "The sauce can simmer for a little while. I thought I'd make you spaghetti, since you eat at fancy restaurants in the hotels all the time."

"I know I'm spoiled when I travel, but yeah, I'm fancied out. Come and sit, Ma."

She sits across from me at the table. "I want to hear everything about the surprise skydiving and the Super Bowl party."

I prop my leg over my knee. "Didn't Tonya and Sully tell you anything?"

"Yes, but I want to hear your version."

Thinking about it again energizes me. "It was beyond amazing. I can't believe Olive pulled that off. Tonya kept asking if we could do it again. And for Sully to show up *and* skydive? I'll never forget his face. He actually looked happy for once." Not that it lasted long.

"I was Smokey's babysitter all weekend. Boy was she a

handful. She doesn't like me very much. I swear she whined the entire time he was gone and hardly ate. It was like I had a toddler again because I couldn't sleep. A soon as Sully walked through the door, she climbed up his clothes and curled up in his arms." She places her hand over her heart and grins. "It tickles me the way he loves that kitten. I think she soothes him somehow. He knows she won't hurt him. Anyway, tell me more."

"Like the others, I was high on adrenaline all weekend. When I jumped, I swore Corey was right there with me. It was out of this world. Skydiving with my friends and family, seeing Olive again, and getting to know her brother Andy better…it was an unforgettable experience.

"Oh, and Andy was hysterical with Sam. They were best buds by the time we left. I wish I could've been there when they met the first time. Andy's cool. He's the goofball in the group. I can't say Tonya liked him. He's also very protective of Olive. He takes their mom down a peg or two when things get heated…which seems to be all the time. It hasn't been easy for Olive."

She grimaces. "Is Evelyn trying to keep you two apart?"

I tilt my head. "Evelyn? How'd you know her name?"

"Olive told me, or you did." She swipes her hand like it's no big deal.

Hmm. Maybe we did. I don't remember, but whatever. It doesn't matter.

"Anyway, things are really tense between them, but Olive's handling it well. I'm proud of her because I'm not sure how I'll act when I see her mom next. Thankfully, there are no plans for that to happen anytime soon."

"Be careful what you say or do. You don't want to add to the tension."

"Easier said than done, Ma." I take a few gulps of

water and change the subject before I get fired up. "So, Olive's looking forward to coming here on Monday. We discussed a lot when we were together in San Francisco."

She sips her wine, hiding her grin. "Like what?"

My throat dries up, and I don't know why I'm nervous. "I want to take the manager position."

She springs from her chair, nearly toppling it, sprints over to me, and wraps me in a hug so tight I'm about to burst. "I can't believe it! My baby boy's staying home!" I feel like I'm seven years old again. "This makes your ole Ma a happy camper." She pats my cheek and returns to her seat. "You'll do a great job. I can't wait to tell everyone."

I love how excited she is. She lists all the people she wants to call tonight. Once she calms down, I explain to her I've quit my job, and this will be the last article I submit. That chapter of my life is now closed.

"I love Olive, and I want to spend the rest of my life with her, Ma."

"And she feels the same?" she asks, a smile dancing across her lips.

"Yes," I mutter, a smile spreading uncontrollably across my face. "And she's open to moving here. But since she's only been here that one week, I want her to get familiar with the island before making such a big decision. If it doesn't feel right for her or us here, I wouldn't hesitate to move."

She leans forward, hands splayed on the table. "Okay…what are you asking me? I can sense there's something else on your mind."

"I want to become manager, but only for two years. If Olive and I decide to stay here, then it'd be for longer."

She doesn't even blink before she responds. "Consider

it done. And you don't have to promise two years. It's your life. Don't worry about what anybody else wants."

I rest my elbows on the table. "But I'm supposed to take over the hotel when you retire. Who would take over then? Tonya doesn't seem too interested."

She reaches across the table for my hand. "We'll worry about that when the time comes. I don't plan on retiring anytime soon. Your happiness is the most important thing here. Watching you move on, in love with your perfect match…it does something funny to my heart."

I rest against the chair and cross my arms. "You really think she's my perfect match? You weren't the friendliest when Olive was here."

She pulls her hand away and looks down. "I know, and I'm sorry. It's a mother's job to protect her child. I don't want you to get hurt if things go south."

"Ma, *nothing* could make me change my mind. She's the one for me."

"Good, because you have no idea what might come your way."

"Olive and I have dealt with a lot in the past. It'd have to be pretty bad to rip us apart."

"Good." She pats my hand and stands. "Time to make the pasta."

42

LEO

In the intimate banquet room where we're holding Corey's memorial lunch, loud chatter fills the air as waiters circulate, clearing away the dirty lunch plates. By the door, Tonya and Louis discuss when to bring in the dessert platters.

Standing around Corey's grave this morning was tough with everyone there, but delivering a speech to the same group will be worse.

"Are you ready?" Olive asks, squeezing my hand. "Say everything that's in your heart. Don't hold back."

"I'll try," I reply, my knee bouncing in sync with my rising heart rate.

Tonya approaches and taps my shoulder. "It's your turn. Take your time."

I push back my chair and head to the front where a large picture of Corey is displayed. Silence takes over the room, and all eyes are on me. I take a few seconds to settle, then begin.

"I wasn't sure I could deliver a speech today. My chest feels like it's going to cave in any second, and the tears want to break free again. But it's okay that I feel sad and angry because emotions prove one thing: I'm alive. Something Corey is not. No matter how hard he fought, the cancer was stronger.

"When Corey died, a part of me died too. I didn't know how to live without my cousin and best friend. Wherever I was, he wasn't too far behind. For the last five years, I've been only existing in this world, not living.

"The day after his funeral, I packed up our memories, adventures, and milestones. They've been collecting dust in boxes as if they had no value. I've pushed friends and family away and replaced them with people who didn't know Corey. As time passed, glimpses of my old self emerged, but never fully returned. Instead of giving myself permission to grieve, I've been pretending it never happened. Traveling gave me an escape. Avoidance was excellent medicine until it didn't numb the pain anymore. I'm not proud of these actions.

"It so happens that someone recently appeared in my life who woke my sorry ass up." I grin at Olive, and Tonya nudges her. "A quiet, troubled, and alluring woman arrived at the hotel on New Year's Eve. One look at Olive, and my whole life changed. She came here to escape *her* troubled life, but her bravery and drive were awe-inspiring. Then I thought to myself, if she can do it, then why can't I? Maybe we could both learn to live again, together."

"I know this speech is supposed to be about Corey, and that's where I'm headed. In that first week Olive spent here, we became close. We talked about the things in our past and how they had affected us. And then she went home. I went directly to Mom's and spent hours in the attic with Sully and Tonya. We looked through photo albums and videos, sifted through travel souvenirs, sorted clothes we wore when we performed, and flipped through little notebooks filled with our ideas. And I cried." My voice cracks, and I look at the ceiling to control myself.

"I cried for Corey and how he suffered. I cried about the unfairness of being alive while he wasn't. I cried because a piece of me will always be missing because he's no longer here. And I cried because I wasted five years of my life, and he would've given anything to have five more.

"And…I cried until there were no tears left because I found a letter from him that was stuck between two of his favorite books. Why I didn't see it when I packed everything up, I don't know. Maybe I wasn't supposed to find it until now."

I pull the letter from my pocket and unfold it. "This is what he wrote."

Leo, sorry about the handwriting. It was always shit, but it's even worse now. Fucking cancer. I see you've finally found this letter. I bet it's years after I left the building. How did I know? Are you really asking that question? We were joined at the hip since birth. I know you better than anyone. I bet you've been wearing your comedian mask and hiding everything else deep down inside since the day I died. You probably don't dance or sing or anything anymore. Am I right?

Don't live like this when you've been given a longer life than me. It was my time to go, not yours. Don't act like you're lying in that rotting, suffocating coffin with me. We had the time of our lives, lived in the moment, and I'm so thankful that I got to spend all my favorite moments with you, doing what we loved. God, did we have fucking fun, or what?

Sully and Tonya crack up, and Aunt Betty shakes her head with a grin. She's probably upset with the language. She was constantly on his ass about swearing. Uncle Mason smiles with watery eyes.

Eventually, you'll find another ride or die along the way. Maybe you already have by the time you find this letter. If not, when you do, don't run away out of fear like a dumbass. Embrace her—yes, her—and dive in, just like you would when I was alive. You always craved adventure and loved life. I'm getting tired and my handwriting looks like a first grader learning how to write the alphabet during a nap. All I ask is that you don't forget me, and don't forget to live because, if you do, I'll kick your ass when I see you again. You know I will. Thanks for being the best friend I ever had. I'll be watching you from above. Make me proud.

And most of all, dance and sing your heart out. You were made to do it!

Peace out, Corey

Laughter fills the room because that's how Corey always said goodbye.

"This is what Corey would want—us laughing at his expense and living our lives to the fullest. We shouldn't take a single moment for granted. He understood this better than anyone, especially me." I stare at his handwriting, then lift up the letter. "I'll never know why I didn't find this until I needed it most. I think it proves there's something magical around us. We all hate the cliché, *everything happens for a reason*, but I think maybe it does. Thanks for listening. I love you all." Then I look up and say, "Love you too, Cor."

I fold up the letter and everyone claps as I return to my seat next to Olive. I hug her and bury my face against her. She rubs the nape of my neck with her hand.

"I'm proud of you," she murmurs. "It was a beautiful speech. I wish I could've met him. What a handful you two must've been."

"You got that right. I'm surprised we have hair left on our heads," Mom says. Aunt Betty is at her side, nodding in agreement. "Wonderful speech, honey."

"Thanks, Ma."

I hold Olive close to my side because I can. We are alive and our future is ahead of us.

43

OLIVE

It's early afternoon, but this has been a long day. Leo and I are both exhausted, but him more than me. At times, he got emotional with the others, which made me choke up because I can't bear to see him suffer. There were many emotional speeches, but Leo's was priceless. I'm proud of him for opening up. I didn't think I could love him more, but I'm proven wrong every day.

This week was nonstop action. Mom and I had another fight right before I came here. She was angry because I didn't tell her about the skydiving plans or who would be at the Super Bowl party. What am I, twelve? Then, because I was pissed, I let it slip that I'm planning to move. I didn't say where, but it's obvious. She didn't like that and stormed off again. If anyone's a raging preteen, it's her. I haven't spoken to her since and I'm fine with that. Andy's flying home for a bachelor party this weekend, and he said he'll check on her.

Leo's been showing me the rest of his favorite parts of the island, hoping to convince me how great living here would be. He doesn't need to influence me—I already want to move here. When? As soon as possible. Where would we live? No idea. It's part of the adventure.

When Corey wasn't the subject of conversation, Corey's side of the family interrogated Leo and me about our relationship. They seemed happy for us and wished us well. Marla has also been more attentive to me. I hate questioning her actions, but that's her fault.

The luncheon is winding down, and some guests have already left. I wrap my arm through Leo's and tug him over to a window away from everyone. "Do you want to go to our bench while the sun's out, or should we go later?" I brush my hand through Leo's soft hair as it shines from the sunlight beaming through the window.

"Let's go now. Later, I want to be alone with you without any interruptions. We've had enough of those this week," he murmurs behind my ear, kissing the skin there.

I squeeze his chin lightly. "Stop doing that or we'll never make it out of here. I don't think your family would appreciate that." Leo steps away and folds his hands behind his back with a cheeky grin.

We mingle a little longer until Betty, Mason, and Marla break up the party, thanking everyone again for coming. Leo and I share a look of relief.

Once the guests are gone and Betty and Mason head home, Leo announces that we're going outside for some air. Tonya says she's going back to her apartment, and Sully quietly pets Smokey, who's perched on his shoulder. Yes, he brought her with him. Marla has to go to her office before she goes home.

We follow Marla as she leads the way, discussing the day and all the remembrances shared. Suddenly, she stops short and grasps Sully's arm. I follow the direction she's looking, and all the air leaves my lungs. I take a second to gather myself because I can't believe it.

I step forward and stand in front of everyone. "Mom? Andy? What are you doing here?" I can't believe she followed me. And with Andy? Are they in cahoots now?

"Evelyn?" Marla exclaims. My head jerks in Marla's direction, then back to Mom.

"Marla." Mom answers back with her chin high. My eyes ping-pong from Marla to Mom, as do everyone else's. *What the fuck?*

"You know each other?" Tonya says before I can.

Leo clenches his jaw, and his eyes turn cold. "Did you know they knew each other? And Andy—why is he here?"

"I had no idea! Did you?" I already know the answer, though.

He shakes his head. "Fucking news to me."

I clench my fists to stay calm and gather my thoughts. I turn to Andy. "What the hell is going on?"

"I tried to stop her, Ol."

"Mind your manners, Olive," Mom says.

Oh, no, she didn't. Leo steps forward to say something, and I throw my arm out to keep him quiet. This is my fight.

"Don't you dare tell me what to do," I snarl, not recognizing my voice. "How the fuck do you know Marla?"

Marla clears her throat. "Keep your voice down. We're attracting attention. Let's go somewhere else. This isn't the place for this discussion. Follow me to my house," she urges.

Marla guides us through the lobby toward the hallway that leads to her personal part of the hotel. Sully and Tonya follow on her heels, Tonya whispering something I can't decipher. Leo is stuck to my side, his jaw tight and ticking. His shock and anger is quite clear.

I'm not only confused, I'm fucking livid. Mom and Andy follow us in dead silence. I can't even hear their footsteps. I want to pull Andy aside to find out what's going on, but there's no time. It must be significant since Andy came with her.

Mom meets Leo once, and she pulls this shit? Good job, Mom, for proving what an obsessive, overprotective parent you are. On top of that, she knows Marla. How fucked up is that? This would make a great "I didn't see that coming" moment in a book.

It feels like forever until we finally arrive at Marla's front door. She opens it, enters, and says, "Let's talk in the living room." Then she tosses her heels aside and hangs her coat. We all do the same, leaving shoes and coats at the door.

I lose track of the moms for a minute as the rest of us look at each other in confusion. When we all finally make it to the living room, the scene before us is fucking absurd.

Marla and Mom are hugging and sniveling.

Mom keeps saying she's sorry.

For fucking what?!

"Okay. That's enough!" Tonya shocks us all with her firm outburst. She may be petite, but she's got spunk. "Someone better start talking or I'm breaking out the alcohol."

"I'll take a beer." Andy raises his hand like he's waving down a waitress. Why is he here again? I need something a lot stronger than wine. *Focus, Olive!*

Leo chimes in, getting us back on track. "How do you two know each other?"

"And why do you keep apologizing to Marla?" I glare at Mom; my voice is harsh and unrelenting.

Our mothers finally separate, swiping the dampness from under their eyes. This must be an alternate universe and we've been taken over by aliens. Maybe Tonya had the right idea. I should suggest a round of shots.

"Ma?" Leo snaps, grabbing Marla's attention this time. "What the hell is going on?"

Marla smooths down her classy beige dress and shakes out her hair, stalling, I think.

"Okay." She fiddles with her pearl necklace. "Yes, we know each other."

Mom stands stock-still, avoiding eye contact with me. Marla reaches out and catches her hand.

"Obviously," Sully says sarcastically. I'd forgotten he was in the room.

Marla clears her throat. "Guys, remember how I had a fight with my best friend years ago?" She looks at Leo, Tonya, and Sully, her eyes soft and pleading.

"What?" Leo reacts first, shaking his head. "No. No fucking way." He points at my mom. "You're the *best friend* who stole Mom's fiancé?" Disgust drips from his voice.

"We weren't actually engaged yet," Marla says, "and her name is Evelyn."

"You're defending her now?" Leo shouts. "What happened to all that manifesting anger every time you talked about being betrayed by your best friend? How you understand what Sully's going through? How can you be so calm with her standing in your living room after all these years?"

Mom shrinks into herself and grimaces. I turn to her, gaping with disbelief. "Best friend? You *stole* her fiancé?"

"*Almost* fiancé," Marla corrects.

"Whatever," I snap. "Do you mean Dad?"

Marla and Mom exchange looks.

"Answer me!"

She eases toward me. "Can we talk in private?"

I step back with my hands up in front of me. "Nope.

You should've thought about this before you sprung this on me in front of Leo's family. Whatever you have to say, say it in front of everyone."

I look at Leo. "Come on now. You really didn't know who my mom was?" My focus turns to Tonya and Sully next. My question loud and clear.

Leo shakes his head. "I knew *of* her, but Ma never said her name. I didn't see any pictures either." Tonya nods in agreement. Sully's expressionless, but his cold, flinty eyes are locked on Mom.

Then something else occurs to me. *Marla.* "Wait a damn second. *You* knew all along who she was. Drilling me with questions about my family. Saying I should bring her here."

Marla's eyes shimmer when she looks at me. "Olive, you have your father's eyes. The more you spoke about your parents and where you lived, the clearer it became."

The corners of her lips droop as she looks at Leo. "I didn't want to jeopardize your relationship with Olive. You were so happy. I didn't have the heart to tell you. I was willing to take the consequences."

He huffs. "When were you planning to tell us? When it was 'time to meet the parents?'"

"Start talking, you two," I demand. "We're not leaving here until we get the full story."

"Why don't we all sit down and discuss this like adults?" Marla suggests.

Sully remains by the fireplace. Tonya sits on the couch with her legs curled under her. Andy plops down next to Tonya, receiving a death glare from her. She's so small next to his bulky frame. Marla sits on the recliner, and Mom stands next to it. Leo and I remain standing. I'm too fidgety to sit.

All our eyes are laser-focused on our moms. Mine begins.

"Marla and I were friends when we were kids."

"*Best* friends," Marla inserts.

Mom nods. "We were. Our families knew each other, and we all spent our summers here on Orcas Island."

I sift my hands through my hair and start pacing. "You're such a great liar, always claiming to not like it here."

"Let me finish," Mom says, surprisingly calm.

"Go ahead. I can't wait to hear what else you lied to me and Andy about," I snarl.

"That last summer, Marla told me she was dating someone she met through a college friend and they were already talking about marriage." Mom sneaks a glance at Marla, then at me. "He was going to visit while we were on the island, and I couldn't wait to meet him. I was so excited that my best friend might be getting married."

Her voice sounds different. It's like she's traveled back in time, and she's listening to Marla spill all the juicy details about "the guy."

My future father.

I curl in to Leo's side and latch onto his hand. He presses a kiss to my temple and whispers, "It's going to be okay." I nod, hoping he's right.

"And then he arrived, and we looked at each other and…there was no going back. We did everything we could to ignore it. But sometimes, you can't ignore life-changing events, no matter how hard you try."

She looks at Marla now, her eyes glassy and guilt-ridden. "I know we betrayed you, and it kills me till this day, but he was everything to me. I couldn't stay away from him. You had every right to cut me out of your life. I deserved it. I still do.

"I regret hurting and losing you, Marla, but I don't regret marrying Pierce. I can't. He became my best friend, my soulmate. He was an amazing husband and father to our children."

Marla's cheeks are soaked from sadness.

"Did you know for sure who Leo's family was before you came here?" I ask.

She wrings her hands over and over. "I put two and two together, yes. Once he talked about this hotel and his mom…Marla."

"For the record," Andy interrupts. "After she shared this tea with me, I tried to convince her not to come here. But Olive, you know how stubborn she is. I had to come along to soften the blow. I sent you a message to warn you, but obviously, you didn't get it."

I see red. How dare she?

"Okay, Mom, now I need to talk to you alone." She opens her mouth to say something, but stops herself. Maybe I look as angry as I feel. She nods.

Andy gets up to follow, and I stop him. "No. Let me be."

"Nope. I'm going with you to make sure you don't kill her. I won't say a word while you duke it out. And I deserve to hear this too."

"Fine," I huff.

"Olive, do you want me to go with you too?" Leo asks. It'd be easy to say yes, but I need to confront Mom by myself. Andy can be her bodyguard.

Before I can respond, Marla answers for me. "Let her go, Leo. We need to talk too."

He looks at me again, his eyes wide with concern. I nod and leave the room, with Mom and Andy following close behind. Instead of going back to the hotel, we don our shoes and jackets, and I lead them out the kitchen door to the garden.

The partly cloudy sky allows some sunrays to beam through, spreading much welcomed warmth through the chilly air. I button my coat and turn around to find Mom roaming around, inspecting little details.

"I haven't been here in over thirty-five years. It's amazing how much has changed, yet looks the same. It was a family tradition to come to Orcas Island and stay at the Madrona Inn during summer vacations, even when your grandparents were kids. Our family and the Gables were good friends. Gable is Marla's maiden name, if you don't already know." I nod.

"This was my favorite place to be. Marla and I were the best of friends. A friendship like that is rare." She hangs her head low and drags her feet over the dewy grass.

I have so much to say, I don't know where to begin. But I start anyway.

"Why did you keep it a secret? I mean, the entire family had to have known since you were all friends. Uncle Bruce? Grandma and Grandpa? Make me understand, Mom." Even Leo's uncle Mason should know who I am.

"No matter how much I loved—*love*—your dad, the guilt ate me alive. Her parents fought with mine, and it caused total chaos because of how devastated Marla was. Our love caused a major rift between the families. Beyond repair. Our family never returned to the island."

"You loved Dad that much to risk everything?"

"Yes," she answers without hesitation. "We couldn't stand the thought of being apart. So I had to be selfish, and I knew I'd be losing my best friend, but there was no question in my mind. He was my forever. I...I'd do it again, Olive. I'd choose him every time."

A look of nostalgia transforms her face, and I can only

imagine it's because she's thinking of Dad. It was crazy, how in love they were. Andy and my friends' parents were all getting divorced when we were teenagers, but ours always acted like they were still on their honeymoon.

"Every day that passes since he died feels like the first day. Some days, it's like I can't even get up—I lie in bed and stare at the wall while I hug one of his business shirts that I kept. Except they don't smell like him anymore." Her voice is tiny.

We cleaned out his closet six months ago. She must have kept some stuff without me knowing. A wave of sadness for her crushes my chest.

"Believe it or not, I still have the last voice message he ever sent me. He asked me to buy his peanut butter cup ice cream when we were shopping. Before he ended the message, he said he loved me more and more each day. I listen to it every morning while I have my first cup of coffee. I'm incredibly fortunate to have spent so many years married to the one person truly made for me." She blinks twice, and tears slide down her face. "God, Olive. The vision of him lying dead in the backyard never goes away. I'm so glad you didn't experience that with me."

Me too. No matter how angry I am, she's my mom. I can't watch her grieve like this. I didn't know—she hides it pretty well.

I wrap her in my arms. "It's okay, Mom. Everyone knows how you two loved each other. He was taken from us too soon and without warning. That makes it harder to let him go. And it wasn't your fault you weren't there."

"I blame myself every day," she whimpers.

Something occurs to me. I drop my embrace and put some space between us.

"So, when I quit my job in LA and moved back home, I was a wreck. Dad told me life was about facing tough choices where I might have to prioritize myself sometimes, where I might hurt innocent people in protecting myself."

Mom looks at me, and I know. "He said that because of what happened with Marla, didn't he?"

She nods. "You made a difficult decision to save yourself. Some people would say it was selfish. I don't think it was, but that doesn't keep the guilt away. You have to learn to live with it. Dad and I both knew about that. But you, confronting your past in LA? It encouraged me to follow you here today. To confront *my* past. It felt like my one chance for redemption."

I release a big breath of air and fist my hair. "Why didn't you say anything when you met Leo? Couldn't you have picked another day? You knew his cousin's memorial was today. Or was it your intention all along to cause problems between Leo and me?"

"I thought keeping you away from him would conceal the truth. I was afraid of what you'd think of me if you found out. My worry turned to anger because my past was catching up with me and I took it out on you. Then you told me you wanted to move. Something had to be done. After Andy showed up, I told him everything. When I mentioned coming here, he tried to convince me to stay put, but I refused."

Andy spreads his hands in a gesture of helplessness. He blew off the bachelor party he was supposed to go to for this shit show. I owe him big-time.

Mom sniffles. "I've acted horribly for months and said despicable things to you, and Leo too. Neither of you deserved my wrath. I'm embarrassed and truly sorry for everything. I hope you can forgive me. I promise I'll apologize for coming here today, and I'll make things better for all of us."

"Good, because I'm not going to lose him due to the

decisions you made all those years ago. You and Marla can fight like cats and dogs, and it won't matter. I will *always* choose Leo. He's my future and who I want to spend the rest of my life with."

"And I'll always choose you too." My favorite voice. I spin around as Leo comes up to me, his arms open wide. Without hesitation, I wrap myself around him because it's my favorite place to be.

44

LEO

We're all quiet until Olive and her family slip out the kitchen door. I don't know what to say or where to begin anyway. Wait, that's not correct. I roll my head between my shoulders, then turn to my mother.

"All this time, you knew who Olive was. I should've known something was up with your constant interrogations. Why didn't you say anything?"

"Every day I was ready to tell you, but I always chickened out. Why would I take away your happiness when you finally found it again with Olive?"

"The first night you met her, you said you had mustard in your eye and that's why your eyes were watering. That wasn't true, was it?" I ask.

Mom looks away. "When I realized who she was and she told us that her father had recently passed, it broke my heart. I couldn't hold back my reaction."

"So let me guess—Uncle Mason and Aunt Betty know too?"

"I told them right after you accepted the manager position and confirmed things were serious between you and Olive."

I bite my lower lip and take a deep breath, trying to rein in my anger. "Thanks for making us look like complete idiots in front of everyone because a guy broke your heart over three decades ago."

"Seriously, Mom," Tonya blurts. "You fooled all of us. And are you still in love with Olive's father?"

"Not at all. Pierce was a big part of my life, and we had a good time together. And he was a good man, despite the fact he broke my heart. I couldn't admit that at first. After a while, I knew I was better off, but I was still bitter and too proud. Anyway, that night, all those emotions and memories flooded back, and I had to leave the room. And then it got me thinking about when *your* dad died. It was far too much for me."

"You were hugging Olive's mom when we got here. Does that mean you forgive her?" Sully pipes in.

"I don't know. I've been doing a lot of thinking since Olive came here. Leo, in some ways, we have something in common. We've both lost our best friends."

I snap my head back. "Are you kidding me? How is that the same damn thing? Evelyn is alive. You might have things in common with Sully—" I stop. No need to go there.

"No, I know it's not the same thing. Far from it. But let me explain myself. You lost your best friend, and there's no chance to get him back. I lost Evelyn, not because she died, but because of a man who wasn't meant for me. It didn't matter how angry I was, I still missed my friend, every day.

"The difference between our situations is that now I have the chance to see my friend again. Maybe we can mend what was broken. I can thank her, too, because without her, I wouldn't have met your dad or had my kids.

"This is how it was meant to be. Like you and Olive are." Mom stands and takes my hands. "Do you realize how incredible it is, despite everything, that Evelyn's daughter showed up at this hotel and you two fell in love? How can I ignore that? Maybe time does heal all wounds."

Sully snorts. "So in thirty to forty years, I should forgive my asshole ex-best friend and ex-fiancée too? I can tell you right now that'll never happen. Fuck them."

"Sully—" Mom reaches for him, but he weaves around us and leaves the room.

"I'll go talk to him," Tonya offers. "It'll give you some time alone." She squeezes my hand, then goes off.

Mom plops back down onto the recliner and puts her head in her hands. "How did this become such a mess?"

"Don't get too comfortable. It's time to find Olive and Evelyn, and we're going to talk it out. Whatever happens between you two, it's not going to come between Olive and me. This is when *I'll* be selfish."

Mom nods and stands. I motion for her to lead the way. We put on our shoes and jackets and head to the kitchen to see if they're outside. Tonya points to the kitchen window, then leaves with Sully following her.

I peer outside. When I see they aren't yelling at each other, I relax. From Olive's body language, she seems pretty calm. Mom nudges me toward the door. I open it quietly and step out. My love for Olive grows to a new level as she expresses her decision.

"I will *always* choose Leo. He's my future and who I want to spend the rest of my life with."

"And I'll always choose you too."

She spins around, her face beaming when she sees me. I forget that our moms are standing there, and I approach her with open arms. She wraps herself around me, right where she belongs.

Hand in hand, Olive and I head to my favorite place. Mom and Evelyn both apologized to us and promised to not interfere any further with our relationship. We left them alone to let them work things out. Andy stayed back with Tonya because she offered to make him a martini when Sully left. I hope she doesn't poison him.

"See, what did I say? Empty. My tree knew we were coming and made sure nobody was sitting on our bench."

"Your tree, huh?" Olive pokes fun. "Isn't it *our* tree now?"

We sit on the cold, squeaky bench and sigh at the same time. I invite the silence as I enjoy the view of the East Sound. She lifts my arm and snuggles up underneath it. I squish her to my side and kiss the top of her head.

"What a day, huh?" Olive's exhaustion is clear.

I hum in agreement. "A lot to process."

"I'm sorry about my mom showing up on the day of Corey's memorial. I don't want it to overshadow his memory."

"No one could do that. And it's not your fault. None of this is. At least she showed up after everyone left."

"Right?" She looks at me with concern. "Do you think your mom will forgive her?"

"Actually, yes. Not that I don't care, but it's their problem. We don't need to be in the middle of it. We have enough to figure out."

She sits up and plays coy. "About our future?"

"Mmm hmm."

"Like what? Give me an example." She bounces on the bench, her energy coming back.

"It's the most important topic. So listen up." Her eyes

widen with excitement. I purposely say nothing to make her squirm a little.

She smacks my leg. "What? Come on. I want to know."

I pick up her left hand and say with a twang, "Like when I'm 'gonna put a ring on it.'"

Her face softens. "I don't need a ring. I can't fathom life without you. To me it's a done deal."

"So you think we're engaged?"

"Maybe." She draws out the word playfully.

I kiss her inviting lips. "Believe me, beautiful. You'll know when we're engaged. I've already got it planned. When, where, and how."

"Did I hear the word *engaged?*" Mom says behind us. Of course she'd know where we'd be. "Is there something you need to tell us?"

We turn around and find her and Evelyn, both with bright faces that don't look forced. In fact, they look… happy? You'd never know there was bad blood between them.

"No. Nothing to tell." Olive smacks a big kiss on my cheek. "But if I have my way, it'll be sooner rather than later."

"Does that mean I'll be planning your wedding soon?" Tonya pops out from behind our moms, her face hopeful and flushed. Where the hell did she come from, and how many cosmos did she drink already? "And don't forget about our bet!"

A bit confused, I mumble to Olive, "Bet?"

The side of her mouth quirks up. "I'll tell you later."

"Do I get to help?" Andy surprises us too.

"No," Tonya responds quickly.

Andy winks at her.

What is with those two?

"Of course you can, brother," Olive says, ignoring Tonya.

"Definitely soon," I say, gazing into Olive's eyes. "I can't wait much longer."

"Me either."

Would it be inappropriate if I thanked Evelyn for stealing Pierce? If she didn't, I wouldn't have been born, and I wouldn't have found the love of my life.

Because that is who Olive is.

The love of my life.

My best friend.

My future.

EPILOGUE
OLIVE

$\mathbf{S}$*ix months later*

I clutch the bouquet of plastic flowers in one hand and squeeze Leo's hand with the other. My skin prickles with nervous excitement. I can't believe we're doing this. Nothing could stop us, though. *Nothing.*

Queen's song, "Don't Stop Me Now" plays in my head.

"Our moms are going to flip," I say, not caring in the least. Well, maybe a little.

"Would you expect any different?" Leo responds, kissing my cheek.

"Not really."

We're in Vegas this weekend with our clan to celebrate Leo's birthday. He surprised me with tickets to see Queen in concert. The others are doing their own thing tonight. When we left the concert hall, we turned to each other and at the same time said, "Let's get married."

We ran to the first chapel we could find, and here we are.

"Maybe we shouldn't tell them. The wedding date's set for New Year's Eve and the planning's begun. Tonya would be pissed."

Leo proposed to me a couple of months ago. Want to know how he did it? Okay, I'll tell you really quick because we have a wedding to attend at this cheesy but perfect chapel.

He mounted a plaque on our bench inscribed with "Olive and Leo," but there was a blank space after our names. He got down on one knee and put a gorgeous diamond ring on my finger, just like he said he would. The blank space will be filled with *Forrest* and our wedding date.

Oh. That'll be interesting. Which date should we use? Never mind. Something to worry about later.

Mom and Marla have made up, and they're good friends again. Mom and I went to therapy together to mend our relationship. So far so good. We moved to the island two months ago. It took some convincing to sell the house, but she gave in. She's working at the Madrona Inn now and lives alone—her choice—in a small apartment in town. Even though she's still grieving, a change in surroundings has helped. I have taken a part-time job at a general practitioner's office. I'm also in charge of the hotel's website and help if someone needs medical attention at the hotel. Life is good.

Leo and I, with Sully's help and connections on the island, have been searching for a house to renovate. Currently, we live in Leo's cottage at the hotel. It's a tight fit, but I love it. Tonya continues to plan our dream wedding with Andy's assistance. It's a good thing he lives in California because they're like oil and vinegar. Either they're going to kill each other one day or end up saying "I do." That would be an interesting story to add to the family history.

Once we're married and settled, Leo wants to give dance lessons to teenagers and maybe start a YouTube channel. He gives me private lessons, but more often than not those lessons end up with us naked. He's hard to resist when he moves his body like that. As for singing, I'm lucky because I get to hear his gorgeous voice in private. We also go to karaoke nights, and he's been invited to sing in a local band. He hasn't decided on that yet. Working at the hotel is his priority.

"What do you think?" Leo brings me back to the present. "Should we keep this a secret?"

I bounce on my toes. "Ooh, yeah. I'm loving this idea. How about until the wedding reception? It shouldn't be that difficult since it's already September. I'd like to have this one thing for ourselves. It'll be something special to tell our kids when they grow up."

"Kids, huh?" He smirks, then kisses my hand. "I'm loving that idea even more. Can we start tonight? Or at least have fun pretending to start. Role play?"

God, I love this man. How did I get so lucky? Waking up next to him in the morning is the most amazing blessing. And, oh man, do I love how compatible we are in the bedroom. And on the kitchen floor and in the shower and...

You get my drift. Life is never boring with him.

"Olivia Hansen and Leonardo Forrest, you're up," the woman with overprocessed pink hair, sky-blue eye shadow, and hot-pink lipstick says. Is she chomping on a wad of gum?

"Ready?" Leo asks me.

"More than anything. Let's do this."

The organ plays the wedding march, and I giggle. It's

tacky, but I love it. Leo's cheerful energy agrees with me, too, as we practically run down the aisle hand in hand.

We stand in front of the officiant, and she begins the vows. I focus on Leo and think about how he kissed me back to life. I'm so grateful for his kind heart, glowing personality, and the love he has for me.

"Do you, Leonardo Forrest, take Olivia Hansen, to be your wedded wife, to have and to hold from this day forward…" The words blend into each other because I'm waiting to hear—

"I do," Leo exclaims, pushing a silver band onto my finger. He looks around like he's ready to high-five someone. We already bought our official wedding bands. His is black, of course.

How am I going to keep this a secret? I want to scream it from the rooftops.

Leo

I can't hold back. I lean in to kiss my wife, but someone clears their throat like they are a heavy smoker.

"Sir, we're not finished yet. You'll have to wait to kiss the bride. We need to move on. There are other couples waiting."

Party pooper.

"Sorry, I can't wait to kiss her as my wife for the first time. You know what I mean, right?"

"No. And she's not your wife yet."

Oops. Hard crowd.

"Babe, come on. It's my turn. I wanted you to be my husband like six months ago. I can't wait any longer."

I glance at the lady. "Sorry. You may proceed."

Olive chuckles. I can always count on her getting my humor.

Then I focus on Olive's vows, and seriousness kicks in. Her soft brown eyes pull me in, and she's all I can see. She's the one who taught me how to live life to the fullest. She's the one who encourages me to take chances no matter the outcome. I hold my breath, waiting to hear those two special words.

"Yes!"

Okay, one word.

She pushes the ring onto my finger. This is a temporary one. I can't wait until she slides on the black one she insisted we buy for the ceremony in December. It's impossible for me to say no to her. It was no hardship because I love black rings too. And I love her.

"*Now* you may ki—" the officiant begins, but I've already pulled Olive into my arms. Our first kiss as husband and wife is full of silent promises. There's no need for words because there aren't any to describe how happy we are. Our bodies blend together as I wrap her up in my arms.

She breaks the kiss, then whispers in my ear, "Does this mean I'm your *ride or die* until the end?"

I pull away and cradle her face in my hands. "No. This means you're my best friend and wife, and *nothing* could ever beat that."

"Not even the *mother* of your *children*?"

"Ooh, maybe that. Now we really need to get back to the hotel. We have some lovin' to do."

I kiss her lips again, then lead her out the door into a world where we'll conquer anything and enjoy every minute of it.

~

I hope you enjoyed *Time To Live Again*. Please consider leaving a review. Tonya and Andy's story is up next in *Time To Love Again*. It's going to be a mix of enemies-to-lovers, second chance, and opposites attract. Sign up for my newsletter or follow me on social media to get updates.

Are you curious about Ellie and Sam's unbelievable love story? Check out *Into Thin Air*. I loved them so much that I had to bring them into this series.

BOOKS BY KRISTINA BECK

Collide Series

Lives Collide

Dreams Collide

Souls Collide

Collide Series Box Set

Four Seasons Series

Snowflakes and Sapphires

Passions and Peonies

Colors and Curves

Maple Trees and Maybes

Four Seasons Complete Box Set

Madrona Inn Series

Time To Live Again

Time To Love Again

Standalone Novels

Into Thin Air

Key To His Heart

Trapped Between Right And Wrong

Free with newsletter subscription

Ring of Hope

ACKNOWLEDGMENTS

This book was a tough one to write. With so much craziness in the world, I wanted to give my readers a book full of hope and redemption, with characters you can't help but love and root for. I hope you had a smile on your face when you finished it. Thank you for your continued support and reading my books.

I'm going to thank my beta readers first. They helped transform this book into the final product and I couldn't be happier with it. Even though it's hard to get negative feedback, it pushed me to improve and mend the cracks. Thank you, Amy, Jamie, Lisa, Maggie, and Rachel. Your input is always priceless!

Now I couldn't have achieved my goals without my editing team. Rachel Overton and Helen Pryke, you are amazing at what you do! Even when I think my book is error free, you always find something. It drives me nuts, but I'm so thankful for it because, by the end, authors become blind to their own work. I hope we'll continue to work together for the rest of the series.

As you all know, designing my book covers is my favorite part. I asked Sarah, Okay Creations, to create my covers for this series. I love the cover for this book, but I love the next covers in the series even more. I don't know how she does it, but she listens to my ideas and somehow knows exactly what I mean. Thank you for your amazing talent.

And as always, thank you to my husband and kids. Your support and enthusiasm helps me get through the stressful process and to continue writing. Love you bunches.

ABOUT THE AUTHOR

Kristina Beck, a New Jersey native, spent the first thirty years of her life in the small state on the East Coast before embarking on a new adventure in Germany. Now, she lives in the wine country there with her German husband and their three lively children, balancing the charm of both worlds. A passionate reader across many genres, Kristina always returns to her first love—romance. When she's not dreaming up swoon-worthy stories, she can be found sipping strong coffee or a crisp white wine, indulging in dark chocolate, or re-watching her favorite '80s movies. She also has a soft spot for flowers and power naps. Outside of writing and reading, Kristina stays active with fitness, all while playfully grappling with her ongoing quest to master the German language.

For updates on her new releases, book news, and sales, check out her website and sign up for her newsletter to receive a free ebook. Want to chat about everything books, join her Facebook group, Krissy's Captivating Reads.

www.kristinabeck.com

facebook.com/krissybeck73

instagram.com/krissybeck96

bookbub.com/authors/kristina-beck

goodreads.com/kristina_beck

www.ingramcontent.com/pod-product-compliance
Lightning Source LLC
La Vergne TN
LVHW091236190726
843491LV00001B/6